i, ENOCH

The Deep Earth Chronicles

Book 1

STEVE STINE

Cover image by: Usman Tariq (U.T.), 99Designs
Author photo by: Kai Sotto
Edited by: Lucy Davis and Piers Pennington
Book design by: SWATT Books Ltd

Printed in the United States
First Printing, 2024

ISBN: 979-8-9907252-0-1 (Paperback)
ISBN: 979-8-9907252-1-8 (Hardback)
ISBN: 979-8-9907252-2-5 (eBook)

Deep Earth Chronicles Publishing
Oregon, 97701

info@deepearthchronicles.com

For Anne—my center

God is a circle whose center is every-
where and circumference nowhere.
                    —Voltaire

An Oath

I, ENOCH, GUARDIAN OF TRUTH AND KEEPER OF ANCIENT MYSTERIES, VOW TO DEFEND THOSE WHO HAVE BEEN VILIFIED, MALIGNED, AND FOREDOOMED BY THE FORCES OF IGNORANCE AND PREJUDICE. I SOLEMNLY SWEAR TO UPHOLD THE VALUES OF JUSTICE, EMPATHY, AND INQUIRY IN THE FACE OF ADVERSITY AND TO RECOGNIZE THAT THE PRESERVATION OF THESE MARGINALIZED VOICES AND THEIR INHERENT TRUTHS IS PARAMOUNT. THEIR STORIES ARE WOVEN INTO THE TAPESTRY OF OUR COLLECTIVE HISTORY, AND THEIR WISDOM HOLDS THE KEY TO A BRIGHTER, MORE HARMONIOUS FUTURE FOR ALL.

I, ENOCH ASSUME THE FULL BURDEN OF RESPONSIBILITY FOR ENSURING THAT THEIR LEGACY ENDURES, UNTIL SUCH TIME AS THOSE WHO HAVE BEEN VILIFIED RETURN TO WALK AMONG US. I PLEDGE TO CARRY FORWARD THEIR STORIES AND THE ANCIENT MYSTERIES THEY EMBODY, PASSING THEM ON TO FUTURE GENERATIONS WITH REVERENCE AND CARE. I WILL STRIVE TO ENSURE THAT THE WORLD NEVER FORGETS THE INJUSTICES THEY ENDURED AND THE WISDOM THEY POSSESSED.

I, ENOCH SHALL REMAIN A CLEAR-EYED OBSERVER OF ALL THAT UNFOLDS IN OUR WORLD. I SHALL DILIGENTLY AND FAITHFULLY RECORD AND PRESERVE THE ABUSES AND TRANSGRESSIONS OF THOSE WHO CLAIM DOMINION OVER THE EARTH. I WILL SHINE A LIGHT ON INJUSTICE, EXPLOITATION, AND THE MISUSE OF POWER, ENSURING THAT THESE ACTIONS ARE NOT HIDDEN OR FORGOTTEN.

I, ENOCH SWEAR THIS TO THE END OF MY DAYS.

PROLOGUE

The forest is Earth's blanket. A quiltwork of creation, it stretches taut over the landscape in folds of flora and fauna. Beneath, the Earth yawns, shudders, and pulsates. She is awake and the water that flows through her veins echoes down canyons. It is the sound of wilderness. Tucked deep in her currents are stories of past times and distant places. They scatter, like pebbles. And this way, they rest for all time on memory's shores, reminding us of what was and what will always be.

From the banks of one such river, a solitary figure—tall and ghostly white—slides into a swirling eddy. The water enfolds him. That old familiar feeling. Deeper now. Edging further, legs planted like pylons against the obsequious tug of the current. Swells rise and lick his thighs, engulfing him, surging past his stomach, chest, and shoulders. Angled into the current, he has only a meter or two to go. With an outstretched leg he probes the sandy bottom. She waits, quivering, to pounce, hoping to sweep him away. It wouldn't be the first time.

An immense boulder rests at the river's midpoint. It juts from the churning waters, parting her currents, carving deep watery depressions and pulsating, repelling, and pleading in quick succession— water, mist, and spray. There is no denying the stone's magnificence, its odd presence. And yet it is the water—not the stone—that draws the attention. Over countless years she has carved away the boulder's craggy undercarriage. The river shapes its contours like a cutler methodically swiping blade on stone. What once was block is now orb. A perfect circle, a round cube, a planet ringed by water. The will of the water is to shave the boulder loose, to let it roll—like all things—downward. Current is to urgency as eddy is to patience. And for the moment, she is patient, prodding the figure floundering along the stone's slippery sides. He stands firm, waiting for just the right moment. Then, in a single motion, he lifts a foot sunk ankle-deep and jackknifes a leg to land a toehold—a single chink against an otherwise smooth surface. The current lifts and spins his torso from leeward to windward. She has him now. He is exposed. But he knows this game and, turning aside, severs her strength and pulls himself free. In one long sweeping gesture, he reaches for the first of three wrought iron rings driven deep and hanging loose against the face of the stone. To cross the full ten-meter expanse requires three well-timed moves.

Pressing chest, stomach, and groin hard against the cold, slick surface, he traverses a thin shelf too small for his large feet, while clinging to the first ring with his left hand and reaching outward with his right. With a wingspan of nearly three meters, he is more giant than man. Back muscles ripple as he dips and swoops, making a firm grab at the second ring. For an instant, he is Prometheus chained, holding the boulder in full embrace. That is when it comes, the first beat of his silent heart. Pressing his cheek against the stone, he turns to one side, then the other, watching as the color in his outstretched arms morphs from white to red, then fades to brown. New blood in his veins gives him the strength to move on.

With gibbon-like grace, he lets go of the first ring, then sweeps down and up to backhand the third and final ring. Facing outward in a dead hang, his gaze pans across the distant riverbank to catch one last glimpse of the old willow, her boughs straining with the weight of a million tiny leaves. Shoulders slack and head hanging, he clings to the half-life that creeps up through his body, reanimating it as it goes. He feels an electric energy scamper up and down his limbs and wonders how many more times he must go through with this. He stares once more, deep into the river, as she swells and coils beneath him. He considers how water rarely surrenders. He smiles, and she smiles back. "I'll see you again," he whispers. Then, taking his first deep breath, he dips and pivots once more to land softly upon a bed of moss, where he draws himself up before swiftly climbing the wind-worn steps.

At the top, the surface is shorn round and flat, the circumference inlaid with a perfect circle of gold. It catches the light and reminds him of all the other times. It takes only three strides to move from the edge to the center. And there he turns, naked and dripping, facing upstream.

whirred to life. With a slight jerk of his head, the drones lifted in unison from their snowy encampment. The climbers shouted their approval. Before them hovered thirty football-sized drones with mounted HD-quality cameras—all awaiting Wit's next retina-controlled command.

"Let's go!" he shouted. Reaching down, he swung his pack over his shoulders. The others followed his lead. Kai, who normally gave the green light for the ascent, stood in stunned silence. The sky was buzzing with drones moving in perfect formation. They formed a virtual oscillating dome over Wit, like guardians. As the CEO headed up the slope, the others followed. They kept a respectful distance, not wanting to disrupt the surreal nature of the moment. *His* moment. He had the quintessential limelight, and no one on his team was going to interfere with that. His media experts and agencies had been prepping for months, taunting the press with the promise of "a great spectacle!" Every question asked was returned with the public relations retort "Watch this space!"

As he climbed, he moved his head in slow, circular motions, tracking, controlling, and making minor adjustments to the formation of the drones. So-called "gesture recognition" had swept the imaginations of Silicon Valley engineers, and for the past twenty-four months, Wit had hired and then hived away some of the best and brightest in a secret R&D facility just outside of Boulder, Colorado. No one knew where Wit was off to every afternoon at 4:00p.m., and many assumed he had finally shrugged off his 24/7 work ethic for an opportune affair somewhere in the Rockies. They should have known better. "Love is a distraction," he once said, when a rising star on his engineering team announced he was getting married. The comment went viral and earned him the moniker of "Midas," in reference to the king who chose wealth over love. Wit took it as a compliment.

At 7,200 meters and nearly three-quarters of the way up the fifty-degree grade of the Lhotse Face, Wit was feeling downright energized. The plan was to stop at Camp Three to regroup, but the others were still far behind. No time to lose, he thought. His flock of drones were performing to spec. Stop now and they might malfunction. Better to push on.

He paused only momentarily. Another 800 meters and he would be crossing into the notorious Everest Death Zone, where oxygen levels ran so low that the body's cells began to die. As if to signal to his live audience that he was pressing on, Wit spread his arms wide and smiled up into the dome of whirring drones—a modern-age Vitruvian Man encircled by an orb of silver-backed legionnaires. From every corner of the world, people were glued to their TV sets, laptops, and smartphones, bearing witness to a man on the path to immortality.

It should have been enough. But Thompson's king-sized ego wanted more. And offer his global audience something more he did. Watching a man ascend Everest, albeit in the most elaborate and high-tech fashion imaginable, wasn't the same as being part of it. What if the entire world could experience Everest with him, in the moment? What would it be for the average Joe to rise through the clouds and into the heavens alongside the mighty Wit Thompson?

He couldn't shake the idea. For months leading up to the climb, he had led a multi-million-dollar product development and marketing campaign in partnership with the world's leading smartphone manufacturer. It was his biggest idea yet. His next-generation drones were the medium. Offering a virtual reality experience to anyone, anywhere—*that* was the endgame. To participate meant owning a pair of SkyBound's state-of-the-art VR glasses. Designing and producing them would prove challenging enough. But getting them to market before the big event? Now *that* required advanced planning. Bundling the glasses with the release of the SamWei VisuLife™ smartphone held promise. To convince the manufacturer, he had to create something special, chock-full of gimmickry and backed by millions of marketing dollars. The packaging, in this case, was as essential as the product, or so he reasoned. The VR glasses would be shrouded in secrecy, locked within an elegant oblong case of jet-black graphite. Embossed in raised gold letters would be "High-Fly 9000™," the words "Watch This Space" beneath. Each case would be secured with a time-release lock underpinned with just two words: "Opening Soon."

It was a Willy Wonka–sized stroke of marketing genius. It was—in a word—audacious! Of course, there would be those who would try to spoil it. Attempts would be made to break open the cylinder and reveal to the world its contents. Wit anticipated this and concocted a fail-safe device. Break the case and the glasses would self-destruct, leaving behind only an ooze of golden goo. His marketing team said it was "mission impossible." His shareholders threatened mutiny. His CFO? Well, he nearly had a heart attack. It was in those intervening fifteen minutes when he learned about Wit's rollout plans that he threatened to quit.

"Do you know what this is going to cost?" he screamed. "Are you out of your mind? Twelve months of astronomical R&D costs to meet your drone delivery timeline, and now this... a gimmick... a fucking marketing gimmick?"

"No gimmick, my friend," Wit replied, donning a Cheshire grin. "Only a stroke of marketing genius."

Naturally, SkyBound's CEO got his way and, true to his word, millions of little black cases with tedious locks and mysterious lettering were delivered to gadget-crazed consumers the world over. For the insatiably curious, the bundled price tag—a hefty $999, not including tax—felt like a grand investment in the future. Just days before the long-awaited ascent up Everest, the firm hired to promote the event reached him via satellite to tell him the good news.

"36 million units sold," shouted the executive. "It's a frickin' miracle."

A miracle it was. The press will go mad, thought Wit. And, of course, they did. News coverage shouted about the conquest *before* the conquest. "From One Summit to the Next," blared one headline. "Wit Thompson's New Vision," rang another. The editors of *TechWorld* were gobsmacked. "Wit Thompson is Edison, Ford, and Jobs all wrapped up into one," they wrote. "To sell a product never seen, touched, or tested at a sky-high price is either the greatest commercial feat in modern history or an act worthy of a snake oil salesman."

So absorbed was he in his own thoughts that he nearly forgot that, at that very moment, 36 million people were wearing replica VR glasses and moving in sync with him, one step at a time, up the steep slopes of the world's highest peak. Thompson and his corporate empire had offered the world a seamlessly engineered virtual experience. "No mountain too high," he whispered under his breath, and the world's consumers swooned.

Shaking off the urge to laugh aloud, Wit stopped, turned, and looked for the other climbers, but they were nowhere to be seen. He set his gaze on two drones to his rear, and with a slight swing of his head, they spun back down the mountain. He tracked their progress via the inner lenses of his glasses, while a digital counter ticked off the altitude range. He could see them now, but their progress was slow. Kai was in the lead, with the others trailing far behind. They had only reached 7,200 meters. Wit stood at 8,600 meters. Had he moved that far ahead? He checked his watch with all its tiny indicators and could see that he had literally halved the time he thought it would take to reach this height. Better yet, he felt great. His breathing was steady and quite normal, no headaches, and he hadn't yet felt a need to take oxygen. The muscles in his legs felt strong and fresh, as if he'd just woken from a good night's rest.

"Mind over matter," he gloated.

The radio he carried in his right pocket was switched off. He now reached for it and flipped it to "on." He noticed the drones all buckle in the air for an instant, then recover. He had anticipated this. He knew from the trials that any intrusion into the limited spectrum could impact drone performance. He held his gaze, then pressed the button and called down to Kai.

"You good, Kai? Over... Kai? Over."

The radio crackled and then stayed silent for longer than he might have expected.

"Here, Wit," Kai answered. "Thought your comms were down. Glad you're okay. Over."

"Better than okay... I'm on fucking fire. Feel like a million bucks. Over."

"More like a billion, you mean. Over."

"Yeah, that too, but the climb, it's not what I expected. Feeling strong, man. I mean unbelievably strong. Over."

"We lost sight of you two hours back. Only your tracks told us you were good. Over."

"I'm at 8,625 now. I'm headed to the Step. If I pick up the pace I can make it to the summit in time for the opening bell on Wall Street. That should get the markets humming, eh? Over."

"Hold on there, Wit. Slow it down, chief. You're gonna blow a gasket if you don't ease off a bit. Trust me on this, Wit. Give us a couple of hours. We'll do this together. Over."

"No can do, Cochise. I'm going solo. See you on top! Over."

Wit flipped off the radio and tucked it back inside his jacket. His breathing remained steady. He returned his pack to his shoulders and, almost intuitively, the drones formed around him and moved forward as one. From his training, he knew that the final 200 meters would be the most difficult. The legendary Hillary Step sat fifty meters from the top along the southeast ridge, and many a climber had made it that far only to fail. Wit bounded forward. He had expected waist-high snowdrifts and slow going at this stage, but oddly enough, his boots sank only a few inches into the snow. The ice ax was unnecessary and remained lashed to the side of his pack, and he knew by the gentle clinking of metal on metal that he had three oxygen tanks at the ready, should he need them. He paused mid-stride and inhaled deeply. The air was thin. But to him, it was ambrosia—nectar of the gods.

"I could fly," he said to himself, leaning into the traverse and wondering if it was possible to "overtrain" for something like this.

Just forty-five minutes later, he found himself at the foot of the famous Step, gazing up at the jagged boulders and outcroppings that signaled the route to the top. The way was marked by ropes and cara-biners that had been pounded permanently into the rock face. He'd traversed over 2,000 meters without clipping in, and he wasn't going to waste time doing it now. Climbers around the world looked on in amazement. No one does Everest without taking all the necessary precautions. Wit Thompson made it look like a stroll in the park.

Kai and the team were still far behind. Knowing that Wit was going to try to summit alone, he urged his climbers to pick up the pace. They were all in peak condition, but the human body could only take so much punishment. By his calculations, they were making good time, so how, he wondered, had Wit been able to get so far ahead? It was verging on superhuman. Forty minutes had passed since radio contact, and he wondered how near Wit was to closing in on the final ascent.

Kai gazed up the side of the mountain to see the long trail of footprints that marked the CEO's ascent.

For the past 100 meters or so, however, something had changed. The impressions in the snow before them were shallow—fifteen centimeters or less—while those behind them sunk knee-deep. Kai suddenly felt nauseous. Was there a melt off? If so, the risk of avalanche just got real. He pulled back the sleeve of his jacket to get a read on the time and temperature: 15:01 and minus twenty degrees Celsius. Plenty cold. While waiting on the others, Kai pondered. Pulling his right leg from the snowbank, he pivoted and placed his foot just above the imprint of Wit's boot, then stepped down. His leg sank to just above the knee. He repeated the movement again, and again his leg plunged down, deep into the snow. As far as Kai knew, Wit was geared up like the rest of them. He had the same La Sportiva boots. The same G10 crampons. Snowshoes would be inoperable in these conditions, not to mention dangerous, and there was no mistaking the outline of the CEO's boot prints. Kai felt queasy, and he wondered whether the altitude was starting to affect his own thinking *and* judgment. He turned his gaze to the summit again, but all he could see was the occasional flash of the silvery drones reflecting the sun's glare.

It was then that the old familiar feeling crept in. A heaviness that weighed down on hope and left in its wake that sour residue of foreboding. Call it climber's intuition—something, he feared, was wrong.

CHAPTER 2

"Come, Enoch. Time to gather."

His mother's voice rang clear. It was the way he would always remember it. As was her daily custom, she removed the woven basket from the hook by the door, took Enoch by the hand, and led him for the thousandth time into the forest. No matter the time of day or the weather, their daily sojourns never lost their mystery. For Enoch, it was like crossing into another world. Tales of the forest peppered his childhood. It was a place, he discovered, that was charged with beauty and laced with danger.

Enoch came to associate his mother's baskets with the forest itself. These, too, were things of beauty. The preparation and time she put into her weaving was not lost on him. She started by removing long strips of bark from the branches of sumac, willow, and honeysuckle. Then, in bowls, she soaked them until they turned soft and supple. With long, strong fingers, she gave them a final knead, before laying them tenderly over low beams. They hung like vines from one end of the tiny house to the other. As they dried, she harvested them, reaching up and pulling down one thread after another and working them seamlessly into tight coils, which she then placed back into wooden bowls.

With mortar and pestle, she ground flesh flowers, berries, and bark. To make yellow, she mixed yarrow and honey locust. For red, sumac and chokecherry. For green, butterfly milkweed and sagebrush. And to make black, she combined mayapple and evening primrose. With a stick, she let Enoch probe the bowls, letting him believe that without his constant prodding the coils would refuse to take the color. Again, she would hang them to dry. And only then would the weaving begin. She began the same way each time, starting from the center and braiding a tight circle of forest green. Every step in the basket's making was accompanied by a tale or instruction. In the years that followed, they would become his catechism—his mantras. He would forever remember the movements of her hands and the sound of her voice. They were interwoven. The two were inseparable.

"That," she said, pointing to the middle, "is the symbol of our Great Mother. And this, the white, is the moment of our birth."

Working outward in ever increasing concentric circles, she introduced a weave of auburn interspersed with yellow, which then went back to dark green. As she wove, the basket took shape—first its sides appeared, gradually, before they then turned upward, more abruptly. She used cedar for the final rung. It stood out, deep black, in stark contrast to the other more subtle hades.

"Why black?" asked Enoch.

"That is death. It is the final step."

"I don't want to die," said Enoch.

"You may not have to, my child," she said, pulling him up from his small stool by the hearth and leading him to the door. "Come. It's time."

Except for the thin line of the footpath that laced its way around the trees, the forest that encircled their tiny home in the glade was lush and undisturbed. Enoch liked it best in the early mornings when the light cast its long beams through the spaces in the branches high above. "God's fingers," his mother called them, fanning out across the forest floor, mist and pollen dancing in and around the shards of light, pirouetting through the ether. Sometimes he would walk holding her hand. At other times, he would run ahead, stop, and turn back to watch her flowing form move in gentle harmony with the pulse of her surroundings. Thick ringlets of auburn hair fell about her shoulders, and he could see through the thin veil of her simple dress her fine, tall form, lithe and alert. She was fair. But then again, she was the only woman Enoch had ever seen. He knew there were others, but he wondered, if he should ever encounter them, would they be anything like his mother?

"Not too far," she cried after him. There was always the footpath, but even so, the wilderness had a way of leading one astray. He was familiar enough with this part of the forest. The scent of the blueberries reassured him. As they approached, he heard rustling in the bushes. The ravens again. They had learned to come early, feast, then flee.

"Shoo!" cried Enoch, as he came into the clearing. Bushes exploded with the sounds of cawing and beating wings. A black shroud hovered above, then darted in all directions to high branches. Black bodies and beady eyes bore down from above. Only the cawing remained.

"We're too late," Enoch sighed. The bushes were bare, with half-eaten berries strewn about.

She stroked Enoch's head and felt his disappointment. "There are more. Just down the way. Stay here and pick what you can. Don't wander, Enoch. If I call, answer back. Do you understand?"

Enoch furrowed his brow as best he could. "Stop worrying, mother. You always worry!"

"Promise me!"

"I promise," he replied.

"Very well. Off with you." And turning, Enoch watched her figure drift away and blend in with the trees.

The forest was his now. He raced across the clearing and into a grove of oaks where the branches hung heavy and low. Good for climbing. With the agility of a ten-year-old, he scurried up the length of one branch, then bounded across the gap to another, mimicking as best he could the movements of monkeys. He soon grew tired and climbed down from the canopy to sit for a while among the mossy patches that grew by the banks of the river, beneath the shade of the willow. There, he was reminded of his mother. It was the place he loved best.

By the river's edge, he witnessed a world divided. On this side was all he knew. On the opposite side, however, all things were foreign. He could see in the distance a tree-lined bank and, on a clear day, what his father called "mountains" jutted up from the land beyond. What of the birds and animals? Were they different from those on this side, he wondered? The only thing more mysterious than the opposite side was the enormous stone boulder that sat at the river's center, parting the currents and causing the water to roar. It was as if it had rolled its way there from some place far upstream, coming to a standstill so that he might do just as he was doing now—pondering it.

The sun settled on the horizon and the water shimmered in response. This was the moment each day when he could let his vision blur to make the boulder disappear, giving him a momentary glimpse of an unobstructed opposite bank. One day, he promised himself, he would make it to the other side. And just like that, he was caught up in a reverie. How long he had been sitting there, he could not say. Enoch snapped to his feet and broke for the path that reached back into the forest. He ran through oak groves and found himself once again in the clearing and among the blueberry shrubs. There, he caught sight of the basket, overturned, with mushrooms, bloodroot, ginseng, and wild ginger scattered across the ground.

"Mother? Where are you?" he shouted. But the forest remained silent, except for the distant fluttering of raven wings and the crackle of grass that was dry and brittle, routed by the heat of the sun.

"Mother. Come out." he insisted, forcing himself to remain still, straining to hear past the more familiar sounds of the forest.

Then a rustle and the thin wisp of a voice beyond the glen.

"Here, Enoch. I'm over here."

Her voice was light and distant and a bit unnatural. He could tell something was wrong. The laughter, always present in her voice, was absent. And that terrified him.

Tearing through a patch of thorns, he winced against the pain, his legs streaked with blood.

"Here, Enoch," he heard her cry. "Come quickly." He was moving as fast as his small legs would carry him. Why had she wandered so far from the clearing? There she was. One leg splayed out at an odd angle. Blood ran down in a crisscross pattern across her thigh. Her dress was torn and her breasts—scratched and bleeding—were exposed. He lunged for her and she winced with pain.

"I'm sorry... I didn't mean..."

"It's all right, Enoch," she moaned, holding him tight against her.

She was trembling and he somehow knew it wasn't the pain. She was afraid.

"I'm all right. I'm going to be all right," she tried to reassure him. Her breath was hot against his neck and he could feel a gurgling in her chest, making him think for a moment of the tiny brook that ran past their home. Enoch didn't move and, for an instant, she went slack in his arms.

"Mother!" he shouted. Her body leapt and Enoch felt her fingers dig into his shoulders, pushing him away.

"You're hurting me," he cried.

Her eyes were wide and distant. But whether from fear or confusion, he couldn't say. And he could see she was working something over in her mind. Enoch waited and studied her tortured face. She lay back, her lips moving, and he drew close, hovering. Her hair was strewn with leaves and matted with blood—the longer he stared, the farther away she seemed to move. All around, the green of the forest was pockmarked with red.

"He's gone now. He's gone." The words came in a whisper, fighting their way back up from the depths.

"Who?" Enoch whispered. "Who did this?"

But she would not, or could not, say. Only the forest responded, cloaking itself in gradual darkness. The dark trunks of the trees and the light rustling in the undergrowth set him on edge. He wondered if the foul creature was still out there. Would he show himself and come back to finish her off? Enoch made ready, but there was no movement. Only the sounds of the forest.

"Is it bad? Can you walk?" he asked, turning his attention back to the woman who lay in a heap beneath him.

"I need you to do something for me. I need you to go back to the clearing and then beyond, back down the trail. You know the way. You've walked it with me a hundred times."

"Not without you."

"But this time you must. Go fetch your father. Show him the way. Hand me that stick. Now go."

Reluctantly, Enoch turned and rushed back through the brambles, wiping away the tears that blinded his way. He found the clearing and the path and started down it. It was bad. No denying that. It was to be his first—but not his last—brush with death.

"She died quickly," his father sought to reassure him. "Too much blood," he muttered. That was all the emotion he could afford, and Enoch resented him for it. In other circumstances, his father's indifference could be easily dismissed. He was unusual that way. Cold and emotionless. Not like his mother. She sometimes made fun of him. "Smile, my husband," she would coax him. "It won't kill you," she teased, nestling into him, tickling his ribs, trying to provoke him. But he never did react. "Stoic," she called him. "Uncaring," thought Enoch. How could he, in this moment, fail to feel for the one person who loved him unconditionally?

For Enoch, losing her was a thing of pure pain. It throbbed in his chest and sides, leaving him breathless. His father offered him nothing in the way of solace, so he took his suffering into the forest, to his spot by the river. The place where the willow hung her head and dipped her branches to play with the current. Arms clasped about his knees, his back to the tree, he saw her figure bending down to search among the shallows for flat stones that she would send skipping from one side of the river to the other. He heard the sound of her laughter when they landed on the opposite bank. "It will never be the same," thought Enoch. And, indeed, it never was.

"We're leaving," his father announced.

It had only been a few days, but Enoch felt almost grateful. In the absence of his mother, the silence in their small house was almost too much to bear. The fresh herbs kept in hanging pots had all withered and died. While his mother had experienced a ritual joy in flinging back the windows and opening the front door each morning to bathe the house in light, Enoch's father forbade it. "Better to be safe," he said.

"Safe from what," thought Enoch? Was the creature that killed his mother still out there? Was this giant who claimed to be his father afraid? Why wasn't he out there now, hunting it down?

Enoch sat hunched on his stool by the hearth, hating the one person who might have saved his mother from death. It had taken him an hour to find his way back to the house and another hour to find his father. By the time Enoch had managed to do so and then show him the way to the clearing, his mother was gone, her body all bled out and part of the earth. Now he was alone with a stranger. An oversized brute with an oblong head. Not even his long beard, braided by his mother with colorful twine and small tokens, could soften the hard-ness that formed itself around him, like bark on a tree. His mother had been everything his father was not—soft, gentle, kind, and joyful. The house suited her perfectly. For him, it was too small. In it, he shifted about like a trapped animal, crouching and ducking to avoid banging his head on the ceiling beams. And when he did finally come to rest, his mind never stopped moving. At all times, he carried with him a faraway expression, as if he was supposed to be someplace else but didn't dare leave.

The object of Enoch's disdain suddenly pivoted and moved from the door to the middle of the room. Without looking his way, he said: "Take only what you need. Leave the rest here. We're going now."

Chapter 3

Traversing the lake and holding close to the shore, Enoch watched as the great body of water transformed itself, absorbing the colors of the sunset before turning liquid black. It had been three full days since leaving the only home he had ever known. His mother was dead, and his father—who moved before him like a great shadow—had barely spoken since their departure. Then, unexpectedly, he stopped.

"Best to be quiet," he said.

"Wolves?" asked Enoch.

"No. The Others."

"Who are The Others?"

"Your mother's people."

"She comes from this place? Where are they now?

"Up ahead. But we must not be seen."

"Shouldn't we tell them what happened to her?"

"*No!*"

His voice was too loud, making the boy jump.

"No, Enoch," his father repeated, his voice now softer. "They did not approve. They will be angry if they learn what has become of her." Enoch detected a trace of remorse. "I broke my promise to them."

"What did you promise?" asked the boy.

Enoch's father made no reply, turning aside and making haste through the trees, forcing Enoch to scramble after him. Before long, they came to a place where the water's edge shone bright. From there, Enoch could see a thin tree line, then a string of huts equally spaced out. Shadows from the flames of scattered fires cast shadows.

"What is this place?" ventured Enoch.

"Your mother's home," his father replied, staring into the dark.

"Do I have family here? A grandmother? A grandfather?"

"I am your family, Enoch. Don't ever forget that. You're not like them."

"How am I different?"

Again, he did not answer.

They drew closer and Enoch could smell meat roasting. He heard the low tones of people speaking. Then came a squeal of laughter and the shadows of three small figures cast against the side of the nearest hut. Enoch felt a mixture of excitement and anxiety well up inside him. He felt drawn to the village. This was his moment. He could break from this man who claimed to be his father. He would rush in and call out at the top of his voice, "It is I, Enoch, son of Ninsun." Would he be received? Would they welcome him in? There was only one way to find out.

He hesitated, and the looming figure of his father sensed what Enoch was about to do.

"No boy! Not this way. Not now. The time will come. We *will* return... but not now!"

His father's words had the intended effect, splitting the air and breaking the spell. It wasn't so much what he said, but *how* he said it that grabbed Enoch's attention. In that moment, there was a different timbre to his voice. It came from somewhere deep inside and down below. It was the tone of voice befitting his given name, Azazel, which meant "spirit of the wilderness." Only when gently chiding him would his mother refer to him in this way. At all other times, he was "my beloved" or "my goodly one" or, on occasion, "my one true love." She had a gift for quelling the wildness that plagued him. Enoch neither understood nor trusted him. He knew him simply as "father."

As they trudged onward, deeper into the forest, Enoch tried not to let his disappointment show. Passing quietly by the village, the sights and smells conjured images of his lost mother. Enoch's melancholy weighed him down. The boy trailed Azazel by only a few paces, but his mood felt like a dead weight. His father must have sensed it. Turning, he scooped up the boy and placed him across his broad shoulders in one smooth motion. Enoch surrendered to it. The fight had gone out of him. "So be it," he thought to himself. "I'll go with him now, but one day, I will return here." It was a promise he made to himself.

It wasn't long before the lengthy, rhythmic strides of his father's gait urged him to sleep. Nodding off, his last image was of the light of the moon cutting its way across the water and pointing to the mountains beyond.

When Enoch woke, the landscape was transformed. The mountains no longer adorned the horizon—a promise of what was to come— but were present, all around and all-consuming. How small he felt in the midst of these giants. They continued to move through peak and valley, and with each step farther into the place that his father called the Upper Realm, Enoch felt the warmth and protection of his native forest seeping away. Here, among the clouds, cruelty reigned. The cold air and rocky ground made a mockery of any two-legged creature that dared to traverse its slopes. Only the winged and cloven-hooved found solace here. With the exception of their vistas and impressive views of the valley below, the mountains, in Enoch's eyes, had little to offer.

"Why is it so hard to breathe?" Enoch called after his father, who was far ahead. Only the deep snow tracks now tied them together.

Azazel turned and Enoch could see that his father, too, was feeling the effects.

"The air is thin," his father called back. The sun was now low on the horizon, and his father's shadow stretched out to reach him.

Enoch lifted one small leg after the other, trying to follow in his father's footsteps.

"Why is it thinner?" he asked, gasping for air and drawing near to Azazel, who stood at twice Enoch's height.

"Perhaps because there is less of it." Azazel bent down and lowered his shoulder. "Come, I'll carry you for a while."

They pushed on, the air growing thinner from one day to the next, the climate becoming colder, and the days becoming longer. Far below, the land spread out before them. There was forest to the south and the east, with more mountains beyond and to the west. There was so much more to this world than anything Enoch had ever imagined.

Days passed and the snow grew deeper. Traversing the ridgeline, Enoch wondered how far the mountains rose into a sky that grew bigger and brighter the higher they went. Passing through the cloud line, he imagined the mountains could rise no further. And yet, when they reemerged, there were only more mountains.

That evening, in a shallow snow cave with only a small fire to keep them warm, Enoch asked the thing he had been wanting to ask for days.

"Are we going to heaven?"

Azazel stopped probing the fire for a moment and looked up. "Why do you ask?"

"Isn't that where we all go when we die?"

"Is that what your mother told you?"

"She said that some believe that when we pass from this world we leave for the sky, move beyond the clouds, and climb high into the heavens."

"That's just a story, Enoch."

"Are you sure?"

"Sure of what?"

"That it's just a story."

"I stopped thinking that way long ago."

"But there are those who believe in a heaven?"

"Yes, I suppose there are."

"Will I ever meet these 'Others'?"

"Yes. If the One wills it," he said.

The irony was not lost on Enoch. The "One" was how Azazel referred to his God. His father rarely spoke of this mysterious being who lived somewhere among the heavens. It appeared to pain him when he did so. But this was not the case for his mother—she saw God in everything.

"God is just another word for what we choose to believe in," she once told him while foraging for food. "God is the way we see the world."

At the time, her explanation was more than Enoch's young mind could manage. His mother, taking pity, leaned over and snatched from the footpath a single acorn. Holding it out in her upturned palm, she said "This is God. It is the promise of a thing. Though small now, it has within it all it takes to become a giant, like this one here," pointing up at a tree that rose 100 meters above them.

"Am I a god?"

His question caught her by surprise, and she smiled.

"In this way, yes, I believe you are," said his mother.

"And will I grow to be tall, like this tree?"

His question made her laugh and Enoch was glad he had asked it.

"Maybe not as tall as this tree. But indeed, tall like your father."

And bending down to let the ringlets of her auburn hair fall all around, he was reminded again of the willow. Enoch felt his feet leave the ground and suddenly he was rotating through space, his mother twirling at its center. This would forever be how he remembered her best.

Coming to a standstill, she knelt and pulled him near.

"My dear Enoch. You are so fine to me. These questions of yours... It doesn't matter in the end. It's what you choose to believe in that matters most. Keep asking your questions, my son, and with this oak tree as my witness, you will come to know your God."

"Why does father not speak of God the way you do?"

"Your father is a private man. He tends to keep his thoughts and opinions to himself. His concerns lie elsewhere."

"He's not like you."

She smiled, and to his surprise, agreed with him. "That is so," she said. "In fact, he is unlike *anyone* I have ever known. He is different in all the obvious ways. His height, his head," she laughed, gently rapping Enoch. "But in less obvious ways as well. He is gentle. Not like the men of my village. He is kind and patient as well. He can be secretive. When he leaves us, he says it is to hunt. But I've seen your father catch a hare or slay a deer with little effort and in no time flat. Sometimes he is gone for days, even weeks. Where he goes and what he thinks about on his journeys remain a mystery. I've learned not to ask, but only to love him on his return."

"Does he love you back?"

"He tries. In his own way. The words and gestures don't come easily. I don't fault him for this. His life—before leaving the Upper Realm— didn't prepare him for a life of love. Or perhaps, he left love behind, far up among those mountains. Those are his secrets, and I've learned to accept it."

"He scares me," confessed Enoch. "When he bids me to follow, I do so. I do my best to keep up with him, but he never slows. He never turns around. I only know him by his backside."

"Enoch, stop," she said, laughing and reaching out to tousle his hair. He leaned in and hugged her about the hips, feeling her softness and wishing he could disappear there.

"He doesn't see things the way you do."

"See what, Enoch?" his mother asked.

"This... all of this. He walks through the world like he's trying to get out. He doesn't see the in-between places. *You* do. I know you do. All the little things that connect one thing to another—the petals to the flowers, the trees to the earth, the river to the bank. Why can't he see them? Why can't he see *me*?"

The words toppled from his mouth and he felt a moment of shame. He dipped his head to let his hair fall across his face, hoping to hide his tears. It made no difference. She knew.

"He loves you, Enoch. He just doesn't know how to show it. It was like this with me in the beginning. He'll come around. You'll see. As you grow, you'll find common ground... a common language. There is a heaviness in him. I don't know why."

It was always his mother's way, to explain away his father's short-comings. To protect him, but from what? That was then. Now, though, she was gone—the victim of some unknown predator.

"It's time," came the sound of Azazel's voice. Light flooded the snow cave as his father threw back the flap. "Today you will meet my brethren."

Prior to that moment, Enoch had never thought of his father as anything other than one of a kind, a loner in the world.

"I will instruct you before we arrive. You must do what I say." And just like that, Azazel turned and headed up the steep slope. Enoch gathered his things and scrambled after him. He had so many questions. But the air was thin and the climb was steep. "Mountain dwellers," he thought. "What would they be like? What would they look like? Large, stern men like his father? Always in motion? Always doing?"

The final ascent proved difficult. The snowy slope turned sharply upward and the boy struggled, with only the thought of arrival keeping him going. After many long and hard hours, the landscape gave way, interrupted by a large fortress with shanks honed from the mighty fir trees far below. The walls stood thirty meters high and at the center was a circular door inlaid with two large cast-iron rings. Beyond the walls, he could see the gentle slopes of rooftops, layered in blood-red tiles and supported by thick wooden beams. Ice daggers framed the fortress and hung precariously above the entranceway.

Enoch's heart raced. His breathing was shallow, and there was a lightness in the air that made him feel like he was floating. The ache in his legs had drained away, replaced by a new energy. He felt the urge to rush forward and lay his hands against the circular doorway, but Azazel held him back.

"Wait." he commanded. There was a sternness in his father's voice, and Enoch obeyed.

Moments passed, and then came a sound like nothing he had ever heard before. It peeled back the surroundings and was then repeated once, twice, a third time. Enoch clasped his gloved hands over his ears and feared that the sound would bring an avalanche of snow down upon them.

He looked up at his father and heard him say, in muffled tones, "They are assembling now. Soon, they will come. Say nothing of your mother."

Before he could ask why, the great door drew back, giving off a sound of metal on metal. From the opening, a phalanx of tall figures emerged in single file, making their way down the sloping gangway. They came dressed in heavy, full-length coats of fur, thick-piled and blinding white. The first among them carried a banner. Upon it was a single embroidered circle with a dot at its center. It was made of a soft, supple material, thin as dragonfly wings, and it snapped and twirled to the timing of the wind. The figures drew near, forming a line along the broad landing at the cliff's edge. From one to the next, they were precisely the same height and could only be told apart by the shape and fashion of their long white braided beards. Their blue-green eyes stared out from beneath prominent foreheads, and their great skulls, smooth and polished, shone bright in the light of the sun. There were nineteen of them, each looking like shaven-headed versions of his own father.

Enoch looked up at Azazel, hoping for a sign of reassurance, but his father held the gaze of the others and waited. His only gesture was to place a hand on Enoch's shoulder, as if to say "Hold steady." The boy could not have moved in that moment if he had tried. He stood riveted in the snow with bated breath, waiting for someone to speak.

Finally, the one in the middle, flanked by nine to the left and nine to the right, broke the silence. "You've come back to us, Azazel?" It was as much a statement as a question. He waited for a reply, but none came. "And who is this by your side?"

The accent was different, but the tone of the voice reminded Enoch of his father's. The boy felt uneasy and reached up to grab hold of Azazel's coat.

"My son, Enoch."

Almost in unison, the expressions on the faces of the nineteen went from stern to shocked, then back to stern again—as if, for an instant, they had lost sight of themselves.

"So it is true. You joined with The Others."

"Not The Others. Just the one. She is... I mean... *was* the boy's mother."

In that instant, he felt the stares of all thirty-eight eyes fall upon him. They were searching for something. It hovered over him, like a hawk circling its prey. Enoch felt their scrutiny pierce into him, and he let his mind go blank. It was a trick he had learned from the forest. A way of disappearing into his surroundings, if only to get closer. A look of surprise passed over his inquisitors' faces, and just as suddenly as Enoch felt the incursion, the connection was lost. The attention shifted once more to Azazel.

"You speak of the woman. Why is she not with you?"

"She has left this world." He hesitated, then added, "It was an accident."

"An accident, you say." The idea seemed to intrigue him. Enoch thought this spokesman for the others might inquire further, but he did not.

"So, your decision was to return to us?" Again, a mixture of a question and a statement.

"It is meant to be. As it was from the beginning."

"So you say!" The reply was sharp. The tone had shifted.

"There is much to explain. I know this. The calling was too strong. I had to leave."

"By whose command?"

The words shattered the air. It was a rebuke and Azazel did not take well to it. Enoch felt his father stiffen and he could see that he was ready to defend himself, but then—just as quickly—his mood softened. And as it did, the sun dipped below the horizon, sending soft, golden rays across the landscape and over all those who had gathered.

"And what did leaving bring you? What questions could the Lower Realm answer that could not be found here, in this place, among your brethren? What more could you want?"

"Your forgiveness."

Azazel's words struck the entourage unexpectedly. A line had been drawn. They waited. And in the waiting, Enoch sensed that whatever Azazel's transgressions might have been, he would, eventually, be forgiven.

Beyond the mountains, the sky turned from dark blue to orange. And as the sun dropped, so did the temperature. Enoch felt his feet go numb. Then came the shivering. It was his chattering teeth that eventually broke the silence.

"Come. We will talk."

And just like that, the nineteen turned aside and, in synchronized steps, headed back up the gangway and through the great round portal of a gate. Enoch and his father followed. As they did so, Enoch felt his father's hand on his shoulder. Leaning down, he whispered to Enoch: "Now you will come to know the ways of the Nephilim."

CHAPTER 4

Carson Spinoza sat in front of the monitor watching the blue line pan from left to right, revealing the jagged patterns of a subterranean world. For more than two decades, he had contemplated this moment. But now that it had arrived, it left him cold. NASA had armed him with some of the most sophisticated Earth-scanning and satellite-imaging technologies in the world. On the fortified grounds of the Goddard Space Flight Center, just ten kilometers northeast of the nation's capital, he had technology and manpower resources at his disposal that most geologists could only dream of. His lab was chockablock with state-of-the-art equipment—so much so that it was hard not to feel a bit self-important at times. Yet, truth be told, the glamor stopped there. Geology was to science what the priesthood was to religion. It was a cloistered life. And that suited Carson just fine.

The coffee rings that stained the surface of his workstation were evidence of the long hours and repeated disappointments of analyzing sonar and satellite data, tweaking the frequencies and displays, all ending in a thin blue line passing across a field of static. Day in and day out, despite each failed attempt, he would return to his charts, reconfigure his equations, and call in his analysts, who would, in turn, generate further sets of calculations in order to run the process again... and again. When applied, these mathematical regressions on the same theme should, in theory, bring Project MEaSUREs one step closer to its ultimate goal—the development of a proven and perfect hologram of the Earth, from surface to core. After some time, Carson stopped measuring his life in hours and days, counting instead the algorithmic variations that were bringing them closer to the completion of the task at hand—a digital rendering of the geological landscape that lay hidden deep within the Earth's interior.

Now, on the blue screen before him, he gazed upon the image of a world that only a few moments earlier had remained entirely hidden from view. Oddly, he felt nothing—it just wasn't the way he had imagined it. He should be ecstatic! The image was more robust than anything he might have hoped for. It was a geologist's fantasy. A complex landscape there for the discovering, were it not encased in countless layers of olivine, pyroxene, and calcium oxide, that is. The Earth's lithosphere finally revealed! It should have been a Vasco da Gama-moment for Carson. But it wasn't.

"Alone again," he muttered to himself. "Maybe this will help." Adjacent to the computer was a row of raised switches. In quick succession, he used his forefinger to flick them all into an upright position. As he did so, the lights dimmed in the large oval room and the domed ceiling above him flickered, then exploded with rivulets of green light—revealing an underworld planetarium exhibiting the thick expanse of the Earth's mantle. It was just a perspective, of course—a way of viewing the ductwork of middle Earth from multiple vantage points. Tunnels, many running through thousands of kilometers of solid rock, were at that very moment transporting molten lava, water, and gasses from one end of the planet to the other. Beyond the mantle, it was assumed that the outer core ran thick in a fiery ocean of liquid iron that burned and swirled at a cool 7,000 degrees Fahrenheit. This molten liquid, in turn, encased an inner core that was believed to comprise a mass of iron, nickel, and elements known as siderophiles, pulsating—red hot—at 10,000 degrees or maybe more. Generating this penetrating look into the Earth's mantle would mean that the book on Earth science would have to be rewritten. And this was just the beginning.

Carson pushed back from the workstation and let the roller chair carry him to the center of the room. There, he reclined as far as the old high-backed beast would allow him, staring up into the constellations of subterranean wormholes, tunnels, and swirling passageways.

"Digital spaghetti," he whispered.

He let his eyes wander across the great expanse, attempting to trace and divide one tunnel from the next, but it was too complex, too entangled. No wonder it was taking his team so long to crack the code on this. Only super-computing and the processing of a trillion giga-bytes of data could have yielded this masterpiece.

Carson was alone in the moment, but he reminded himself that he had wanted it that way. It was he who had volunteered to work through the night. That was the best time for reviewing each day's discoveries, reworking the calculations, and making all the necessary adjustments. It was his way. To have others milling about was only a distraction. His fellow researchers understood this about Carson, and more often than not left him alone. Perhaps, he thought, at least on this occasion, it would have been nice to have had someone else around. Only he was there to witness what could well prove to be one of the greatest discoveries of the twenty-first century. No cheering team members. No congratulatory benefactors. Just one man, alone, at the center of a holographic world that was grander and more myste-rious than anything he might ever have imagined.

He felt his stomach rumble and reached for the leftover half of his store-bought beef and bean burrito. He took one last bite before lifting the lid of the garbage pail and tossing the remainder away. Bad decision, he thought to himself, sitting bolt upright and clutching his stomach, before making a dash for the men's room. As he moved through the long corridor, motion sensors tripped the fluorescent lights one section at a time, guiding his way.

He bounded into the nearest stall and let his pants fall around his ankles. His stomach spasmed and relief soon followed. He sat there longer than necessary, head in hands, then eventually stood up, pulled up his trousers, and left the stall to stand before the sink, splashing cold water on his face and hating burritos. He felt weak, and his mind began to wander until, suddenly, he heard a bang and a clatter from the corridor outside. Jerking two paper towels from the dispenser and quickly drying his hands, he swung back the restroom door and made for the lab. His quick steps echoed along the corridor. Pausing at the entrance, he removed his glasses and leaned forward, allowing the tiny laser to scan his eye, confirming the retinal image. The door flew open and he stepped into the large, domed lab. He paused once more, admiring the digital hieroglyphics of his new underworld discovery. In that moment, he felt cradled by the great green glowing images of a thousand intertwining wormholes, standing—as it were—at the center of the Earth, looking upward and outward. The detail was astounding, glowing with precision. Carson's eyes welled up. He felt his throat tighten.

"What's wrong with me?" he said out loud. "It's not like I didn't work for it," he then said to himself, coaxing away the emotion. This was no *Treasure Island*, and he was no Jim Hawkins. This was real. A true scientific discovery. He felt vindicated. Years of going cap in hand to the Appropriations Committee, where he endured the same questions year in and year out. It was humiliating. Carson despised politics and politicians. Too many times had he and his program been subject to their indiscretions. If it wasn't the amount of money required to continue his research, then it was the nature of his work that gave certain members of Congress a rise.

"Space exploration," cried the conservative senator from Wyoming. "That's what NASA is all about. How many more billions are we going to spend on topsoil and truncations? It's tomfoolery... nothing more than an exercise in navel-gazing! You wanna get a bang for the buck? Look to the stars. That's the future!"

"Here, here," came the responses from the partisan members.

"More grandstanding," thought Carson. "Don't they ever tire of it?" Fortunately for him, there were members of both the House and Senate Intelligence Committees who favored his research and saw the merits of inner-Earth exploration. This left him with no choice but to share the details of his progress. The idea of appearing before them again and showing them the final result made his stomach churn, leaving a peptic taste in his mouth—or maybe that was the burrito.

Standing over his desk, he tapped his password into the console.

"Error" flashed across the screen.

He hit the return button and typed the password again.

"Error."

He wiped his hands down the front of the shirt, thinking they might still be wet. Then he reached out and, once again, typed in the password.

"Error."

"What the..."

The other entryway at the far end of the lab made its familiar swooshing sound, and Carson spun around to see who had entered.

No one. Except for the dim, dull pulsing of green light from the domed ceiling, the expanse of the circular lab—with its forty terminals and wall-mounted servers emanating their soft and succulent hum—remained for the most part in the dark. Carson reached for the panel and, flipping the main switch, doused the room in white light. Shielding his eyes, he cast about. No one.

"Is anyone here?" he hollered. The only sound came from the quiet drone of the servers. Moving from his workstation and gently pushing aside one chair from the next, he approached the far entrance. The familiar red and green light glowed at eye level, and the thick steel-plated glass door was still firmly in place. He pushed the red release button and the door glided open again. Carson stepped into the hallway and called out.

"Is anyone there?" His voice echoed down the length of the corridor. No reply.

"Sleep," he said, turning back to the lab. "I need sleep."

Approaching his workstation, he took hold of the back of his swivel chair and swung it around. There, in the middle of the desk, sat a box of black lacquer, its top inlaid with a gold circle, a single dot at its center.

Chapter 5

Enoch's reception was not what he expected. It was as if he didn't exist—as if he was a ghost in their midst. Day in and day out, the Nephilim went about their business. Everything was structured, from their morning ablutions to the way they sat at and ate their meals, completed their chores, and pursued their studies. Nothing, it seemed, was left to chance. Discipline ruled their world. From where he stood— as a boy of ten—their lives felt monotonous.

"Why do they ignore me?" Enoch asked one afternoon, trailing his father as he made his way from the fortress gates to the mines just beyond.

"In time," he said, "you will know all that you need to know."

Asking Enoch to be patient was like asking the sun not to rise. It was maddening, this place, with all its cold and calculated routines. How he missed his home, the forest, and all the unexpected things that kept him infinitely entertained. The contrast between the two realms could not have been starker. Here, in the place they called Dinas Affaraon, within the Upper Realm, roles were assigned and duties were performed in rigorous accordance with something the Nephilim referred to as "the Book." The goal, Enoch assumed, was perfection, if only because everything around him exuded perfection. His father offered little by way of explanation, but he did mention one day, when Enoch was particularly insistent, that *everything* within and around Dinas Affaraon had its place and its purpose. To what end, though, Enoch could not imagine.

Mealtimes were no less rigid, and the food proved as dull and life- less as the gathering. The Nephilim ate only once a day—a habit that Enoch found difficult to get used to. Back home, he was accustomed to three meals a day, and when those weren't enough, the forest would provide. In their small hut, meals normally came with conversation, stories, and laughter. In the Great Hall, dining remained a silent affair, with the doldrums only being broken by the sound of masticating.

It was after dinner, however, when things got interesting—or at least as interesting as matters could get in the Upper Realm. This was the time they reserved for "debate." Enoch was forbidden from interrupting or asking any questions of his own. But he was allowed to sit and listen. It was by virtue of these gatherings that he began to learn to tell The Twenty apart. And he did so by identifying subtle, almost undetectable, discrepancies. It was a skill that would serve him well for the remainder of his days.

The one called Chazaqiel, for instance. He had a small blemish at the tip of his nose. Another, Araqiel, had a twitch. Each time, without fail, when he was asked a question, he would blink and tremble before answering. The one called Danel would sit with his head bowed, as if napping. Upon the shiny crown of his head was a brown patch in the shape of a wilting tulip. With Samyaza, it was his voice. He was the one who spoke for the others on the day they arrived. All the brethren spoke in thunderous tones, but there was something in Samyaza's voice that rose above the others, sonorous and mesmerizing.

As if discerning the members of the group from each other wasn't difficult enough, trying to make heads or tails of their conversations was enough to put a novice into a trance. Perhaps it was their accents, or maybe it was the general tone, but Enoch discovered it took his full concentration to decipher the voice of one from another. No one ever interrupted. And each was afforded whatever time was necessary to report on what they deemed to be most important. To Enoch, however, it was all gobbledygook. They spoke of weather patterns, of the configuration of the stars, of the strength and direction of the wind. They shared details about the quantities and ratios of the minerals extracted from their mines, the number of trees that were growing and were felled, as well as the amount of one mineral that was to be mixed with another in order to strengthen a compound or render it useless. All the details, Enoch noted, were carefully captured on chiseled slabs of granite that filled the catacombs running long and deep beneath the fortress. It went on like this, each evening, until there was no more to report. Then, one by one, The Twenty—as he came to know them—rose from their chairs and made their way to their respective bed chambers to await another day.

Months passed and Enoch began to question his place among the Nephilim. Then one evening, when everyone except Samyaza and his father had retired, they called him over to join them.

"Enoch. Come here, boy," his father beckoned.

Enoch thought himself to be invisible to them all, so he wasn't sure how to respond.

"Come now."

Standing, he approached with caution.

"There's nothing to fear, boy. Stand here before us. This, as I'm sure you've discerned, is Samyaza. He is the first among us. In my absence, there has been a prophecy. It appears that you may have some role to play here, but it is too early to say. Samyaza has agreed to allow you— both of us—to remain. You will receive instruction."

So unexpected was the proclamation that Enoch was left speechless, and it was all Azazel could do to suppress a smile.

"All of these brethren are keepers of the Great Blessings. Each carries some wisdom as borne through the ages, and if you tend to their instruction, these lessons will serve you well. Do you understand?"

Enoch was still at a loss for words but managed to blurt out an eager "Yes!"

"Do you have anything else to say?"

"No!" he replied. And, quite unexpectedly, both Samyaza and Azazel burst out laughing. It would be a turning point for the boy. Years later, he would remember it as the moment of his making.

"Instruction" turned out to be far less than what Enoch might have hoped for. Questions, it seemed, were forbidden. All he was allowed to do was observe The Twenty as they went about their work. At first, it was difficult to make sense of it all. But what he did learn was this— their methods were solitary. When the Nephilim worked, they worked separately, cloistered away in separate rooms specifically outfitted for the task at hand. It was in this way that Enoch first began to journal. He recorded everything—how they began their day, how they reviewed the records from the previous day, how they approached each step of the process with close attention to the smallest detail. At first, it was exasperating. Over time, however, he learned to admire the way The Twenty placed a premium on focus and discipline.

Enoch had almost given up on the possibility of ever being able to ask a question or hold a discussion with the brethren, but on the day of his sixteenth birthday, the one called Amaros walked out from the fortress gates.

"What are you looking at?"

The words startled the boy. Not since Samyaza had conferred upon him the right of instruction four years prior had *any* member of The Twenty spoken a word to him. At fourteen years of age, he had assumed his life would be one of solitude.

"I ask again, what are you looking at?"

"Are you talking to me?"

"Well, I wouldn't be talking to myself, would I?"

Enoch thought for a moment. "Well... you do that."

"Do what?"

"Talk to yourself."

Wrinkles formed across his smooth forehead. "You must be mistaken."

"I think not. I even wrote down some of the things you've said." Reaching behind him, Enoch pulled out his leather-bound journal, then turned to a dog-eared page and held the entry before Amaros so that he could see for himself.

"Hmph!" he grunted. "Must have caught me off guard."

"Not at all. It's a habit of yours. It's why I think I understand what you do best."

Now it was Amaros' turn to look startled. "And what is it, pray tell, that you think I do?"

"You study the way the elements are drawn together or driven apart."

Amaros tried to hide his surprise. He studied the boy, who seemed to delight in his own cleverness. "So, you think you understand what I do?"

For the next many hours, Enoch and Amaros found themselves deep in conversation. It had taken many long months to arrive at this point, but, at long last, one of the brothers had seen fit to engage, treating him—so Enoch felt—like an equal. One by one, the others followed suit. And in only a few short months, they were able to find some common points of interest and arrive at some deeper level of understanding.

There were some questions, however, for which the Nephilim appeared to have no answers. None, for instance, could say for how long they had dwelled in the Upper Realm, nor how they had arrived in the world in the first place. The Book—the object that bound them to their ways—served as their sole point of reference. Within its pages, it mentioned only once their "descent" into the world, for the sole purpose of preserving and advancing what the Book referred to as the Great Blessings.

"What makes The Twenty special?" Enoch asked Amaros.

"We are keepers of the Great Blessings."

"And who are these blessings for?"

"They are for all the world."

Enoch frowned on hearing this. Amaros was simply mouthing the words as they were written in the Book. What he really wanted to know was what set the Nephilim apart.

"Who then are The Twenty to be blessed with such a task? Who appointed you?"

Enoch hadn't intended his words to sound accusatory, but they did, and he could see that Amaros was either hurt or shamed by them.

"Fallen or not, it's what we angels do!"

CHAPTER 6

"Hey-ho! Hands off. Can't you read?" hollered Philomena from the back of the store.

The two college-age girls turned with a start.

"Sorry, we didn't know," said one.

Philomena jumped down from the stool behind the register and came out from behind the counter. She had an unnaturally long gait for someone so short. In less than ten strides, she made her way from the back to the front of the store. The two girls stared wide-eyed at this little woman adorned in a long patchwork skirt of taffeta and lace, with a leather-and-stud halter top—plus an attitude to match. Her long sandy brown hair fell loose about her shoulders, and woven within the curls and tangles were tiny beads, medallions, and bird feathers. Bracelets of all sorts ran up and down her arms and jangled and clinked as she moved. Her face was dark and sunbaked. And while she was doing her best at that moment to look cross, there was nonetheless an air of humor about her that could not be disguised.

"That's an heirloom," she said to the girls, primping and adjusting the flapper dress that clung to the lithe mannequin.

"Oh," said one of them. "Was it yours?"

Philomena knew when she was being teased.

"I guess you might say it is mine, seeing that this is *my* store and these are *my* items."

"So is it for sale or not?" asked the girl.

"Are you blind, missy?" said Philomena. "Can't you read the sign?"

"What sign?"

"The one hanging… Oh dear…" Philomena cast her eyes about the mannequin, then searched the floor. Stooping down, she snatched the "For Display Only" sign, dusted it against her long sleeve, and rehung it over the mannequin's neck.

"Well, pardon me then. Not quite myself today. Full moon and all, you know... Have yourselves a look around. New batch of vintage tops over there," she said, pointing to the racks along the back wall. Giggling, the girls drifted in the direction of Philomena's outstretched arm.

For the past twelve years Philomena Pettibone had owned, run, and fussed over the little shop she called *De Cru*. During that time, its contents had morphed from one theme to another. When the shop first opened, she featured small glass-blown angels that she had purchased lock, stock, and barrel from the closing down sale of a department store in Boulder. She had spent days painting the ceiling of her shop with puffy clouds on a blue background, before stringing the little glass figurines on long strands of fishline. She hung mirrors along both walls, added soft lighting, and played celestial music on the little stereo behind the counter. It was perfect! Perfect, that is, until she opened for business. In one day, she lost eight of the little figurines to what she would later call an "occupational mishap." Customers—on average a fair bit taller than she was—with their heads in the clouds, collided with the swinging glass angels, relieving them of their trumpets, limbs, and wings.

Indeed, within three days, half her stock had been decimated on the hard tiles of the little shop. First there was a clatter, then a tinkle, and then a sound of shattering glass. As one customer, then another, back-pedaled from the store while voicing their apologies, the celestial—and sacrificial—shards of glass lay strewn about the floor. Few offered to pay. And Philomena, reluctant to make a stir, rarely asked. It seemed wrong to blame the customer in a store engineered for disaster. She thought about hanging a sign that read: "You break it. You buy it." But the tone did not befit the beatific setting. Instead, she took the path of least resistance, and closed up shop after only five days. Balanced tippy-toe on her step stool, one by one she removed the wounded angels from their airy orbit.

In the months that followed, Philomena swapped out one retail concept for another. Each effort would start with a bang. But nary a month would pass before shoppers—and sales—waned. Scented candles, Nepalese curios, beads and bangles, antique photos. You name it, Philomena had tried it. Vintage clothing was now in vogue, so she reached out to an old classmate who had moved from Chicago to

New York and made it big in secondhand clothing. "More than happy to help out an old friend," said her classmate—and two weeks later, a container of old clothing arrived on Philomena's doorstep.

It was more than the little store could handle, so she put out an all-points bulletin to her fellow shop owners and, as was customary, they all pitched in. It took ten hours of lifting, stacking, and hanging, but when it was done, Philomena was officially a vintage clothier.

"This calls for a celebration," she shouted, and running to the front, she locked the door and lit every candle she could find. The party went hunting among the loose piles of clothing for the most outlandish outfits they could find. Justin from the cannabis shop snuck out the back and returned with a jug of his precious moonshine. Philomena produced a ziplock bag of dried mushrooms. And Candice, the druggist, handed out licorice sticks. Now dressed up, they imagined themselves as a pack of troubadours. While Eugene (the pet store owner) played the flute and Angelina (the tarot card reader) strummed the mandolin, the others skipped and twirled through piles of clothing until they fell to the floor in a heap, then for the next several hours watched candles cast their shadows across the ceiling.

In Manitou Springs, tourists outnumbered the locals three to one. The novelty shops that ran up and down Canon Street had been a regular feature of this town since the 1960s when it was discovered by a colony of hippies who moved there in search of the quintessential "alternative lifestyle." Over the years, the town had attracted all kinds, and it was a little more than a decade earlier when Philomena and her then lover had first turned up to partake in the annual "Great Fruitcake Toss."

She rode into town on the back of a Harley-Davidson FXS Low Rider. Stepping off the bike and into the circle of fruitcake-launching enthusiasts, she felt oddly at home. And so she stayed. It was the "feeling" that Philomena had in Manitou Springs, rather than the novelty shops or fruitcakes, that kept her firmly affixed to this western outpost— what she would describe as "an energy."

If "thrift store owner" was her vocation, it was "Earth art" that reigned as her life's great passion. Growing up in Chicago as the youngest of four, Philomena spent the first half of her life living in a cement jungle. In the Windy City, the only green thing was money. For most of her childhood, concrete corridors and traffic lights framed her world.

That all changed some six weeks before her high school graduation, when her English teacher—a hangover from the Flower Power generation—introduced the class to Jack Kerouac's novel *On the Road*. To set the mood, he proposed a road trip. Philomena was dead set against it.

"I have a science project to finish," she told her teacher.

"You aren't taking science," he replied.

"I'm allergic to grass!"

"Wear shoes."

"I get carsick!"

"You can ride in front."

There was no escape. On the appointed day in early May, twelve students with permission slips piled into two '49 Hudson sedans. And like Jack and Neal some thirty years prior, they headed out of the big city, past go-downs, train stations, warehouses, and housing projects. Within half an hour, the urban landscape had given way to suburban sprawls—living hells for any self-respecting city-dweller.

An hour in, and the old cars with their beating engines emerged onto an open two-lane highway. Fields of green spread out peacefully around them, and the engines followed suit, settling into a dull hum. Philomena closed her eyes and pressed her head into the soft leather headrest. The slight smell of mildew filled her nostrils. She rolled down the window and a light wind caused her hair dance around her face. The scent of farmland now filled the car.

The two Hudsons, bumper to bumper, drifted into the hills and onto a smooth curving road that cut its way through thick forest. Philomena half opened her eyes, dazzled by the light that now flickered through the trees. She felt herself drift off, then awoke when the car turned with a bump and a rumble onto a narrow dirt road. She rolled the window down all the way and took in the sweet smell of pine. After a quarter of an hour, they emerged from the trees. In front of them was an expanse of water. The light played off the water's surface and the lake was lined with trees as far as the eye could see.

One by one, the students rolled out of the sedans and wandered in different directions, stretching and enjoying the warmth of the day. Picnic benches stood along the lake's edge and, after a while, the group gathered around them. Lunch consisted of ham sandwiches and potato chips, but Philomena was not hungry. Instead, she drank cold iced tea from a thermos. The more she drank, the thirstier she became.

Nestling among the roots of an old oak tree, she pulled her paperback out of her daypack. Folding the book back, she wiggled her hips to make an indent in the ground, where the soil ran thick and dark around the base of the tree. And there she bathed in Kerouac's prose, while the breeze tousled her hair and tried calling her away.

She woke with a start. The book had toppled over, leaving the wind to rifle through its pages. Beneath her, the ground was wet and moist. Had it rained, she wondered? How long had she been asleep for? Her body felt heavy and her impulse was to remain exactly where she was, cradled and rooted by the tree. She reached down with both hands and clutched at the soil, bringing two handfuls close to her face. Unclenching them, she watched as it toppled through her fingers, soft and dark, leaving her hands wet and deep red.

"Blood," she whispered.

Wiping her hands against the exposed roots of the tree, she then gently reached beneath her dress, feeling the dampness. It clung to her and the air around her, that familiar sweet metallic scent, reminding her that life is both a cycle and a circle.

She lay still, close to the earth. Closing her eyes, she imagined herself naked, bathing in the warming currents of a natural hot spring, with water welling up from somewhere deep beneath the surface, lapping across her thighs, seeping into her groin, and creeping up and across her stomach. She felt pools of steaming wetness cascade and bubble around her, before seeping back into the earth. From where the water sprang and then receded, small green shoots appeared—fiddleheads unfurling and beckoning to her, stroking her inner thighs and braiding their way through the soft hair at her groin. They were calling to her, beseeching her, growing fast and wild from the blood-soaked soil that encircled them both.

Philomena's eyes sprung open as if a spell had been broken. With that "Awww!" the world went technicolor. Like Dorothy pushing back the door, she woke to a Munchkinland of her own making. It was as if all her senses had suddenly burst through the surface and she felt... really *felt*... for the first time. All around, the world shimmered. If this was rapture, she thought, I'm most certainly in it. Every ounce of her body squirmed to contain the euphoria of the moment. She rose from the spot, gathering the ends of her dress, and walked to where a small stream pushed free from the forest. While the trees looked on, she straddled the flowing water, then squatted down and gently cleaned herself, sending a ribbon of red into the slow-moving current.

The world, she discovered, looked different from among the trees. Hues of green gathered and separated before her eyes, and she saw things hidden in the spaces in between. Drying her hands as she walked, she entered a clearing where moss lay thick as a carpet over the forest floor. She dropped to her knees, leaned over, and placed her ear against the cool earth. She closed her eyes and listened, and she knew then that anything worth knowing lay beneath the surface.

Nothing would ever again be the same. She knew this now. How much time had passed, she could not say. But when the others called out for her, she reemerged from the woods without a word and climbed back into the '49 Hudson, while everyone stared. They were driving, but she might as well have been flying. Two days later, once the trip had ended, she informed her parents that she had places to go—with a duffle bag, $43, and some loose change, she left Chicago and the city forever.

CHAPTER 7

"Clear!" came the shout from the tower. The men stood back and the rat-a-tat-tat of the wheelhead resumed. Jets of water and steam poured from the hole in the platform and swirled around the bell nipple at the top of the casing string. The air was thick with heat and humidity. Spike felt the sweat pour down his back, under thick layers of fire-retardant clothing. His feet felt hot and clammy in his steel toe boots. Sixteen days of back-to-back shifts and four days to go before the end of the hitch and some R & R. Landing on this oil rig deep in the Persian Gulf wasn't what he had had in mind, but it paid well and he knew that "roustabouts" couldn't be choosy.

"Back it out, you ginzels!" cried the foreman, leaning out over the elevator, his words muffled through the noise-protective headgear. Spike and the two other men hauled back on the big bear hitch and Spike leaned in to release the drill string. It belched with the easing of the pressure. J.D., the motorman, stepped forward and examined the bell nipple.

"There's a moon pool down there, I swear by it," he shouted.

"Not possible," screamed the foreman. "We've been over the Horner plot a thousand times. It's clear!"

"I'm tellin' ya, it ain't," hollered J.D. "She's gonna kick if we don't back it out."

"Fuck that. You wanna stay on it, then stay on it. Otherwise, hand it over to Shrill there. He'll do what he's told."

For the past five days, the drill had been acting up. The well log showed no obstruction—a clear shot at the target, some thousand meters below. Their deepest attempt yet. At 500 meters, they unexpectedly struck basalt, forcing a change in plans and a "kickoff" to the west. End-rounding the obstruction had taken them three days longer than planned, and corporate was not happy about it. Now edging down to 850 meters, the drill again stopped biting.

"You're gonna go fishing for the shards if this point blows?" challenged J.D.

"Fine, pull it and drop the pig. Clean her out and we'll try again at 18:00."

"Get yer ass over here, Shrill. Jerk that thing out," yelled J.D.

Shrill had earned his name from his high-pitched voice. It was an odd sound to come out of a man standing nearly six foot eight. It gave the others an odd pleasure, making the giant do all the scutwork. He didn't protest. He was a newbie among veterans, the "worm" of the lot. "Pigging" was as tough as it got. Like cleaning a clogged toilet three kilometers deep. Shrill shrugged and got to it.

"You stay with him," said J.D., pointing at Spike while removing his gloves. The crew lumbered off in the direction of the wet room, where they'd peel back their sweat-soaked pullovers before heading to the canteen for coffee.

Spike looked at Shrill and muttered, "Let's git her done."

The two men hauled back the safety locks. Spike reached for the casing hanger and swung it into place. Shrill jumped over the well to the left and lifted the hatch. He dropped the wire line to measure the free point, the place where the drill had seized up.

"If we gotta sidetrack this bitch again, we won't be seeing beach and booze for another week," grumbled Shrill.

"Might just be the drill string, let's see first," said Spike.

Together they bore down on the accelerator and started the cleaning-out process.

"I'll go for the floorhand. See if he can help," said Shrill, already thinking about how he might hand this one off. He hated this part of the job.

"I'm good," replied Spike.

Shrill headed across the expanse of metal walkway that led to the far end of the rig. His tall figure, wearing an orange pullover, stood out against the dark and cold metal of the rig and scaffolding. Spike shrank back against the bulwark and sat down with his back against the railing. It was a good 100-foot drop from there to the surface of the ocean. He turned and peered over the side. Long swells of dark water moved from east to west and cut across the pylons—intruders in their midst. The ocean was black from that height. No sign of life.

"Miserable fuckin' existence," he muttered under his breath.

As he was frequently reminded by his foreman, Spike was relatively new to oil rigs. He had spent one hitch—twenty days—on another rig in the Gulf of Mexico. It was a lot easier there. He had struck out after graduation, looking to make some quick money. Dallas or Houston seemed like good choices. Spike came from a long line of riggers. He was a third-generation Gulf Coaster out of the greater Austin area. His father spent twenty-three years as a toolpusher—a rig boss—driving men through twelve-hour shifts, day in and day out. Too young at the time to know any better, Spike thought his father drank and slept for a living. When he was home, which wasn't often, that's all he did. The old man didn't even wake up for college ball games—and in the state of Texas, that counted as odd behavior.

Petroburton Corporation had been good to the old man. They gave him steady work, offered first-class healthcare, and helped his family pay off the mortgage on their home. The house wasn't much, just a one-story structure with a few rooms and a screened-in porch, but it meant something to Spike's father. His mother worked as a waitress at Callie's. She had been there only a few months when Spike's father walked in for a cup of coffee. "She had attitude and a fine pair of taillights," he used to say. There weren't too many options in a town the size of Bastrop, so she agreed to marry, and when he wasn't rigging and she wasn't waitressing, they spent all their time in bed. Spike was the product of their efforts. When the old man got promoted to toolpusher, he got busy and stopped coming home as much. Down at Callie's, the truckers teased his mother about the long dry spells, and she took a few of them up on their offers to make things right. But most of the time, she would just come home dog-tired, wanting to put her feet up and looking for attention from the one person in her life who served as a constant—her one and only son.

"Rub my shoulders for me, Spike honey," she used to coo, her silk robe tied loosely around her hourglass figure, the fan on its stand caressing the robe and tousling her hair. When he was younger, Spike obliged, doing as he was told and applying lotion to her neck and shoulders. As he got older, though, he became more reluctant.

"Come over here sugar. Now tell me 'bout them girlfriends of yours," she'd tease.

"You know I ain't got no girlfriend," Spike shot back. "What's so damn special about girls, anyway?"

"We women know things, honey. You just startin' out. You'll see what I mean soon 'nuff," she'd say, lifting herself from the couch and walking to the kitchen with a hip roll perfected from years of waitressing.

It seemed the older he got, the more his mother needed him. She would ask him to run errands, sit with her at the beauty parlor, and, when they were back at home, take the silver-handled brush and comb out her hair, now grown thin with age. By the time he entered his teens, Spike had had about enough of it. He started looking for ways to stay away from home. At age thirteen, he built his own motorbike by scavenging used car lots for spare parts. At age fourteen, he developed an appetite for making money and would sometimes hold down three jobs at once, before and after school. He'd haul rebar to new building sites in the morning, work as a roofer most afternoons, and substitute as a dishwasher at the American Legion when the regular guy didn't show up.

"Whaddya saving for, boy?" asked one of the regulars at the Legion. "Got big plans, do ya?"

"Just planning to get outta here," said Spike to the old-timer, rolling past him as he hauled one last load to the dumpster before calling it quits.

He was only fifteen, sitting at home and watching reruns of the TV show 24, when the phone rang with the news. The old man had died.

"It was a blowout," reported the employee relations manager. "No one saw it coming. We regret the incident and offer our prayers," he said in that scripted voice.

They may have prayed, but they didn't pay. And when Spike and his mother learned that the old man had stopped submitting his union dues as early as 2003, there wasn't much to be done. There were a few phone calls and visits from lawyers, but ultimately Spike's mother received a check for $3,420.10 and a promissory note stating that Petroburton Corporation would not take legal action to recover his father's unpaid loan.

It seems that Spike's father did have dreams after all—when he wasn't sleeping, drinking, or working on rigs, he was speculating on a group of wildcatters from West Texas. The old man had worked with a few of them in the late 1990s. The three of them used to talk about "making it big" one day, so they started pumping money—just a few hundred dollars at first, which soon became thousands—into speculative claims. Spike's father never spoke of it, but he'd secretly enrolled in an employee loan program without mentioning it.

"He dug himself quite a hole," said the lawyer, who showed up at the house with a stack of documents for Spike's mother to sign. "He was well-liked, Mrs. Morrison. I assure you that. The men all showed him lots of respect." And with that, the lawyer—pink-faced and paunchy—stuck out his meaty hand, said his farewells, then turned and walked away.

Spike lost his appetite for odd jobs after that and ended up hanging out in the school weight room most afternoons. Lifting weights was a solitary affair. The sound of clanging metal and the smell of old sweat gave him odd comfort. By age sixteen, he had bulked out, and one afternoon the football team poured in for preseason training. He moved to the bench press, trying to keep to himself. A few of the players came closer, waiting their turn.

"How much you bench?" asked one of them.

Spike looked down, hesitated, then said "I'm up to 315."

"Bullshit!" said the player.

"Bullshit yourself," Spike shot back.

"Show us," said another, who had walked up to join the first.

Spike hauled off the rack one forty-five-pound plate after another, loading them onto the barbell. The bench groaned, and a few of the other players started gathering around. He placed himself beneath the bar and, seeing a crowd of heads hovering above him, closed his eyes, before taking three deep breaths. Months had passed since Spike had given up work for weights. Lifting gave him something to do—he didn't really care how much he could lift or how his body had changed. The iron bar pressed hard into his palms. He tightened his jaw and, with a grunt, lifted the bar from the rack. Arms quivering, he let the bar down gradually until it grazed his bulging pecs. He hesitated only a moment, then he arched his back and drove the bar—and 315 pounds of metal—skyward.

"Shit!" exclaimed one of the onlookers.

"Check this out," called another.

Spike returned the bar to the rack and sat up. Coach Ripple pushed through the group of players. His head seemed too small for his body, and the bill of his cap was curled tight, making it look that much smaller. He clutched a clipboard in his meaty right hand, and the muscles of his forearm spasmed. His thin-lipped mouth pursed out when he squinted, and he was squinting at Spike now.

"What's your name, son?"

"Spike Morrison."

"Where'd you learn to do that, Spike?"

"Do what, sir?" Spike replied.

"Lift that kind of weight."

The coach gestured to one of the bigger players standing at the foot of the bench.

"John Ross over there can hardly push 300. How'd you manage 315?"

"Practice, I guess, sir," said Spike.

"You play ball, boy?"

"I don't, sir."

"You wanna play ball?"

"Not particularly."

"Why the hell not?" shouted the coach.

"I guess you might say I'm not much of a team player."

"You know about the front line, Spike?"

"Yeah, I guess I do."

"Well, you don't have to know how to play ball, but you gotta know how to hit. You wanna hit someone, son?"

"S'pose I do," answered Spike.

For the rest of that season and the two seasons that followed, Spike became something of a legend in his small town. At first people joked about it. "Bench lifter turned bench warmer," they quipped. For a kid who had never played, he surprised everyone by making the first string that season and All American the next. He had speed and grit, and as he told the coach, he liked to hit. His senior year, they moved him off the line and turned him into a free safety. There he showed the county and the state just how talented a ballplayer he was. Then came the scouts and recruiters. They poured into the little town of Bastrop for one reason and one reason only: to recruit the young Morrison boy. Texas A&M, Ole Miss, Oklahoma—they all showed up, waving their school colors and wooing him with tales of fame, glory, and women.

"Come down our way and you'll have all the ass you can handle," said one overzealous scout.

But Spike couldn't have cared less. "I'm done with football," he announced.

And just like that, at the close of the season, Spike quit football for good. "Problem with that boy is that he's got no ambition," said one recruiter. While dozens of his teammates headed off to football training camp that summer, Spike struck out for the coast.

Working the rigs in the Gulf of Mexico that summer wasn't as short-lived as he had first imagined. He stayed on through the fall and into the winter. After a year, some of his crew drifted off with vague notions of "better work somewhere else," but Spike stuck around. From one hitch to the next, he hung with the rigs, and like his old man, he'd head back home in between stints to sleep and drink.

That was two years ago, and now he sat here, propped up against the railing in some godforsaken place in the Persian Gulf.

"Some shit," he muttered.

Shrill hadn't returned, and Spike was about to throw it in and head to the canteen when the drill tower started rattling—lightly at first, then louder. By the time he lunged from the railing to the hole, the entire structure was convulsing. He pulled the headgear over his ears while reaching for the bell nipple at the same time. It shuddered and quaked, and even with Spike's kind of upper body strength, he found it hard to swing the nipple back from the hole. The minute he did so, the shaking and high-pitched whistling stopped. Pulling back his headgear, Spike listened. The whole rig was still and quiet. The engines had stopped. All he could hear was the lapping of waves far below. Even the air was still.

The bull chains that hung from the rigging allowed Spike to reach up and take a firm grip. The Kelly drive hung limp over the hole. He planted his feet, then angled himself over the well, holding tight to the chains, shoulder muscles flexing. By lowering his gaze, Spike could now look directly down into the well shaft. With the remaining light of day, he could only see three to four meters down, and for a minute, he smiled at his own foolishness. What could he really expect to see? But there it was, deep at the bottom of the well—a light pulsing and throbbing liquid blue. As if suddenly and inexplicably blessed with periscope vision, Spike found himself staring 550 meters into the Earth's crust. His mind raced, trying to keep up with what his eyes were telling him. For a minute, vertigo got the best of him. His legs started to buckle, but he pulled on the chains and righted himself, never taking his gaze away from the beating blue light. Somewhere far away, Spike heard Shrill's high-pitched voice.

"What the hell you doin'?" he heard him cry.

Spike could hear Shrill racing across the metal walkways from the direction of the canteen, the clang, clang, clang of his metal-tipped boots against the scaffolding. It was at that instant that the light billowed, receded, and then shot upward in one ominous burst. Spike's eyes opened wide as aqua blue light flooded his head, slamming against the back of his skull. Spike let go of the chains with his right hand, clutching his face. His body arched over the hole, consumed by the explosion of crystalline light that shot from the well. His left arm remained coiled in the chains, though, and he started to spin back and forth across the opening like a pendulum gone haywire. He felt himself slipping into unconsciousness when the force of Shrill's six-foot-eight frame suddenly came crashing into him, heaving him across the hole. The chains gave way, the two men collapsing into a heap, half splayed over the edge of the platform. The last thing Spike remembered hearing before passing out was the high-pitched wail of Shrill's voice.

CHAPTER 8

"What news?"

"It's begun."

"How can you be sure?"

"There's been a shift."

"How do you know this is the one?"

"Do you need to ask me this?"

"No, I suppose not."

The man in the long dark coat walked the length of the table to where floor-to-ceiling windows offered a panoramic view of snow-capped mountains. He stood there, saying nothing but letting loose an audible sigh.

"Have you chosen?" he asked.

"It's not for me to choose."

"Who else, if not you?"

"They aren't ready."

"Were we ready?"

The question fell like darkness across the room. For a long time, neither of them spoke.

"I had no choice. You know that."

"Yes, I know. You did what you had to do. But this time it will be different. No one will be forced. They can say no."

"Can they? *Will* they? They can't even know what's at stake."

"None of us do. We have to find out."

"Then why don't you and the others go?"

"You know that's not possible. We need them. They feel the world in ways we do not. It's gnawing at their souls. That's why *you* must choose for them. Only you can free them from the darkness of not knowing."

"I don't even know!"

"Oh, yes you do. You've known for a long time now. And now there's evidence."

"Perhaps I should go alone."

"You are resourceful, my boy. But even you, the solitary one... our chosen one, don't have what it takes to discover alone what we believe to be true. You need them! The *world* needs them! Now, go!"

CHAPTER 9

Wit Thompson's "disappearance" from the top of Everest had every media outlet in the world buzzing. For weeks, news agencies had ushered through studio experts of every ilk: professional climbers, meteorologists, cosmologists, astrophysicists, even climate change experts. They were all asked the same question: what happened to Wit Thompson? But no one could explain what had been so evidently portrayed in high-definition 3D. Scientific rationale, at least for the moment, remained elusive. Every interview was a mind-numbing display of gross speculation, which only prompted other theories, causing the media to roll out a cavalcade of philosophers, metaphysicists, mystics, and, of course, religious leaders.

Reverend Avon Caulfield was the first to say it. "Our time has come," he told the CNN anchor. "This is God's way of saying, '*Prepare yourself!*'"

The response was predictable. The airwaves, blogs, and social media sites exploded with all manner of further speculation. Self-professed experts began recounting Bible passages—some real, some not—that spoke of the "Second Coming" and a "Day of Reckoning." Church numbers nationwide had been declining for years. But in the time between Thompson's disappearance and Caulfield's declaration, attendance had rebounded. Now, each Sunday, nearly 200 million Americans clamored to enter churches ill-equipped to manage the demand. In North America, Latin America, Africa, and North Asia, converts flocked to the Pentecostal message. Tents sprang up everywhere to welcome "sinners" in search of redemption—a call to worship, *before it was too late*. Not only Christians, but also Muslims, Jews, Hindus, and Buddhists all found references in their own scriptures to a time of pending doom, meaning that the end-of-days banter was the one subject that, for the first time ever, united people of all religions.

Avon Caulfield—a television evangelist who five years earlier had faced accusations of money laundering and tax evasion—found himself at the head of this movement. Oh, how things had changed. Fear, it seemed, had proven to be a powerful motivator for people returning to faith. The image of Avon, heavy-set and thick-jowled, had become a feature of the media, like the image of Wit Thompson before him. Avon was made for the part. Cut from the cloth of the many "fire and brimstone" preachers that had gone before him, he knew just enough Scripture to be convincing, but not enough to appear conceited.

His gift was his rhetoric. His curse was his ego. Early on, Avon had floundered as an associate minister at the Church of God in Shelbyville, ending up at the Calvary Christian Center, where he ran prayer groups twice a week. There, he discovered that he had a knack for "riling the senses," as he put it, and he decided that he would start his own movement, rather than conform to church doctrine. Within six months, he had garnered enough support to launch an evangelical radio program. And with the help of his young converts, he wiggled his way into the world of digital podcasting, where his unique message of power through God combined with brazen materialism went viral.

Avon's message resonated, and the Pentecostal Order took notice. The elders hated how Avon, the upstart, was setting the pace for born-again conversions, but they knew that the movement would languish without him. Rather than reject Avon, they embraced him *and* his followers. From a backcountry nobody to an evangelical rock star, Avon now stood at the helm of a media empire. His Sunday morning services were streamed live and boasted viewership from around the world. They offered simultaneous translation, real-time interactive messaging, and virtual "salvations." Avon's phalanx of social media wizards built the entire enterprise under one brand—*GODacious Ministries*. And it was under that banner that Avon Caulfield was on a fast track to become the Mark Zuckerberg of religion.

Even before Wit Thompson's disappearance, Caulfield's message was on the rise. With the CEO's "emancipation," as it would later be called, Avon and his followers found a foothold that would lift them—so to speak—to new heights.

"God is merciful," boomed Avon. "But only to those who pave the way! Don't listen to me. Listen to God! For he was the one who delivered our dear Mr. Thompson to a better place. Others *will* follow. As it is written, so shall it be done," Avon bellowed.

Pearls of perspiration broke out across his broad forehead and thick upper lip. He quietly cursed the station. They had agreed to chill the studio to a crisp sixteen degrees Celsius. Avon, as was widely known, had a propensity to sweat when infused with the Holy Spirit.

"You keep saying this, Reverend, but where's the evidence?" asked the interviewer.

"Evidence?!" Avon blustered. "What more do you need, ye of little faith?! We all saw it. Dear God, the whole *world* saw it. Swept up to the heavenly gates was our Mr. Thompson. *Freed* from the chains that bind us to this life... tethered... I say *tethered*... can I get an amen... to the demon of our nature? *He* is the one! *He* is the messenger... our John the Baptist. *He* is the one who shall prepare the way for the Second Coming of Christ, our Lord and Savior. What greater proof do you need?"

Avon had been testing this message for days now, and the analytics across all social media feeds had proven to be encouraging. It was a winning narrative, and he was sticking to it.

"Reverend Caulfield, with all due respect, sir, there is—at least for now—no universal explanation for Wit Thompson's mishap. Some suggest a sudden shift in weather patterns, not unlike a rogue wave. They say the winds might have knocked him clear off the summit that day. There are other theories as well. The jury is out. Would it not be best to see what science has to say on the subject?"

"The jury is out, you say?" There is no jury in the court of God, for it is his divine wisdom that determines our destiny. The Lord Almighty chooses who lives and who dies! Mark my words, the rapture has begun, and Mr. Wit Thompson is the one who goes before us. *Praaaaise* the Lord... our *chosen* one. It is all part of God's plan. Can I get an *amen*?"

"Well, I..."

"No, sir. No, sir. It was *not* a coincidence," he interrupted, now feeling the Spirit pulse in his veins. "Why not a poor child from the jungles of the Congo or an old woman from the highest hills of old Nepal? I'll tell you why. Because where God strikes, thunder follows. And thunder, my good man, is here wrought in the wonder

of modern media. God chose the time and place, and we—all of us—
were watching. 40 million believers from around the world looked
on as our SkyBound CEO mounted the heavens and rose to meet his
maker. Moses on the Mount was Mr. Wit Thompson. What can science
tell us that we didn't see with our own eyes? *Praise* be to God! Lord
have mercy! There is no explainin' for what needs no explainin'! Wit
Thompson *rose* atop mighty Everest! He *defied* the very laws of nature!
He was *reborn! Cradled,* dare I say, in the arms of the Lord Almighty.
SkyBound! The very name of that man's company bears witness to his
divine liberation. This was no mortal feat. This was *God's* work, I tell
you. Can I get an *Amen?*"

On the point of defying logic, Avon's words rang true. Wit
Thompson, at the moment of his "flight" into thin air, had looked
otherworldly, imbued with a supernatural energy that made nearly a
billion viewers gape in wonder. For those who had virtually traversed
the mountain that day alongside the CEO, with his customized VR
glasses and white-toothed smile, it was hard not to imagine that
something extraordinary, magical, or even metaphysical might have
occurred. Viewers from around the world were both participants in
and witnesses to Wit Thompson's demise. Or was it his liberation?
Against this backdrop, Reverend Caulfield's words rang true.

CHAPTER 10

Kai Horner sat in his cottage on the outskirts of Christchurch watching the interview with Avon Caulfield. Losing a client was never easy. It had happened before, but not like this. For weeks now, he had been vilified by the climbing community. They called him callous, irresponsible, reckless. He was none of those things. Of course, the live footage of Wit Thompson's ascent might have suggested otherwise. The sheer fact that he and the other climbers had trailed Thompson by such a distance was clear evidence that Horner was not in control of the situation. Others—the Nepalese in particular—were less critical of how he "managed" the situation and more disturbed by the "spectacle" that the SkyBound CEO had created. Such an intrusion of technology onto the slopes of their sacred mountain amounted to apostasy, an affront to their culture and beliefs. Everest, or *Chomolungma*, as it was known to them, meant "Holy Mother," a sacred domain, impenetrable and unknowable. The High-Fly 9000™ changed all that, exposing all aspects of her majesty to the prying eyes of armchair adventurers scattered across the world.

In short order, Kai was made *persona non grata* and forbidden from ever returning to Nepal. It was the final nail in the coffin of his fledgling mountaineering business. His career and reputation were in shambles. He was ruined. And now this—some half-cocked reverend halfway around the world alluding to Thompson as "the chosen one." That made him the Judas in this tale of misfortune. The press would eat him alive.

"Bullshit," he grumbled, flipping with thumb and forefinger the cap from another bottle of beer.

He had known Wit Thompson. He was no saint. Far from it. He didn't even believe in God. For him, technology was the Second Coming. Thompson scoffed at the entire religious order, its belief in faith over facts and what he considered the mass manipulation of people who were either too gullible or too stupid to see things as they were.

Kai lifted the remote control and lowered the volume, reducing Caulfield's rant to a dull moan. He surrendered to the armchair, kicked back, and gazed up at the ceiling. He recalled, as best he could, the events that had unfolded that day: Thompson switching off the radio, the glint of the sun on the distant drones, the pain in his chest and legs as he drove himself up the side of Everest, leaving the others under the care of his Sherpas, and the horror of his discovery as he arrived at the summit.

That arrogant prick of a CEO should have been there, poised against the backdrop of the Himalayas. But he was nowhere to be seen. No footprints. "What happened?" he wondered. Perhaps the nefarious asshole had wandered off the trail, fallen to his death, or, at that very minute, lay frozen in an icy tomb. Anything was possible. What Kai ultimately discovered was the last thing he expected. At the peak of the world's highest point there was... nothing. There was no one! Thompson had simply disappeared.

The snow, a thick coat of powder, had lain smooth and unsullied, dusted. No human—at least not on that day—had set foot on Earth's highest spot. Short of breath and head pounding, Kai had scoured the horizon, before concentrating his gaze on every square meter of the mountain's sharp slopes. It was then that he saw them—dozens of tiny indentations in the snow's gentle surface, pockmarks on an otherwise smooth complexion. He carefully maneuvered his way down to the nearest hole and discovered a glistening silver drone, dormant and silent in its snowy nest. He scaled back to the summit and methodically counted the places where the snow had given way. The light was intense and the altitude was taking its toll. Kai found it difficult to concentrate. Fifteen, maybe sixteen, hard to tell.

Then it struck him. The drones were inextricably linked to Thompson and his eyewear, which had been designed specifically to control and direct the drones. They were down because Thompson was down. But where? Kai's heart was racing. He felt dizzy.

"Think man, think!" he said out loud. "Don't fuck with me, Wit!" he yelled, his voice raspy and his throat aching. "Come out, you bastard!"

But even as he screamed the words, he knew the story of Thompson and his personal drones would not have a happy ending. Kai fell to his knees and inexplicably began sobbing. What he didn't know then, but would discover later, is that a lone drone was still operative, its camera peaking just above the snow line and, at that very moment, feeding live footage to more than a billion viewers. Just two hours earlier, the world had witnessed Wit Thompson catapulting into the heavens. Now they watched as the mountaineer wept for the SkyBound CEO.

The image left an indelible mark on the minds of the viewers. Kai initially received an outpouring of support, but thanks to the lawsuit that was filed by SkyBound Inc and the public relations onslaught that followed, the alpinist was quickly recast as reckless and held solely responsible for Wit's untimely disappearance.

Without the incontrovertible Wit Thompson at the helm, SkyBound's share price plummeted. Thompson was more than an accomplished engineer and a great entrepreneur—he was a dreamer. The only things outperforming the quality of his innovations were the tales he told to promote each new venture. These extravagant claims were a matter of public record. Wit played the media like a fiddle. He could whip them into a frenzy, grab headlines, and woo the press and the public into submission with his visions of superhuman endeavor. The High-Fly 9000™ was to be his crowning glory, the firm's finest moment, a substantial payday after years of financial and professional sacrifice. Instead, the plan had failed. Wit was gone. And the company he built lay in waste, its parts strewn about like so many downed drones. SkyBound's investors had to blame someone, and Kai Horner was the obvious choice.

"It's all bullshit," he mumbled once more, reaching for another beer and reclining on the big couch. "Guy was a bastard."

What the world did not know was that the tears he shed that day for all to see were not for Wit, but for another. Alone, atop the world's highest mountain, cold and snowbound, the pangs of loss hit Kai unexpectedly, bringing him to his knees. She was gone and he was to blame. Seven years had passed, but her memory would not leave him alone. That failure had framed his life, causing him to quit academia and turn to a career in mountaineering instead. His discipline had proved legendary, leading him to become one of the most accomplished high-altitude fast-track climbers the world had ever seen. His list of conquests outstripped all others, earning him some celebrity.

He had never planned it that way. His future, he had thought, lay within the confines of academia. As a young and accomplished glaciologist, Kai had found the perfect balance between research and exploration. A fast riser within this exclusive group, he specialized in the subterranean formations of the Transantarctic Mountains—3,500 kilometers of jagged, snow-crusted mountains dividing East Antarctica from West. It remained one of the world's last great unexplored territories—and for good reason. The conditions were harsh beyond compare, and there was only a narrow window each season when exploration was possible.

The first team of climbers to attempt the crossing dated back to 1902, and it was not until the mid-1950s that others were emboldened to test their luck. Kai represented the new generation of Arctic explorers, armed with advanced technology and some radical theories. Climate change, of all things, had created an opening—literally. With each passing season, glacial retreat revealed hidden landscapes that had been trapped for centuries beneath kilometers of ice. On the upside, discoveries of new soil and fossil samples had helped to address unanswered questions as to Earth's origin. On the downside, somewhere in the range of 1,500 billion metric tons of organic carbon stored in Arctic permafrost were thawing, accelerating levels of global greenhouse emissions. Of course, it was the latter point that attracted the headlines, which suited him fine. Kai's ambitions spoke to something deeper—4,000 meters deeper, to be exact.

Glaciers are like elves. They move about unnoticed. But turn away, then turn back, and inevitably they leave clues. By returning year in and year out to the same glacial sites along the Transantarctic Range, Kai was able to pick up on those clues, homing in on a twenty-kilometer-wide expanse where, season after season, he probed away in search of a lost world hidden deep beneath the ice.

Alluvial sediment, he discovered, had a fingerprint quality, and by tracing the path of the deposits, he hoped to one day find that elusive opening to the underworld. Neither seismic testing nor satellite imagery had revealed anything to match his hypothetical claims. But this, he suspected, had more to do with the technology's limitations than any hard evidence against the possibility.

Kai received his fair share of goading for such fantastic claims. Soon after his theory was published, his students removed the antique globe from the library and placed it in the lecture hall. Scrolled across the outline of the Antarctic in bold red letters were the words "Thar Be Dragons." He had to admit, for anyone not specializing in ice formations and shifting climate patterns, the claims of a subterranean passage through the Earth's mantle did feel rather far-fetched.

One more expedition to the Transantarctics, though, and he was sure to be vindicated. All he required was funding, and his best bet was the National Geographic Society. Unfortunately, it was not meant to be. The selection committee, he was told, could not agree. Some argued that his claims were too controversial, that his methods were too unorthodox. Others felt that digging around beneath the ice sent the wrong message, when well-documented glaciers were melting and collapsing in full view. Providing money to explore snow caves when climate change was on full display felt misguided, they argued. As a result, funding was not forthcoming, leaving the expedition high and dry.

Days passed and disappointment gave way to disillusionment. He was ready to give it up and return to teaching full time, but not before taking a few days off to go climbing. While packing and checking his gear one last time, the phone rang.

"Kai Horner?"

"Speaking."

"This is Abigail Clarke."

Kai didn't recognize the name and assumed she was a new transfer student. "What can I do for you, Ms. Clarke?"

"I want to show you something."

"Excuse me?"

"There's something you need to see."

"New discoveries await us in the new term, Ms. Clarke. Can you hold off for a few days?"

"Please... I only need a few moments, but it needs to be in person."

"This really isn't the best time."

"I only need ten minutes."

Kai's initial curiosity gave way to irritation.

"I don't think so. It's late."

"Your article, Dr. Horner. You missed something. Something big."

Kai found himself caught off guard. He remained silent.

"Are you there?"

"I'm here," he said.

"What you're looking for exists. It's just that you've been looking in the wrong place."

Chapter 11

The days ran long in Dinas Affaraon. High in the mountains, the sun rose early and set late, which suited the Nephilim just fine. They had little use for sleep and seemed most content when absorbed in their respective fields of expertise.

Over time, Enoch discovered that the Nephilim Way was more complicated than he had first imagined. Their mission was not personal, he learned, but universal. They worked separately, but toward what they claimed was a common goal. And yet none of them could agree on the nature of that goal. It remained as elusive as the Nephilim themselves. They operated with a seriousness and conviction that could only be described as reverential. When combined, it was as if they possessed the full spectrum of all earthly knowledge. At the heart of it, The Twenty were *naturalists*—astute observers of the natural world. They lived and worked with precision, and their efforts—as far as Enoch could tell—were an attempt to preserve all that was most meaningful and essential as it related to life on Earth. What compelled them to spend all their time in pursuit of this knowledge was kept hidden from him.

Although they never acknowledged it, Enoch's charms were not lost on them. The Nephilim, though stoic by nature, were not entirely void of emotion. Indeed, they were fully aware of his many attempts to draw them into conversations about questions that they might prefer to leave unanswered. In this respect, Enoch was like running water that, over time, wears away stone. His very presence had a subliminal effect. He was a constant reminder to them that somewhere far below their mountain fortress, there was another way of life. Another way of being. It intrigued them, and so they were drawn to him.

Long after his sixteenth birthday, when he had quite suddenly been officially acknowledged by The Twenty and granted the right of inquiry, Enoch had learned to frame his questions carefully. Practical queries were tolerated. Rhetorical ones were not.

"Why do you not visit The Others who live by the lake as my father once did?" he asked them one evening, disrupting their silent supper of broth and bread.

The Twenty all looked up from their bowls in unison, staring first at Enoch, then at Azazel, whose eyes were now firmly fixed upon his impudent son. Enoch fought to conceal the sheepish grin that crept across his face. "I have their attention now," he thought to himself.

"Azazel, what sayest?" Samyaza had clearly decided that since the question had been asked, it should be answered. And Azazel—the only one among them who had ventured to the Lower Realm to observe The Others—understood that only an answer from him would suffice. Enoch could see that his father was not entirely displeased to be called upon.

"I will answer," he said stoically. "Many years have passed and not once have any of you raised the subject or pressed me for an account of my time away. I am grateful to you for that. But there are subjects, long forbidden, that we must discuss. First, though, my son, who believes it is his place to ask such a question, must now leave us. I bid you go now!"

Azazel stood and gestured for the boy to take his leave. Enoch stood, gave a sarcastic bow, and left the room. As the doors closed behind him, he caught a glimpse of his father's disquieted expression. What had he done? He thought he would head down the hall to the bed chambers, but then he thought again. Whatever his father was preparing to say, he wanted to hear it for himself. Climbing the stairs, he crept to where the beams of the Great Hall curved upward, and looked down on the gathering from there. The acoustics were such that he could hear perfectly, as if he were sitting among them.

"They grow in numbers," he heard his father say. "The Others multiply. We passed that way on our journey here. The village is ten times as large as it was when I left for the forest with Ninsun."

Enoch had rarely, if ever, heard his father use his mother's familiar name. A lump formed in his throat, and he gulped, then wondered if those below had heard him.

Over the next hour, Enoch hovered as his father recounted his sojourns in the days before he knew his mother. His search for new minerals, he told them, had led him to the Lower Realm. While crouching among the reeds by the river's edge, he witnessed a sight that would forever change him. She entered from the opposite shore, slender, brown, and naked, and the image of her against the low setting sun shifted something inside him. After seeing her, no gemstone, rare mineral, or composite would ever hold the same allure. In an instant, his world was inverted. She was just one among The Others. But for Azazel, she was *the* one.

"I cannot explain to you what I felt," Enoch heard him tell them. "But no feeling in the Upper Realm can compare. My eyes were opened. And most importantly, I *had* to see her again," he confessed.

Azazel looked up to see how his admission had landed. But there was no shocked surprise. Only blank stares. And then it dawned on him. They had no way of knowing what he felt. For they had yet to experience love—or lust—themselves. Their childlike expressions were laced with anticipation. They were leaning in, as if waiting for the point of his whole story.

"Go on," Samyaza urged. "What more?"

Azazel shook his head slightly, concealing a smile, then continued.

"I followed her from a distance until she came to a village. There, I hid just beyond the glow of their campfires. I began to see her as part of a complex system, always intermingled with The Others. Their ways are nothing like ours. They have no order. No structure. In fact, it's hard to know if they have any purpose at all, other than eating, talking, arguing, and singing. Yes, they have something called *song*, and when they do it together, it reminds them of who they are and why they walk together upon this Earth. At first, I couldn't understand why they needed to remind themselves of these things. Perhaps, I thought, they don't record on stone tablets the way we do. It took many years and time alone with Ninsun before the meaning of their singing became clear to me."

The Twenty leaned in, as if hoping Azazel would reveal to them the secret of song.

"And what do they make with the song?" Samyaza asked.

"Nothing at all," said Azazel. "But the sounds make them happy. And this, I believe, is something very important to them. I know it was important to Ninsun. Although, I never thought to ask her why."

Enoch's throat tightened as he recalled the sound of his mother's voice. She would sing when alone and oftentimes while performing the most mundane tasks. As a young boy, he would creep close and stay hidden, not wanting her to stop, basking in the sound of her song.

Looking down across the Great Hall, Enoch could see how gradually The Twenty were drawn in by Azazel's stories of these strange and distant people. But it was his description of their numbers that interested them most. They multiply, he told them.

"And how do they make their numbers grow?" asked Danel.

Enoch could see his father was unprepared for the question. He let his eyes rove over the brethren, searching for the best way to reveal this greatest mystery of all.

"They join together," he said softly, bowing his head and trying to push past the memory of his now deceased wife. "And from their joining they produce children—small versions of their combined selves."

"Ahh, so they do make some useful things," rejoined Danel.

Enoch guffawed—and thought for certain he had given himself away. But The Twenty were engrossed. Azazel had them enraptured.

"My brethren... There is more," Azazel continued. "The boy's mother... she was also my wife. I married her in accordance with the laws of The Others. You must understand, I loved her!"

The collective gasp that went up from the gathering was almost enough to loosen Enoch from the rafters. The Nephilim erupted. There was no mistaking the shock and displeasure.

Samyaza was the first to speak. "You know it is forbidden. On this point, the Book is clear! Bonding with women is for The Others. Not for us. Our duties are to the One." The rebuke landed hard, and Azazel bowed his head. The brethren all began to speak at once—an occurrence that Enoch had never before witnessed. He could see from on high the shame that swept across Azazel's face, and in a fit of compassion, Enoch thought to call out in his defense. But just as he was about to do so, Samyaza, in a thunderous voice, brought the group to order.

"Silence!"

The Twenty all had a look of surprise that under different circumstances might have been humorous.

"Please, brothers," Samyaza continued, this time using a much softer tone. "I beg you."

Samyaza bowed his head and each of them did the same. Azazel, perhaps in the hope of intervention, or possibly as an act of defiance, turned his gaze skyward to find himself locking eyes with Enoch. His expression was neither sad nor stern. Indeed, tears streamed down his face. Enoch had never before—and would never again—see his father cry.

After what felt like an eternity, Samyaza raised his head and silently stared into the faces of each of the brethren. They were speaking, but with eyes only.

"It is heresy, Azazel. No one knows this better than you. And yet you are changed. You cannot hide it from us. You have tasted the fruits of another world. You are a part of it now. And it is a part of you. It would be rash not to hear you out. Go on," said Samyaza. "We're listening."

In an instant, the tension drained out of the Great Hall. The Twenty—perhaps—were open to new possibilities. Azazel's sense of relief was apparent. His eyes widened with a look of encouragement and hope. Silently he had suffered. He had returned and been accepted back into the fold. But the loss of Ninsun and his former life stuck with him. He had known the love of a woman. It had opened in him a new realm of feeling and possibility. Never again would life in the Upper Realm hold the same sense of purpose. There was more to this life than following the dictates of a book, written by whom and for what purpose none of them knew. For the Nephilim, time stretched eternal. It went deep into the past and stretched far into the future. A continuum. Surely there was more to their eternal lives than what was prescribed by the Book. Azazel could not say why or how, but something in his soul spoke of a greater purpose. The Lower Realm held many secrets.

As the hours unfolded, Enoch's father regaled his listeners with tales of this other world. The more he spoke, the more they wanted to know. Enoch listened in awe. How could it be that this being of so few words could suddenly flood the room with descriptions of a foreign land, its forests, and its people? As the evening played out, Enoch witnessed his father grow increasingly animated and noted a change in the attitudes of the brethren, who from time to time mumbled their approval and nodded their heads. Azazel's words flowed like the river of Enoch's youth. Life sprang up in every direction. The Great Hall was filled with images, and in the expressions of the brethren, there emerged a longing for new experiences like those made possible by life in the Lower Realm.

Azazel spoke until he had no more to say. And for a while, no one in the Hall said a word. Finally, Samyaza spoke.

"The time of the prophecy may be at hand," he proclaimed. "We have not spoken of this for many long years. Maybe your returning to us now with your tales of another world is more than a timely coincidence."

Azazel knew the mind of Samyaza well enough to know that a justification was what he needed most. By citing the Book, he would find a way that would lead the Nephilim into the Lower Realm.

"It was foretold that a Twenty-first would come to live among us, and when he did, a new destiny would unfold before us. Perhaps Enoch is that one."

The sound of his name nearly loosened Enoch from the rafters.

From the morrow onward, his life would be forever changed.

CHAPTER 12

For most, the Garden of the Gods had earned its name in witness to the tall stone monoliths that dotted the landscape, thrust from the Earth like offerings to a higher power. But for Philomena, this spit of national park carried deeper secrets.

More than two decades had passed since she made her abrupt departure from inner-city Chicago. She had left without a plan or a destination, drifting from one place to the next, picking up odd jobs and spending as much time as she could afford to occupying places untouched by people.

As she made her way from east to west, a parkland called the Garden of the Gods felt like something not to be missed. In the nearby town of Manitou Springs, she dismounted her Harley—too long in the saddle—and gave her thighs a good hard rub. The second her feet hit the ground, she knew she would soon be calling the place home—although the reason for her attraction to this hamlet in the Colorado desert was anything but apparent. It certainly wasn't the tiny rows of touristy shops that lined Main Street. Nor was it the town's proximity to the US Air Force Academy and its mysterious underground silos that purportedly cocooned stockpiles of long-range nuclear missiles. It was definitely not that! Perhaps it was the people? Eclectic, to say the least. A community of old hippies, outdoor enthusiasts, budding artisans, and Buddhist converts. This made for interesting conversations and some screwball gatherings, but it wasn't until Philomena first ventured seventeen kilometers west, to the Garden of the Gods, that she knew—with certainty—why she was there. There, beneath her feet, the earth spoke to her. And from that day onward, nothing could dissuade her from getting to the bottom of it. So, year in and year out, she took to every bookstore and library in the county, searching for answers.

It was while browsing through a second-hand bookstore three doors down from her own shop that Philomena happened upon *The Yellow Emperor's Classic of Medicine*. The book was worn, its pages dog-eared and smudged. The margins had been filled with scribbled notes and symbols, and one enthusiastic owner had let loose on the text with a hot pink highlighter.

"Not much left of that one," the proprietor said as he rang up the $1.50 on an old dime store register. "You know anything about acupuncture?" he enquired.

"All new to me," said Philomena, reaching into her beaded satchel and pulling out a handful of change.

"The guy who last owned it lives 'round here, I think. He fancied himself some kind of 'Eastern healer' for a while, but then gave it up. I heard he took up stargazing instead," said the shopkeeper with a little grin. Philomena couldn't tell if he was being serious or sarcastic.

"He just walked in one day, plunked down a full crate of books, and said he'd had enough. I never asked why, and he never offered to tell me. Didn't ask nothing for the books, neither."

"You know where he lives?"

"Not too sure. Head on up to the Penny Arcade and ask around. His name is Boney Grazier. He's a Buddhist. Not your typical Buddhist, mind ya. I don't know too many Native American Buddhists, do you?"

"Can't say I do," answered Philomena. "What does he look like?"

"Tall feller. He's got a mound of gray hair tucked up under his Stetson, and he likes wearin' them big baggy *I Dream of Jeannie* pants. I'll tell him you're looking for him if he comes round."

"I don't mind if you do," she replied, tucking the book in her satchel before making her way through the front door.

Three days later, Philomena sat in the public courtyard with the coin-filled fountain to her back. She had an egg salad sandwich and was bent over the *Yellow Emperor*, trying to decipher the symbols that ran up and down the margins.

"Those are earth symbols."

"Pardon?" said Philomena, lifting her head and shading her eyes from the sun that silhouetted the tall figure before her.

"I said, those are earth symbols," repeated the man, pivoting on his snakeskin boots and plunking down beside her. Philomena found herself staring back at herself, her wild hair and tanned face reflected full in the mirrored sunglasses that bookended a fender bender of a nose, broken in two places. The rest of his face was shrouded in a mottled and unkempt beard. So unusual was the man's appearance that she momentarily lost track of what he had said.

"You deaf, missy?" came his raspy voice.

"Why no, not in the least," she replied.

"Okay then, just checkin'. I was tellin' ya those are earth symbols. I drew them there myself."

"Oh, you're that Boney guy."

"Pardon?"

"Boney Grazier? That's what the man at the bookstore told me... I'm sorry... Please go on. What do they mean—the symbols, that is?"

"Just a theory. Came to me one day when I was poking around the salt mines, smokin' a doobie and communin' with nature, if you know what I mean."

"Sorry, I'm not following you."

"No matter... It's not common knowledge. But drop down two clicks from the salt mines and you'll find a string of caves. You gotta hop the fence. Lawyers got the place tied up in paperwork—it's been closed off for years. Anyway... there's a little drop-off and a foot trail, and if you stay close to the western slope you'll see 'em through the scrub. Good spot for rattlers, I thought, and sure enough, I stuck my boot in there and nearly got bit."

"Bit by a rattlesnake?"

"Sure 'nuff," he said. "I grabbed a stick and pulled that mean mother outta the way. He got to rattlin' and puttin' up quite the fuss. I told him I meant him no harm, and he just turned and sidesaddled away. That's when I noticed it."

"Noticed what?"

"The cave. Right there in front of me. I ducked down and went through, holding my lighter up high so I could see. It opens up inside. Plenty of space. Got to thinking maybe I'd stay a while."

He gave a little wink. But Philomena was too absorbed in his story to see that he was joking, so he went on.

"It was like a big dome inside, nice and smooth up top, as if someone had carved it out of solid rock. In the center of the ceiling there was a single bump, like someone was thinking about hanging a chandelier or something. But that wasn't the best part," he said, pausing.

"Yeah? What was the best part?"

"You sure you wanna know?" he teased.

"Hell yeah, I wanna know."

"Those symbols," he said, pointing to the book. "They were all chiseled into the wall and ran full circle round the cave. Must have been twenty or more. Most, you could make out, like they were fresh-carved. Others were faded. I just stood there under that dome and turned myself 360. 'Hot damn,' I thought. 'I'm a regular Indiana Jones,'" he said with a big grin and a guffaw.

He had Philomena where he wanted her. "What then?" she asked.

Boney sprang to his feet.

"Why, I grabbed me a big handful of gold and hightailed it out of there," he said, lifting a leg and doing his best Wylie Coyote imitation. "I was just waitin' for that big stone ball to drop on down and chase me right outta that thar cave."

Philomena was transfixed. "What big ball, and why was it chasing you out of the cave?" she teased, not wanting to give him the satisfaction of thinking she could be easily entertained.

Boney pretty much gave up at that point. He could see she wasn't putting up with any of his shenanigans.

"I'm sorry Miss... what's your name, anyway?"

"Philomena," she said. "But never mind that. What did you do with all that gold?"

"Well shoot, Miss Philomena, I was just joshin' ya about the gold and the big stone ball, too. But the rest is surefire true," he said, crossing his chest with a crooked finger.

Philomena let out a laugh and Boney could see he'd been had.

"You done flipped 'er on me, didn't ya?" he chuckled. "Just leading me along, you were."

"Maybe I was, but now you listen here," said Philomena, drawing herself up to her full five foot two. "I'm not sure I like being fooled with, so why don't you get along now. I'm reading and you're bothering me. Now go on," she said, pointing the way out of the little park.

"Hold on there, little lady. I meant no harm. Now let me explain."

"I think you've explained enough!"

"Not hardly. You still wanna know about those symbols?"

Philomena snapped back to attention and sheepishly said, "Well, yes I do, but tell me for a fact, are you really Boney Grazier, and did you really draw these symbols?" pointing again to the book.

"I am and I did," he replied.

"Well then, let's start again. I'm Philomena Pettibone. I like plants, and they like me. I own a shop. But soon enough, I'll be leaving that all behind. And that's because I'm an acupuncturist in training. An *Earth* acupuncturist, to be exact. Pleased to meet you," she said, extending a hand.

"You are quite the spark plug, Ms. Philomena," said Boney, who could see at last that he had met his match. "The pleasure is mine."

For the next three hours, the two erstwhile strangers sat in the courtyard and pored over *The Yellow Emperor.* In another time and place, they might have been mistaken for witch and warlock, but on that sunny May day in Manitou Springs, they were just two eccentrics, sharing a book, wrapped in conjecture.

Chapter 13

"Billionaire Bound for Heaven," screamed one banner. "Where Is Wit?" read another. So ran the headlines on the day of Wit Thompson's disappearance. Had it not been witnessed in real time by tens of millions of people around the world, the story would have been unbelievable. For days following the event, the whereabouts of Wit Thompson were not just a story, they were *the story*. It was only seconds before it was posted on YouTube, generating 450 million views in the first week alone. If this was indeed a publicity stunt, it would no doubt rank as the greatest media spectacle of all time.

The footage was stunning. A 360-degree view of a single man, scaling the world's tallest mountain. Wit looked the part of a conqueror in every way—chiseled jaw, powerful shoulders. The man didn't huff and puff his way to the top, he practically ran. Nothing topped the moment of glory when he was standing at the highest point on Earth, however, hands outstretched to the heavens—he was the very image of immortal conquest. Simply put, he reigned triumphant. His impossibly white-toothed smile flashed and his azure glasses reflected the flying machines forming a perfect sphere around him, a man who had done the impossible. But what happened next was anyone's guess.

It was almost undetectable at first. Wit's powerful figure rose from the surface of the snow. He seemed to hover for a moment, then continued skyward. His drones kept pace and held their tight formation, orbiting him and sending real-time footage to millions of stunned viewers. For a moment, the world held its breath. Then, in a whisk, it was over. The last recorded image of the CEO showed a flicker of surprise, followed by a flash of panic, before he disappeared forever. In the space of a few seconds, his hapless figure shot up, straight into the heavens, his final ascent captured by the video drones as they, in turn, fell to Earth. Their connection with Wit had been severed, leaving a small legion of metal hoods across Everest's peak.

For the evangelicals, however, the footage was heaven-sent.

For the Lord himself will come down from heaven, with a loud command, with the voice of the archangel and with the trumpet call of God, and the dead in Christ will rise first. After that, we who are still alive and are left will be caught up together with them in the clouds to meet the Lord in the air. And so we will be with the Lord forever.
—1 Thessalonians 4:16

Reverend Avon Caulfield read each word from his Bible with clarity and conviction, "channeling" God's will. He lifted his head momentarily, letting the passage sink in. His eyes drifted over the throngs. This was his flock, gathered today in their thousands, not to mention the tens of thousands of others who were also tuning in via satellite, to hear him—Avon Caulfield—deliver his message of repentance and salvation.

As the fates would have it, only three months earlier *60 Minutes* had aired a segment on the surge in Pentecostal Christianity all around the world. The program cited a study that found twenty-two percent of the world's estimated Christian population, or nearly 820 million people, declared themselves to be "Pentecostal"—an evangelical brand of Christianity that outstripped every other denomination combined. This popular weekly news program set out to discover the reason for the rise. Not surprisingly, America's most visible Pentecostal preacher featured heavily in the segment. It boosted Avon's ratings, placing him on top of the world.

For evangelicals everywhere, Wit Thompson's disappearance was a script for the ages. "The rapture" lived large in the lives of Pentecostals. Now the SkyBound CEO had delivered to them the necessary evidence to suggest that God's Day of Judgment was at hand. Of course, not everyone agreed. It was hard to align the subtext of the rapture with the likes of Wit Thompson. He was an avowed atheist and a far cry from the God-fearing type. Wit worshipped at the altar of his own image and paid tribute to the capitalist system. That was all the god that he needed.

Rather than roll over on the idea that Wit Thompson was a nonbeliever, born-again Christians gave wind to rumors that Wit was, in fact, a closet Christian who had for years been following the Scripture, which, in turn, guided his decisions and fueled his success. The lengths to which Thompson went to shield his private life only heightened the speculation. And in the absence of any form of public denial, the rumors spread like wildfire.

Avon Caulfield didn't start the rumors, but that didn't stop him from taking credit. No other evangelical leader of his time had done more to leverage social media's power for propaganda. Within days of Thompson's disappearance, he unleashed his platoons of digital crusaders, and through Facebook posts, Instagram feeds, WhatsApp blasts, and YouTube "likes," the story of SkyBound's CEO and his silent conversion to "the one true faith" became God's own truth for all those who chose to believe.

Avon seized upon the event as a pivotal moment for the evangelical cause. It wasn't enough to promote the Second Coming. He and his minions were on a mission to fundamentally discredit anyone who dared put forward a scientific explanation—assuming there was one—for the CEO's untimely disappearance. To this end, Caulfield's media empire rolled out one pseudo-scientist after the next, unleashing a media blitzkrieg. Credentials mattered less than soundbites. The minute a researcher put forward a hypothesis, one of the reverend's paid commentators would step in and cast doubt upon it. If science could not offer a rational explanation, he and his team of data specialists would do the next best thing: they would *create* one!

So astute were Avon and his team in the art of story manipulation that they were gradually able to shape public opinion through exhaustive analysis accompanied by precise selections of keywords. The word "emancipation," for instance, took center stage. It was an outright invention of Avon's media machine. By carefully "placing" the word in the subtext of his "sources," he began to build support for the term, which had a somewhat more modernist ring to the otherwise anti-quated notion of "rapture." Before long, "emancipation" caught on. From pulpit-pounding preachers to talk show pundits, it reigned as the epitome of a world gone mad. It was God's plan in play. The fact that there was no scientific explanation for Thompson's catapult into the stratosphere only complicated matters. That didn't stop a special congressional commission from trying, though. Certainly, many hoped that science would come to the rescue.

On the day the commission's report was due for release, Washington, DC was in the throes of a July heatwave. Even so, the committed and curious descended on the capital by the thousands. By 7:00a.m., the National Mall was teeming. "Believers," bent on perpetuating the view that Wit's disappearance was all part of God's plan, held up posters scrawled with quotations from Scripture and images of the apocalypse. Opposite them, facing off, ran a long line of avowed atheists, rational-ists, and stern-faced intellectuals. For the best part of an hour, shouts of "Repent!" from one side were countered by shouts of "Invent!" from the other. At 8:15a.m. sharp, the doors of the Department of Justice flew open, and an entourage of politicians, scientists, and members of the Secret Service poured into the intersection between Pennsylvania and 10th street. The special counsel took the podium and urged the crowd to settle down.

"For the past two weeks, our commission has pored over every possible aspect of the failed mission that resulted in the unfortunate disappearance of Mr. Wit Thompson. We have examined and authen-ticated the documents presented to us by SkyBound and thoroughly examined the drones recovered from that fateful expedition."

The speaker paused and looked out across the ocean of onlookers.

"We have concluded with absolute certainty that the drones designed, prototyped, and tested by SkyBound are entirely incapable of enabling or supporting human flight."

An audible gasp went up from the crowd, followed by wails of "Hallelujah!" For the next several minutes, the speaker struggled to calm the crowd down so that he might wrap up his statement.

"In light of these findings and in collaboration with independent experts who have conducted a thorough review of the meteorolog-ical conditions on the day of Mr. Thompson's disappearance, we are unable to offer any empirical explanation for his... *emancipation*. We thank you for your attention and hereby conclude our investigation."

In the battle for public opinion, evangelicals marked the moment as a great victory. It was lost on no one that the special counsel had used the word "emancipation" to describe Thompson's disappearance. In so many ways, it was the final legitimization of the evangelical community's hard-fought position. In the weeks that followed, the *cause célèbre* would assume new and fanatical heights of public discourse.

Chapter 14

Time passed more quickly in the world of humans than in the mountains, where the tedium of a cloistered and ritualized existence made life dull, predictable, and slow-moving. In the Lower Realm, by contrast, every day was marked by some new development, drama, delight, or tragedy. It was life as Enoch remembered it. And the life he had returned to.

From that evening when Azazel had first shared with the brethren his tales of his sojourn in the Lower Realm, change was inevitable. All that Azazel said could not be unsaid or unheard. He had planted in the minds of the Nephilim the seeds of imagination. And for The Twenty who had plodded from one task to the next for countless years, the prospect of life in the Lower Realm grew intoxicating. The brethren—creatures of habit that they were—became excited and impulsive. Their daily routines were thrown out and replaced by a new list of tasks prepared by Samyaza and Azazel. Leaving the Upper Realm meant securing Dinas Affaraon, locking away the stone tablets, and otherwise putting the fortress in good order.

There were also rituals to be performed. As anticipated, Enoch joined the ranks of the Nephilim, ceremoniously accepting his place as the Twenty-first among them, as foretold by the prophecy. It was the justification that Samyaza needed in order to make plans to put their departure in motion. Enoch would go first, entering the Lower Realm as an emissary. He was instructed to observe, engage, and report back without revealing to The Others the true purpose of his mission, which was to prepare the way for the Nephilim.

Enoch did as he was instructed, entering the village to the gasps of all those who witnessed his arrival. He was a fully grown man now— tall, powerfully built, and handsome, like his father, yet soft in gesture and expression, like his mother. When they discovered he was the son of Ninsun and the grandson of their chieftain, fear gave way to curiosity. In contrast to the Nephilim, The Others warmed quickly to Enoch, welcoming him wholeheartedly into their daily lives. So as not to offend, he took care to learn their customs and follow their practices, remaining observant and vigilant at all times. In this regard—and thanks to his time among the Nephilim—he was well trained and prepared.

All his father had told him about The Others was true. They were social by nature and prone to work as members of a team, but they could also prove unpredictable and flighty if they were distracted or provoked. Their lives—in contrast to those of the Nephilim—were ruled by their hearts, not their heads. Being half-human himself, Enoch understood this, perhaps more than his father ever could.

It took months, but once Enoch had earned their trust and confidence, he asked the elders if The Twenty might be granted permission to enter the village and stay among them for some time. Most were receptive, but some were suspicious. Besides Enoch, the only other Nephilim they had ever encountered was Azazel, who many years prior had quietly slipped away with the chieftain's daughter and disappeared with her into the forest. They knew and remembered how Azazel's love for Ninsun made the young men of the village resentful. He was not like The Others. He was much larger, stronger, faster, and cleverer—and, if truth be told, much kinder as well. Compared to Azazel, none could compete. These feelings festered, but rather than suffer their disdain, Azazel and Ninsun chose to leave. It was the last time the villagers set eyes on them, and soon they were forgotten.

After some debate, and some dissent from a handful of the younger men, the elders agreed to receive the Nephilim. In the days preceding their arrival, the villagers busied themselves, prepping their homes and the common areas, putting all things in order. The path leading into the village was strewn with flowers and lined with candles, for they were told the Nephilim would arrive by night. Years later, tales would be told and repeated describing the moment the tall ghostly figures of The Twenty emerged from the forest and passed beneath the candlelit trees. They came in procession and full regalia—white robes and breastplates. It was unlike anything The Others had ever witnessed.

Enoch stood among the elders and watched with giddy pride as The Twenty—his brethren—entered the village in perfect formation. They fanned out, first one to the left and then the next to the right, until they all stood in a line facing the elders. The chieftain stepped forward and came toe to toe with Azazel. She was half his size, but she had the presence of a giant.

"So you have returned to us?" she said to him.

Azazel bowed his head so that he could see into her eyes.

"With your blessing," he replied, searching her face for a sign.

"My blessing, you say. Perhaps a blessing might have been best given the night you took my Ninsun away."

"I see this now. I hope that one day you can forgive me."

She gave no reply, but instead turned her attention to Samyaza.

"And who is this noble creature?"

"He goes by the name of Samyaza. He is the first among us."

"Your leader?"

"We have no leader. We are of the One."

"And has 'the One' given you leave?"

She was clever, the old woman. She sensed some division among The Twenty and was now testing her theory.

Samyaza spoke: "We have come of our own free will to know you and The Others."

"And once you *know* us, what will you do next?"

Samyaza was unprepared for this question. In their world, decisions were taken one at a time. Being accepted by The Others was the first step. What the future held was anyone's guess.

"Our intention is not to take, but to give."

It was the perfect segue. Each of The Twenty carried a small chest, and one after the other they stepped forward and placed the black lacquered boxes with gold inlay at the feet of the elders. As the villagers pressed forward, the boxes were opened and their contents revealed. Legends arose from that first night—tales of how the world's secrets were made known to The Others and how, from that point forward, they were aroused to the possibilities of the human race.

As the days and weeks unfolded, Enoch's assurances to the villagers proved true. The Twenty offered up all they could, willingly and without hesitation. The Others were astounded. These giants from the north possessed knowledge and know-how that surpassed anything they might have imagined. If there were any lingering misgivings among the people, they soon gave way to curiosity and a hunger to grasp all that the Nephilim had to offer.

The Nephilim found it curious that some of their Great Blessings were preferred over others. In their world, all of the godsends held equal merit. The villagers, by contrast, gravitated only to those gifts that could produce for them what they most desired. And in this regard, Azazel's gifts ranked as the first among many.

As an alchemist, he had perfected the art of melding minerals to produce tools and weapons of the most enduring quality. To demonstrate his skill, he built a forge on the outskirts of the village. He took on apprentices and showed them the fine art of transmuting base metals into supple alloys that, when heated at precise temperatures under specific conditions, yielded all kinds of useful and durable instruments. The men of the village were fast learners, and soon Azazel was able to step back, allowing them to experiment on their own. Azazel soon discovered just how quickly these villagers learned to innovate. While the way of the Nephilim was singular, meticulous, and in many ways predictable, the human approach to problem solving was more intuitive, experimental, and random.

Only second to the forging of weapons was the making of fine jewelry. The people of the Lower Realm had never seen gold or silver before, and when Azazel fashioned a mold and poured the scalding liquid to create a bracelet imprinted with images of deer, bison, and rabbit, the villagers were enraptured. From that point forward, Azazel was overrun with requests. A ring for one's father-in-law, a broach for someone else's mother, a necklace to woo a lover, or a bracelet for a wife. Whatever they wanted, Azazel made it. Their infatuation with these objects confused The Twenty. Most of these objects had little practical use. And yet the rings, bracelets, and necklaces that he was urged to create carried some weight with all those who came to see him work.

While the efforts of Azazel were always in demand, those among The Twenty who possessed more esoteric skills were largely left alone. For the villagers, thunderstorms, floods, or earthquakes were seen as nuisances, at best, and causes of fear, at worst. They watched as Baraqiel, Armaros, Zaqiel, Sariel, and the others carried out their daily rituals—staring up at the stars, measuring the trajectory of the sun, poking and probing the earth, and taking samples of flora and fauna. They marveled, then mocked the ways these strange giants from the north set up their equipment, fiddled with their bizarre instruments, and recorded on stone tablets one inconsequential detail after the next. "What odd behavior," commented the villagers. "So serious," they chided.

There were many differences between the Nephilim and the humans, but they perhaps differed the most in terms of their divergent views on "time." While The Others had a propensity to embrace anything that offered a short-term gain, the Nephilim, by contrast, took the long view, believing that every new insight, no matter how trivial, would serve them well over time. They honored and revered each and every new discovery, ranging from Zaqiel's search for subtle shifts in the Earth's atmosphere to Kokaiel's careful assessment of the meanings in the movements of the stars. For the Nephilim, it was a matter of gradually and precisely unlocking the secret of the One and the mysteries of the planet and the cosmos. For the villagers, by contrast, if a thing offered neither sustenance nor pleasure, then they had little time or use for it.

Enoch observed these differing points of view initially with curiosity, then later with some concern. As he felt the conflict within his own being, so he saw these differences playing out between the two parties. On one such occasion, a dispute broke out among The Others over the production of some new weapon. To help resolve the issue, Enoch was summoned to meet with the village elders. When he entered, the council was already in session. The atmosphere was charged, and Enoch could sense a mixture of excitement and tension.

From the start, Enoch was impressed by the equal weighting of the council, in accordance with tradition. There were thirteen in all—six men and six women, with the chieftain serving as the thirteenth. She never took sides. Her role was to facilitate. As a young boy, Enoch had known only one woman—his mother. At one time, she was the center of his existence. Spending time with the councilwomen for many months had helped to ease his suffering, but doing so had also left him with a deeper longing, as well. Unlike his mother, these women were older. And yet, like her, they were healers. Each had perfected the art, and it was because of them that the entire community thrived. No one, no matter how sick or seriously injured, was left unattended. It was the unspoken code that separated The Others from all other creatures on Earth.

The men on the council were deferential to the women in this regard. They understood without question that the women were the glue who held the community together. The male members had earned their places on the council through their prowess—their ability to provide for the community, as primarily defined by the hunt. And it was the role of the chieftain to ensure and maintain this balance. On this particular day, though, Enoch could sense dissension among their ranks.

"We have news, young Enoch," the chieftain declared. "But we are concerned that it may not sit well with The Twenty. You have proven yourself true. All that you promised us with respect to the Nephilim has come to pass. In only a few short years, our eyes have been opened to the possibilities. While we have long believed that nature holds many secrets, the Nephilim have unlocked this mystery. For this, we remain eternally grateful."

Enoch listened thoughtfully, pleased that his reputation and stature had grown as a result of his candor. But there was more.

"For many generations now, we have lived at the mercy of the natural world. We have known hunger, disease, and suffering. We have believed through the ages that our life cycle is like that of the budding flower. There is a time to live, and a time to die; a time to celebrate and a time to suffer. The Twenty have changed this. For nearly four years now, we have not suffered disease, gone hungry, or wanted for anything. They have offered us tools, seeds, elixirs, and defenses against all things that might otherwise cause us harm. We are stronger, wiser, and better equipped than at any other time in our history. Our numbers have grown, and there are those among us who believe it is time to test this advantage."

The chieftain, from the outset, had always spoken on behalf of the other council members. For the first time that he could recall, she deferred.

"Lock, you are outspoken on these matters. Tell Enoch what you have told us."

The man rose, and his expression showed that he was pleased to be called upon. He got right to the point.

"We are assembling a war party. In three days' journey from here, we will meet our foe and smite them."

Enoch could not believe his ears. He felt his mind racing. This was most unexpected.

"Foe? You have no foe! The other groups who live on the far side of the lake do you no harm. Why would you set upon them for no reason? You are right. This will not sit well with The Twenty. You threaten the alliance. The Nephilim will not approve."

As soon as the words left his lips, Enoch realized he had let down his guard. Lock pounced.

"We do not *need* your approval or theirs. Nor do we ask for it."

Lock's words drove deep. They made Enoch flinch. Was this the same man who, from the outset, had ingratiated himself with the brethren? The one who spent long days listening to and learning from The Twenty, long after the other villagers had grown bored and drifted away? Was he not the one who could be counted on to rush to the defense of the Nephilim when some disparaging remark was made? Yes, it was the same Lock. And yet he was changed. The man before him now was agitated and enraged. Anger was an emotion to which Enoch was not accustomed. He was unsure how to respond, but before he could do so, the chieftain stepped in.

"Lock," she chided. "You forget yourself."

Her words were like water to a flame. For a moment, it looked as if he would resist, but just as quickly, he bowed and withdrew. From the shadows, Enoch could still feel Lock's eyes upon him. A fight was brewing in the man. Enoch could feel it smoldering.

"Forgive his impertinence. But I and the other members of this council believe he is not wrong. Our destiny is to greatness. Whether by the will of nature or that of the Nephilim, The Twenty have offered us an advantage. Our coming together has set events in motion. It has freed us from all limitations. And unless I am mistaken, the Nephilim are free as well. Some among you have feared divine retribution. And yet here you are. Are the lives of The Twenty not richer and more meaningful now that they have wives and families of their own? Now it is our turn to test the thresholds of our potential. We will venture to the Outer Realm, come what may. This is our time!"

The more she spoke, the harder it was for Enoch to find fault with her logic. Who was he to judge their ambitions to venture further? And yet, in her eyes, he saw a trace of doubt. No, not doubt. It was fear. It would be the first of many moments where Enoch's powers of observation would serve him well. He had learned through the years—and he would learn for many years to come—how to detect meaning that lay hidden behind the spoken word. "Beware," warned her eyes. "Lock cannot be trusted!"

Then, for all to hear, she said: "Go tell Azazel and the others that Lock and his men will raid at dawn. It will be better coming from you!"

Somewhere, out of sight, Enoch felt Lock silently celebrate his first great victory.

Dismissed, Enoch left the council hall, and not knowing how he would share the news with The Twenty, he entered the forest, but it was not the same. He felt squeamish and dizzy, and the plants and trees all around glowed fluorescent green. Far above, in the branches, the leaves twitched in unison, despite the absence of wind, sending a cry out across the land.

Chapter 15

Nearly two weeks had passed since Philomena first felt the pangs of nausea. It came in waves and sometimes resulted in vomiting, followed by headaches and dizziness. She recalled feeling this way one other time in her twenties, and hoped to God that she wasn't down with the same thing this time. Pregnancy wasn't part of the plan—then or now.

Days passed and the feeling only grew stronger. It was as if her body was mirroring her surroundings. By day, the weather was hot and humid—unseasonably so for Manitou Springs. By night, the land would cool, going dry and dusty, as if the earth was lapping up every bit of moisture before falling asleep. As the weather shifted, so did she, moving from fits of high fever to spasms of teeth-chattering chills. Late each night, dry lightning filled the sky, leaving the air roiled with static electricity. It was enough to make her already unruly hair stand on end.

"What the heck is going on?" she wondered, between frequent trips from the front porch to the bathroom.

The nausea was getting worse and so was she. Then came the migraines. A trip back to the doctor was out of the question. She barely had the strength to sit up. Hours turned into days, and Philomena found herself in a state of delirium, to the point where she barely heard the repeated rap-a-tap-tap on the window. Hands clenched over her ears, she sank deep beneath the covers. The head-splitting sound of the bedroom door being thrown open jolted her upright.

"What's up with you, girl?" came a voice, traveling a million kilometers through the corridors of her inner ear to arrive at the reserves of her brain.

She looked up and found herself staring at close range into the eyes of a wild-haired demon with a long broken nose.

"Don't hurt me!" she cried.

"Hurt you? Good God girl, I'm here to help you... Lord, you're burning up. We need to get you to doc," he said, lifting her body from the bed.

She hung limp and wasted in his gangly arms. Each movement sent shards of light through her skull. Philomena clamped her eyes, trying to shut out the pain. Her body moved and bounced in rhythm to Boney's long stride. He turned sideways to get through the door frame, then accelerated down the front hall. She heard him push against the screen door and imagined him lunging across the door mat that read *Good Vibes Only.* It was then that he must have lost his footing. One moment she was skybound, the next she was knocked senseless as her head hit the pavement.

Philomena's friendship with Boney had been most unexpected. Over the months, their relationship had grown. Now, it was safe to say he was her confidant... her *person.* It wasn't just his endless supply of books and manuscripts with odd titles—like *The Tao Te Ching, The Tibetan Book of the Dead,* and *Secret Signs and Symbols*—that made him special, it was the way that he engaged. He listened and asked the kinds of questions that only those with a special wisdom might ask. He also had a gift for mixing and matching the principles of traditional medicine with modern philosophy, which opened up little windows onto the world of knowing. Above all else, he was humble. And by virtue of his gifts as a facilitator—never pushing, always probing— he imbued in Philomena a newfound belief in herself and her unique ability to sense subtle shifts in all the deep places. For decades, these impulses had confused and frightened her. Then Boney entered her life, and like a spiritual paleontologist, he knew where to dig, how to exhume, and how to brush all doubts and misgivings from her hidden gift. It was knowledge locked away, and Boney offered her the means to unearth it.

"What are those?" he asked, pointing to a string of symbols layered over an enormous double helix drawing of Earth, sketched in detail on the back wall of her shop.

Philomena had meticulously drawn in red, green, and blue marker a complex grid that overlaid a map. It had taken her weeks to complete.

"Those are meridians," she said, tracing her fingers along the long sloping lines. "And those are *chakras*," she added, pointing to a network of intricate symbols plotted against the lines. "Each symbol is associated with a form of energy," she explained. "Like acupuncture points on the body."

"But over the face of the planet instead," he noted.

"Precisely," she said.

Philomena moved to the point where the two circles met and with a black marker wrote "7.83 Hz." She'd used the same marker in previous days to place hundreds of plus and minus signs over the face of the drawing.

"What does '7.83 Hz' mean?" asked Boney.

"It's the frequency."

"The frequency of what?"

"The Earth," said Philomena.

Lifting a book from the table and folding back a dog-eared page, she read: "The fundamental mode of a Schumann resonance is a standing wave in the Earth–ionosphere cavity with a wavelength equal to the circumference of the Earth."

"Say what?" said Boney.

"In 1952, Otto Schumann presented a mathematical proof that suggested the presence of a kind of energy or 'force' field that encompassed the Earth. At 7.83 hertz, he argued, the Earth remains in a state of balance. Disruptions, he theorized, could fundamentally alter both atmospheric pressure and gravitational force."

"Theory, you say?"

"Yes, theory. He died before he was able to prove it. But there's evidence to suggest that extreme weather patterns can alter the Earth's foundational frequency. Meteorologists use Schumann's theory to track lightning activity and climate change," she said.

She lifted the book and continued to read aloud: "Schumann resonances have been used for research and monitoring of the lower ionosphere on Earth and were suggested for the exploration of lower-ionosphere parameters on celestial bodies... More recently, Schumann resonances have been used for monitoring transient luminous events—sprites, elves, jets, and other upper-atmospheric lightning. A new field of interest using Schumann resonances is related to short-term earthquake predictions. Schumann resonances have gone beyond the boundaries of physics, invading medicine, raising interest in artists and musicians, and gaining interest from fringe fields such as psychobiology."

Snapping the book closed and laying it back down on the table, she looked up as if to say "What more proof do you need?"

Boney stared back, trying to mask his surprise.

"Sprites, elves, and jets?" he repeated.

"Oh, that's all just conjecture. It misses the main point. Earth—like the human body—operates best when in harmonic resonance."

"Harmonic resonance."

"That's right. Darn it, Boney, are you trying to test me? I'm telling you, things are out of balance."

"You're telling me," he said, with a wink.

Philomena's eyes narrowed and her cheeks flushed, and Boney could see he had kicked up a storm.

"Hold on, hold on. I don't mean no disrespect, Miss Philomena. Go on now. I'm a listenin'."

She further narrowed her gaze. "Schumann spent his life trying to prove the potential negative impact of radio frequencies on the Earth's atmosphere. Theories of radio waves had been around since the 1880s, thanks to the likes of Heinrich Hertz and Nikola Tesla. But it wasn't until 1920 that radio broadcasting went mainstream. Schumann had a lot to say about it. He expressed concern that our use of the airwaves could interfere with Earth's frequency, but he couldn't prove it mathematically."

Philomena paused to make sure Boney was following her before continuing. "Then in 1993, Iridium Communications launched and placed into orbit 66 satellites that effectively encased the globe in a 1616 and 1626.5 megahertz operating spectrum."

"Gracious, Miss Philomena, where'd you learn all this?"

She shot Boney a look as if to tell him to hold his questions until she was done.

"Schumann anticipated this and released his definitive study, ten years in the making: *Global Wireless Communications and Their Implications on Earth's Gravitational and Atmospheric Balance*. He effectively denounced the use of new cellular technologies and called for an intergovernmental moratorium. In certain academic circles, Schumann's research gained a following. Corporations were less receptive. They argued that the benefits of cheap, ubiquitous communications far outweighed any negative effects of tampering with the Earth's so-called 'natural harmonics.' They declared Schumann a quack. Then, nine months later, quite unexpectedly, he died. Earth's foremost expert on Earth harmonics was found in his lab, eardrums shattered. Official reports attributed his death to one of his sound experiments gone wrong. You know the rest of the story... Today there are 10 billion cellular phones in use, consuming an enormous block of available spectrum. It's like wrapping a plant in layers of cellophane, then asking it to grow."

Philomena paused to let the story sink in, then turned to her drawings on the wall.

"These marks on the map," said Philomena, pointing to the plus and minus signs, "show what forty years of cellular networks have done to the 7.83 hertz field. It's gone haywire. And there's more..."

Philomena walked back from the wall and flipped a switch on a projector mounted atop a pile of books. The twin circles on the wall were now framed in blue light. She connected her laptop to the projector and, following a few keystrokes, an elaborate and detailed grid filled the twin spheres. Boney let out an audible gasp. It was the cartological equivalent of lighting up a Christmas tree.

"Good Lordy, Miss Philomena. What have you done?"

"What have *I* done? What have *they* done is the question. This shows that whether planned or coincidental, the surface of our planet is pockmarked with what I'm calling 'spectrum contusions.' All these points," she said, tracing her hand over the projected image, "are man-made disruptions of Earth's energy field. If Schumann's principle holds true, our planet is suffering a kind of cognitive dissonance. It's like putting her in a small room and blasting her with blinding light and blaring music. It severs the lines. She can't think or function, so she starts to die. You can see how it takes this climate change discussion to a whole new level."

She was reminded of how her theory had left Boney speechless as she slowly regained consciousness. She opened her eyes and scanned the room. Boney lay nearby on top of a hospital gurney. The curtains were drawn around both of them. She lifted a hand to feel a tight row of stitches across her forehead. He lay still, looking peaceful. Between them was a small side table and upon it was a black lacquer box, about the size of a shoebox. On the lid was a carved circle, inlaid with gold, with a single dot at its center.

Chapter 16

"She knows, doesn't she?"

"She senses. And that's all that matters."

"How will you convince her?"

"She won't need convincing. She already knows what needs to be done. She's been searching her whole life for this. It's a quest now."

"Is that what she's on... a quest?"

"Precisely! That's why she—among all others—is right for the journey."

"Has she responded?"

"Not yet."

"Does she need encouragement?"

"Not from you."

"Going it alone again, I see. When will you learn? This is not just yours to bear."

"With respect, it is mine to finish. It's coming together. The assembling has begun. You and the others have already proven invaluable. We would not be where we are had it not been for you."

"We are where we are. Time has made sure of that."

"You have all been so very patient. But time is running out."

"Time is plentiful. All else is fleeting."

Chapter 17

Carson hated politics. In fact, he hated the whole political process. His regular trips to the nation's capital intruded upon his time and energy. All he wanted was to be left alone to do his job and keep his finger on Earth's pulse. Under the circumstances, and after alerting his superiors to his findings, he had no choice but to return to the corridors of power. He was summoned to sit before the audacious yet essential House Appropriations Committee—audacious because of its members and their tendency to grandstand, essential because each year the committee decided whether to fund or defund his work. Failure to produce results had big consequences.

For years now, Carson's Earth Science Division under NASA's Science Mission Directorate had come under increased scrutiny. Any discussion of climate change was a political hot potato. Carson would not be deterred. His goal from the beginning had been to prove how human activity was destroying the planet. His plan was to map Earth's mantle to show just how severe the problem had become. Years of drilling for oil had compromised the planet's water tables and the aquifers supporting them. Fracking for natural gas had unleashed earthquakes. And most shocking of all, the angle of Earth's axis had started to shift. Water, Carson theorized, was retreating to the core.

As a scientist, Carson struggled with the idea that politicians were wary of research and what it might reveal. Wasn't that the point? Search for the cause, then find a solution? Time spent before the committee only reaffirmed his apprehension.

"NASA. That stands for National Aeronautics and Space Administration," hollered the Republican member from the state of Wyoming. "What on Earth—and I mean that literally—are you people doing staring at the ground?" he chided.

It was the same thing every year. One member of the committee or another would crack a joke about a space agency not observing space. Members of the Appropriations Committee were always the worst. They were a privileged lot and behaved accordingly. And while they were not able to reject programs outright, they placed special conditions on funding as their legislative forte. For most, NASA's Earth Science Division was little more than a line item in an annual budget of billions of dollars. Unfortunately for Carson, a few select members took disproportionate interest in his work and results.

"Professor Spinoza," intoned the corpulent chairman from Arizona, "please enlighten my esteemed colleagues as to the import of your work. And please be as specific as you can."

Carson flinched at the sarcasm but maintained his composure.

"With all due respect, Mr. Chairman, the funding you and your colleagues have provided through the years has allowed us to observe the subtle yet important changes in the Earth's composition. Note the evident effects of climate change. Erratic weather patterns, melting ice caps, rising sea levels. You name it. But it's the more subtle shifts *beneath* the Earth's crust that have raised the greatest concern of late. Which brings me to our recent discovery..."

"Professor Carson," interrupted the chairman. "Do forgive me. I am but a simple man and my knowledge of such things is quite limited in comparison to one such as yourself... But this use of the term 'evident'—would you care to explain to the committee what you mean by 'evident'?"

Here we go, thought Carson. As a former oil and gas executive, the chairman had a reputation for casting doubt on any role that industry played in altering the climate. It was his method and the disingenuous nature of his questions that bothered Carson the most. Bait and switch. His predecessor had succumbed to such tactics and, based on one small misstep, was ousted from her post and castigated by the ranks of conservatives who had despised her from the outset. Carson took a deep breath and settled into the possibility that he was in for a long and torturous interrogation.

"Mr. Chairman, I do believe we've had this conversation before. I've presented our division's findings on countless occasions. You've read the reports. The evidence is clear, or as I've just suggested, 'evident.' I come to you today with a new discovery, something that I do believe will interest you and the esteemed members of this committee. If you would allow me, we have qualified evidence of a subterranean landscape. It exceeds every expectation."

Carson felt the shift. He had them where he wanted them. Nothing like a good Hollywood-style lead-in to flatline a sarcastic rebuttal.

The chairman peered over his bifocals, then looked sidelong at his fellow committee members, gauging their willingness to entertain the request. The members nodded in unison.

"We will allow it, professor. Please proceed."

Carson was prepared. He signaled to his colleague who pulled a series of high-resolution charts from a large portfolio. Mounting them on an easel, Carson flipped back the cover to reveal a bright orange orb with highly pixelated imagery, patchworked with browns, greens, reds, and blues. Carson remained silent, letting the image speak for itself.

"What exactly are we looking at?" asked the chairman. "Have you discovered a new planet, Professor Spinoza?"

"No, sir. This is not a *new* planet. This is *our* planet... planet Earth!"

"Not mine. Looks nothing like it!"

"It's a satellite image. It is in the name of GRACE that I'm able to show them to you today."

"Are you trying to be funny, professor?"

"I am not, sir," though Carson was pleased with the pun. "These are the findings from the Gravity Recovery and Climate Experiment—G, R, A, C, E—mission, funded by this committee between March 2002 and June 2017. The program was subsequently defunded, but we didn't let fifteen years of research go to waste. For the past several years, my team and I have been building models based on the initial images. By combining key data with seismic-wave research, adjusting for anomalies, and using advanced scanning techniques, we have—for the first time—penetrated beyond the precinct of the Earth's crust."

"Go on."

"I have good news and bad news, I'm afraid."

"First the good news, if you don't mind," said the chairman.

"We've discovered and have been able to map in detail an elaborate series of interconnected passageways that snake their way through the Earth's crust and penetrate the mantle." Carson flipped the chart to reveal an elaborate image of what appeared to be a cross section of Earth's crust.

"Catacombs," said Carson. Tens of thousands of kilometers of underground catacombs."

"Made by whom, professor?"

"Not by *whom*, Mr. Chairman, but by *what*. And this brings us to the bad news."

"Which is?" asked the chairman.

"A massive depletion of our Earth's natural fresh water supply."

"What are you saying?"

"I'm saying that, prior to shuttering the GRACE program, we were on the path to understanding the severity of a pending global water shortage. For the first time, we were able to reveal the depth and complexity of the Earth's aquifers. As long as water ran flush in the veins of these underwater ducts, our planet thrived. To verify our findings, we ran bore holes in these 141 locations. It confirmed our worst fears. We're on the threshold of a global water crisis. And we can't even explain why."

Carson paused and waited for questions. The committee members were sitting somewhere between confused and dumbstruck. He thought for a moment about how to bring the message home. "The facts," thought Carson to himself. "Show them the numbers."

"If you consider that the Earth's aquifers store approximately 23.4 by 106 cubic kilometers, representing about one half of the 2.5 percent of Earth's total water sources, then these images show what we would refer to as a planetary halcyon effect."

"A what?" asked the chairman.

"A halcyon effect. When the body is in crisis, blood rushes to the core. It would appear that the Earth is responding not unlike the human body. In other words, water is to the planet what blood is to the body, and it's retreating through these networks of chambers and aqueducts to a source deep beneath the Earth's crust, penetrating to the mantle, and perhaps to the core itself. This would appear to be our planet's fundamental geological response in the interest of self-preservation."

"Have you lost your mind, Dr. Spinoza? Did you not say yourself that the loss of water defied explanation? State your case as a hypothesis, professor, then move on."

He had a point. Carson had allowed himself to move into the realm of speculation. That wouldn't do. Not before this lot, at least.

"I stand corrected, Mr. Chairman. I have no proof of this."

"Then what proof do you have?"

"These catacombs... tens of thousands of kilometers of them. If we want answers, we'll find them there."

It was bold, but he had to try.

"So now you're a *terra*naut," chided the congressman from Wyoming. "I suppose you'd have us shut down the space program and redirect our resources to exploring Earth's core."

"Yes. In fact, that's exactly what I'd suggest."

Perhaps Carson's idealism had got the best of him. Or perhaps he had simply spent too much time in the lab contemplating the world beneath him, but the next reaction from the committee caught him completely by surprise. Laughter erupted from one end of the table to the next, then reverberated back again. The chairman, now flush-faced, was the first to compose himself. By banging the gavel, he called the room to order.

"Dr. Spinoza... Carson... may I call you Carson?" It was that patronizing tone that he was all too familiar with. "What you're suggesting verges on the absurd. You come to us with a series of fancy, full-colored X-rays of Earth, tell us we're having a water crisis, then suggest we take tens of billions of dollars in NASA funding and flush it down your 10,000 kilometers of underground tunnels. Does that sound at all absurd to you?"

When put that way, Carson had to admit that it did sound a bit outlandish. But this time things were different. For the first time in history, they had evidence that a subterranean world lay just beneath their feet. Here, before them, his map charted clear passageways to the underworld. The role these channels played in the retreat of Earth's fresh water supply was not merely worthy of exploration, it was critical. The entire human race depended on it.

"The only absurdity would be to do nothing!" he shouted.

"Mind your tone, professor. I and the other members of this committee know what you're up to."

"And what might that be, sir?"

"Money. That's what it's always about. Am I right?"

"Money? I tell you we're facing the possibility of extinction, and you think all I care about is money?"

"It's always about money. Why else would you come to us with this elaborate tale of a planet, trying to rescue its core from disappearing water and tunnels to hell? The whole thing is poppycock, and I for one say it's time to cut you off, professor. I move that we adjourn."

"I second that," came the response."

"This gentleman from the Earth Science Division has wasted enough of our time."

The committee erupted in protest.

"Hear him out," cried one member.

"Shut it down," cried another.

The chairman grabbed for his gavel. Pounding it over and over, he shouted, "Order. I'll have order!"

After some grumbling and a few final few protests, the room settled. A change in the chairman was evident. He looked winded. Less confident. A thin line of perspiration appeared across his meaty face. For an instant, Carson saw the man lock eyes with a lone aide who was standing solemnly at the far end of the table.

"We will take a brief recess. Dr. Spinoza, I suggest you collect yourself and consider for a moment what you are telling us. When we return, I want the real explanation for this charade."

Before Carson could respond, the chairman raised the gavel and then threw it down with such force that it made the other committee members jump.

Retreating to the adjacent conference room, the chairman and his aide sat in silence waiting for the videoconference to begin. While the senator twisted and untwisted a paperclip, his companion tapped the legal pad with the eraser of his pencil. They knew what was coming.

The blue screen flickered, then the word *Connecting* appeared. Seconds later, the image of the one who asked all the questions appeared before them. From where he called, they never knew. Always the same dimly lit surroundings that mirrored the figure's predictably dark mood. His countenance never betrayed him. He wore calm the way a fox wears fur. Anyone unaware of the role he played would have interpreted his behavior as something akin to cold indifference, but nothing could be further from the truth. A passion burned somewhere deep inside. Those who knew him—of whom there were very few—called him uncompromising. He wore it like a compliment.

"There's been a development," said the aide. The chairman kept working his paperclip, resisting the urge to lift his head and stare into the face of the one man who made him feel small.

"And what development is that?"

"A researcher. One of ours. He's made a discovery."

"I'm listening."

"It shouldn't have happened. We pulled funding years ago. But he found a way around it. Now he knows."

"Who else knows?"

"His team. The committee. Maybe one or two others."

No response. The image on the screen was so still that, for a minute, the two men wondered if the video link had frozen. The chairman dropped the paperclip and reached for the console to redial.

"Allow it." The chairman withdrew his hand and resumed fidgeting with the paperclip.

"But…"

"I said, allow it. He may be of some use. Access his files. You know what to do."

The image went dark and so did the room. The two men sat in silence. The only sound was the tap, tap, tap of the eraser head.

Less than forty-eight hours had passed since Carson's inquisition at the hands of the House Committee. They had adjourned but failed to reconvene, leaving Carson alone in the antechamber rethinking his next move. Had it been a mistake to reveal so much so quickly? Were they at that very minute voting to rescind funding? What would he tell his team back at the lab? Eventually, someone did come for him.

"Professor Spinoza?"

"Ah... yes. You're looking for me?"

"This is for you," said the clerk, shoving a note into his hand. It was more jumbled than folded. In the chairman's bold and familiar hand, the note read: "The committee has heard you. Say nothing more."

Carson returned to the lab only to find it overrun with black-shirted members of Homeland Security. All he could do was watch while they pried open desk drawers, carried away computer terminals, and unplugged servers. He was ordered to remain where he stood, should anyone have any questions. His team members had all been turned away, relieved of their security passes, and told to go home. He knew that no degree of protest would make a difference. He stood aside and let the marauders do their dirty work.

When the last agent had left the room, Carson retreated to his swivel chair and collapsed into it. He pushed once more to the center of the room and reclined back, looking up into the darkened dome ceiling. Only days earlier he had sat in this very spot looking up into what lay below. It was over now. Years of work. And for what? He wasn't even sure who to blame. Was it the chairman and members of the committee? Or had some other branch of the government made the decision to shut him down? Had he stumbled upon something, not knowing what it was? Or perhaps the idea of an underworld explanation was simply—as the chairman had suggested—absurd. He had spent a lifetime in search of something that he knew existed. "Discovered," he thought to himself. "But forever hidden away." Is this what the end felt like?"

"Fuck it," he said, working his legs and causing the chair to spin around and around, before it gradually slowed to a stop. He stared into the reserves of his workstation, and there, atop the surface stained with countless rings of coffee cups, sat the black lacquer box. How had they missed it? They had taken everything else.

He leaned in and studied the object more carefully, then moved over it and gently traced the gold circle with his finger. The box vibrated, and Carson quickly withdrew his hand. From the dot in the middle, a pure beam of blue light appeared, then stretched up into the reaches of the dark ceiling. It quivered before fanning out, creating a cone of light. Within it, he saw a slowly rotating image of planet Earth.

CHAPTER 18

Because the Nephilim were so entirely predictable, their reaction to the news of the planned raiding parties was just as Enoch had anticipated. They were not at all pleased—but they were not prepared to protest, either. Rather than challenge the council's decision, they withdrew. And with their newly acquired families, they retreated far from the village, deep into the forest.

Confrontation was never their way. But truth be told, their decision to leave had more to do with their personal lives than with the misguided intentions of Lock and his minions. After living an eternity in relative isolation in the Upper Realm, their few short years in the Lower Realm had transformed them. In this place, they had discovered a gift more profound than all of the Great Blessings put together. And while the historical record would forever claim otherwise, their union with mortal women unleashed something in The Twenty that could never be put back.

Love was the culprit. It moved through the Nephilim like a contagion, gradually working its way into their oblong heads and breaking apart the tedious little compartments of their calculating minds. Confusion followed. But after that, a kind of wonderment. The daily rituals that had forever dictated their measured lives fell by the wayside. And on frequent occasions, Enoch would spot one of the brethren or another sitting idly, basking in the simple delights of family life.

The act of making love had set Nephilim sensibilities reeling. And as far as he could see, The Twenty spent ample time making up for centuries of solitude. Pregnancy proved as mysterious to them as the alchemical fusion of metals or the movements of the planets. And yet, this time, it was enough for them to relinquish their clinical curiosity, submitting to a state of awe instead.

Among all the metamorphic changes occurring within the world of the Nephilim, none proved more impactful than the arrival of children. For beings that had grown accustomed to the idea of constants, their progeny were living proof that vitality and change went hand in hand. These small creatures electrified The Twenty. For the Nephilim, they redefined the meanings of chaos and disorder—and, for the first time in their long lives, it lent substance to their otherwise mundane existence.

All this, Enoch observed. And, as was his way, he kept meticulous notes, documenting his brethren's awakening. He felt obligated to do so, shunning all opportunities—of which there were many—to find a wife and raise a family of his own, lest he forfeit his objectivity.

Beyond the jealousies that were inevitably stirred, the men of the village could not have cared less that the Nephilim were undergoing an existential catharsis. They barely took note when the Nephilim left the village for the forest. Most were happy to see them go, claiming that they were never at ease in the presence of giants. For Lock, The Twenty had become a distraction. Their presence had a way of drawing attention away from him and his men. Indeed, he began to resent the way they hovered about, always listening, yet saying nothing.

"Who needs them?" he argued before his war council. "Let them have their time with their women. They have nothing more to offer."

The raids went ahead as planned. It was no contest. During a pause in the celebrations on the evening of their return, Lock described to the elders how his men had entered the village—a place not unlike their own—pillaging, burning, and killing as required.

"Brutal work," confessed Lock. "But worth the effort," directing the elders' attention to the women in the courtyard bound in chains, their naked bodies bruised and torn from their abduction.

"They will bear children. Our numbers will grow," he insisted. "Soon enough, no one will be able to resist us. We will take what we want."

As the months stretched into years, Lock's vision became reality. One village after another fell to the superior power of Lock's army. As he promised, they took all that they could carry. And what was once a small village became a metropolis, 150,000 people strong. No one seemed to recall that it was the Nephilim who had generously provided The Others with the means to wage war. Their good fortune, the people agreed, was a result of Lock's leadership and the bravery of the men who fought by his side.

Throughout this time, Enoch stayed close. He observed these changes and recorded them meticulously in the journal that he always kept with him. As he watched, the village was transformed: walls were erected, a temple was built, and the humble dwellings that were once dotted along the lakefront were replaced by large, stone-fortified lodges—symbols of wartime success.

For Enoch, it was the subtle, almost undetectable changes that concerned him the most. It was as if the bonds between the families had been severed and then rebuilt around the institutions that Lock erected in their place. The army—not the elders—now held sway, and Enoch witnessed its effects. He could see the growing preoccupation with marauding and conquest, and how the ways of men overshadowed the rites that had long been practiced by women. The healing arts, natural rituals, and goodwill offered to all sentient beings lost its vitality. The villagers still went through the motions, but without the conviction that once served as the community's spiritual epicenter.

What surprised and disturbed Enoch the most was the fact that no one seemed to notice the change. The Others—if nothing else—were shockingly adaptive and forgetful at the same time. Indeed, on the face of it, most appeared happy. And while it was true that the villagers operated with newfound senses of security and prosperity, he could see that some essential part of who they were was being lost in the way that they thought more of themselves and less of one another, perhaps forever. The bustle and excitement of this new way of life made the old ways feel dull. The plundering and killing didn't seem to concern them in the least. Lock made sure of that.

For all his prowess on the battlefield, the warlord's hidden talent lay in his ability to manipulate the truth. At first, it was unclear why Lock went to such lengths to raise his own profile at the expense of The Twenty. What harm had they ever caused him? But gradually, the intent of his sinister plan became clear, and Enoch was awakened to a side of humanity that until then had remained hidden, waiting—perhaps—for the right opportunity to reveal itself.

"How did I not see it?" Enoch wondered. He was half-human himself, was he not? Perhaps he had chosen to notice only what he wanted to see: people, like his mother, in love with the world and grateful for all that life offered. Enoch thought back to only four years earlier, when The Others had welcomed him and The Twenty into their homes. He saw how easily they gave of themselves—their friendship, their generosity. "Where did it all go wrong?" he thought.

Into the narrow spaces of the human imagination, Lock poured fear and mistrust. He turned the hearts of the villagers against all outsiders and spoke at length about the importance of striking first, always taking the offensive. It was a new language and a new way of thinking. Passivity was a weakness of the ancestors, as they waited patiently for nature to offer up what she might. Raids and constant warfare were signs of strength, particularly when aided by weapons and the will to use them. More was better, they discovered. At the heart of it, this was Lock's new vision.

"Our enemies surround us," shouted Lock.

He stood at the center of the temple courtyard, his warrior council squared off around him, ten to a side. He had long ago cast aside the simple garb of a hunter in favor of more elaborate dress. On his forearms and thighs, he wore thick leather sheaths to protect himself in combat. Over his shoulders, he wore a cape adorned in shells and colorful feathers snatched from rare and exotic birds. As was the new custom, his body had been ceremoniously cut open and layered with small stones. The scarification formed elaborate patterns across his chest, arms, and legs. Around his neck, he wore amulets forged from precious metals, each one representing a conquest of one kind or another. The pubescent pestilence that provoked him to defy the elders early on had been replaced by a cold and abiding confidence. He still knew how to rally his followers to a cause, but he relied less on passionate pleas and more on insidious forms of manipulation.

"What enemies, my Lord? Who do you speak of? From here to the mountains in the north and the ocean to the south, all have submitted. You rule supreme."

Lock found it hard to hide his pleasure in hearing this from those most loyal to him, but he disguised it well.

"So you say! Have you forgotten those who lurk deep in the forest? Do they not lie in wait? Are they not simply biding their time, waiting for us to do their dirty work before they lay claim to what is ours?"

Lock turned slowly, looking into the eyes of the men who he himself had trained to become the realm's most ruthless warriors.

"Come now, not one of you knows of whom I speak?"

"Not The Twenty?!"

"*Yes*, The Twenty. And their whole brood of freakish brats as well. While we've waged war from here to the oceans, they've grown their ranks, copulating and producing like the rats they are. While we slumber, they breed an army... of giants, no less! Are you prepared to go to war with giants?"

Clearly the idea had never crossed the minds of these men, but they took notice now. And Lock wanted it that way. Plant the images deep, so they were all but impossible to dispel. Lock knew better than most that stories—true or not—can leave an indelible mark on the mind.

"The time has come. We must exterminate them!"

"But they are immortal!" came a cry.

Lock spun about to see who dared voice what had long since been discredited.

"Who says? That's what they want you to believe. And if you do believe it, they have already won. Have you forgotten how the Nephilim not so long ago slithered like snakes into our village, asking for favors and ogling our women. They took from us and then they disappeared. Are you fooled by their subtle ways?"

Lock could see his narrative beginning to take root. They wanted to believe him. He could see it in their eyes. This was the way of power. And he—Lock—had perfected the art.

The following day, Enoch emerged from the forest and entered the gates to the temple square. On most days, merchants would be gathered here in droves, trading gossip while hawking their wares. But this day was different. Rumors were swirling that Lock was planning a new offensive. The square was oddly quiet. Enoch was about to go in search of answers elsewhere when he noticed an old woman—his grandmother—sitting in the shadow of the temple. Months earlier, she had been stripped of her title as village chieftain. He could see she was lost in thought, so he moved slowly and sat down quietly beside her. For a long time, they said nothing. Then Enoch spoke.

"What have I done?"

There was no need for him to explain. She was well aware of how her people had changed and she knew Enoch blamed himself.

"It's not your fault, Enoch. These were choices we made. The Nephilim offered us knowledge. We took it. And this is what we've done with it," she said, giving a dismissive nod to the temple that loomed before them. "The Twenty could not have known that the gifts of the ages would be used in this way. We are children compared to the Nephilim. They offered us fire to warm and feed ourselves. We used it to burn and destroy instead. This Lock... he is the tinder that forms the flame."

"Not Lock. It's my fault. I urged you to accept the Nephilim into your lives."

"But I was the one who agreed to it," said the old woman. "I thought I knew my own people. The Nephilim offered us ways to plant gardens, cure illnesses, and read the signs in the night sky. These were beautiful gifts. We were unworthy of them. We are self-serving creatures, often-times incapable of seeing past our next meal. In earlier times, when we had less, we shared. Now, we fight over trifles. We make war on others and care not for their suffering."

The old woman seemed to disappear into herself for a moment. Enoch did not try to stop her. She was right. The Nephilim were not to blame. How could they know that The Others would squander the knowledge offered?

Reemerging from her reverie, the old woman turned suddenly, placing her small hand on Enoch's forearm: "You are in danger. It is best that you leave this place... there is no time to lose. I hope The Twenty are able to protect their wives and family better than your father protected my daughter..."

The old woman reached to retrieve the words, but it was too late.

"Forgive me, my boy. Clearly, I still harbor some resentment... But not for you... Not for The Twenty. I see them now for what they are. I believe they have found life's meaning. How ironic that after searching in the Upper Realm for an eternity, they have come to know what is most essential by living among us. Have they stolen the truth from us, or have they merely found what we have lost? Come, one last embrace, then off with you."

Enoch felt the thin arms of the old woman gather about his waste. He held her quivering shoulders for only a moment. Then she was gone, the tail of her robe leaving a small trail of dust in her wake.

Enoch did not wait to confirm the lies Lock told his warriors. He had heard enough and now understood that he and The Twenty had no time to lose. He turned immediately from the village and, passing through the gates, headed toward the forest. As he entered, he broke into a run. It had been months since his last visit to the dwelling place of the Nephilim and their families. Walking it would take him all day and all night. Running, he might reach them before sundown. How would he explain this? Enoch knew the brethren well enough to know they would not be able to comprehend Lock's plan to wipe them out. There was no good reason for The Others to do them harm. Had they not offered the villagers all their worldly wisdom, shared with them the secrets of the Earth and the cosmos, given them means to evolve in ways they never imagined possible? If they were human, the Nephilim would have found the idea laughable. But the Nephilim were not human. They viewed the world through a stoic lens. And therein lay the problem.

In the way of a thousand small cuts, Lock had chipped away at the idea that the Nephilim had rescued The Others from lives of mundanity. Just over four years had passed since the first night of their arrival. They had been a vision in the eyes of the villagers—gods descending from on high, offering gifts that would forever transform their lives as well as the lives of their descendants. At first, they had been feared. They were strangers after all—and giants, no less. Though only twenty, each had the strength of ten ordinary men. Within days, however, fear had given way to curiosity. The Twenty had proved gentle and patient. How could it have come to this?

The thought forced him to pick up his pace. How quickly, he wondered, could Lock assemble his troops? Could they be *en route* now? Would he have time to warn The Twenty and urge them to leave while they still could? And would they? After all, the Nephilim had no reason to believe The Others would do them harm. Why would they? And even if Lock's army did lay siege, what chance would they have against the combined strength and skill of The Twenty? Besides, the Nephilim were immortal. They couldn't be killed. What else might they do? Capture and put them in chains? The very possibility would strike the brethren as absurd.

It was then that Enoch had an idea. "The prophecy," he said out loud, coming to a halt.

The Book—the one tablet in which the Nephilim vested their full belief and trust—told of a Twenty-first who would appear to them, carrying the wishes of the One. Enoch, they believed, was that messenger. When Samyaza first raised it as a possibility, Azazel did not object. His hope was to persuade The Twenty to leave their mountain fortress and venture into the Lower Realm. There, he believed, the Nephilim would discover their true purpose. At the time, using the boy as a means to an end seemed to make sense. Enoch's first mission was to serve as emissary and prepare the way for the brethren's arrival in the Lower Realm. It went well. The Nephilim were given a chance to share their knowledge, and they were allowed to intermarry in exchange. The lives of The Twenty had been transformed. Daily drudgery was replaced by a lust for life, a chance to love, and the blessings of children. *The prophecy had proven true!* Or so the Nephilim believed...

Enoch knew what he had to do. He had watched Lock's deceit in pursuit of his own self-interest. Now he would have to do some deceiving of his own—not to benefit himself, but to save the Nephilim both from themselves and the misguided hatred of The Others.

"Hurry," he whispered. "No time to lose."

But it was too late. As Enoch's world faded to black, the last thing he remembered was reaching for the back of his head, his fingers caked in blood.

Chapter 19

When Enoch came to, he could not see. Blindfolded and bound, he tried to roll over, but a foot came down in the center of his back, forcing his face into the ground and leaving a taste of blood-soaked mud on his lips. He could feel that his body was bruised and torn. His head throbbed incessantly. Through the din of a crowd, he heard a familiar voice ring out from far above.

"Hear me!"

Gradually, a hush fell over the crowd.

"Did I not warn you that no one is to be trusted. Enemies all around. And enemies within as well!"

Enoch felt rough hands reach down and haul him to his knees. The blindfold was torn from his face, and blinking into the sun, he saw the silhouette of a man standing at the apex of the temple. All around him, warriors, villagers, and children huddled in rapt attention, Lock's accusatory finger was pointing directly at him.

Shouts and curses rang out, and Enoch, for the first time in his life, felt genuine fear. The faces—some familiar and some strange—held him in contempt. These were the people he had come to know. But they were all strangers to him now.

At the foot of the temple were two pyres—large stakes driven into the ground and surrounded by firewood. Tied to one was his grandmother. The other one was empty. Even from that distance, Enoch could see the sadness and resignation in her eyes.

"Our Great Mother—your chieftain—in chains," Lock shouted. "How can that be, you ask? Well, I shall tell you what has come to pass since I last stood before you. Had I not found her conspiring with the enemy, I, too, would feel your shock. But here are the facts. She has betrayed us. She has warned the enemy! Told them of our plans. And now, mark my words, the Nephilim make ready. They are coming for vengeance, and *she* is to blame!

Lock's disgust passed over the crowd like a noxious gas, seeking to snuff out any lingering empathy the crowd might have felt for the old woman. Enoch strained to lift his head. Looking sideways, he glimpsed the pitiful image of the old woman tied to the stake. Her confusion and pained expression reminded him of the day that he had found his own mother lying in the clearing, wounded and broken.

"Look at her. Look upon the face of your Great Mother. Does she show shame? No. Remorse? None whatsoever. If she suffers at all, it is with guilt!"

The crowd grumbled in response, but Enoch could see that there were still doubters among them.

"And there... groveling before you... the messenger. We allowed him to roam among us for too long. He is *not* one of us. He is one of *them!* He killed his own mother, no doubt, and fled with the devil Azazel into the mountains. He sided with the Nephilim long ago. Now he will die by that decision!"

The chanting began, and Enoch was lifted to his feet and marched to the base of the pyre. Six men were required to haul him up and bind him to the stake. As they did so, Lock approached and, leaning in, spoke to Enoch so that the others could not hear.

"It was I, Enoch," he whispered. "I preyed upon her when you went running off."

At first, Enoch thought Lock was referring to his grandmother, but then he understood.

"Yes. Like a wolf I set upon her. She fought, but I planted my seed anyway. She was mine. That was the plan. Your bastard of a father ruined all that. He took her away. I only reclaimed what was stolen from me."

Hearing his words, Enoch tensed, and his bindings groaned. The crowd was yelling and raving now. But all Enoch could hear was Lock's vile confession as it poured from his lips.

"She died that day," said Enoch through clenched teeth.

"Death was a blessing. Corrupted, she was, by Nephilim blood."

Enoch could smell the man's hatred. It permeated his every pore. He was so close now. And yet Enoch could do nothing. He was bound fast. The end was near.

Pulling away, and taking a sidelong glance at the raving crowd, Lock spat on Enoch for effect, then bounded down from the pyre and made his way back to the platform. Enoch pressed his eyes closed, struggling to contain the anger that was welling up inside him, then glanced across to see his grandmother staring back. Her eyes shone with kindness, her mouth tight with regret. Gently, she nodded. She knew from his expression what had been said.

Buckets of oil were lifted and poured over their heads, shoulders, and flanks. The liquid blurred Enoch's vision and he gasped for air. There was silence, then the crackle of a fire being lit. As the smoke began to rise, he braced for the horrific pain that would most surely follow—and follow it did. It started at the bottom of his feet and quickly went up his legs. He wanted to scream out, but his lungs were empty, as if his very breath had been whisked away. Through the smoke, he took one last look at the woman beside him, her eyes locked on his. Before passing out, he heard her say "Travel well, Enoch. We shall meet again." That was all. It was done.

Death came quickly. It started as a whisper, in soft tones making their way through the smoke and flame. Then, the pain came in waves. Pain is the shadow that accompanies death. It clings to you. In the beginning, there is no separating yourself from it. A whirring in the mind tells you it is ending. Like a rush of wind, it buffets the body and shakes the soul. There are pops and clatters as blood hardens and bones crack. And yet the awareness never leaves you. It is as if you are seeing yourself while being seen at the same time. You turn to look for the one who is looking and you discover there is nothing. There is no one. Colors meld and the sky becomes a kaleidoscope. It twists and turns and morphs into shapes, hues, and textures as if memory itself were being torn apart, scattered, and reassembled. The body evaporates, but the senses remain. They vibrate on the wind, untethered and unencumbered, while the universe expands and contracts all around. In one moment, there is an overwhelming sense of loss. In the next, a deep throb of hope. It wells up. Not from within the body, because the body has vanished. But from some other place—somewhere deep. It is dark and unseen, and if not for the hope, it might feel foreboding. The universe bends like the archer's bow, and you pass through it, as it passes through you. There is no beginning and no end. Time is meaningless. Then, you are there, in the midst and at the very core. And as you move, the world moves with you. You are *the circle whose center is everywhere and circumference nowhere.*[1]

It was from this dream that Enoch awoke, close to his childhood home, in the glade by the river. In quick succession, his senses returned to him. First sound, and the river. Then smell, and the trees. These were followed by the tickle of grass beneath him and the taste of sweet air all around. Last came sight. He opened his eyes as if for the first time. The trees swayed and the leaves rustled above him. The sky was blue, cloudless, and clear. He was home and at the center of his own being. He felt life in his limbs, clasping and unclasping his hands. Had it all been a dream? How was it possible? He was entirely naked. The bumps and scars from his 28 years were gone, as if they had never existed.

Enoch waited for as long as he could, relishing the reification, allowing his body to catch up with his mind. And yet he felt muted.

"What miracle is this?" he whispered, gradually standing and raising his arms to the sky.

He was white, like snow, and just as cold. Then came the call. It was soft at first, pulsating from somewhere upstream. Looking out, he saw the familiar boulder at the river's center. It was just as he remembered it. Forever fixed among the currents. A breeze cast itself along the shoreline. It beckoned him, and he moved uncertainly to the

---

1   Voltaire.

water's edge, then into the wake. He felt nothing, perhaps because his own body had no warmth of its own. Then came the tug and he found himself moving—pulled magnetically—toward the boulder.

As a child, he had been warned never to attempt the crossing. But now, fully grown, he had the strength to withstand the river as she tried desperately to pry his feet from the sandy bottom. Reaching its edge, he could see far above the heavy iron rings that had been pounded deep into the stone. He would need to climb from the water to reach them. His movements were slow and calculated, as if he had climbed this way before. Grasping the first ring tightly, he let his body swing down, then out, before grasping the second and then the third. As he did so, he felt strength return to his limbs and his lungs fill with air.

By the time he crawled his way to the boulder's broad, flat surface, his skin's familiar color had returned. Hair sprouted from his head and all across his body. Sights, sounds, and smells moved in waves, as he tuned himself to the world around him. Falling to his knees, Enoch felt his entire frame shudder at the sudden memory of death. He wept for his mother, for his grandmother, and for the Nephilim, whose fate now seemed certain. But most of all, he cried for The Others, who had fallen prey to power.

He had lost all sense of time. Had this transference from life to death and back to life again taken only moments or had it occurred over a lifetime? Ever so slowly, he stood, as if to test his legs for the first time. His back, torso, and thighs ran thick with perspiration. His pores, like a million tiny mouths, were gasping and playing their part in giving his new body life.

The call upriver came once more. And he responded by moving to the center and turning into the breeze. Then she came. In her, he saw the shape of the wind. Or perhaps it was in the wind that he saw the shape of her. She came softly, then strongly, swirling about and enveloping him to the point that his feet were lifted off the ground, with only his toes still touching the stone's cool surface. It was then that he heard his mother's voice. He saw in his mind's eye the two of them sitting on the riverbank. She was telling him something.

"What is the wind, mother?"

"It is spirit, my child."

"Why does spirit come as wind?"

"Because it must travel far and fast. Without wind, life stands still. Spirit fills all that is empty. It's what ties us together. Me to you. You to this river. The river to all the trees along her shore, and so on, and so forth."

"What is the wind saying to you now, Enoch?"

"It's telling me I must go."

"Go where?"

"To the Nephilim. Time is running short. They need me."

"Then go, my boy. Go like the wind!"

If he was under a spell for that moment, it was broken in an instant. With no time to lose, Enoch leapt from the boulder into the rushing water. He moved with the current and, coming to the shore, lifted himself out, then headed south without breaking stride. He knew this part of the forest well, and while the narrow path was less evident than it once had been, he was able to pick his way through the trees, keeping the sound of the river just within earshot. As he ran, he wondered if he would be too late.

CHAPTER 20

"What was it like for you... your first death?"

"It is hard for me to remember, as it was so long ago. I wasn't prepared."

"Where were you?"

"In the mines."

"How did it happen?"

"I don't recall. I only remember waking up and wondering how I got there."

"Where were you?"

"In the foothills, below the ice, where blue flowers cover the west hill and yellow ones blanket the east. I was lying at the crux, the division between the two. I remember feeling the soft grass beneath me and the sound of insects working their way beneath the soil. I opened my eyes and there I was, staring up at the sky. I couldn't move, or perhaps I didn't want to. She came to me the way she comes to all of us—on the wind."

"If we die, then live again, does that make us immortal?"

"It depends on what you mean by immortal. If you mean one life, unbroken, never changing, I would call that inertia, not immortality. Change is what we strive for. And change only comes from death and rebirth. Change breeds hope. It speaks of new beginnings. It reminds us of what is most essential. It is woven deep into the fabric of this planet. All we need to do is observe and emulate. The rest will take care of itself."

"And yet each of you labor after the hidden mysteries of the Great Blessings?"

"Our labor is our gift. It is not for the world to shape us, but for us to shape the world. Enter into her, and she will enter into you.

"Do you do this for them?"

"We do it for the world and all those who find themselves in the world."

"I'm afraid they do not see the world the way you do. They mean to take from it what they can."

"It was not always this way. There was a time. And perhaps there will be a time again. The pendulum swings. Our destiny points downward. Alone, or together, we will soon know the truth."

"What if we fail?"

"You will not fail. Because you—above all others—are as one with the world."

CHAPTER 21

Kai's flight was uneventful.

"Welcome to Helsinki. I hope your flight was comfortable."

If she had been on the plane from the beginning, he had not noticed. It was his first time on a private jet—and a luxurious one at that. On boarding, he flopped into the plush leather seat, hit recline, and was asleep before they took off.

"Helsinki?"

"That's right. Follow me, please," she said.

"Finland, huh. Didn't see that coming," he mumbled to himself.

"No need," she said as he reached toward the overhead compartment. "Someone will come for your things."

"Nice touch. Any chance you can tell me who I'm meeting?"

Too late. She was out the door and halfway down the gangway. Tired and disheveled, he found it strangely difficult to keep up. As they approached the end of the corridor, twin doors flew open, flooding the hallway with light. He held up a hand, giving his eyes a chance to adjust. A chopper sat waiting, its engines roaring. The air was crisp and clean, and Kai inhaled the smell of the ocean. The woman, wind fluttering her white dress, gestured for him to climb aboard. The door slid back and the pilot in a dark blue flight suit—adorned with a gold circle and dot—welcomed him on board. He stepped through, then his escort climbed in after him.

"Your headset is to your right. Please make yourself comfortable," she said. "It won't be long."

Kai did as he was told, resisting the urge to ask where they were headed. The chopper nosed into the wind and then soared out from the land toward the shimmering horizon of the North Sea. Twenty minutes later, the helicopter banked, then circled a small island. They hovered long enough for Kai to decipher a series of low-slung buildings made of wood and stone clinging to the west side of the island and blending perfectly into the landscape. Indeed, only at low altitude could one see the contours of the half-dozen structures. "Eco-friendly or trying to hide something?" he wondered.

No sooner had they landed than his escort bade him farewell. "I hope your stay is a pleasant one. Your quarters have been arranged. Your host will see you in due course. Head that way and you'll see the path."

And just like that, she and the chopper took flight. "A woman of few words," he muttered to himself, unaccustomed to being left in the dark.

From the cliff edge, he had no choice but to head inland, and as she promised, a path reached out to greet him. He passed through a grove of trees and reemerged to find the trail dead-ending into the side of a hill.

"How poetic," he scoffed. "A path to nowhere." He was giving the hillside a pat with his hand as if to say "Thanks for nothing" when, unexpectedly, a large moss-and-stone-covered oval door swiveled inward. Beyond it lay living quarters of unsurpassed beauty: at the far end, a large concave portal made entirely of glass jutted outward from the cliff to give a 180-degree view of the ocean horizon. The sun was setting, and it cast its orange glow back through the portal into the circular room. In the middle was a large round bed, covered in silk pillows, and from the ceiling and along the walls hung flowered vines which released a scent as fragrant as it was bewildering. The bedroom opened onto a bathing area that was more cave than room. Stalactites hung from the ceiling, releasing soft streams of water that gathered and flowed into a small waterfall that extended along the floor, then headed out and over the exposed edge. A natural hot spring was carved from the stone, and fresh towels were draped along its edge.

"Not too shabby," he said aloud.

But the room, the island, and the whole journey, for that matter, were starting to grate on him. "Either somebody wants something from me or I hit the jackpot and just don't know it," he thought to himself. Planning mountain expeditions for billionaires had made him cynical. People with money liked to jump the queue. "Maybe this one didn't get the memo. I'm outta the business. Done with Everest. Done with the whole damn thing. Guess I should enjoy this while I can," he mumbled. And stripping down, he eased his body into the spring. Steam bathed his face and Kai let his mind wander.

When he opened his eyes, he was still in the bath, but the room was dark. "How long was I out?" he wondered, leaping from the tub and drying himself off. He reentered the bedroom to see his bag open and empty by the front doorway. His clothes had been placed in the closet and his shaving kit by the sink. "What's your rush? Stay a while," he said to himself with a smile. "Elves, no doubt."

It suddenly occurred to him that he hadn't eaten in nearly a day. "Time to do some foraging," he thought. A trail bordered by lights led away from the shoreline and the villa, toward the island's center. He followed it until he came across an A-frame archway that mirrored the hill behind it. There were no doors—only a frame. He stepped through it to find himself standing near the center of an enormous grotto. Stalagmites thrust upward from the floor of the cave, and all around him was the sound of cascading water. At the center, in a clearing beneath the great domed ceiling, there stood a large round table of polished stone. Light rose from the stone floor and illuminated the symbol of the gold circle. Out of the shadows, a woman approached. She had long dark hair and wore a full-length, form-fitting jacket. But it was her gait that gave her away. As she drew closer, Kai felt a sudden rush of excitement and nausea.

"Abby?"

"Hello, Kai."

"But how... how is it possible?" He reached out and held her by the shoulders, not sure whether she was real. Her eyes reassured him, and he drew her near, holding her tight. This time, he would not let go. Overcome with relief, he surrendered to tears. A full minute passed before he tried to speak.

"I let go. I'm so damn sorry. Why did I let go?"

"It's not your fault. It happened a long time ago," she answered. "And I'm the one who should apologize. I let you believe I was dead. There were moments when I couldn't bear it, when I was ready to call and tell you everything, but I couldn't. It would have compromised everything. This place. Our mission. My role. It came with conditions."

"Conditions? What conditions?"

"I've played this moment in my mind a thousand times now," she said. "I knew it wouldn't be easy. Where to begin...?"

"How about from the start... like the moment when I lost you?"

She reached out and took his hands into her own. "Walk with me. I'll explain."

Abby told him everything. How she had fallen when the rope gave way, sending her body careening down the icy expanse and into the bowels of the glacier. She described the panic and flash realization that it was over, twirling and spinning to her death. But then there had come a sudden shift in the angle of the ice. She told him how the crevasse had flattened, then angled upward, slowing her descent. She had crested in a pool of shallow water and sat up, shivering as much from the cold as from the shock. The only thing keeping her alive there in the pitch black, thousands of meters below the surface, was the adrenaline that was surging through her veins. She told him how, after recovering her senses, she had forced her hands to move down and across her body, searching for open wounds or broken bones, but found none. She had survived, in one piece. But not for long—she felt hypothermia setting in.

Mustering the last of her energy, she had called out. It had seemed futile to do so—all around her was the crashing sound of cascading water. The odds of Kai hearing her, let alone locating her, had seemed impossible. "It was hopeless. I was entirely disoriented. I was cold and I knew that unless you, too, had fallen, I would be left there alone to die in the dark."

Kai listened to Abby recall all that had happened and felt sick to his stomach. She was right, he was sure that she had died. No one could have survived that fall. He remembered clinging to the ice wall, looking down, and realizing that he had neither the length of rope nor any other gear to reach her.

"I tried. I kept calling, but there was no answer, no sign that you were alive. I should have come after you, Abby. I'm so sorry I didn't."

The memory of that day was all too clear. Kai thought back to the moment when they decided to descend into the caves. It wasn't part of the plan. But with the weather deteriorating, they had no choice. It was either that or brave the katabatic winds that carried high-density air from the higher elevations under the force of gravity. Those demonic winds were commonplace at that time of year. They could well up suddenly and sweep an unexpecting climber off the ice. Making it back to the compound was not an option. It was Abby who had led them to this frigid expanse of coastline months earlier. She had been right. His search for the elusive subterranean caves had not been along the fault line in the Transantarctic Mountains, but along the upper reaches of Elephant Island. Together they had mapped the area, just the two of them working on snowcats and by foot. The retreating ice had created new openings, revealing tunnels beneath snow and ice. They used sonar and drones and other reconnaissance techniques, soon discovering a network of interconnected passageways that ran for hundreds—perhaps thousands—of kilometers beneath the surface.

Abby's phone call months earlier and her insistence that they meet in person had been the precursor to it all. As a theoretical physicist, she had come to the study of glaciers in a circuitous fashion. Early on, her research into quantum gravity had suggested that anomalies could occur deep within the reaches of Earth's mantle. At first, she had tried to raise interest among the drilling and mining companies, but their decisions were driven by profit, not research, so her requests for sponsorship and technical support were quickly rejected. The societies and foundations that at one time had clamored to support expeditions of this kind had grown conservative and cynical. Those she spoke to voiced skepticism. She lacked the necessary credentials, she was told.

For a time, she had considered giving up. Then Kai's article appeared, outlining his theory of subterranean passageways. At around the same time, she had detected magnetic dissonance while in residence on the southern reaches of the Chilean coast. Within weeks, she had located the first of the moulins—large holes that formed on the surface of ice as the glaciers receded. It was a record melt, and while the press focused on the wider implications and the prospect of rising ocean levels, the openings themselves received little attention.

Kai, she had hoped, was someone she would be able to trust in helping her make sense of it all. After her phone call and their initial meeting, it had taken little convincing. They were the perfect match for pursuing what lay deep beneath the Arctic ice. The days were long at that time of year, so sleep felt more like a luxury than a necessity.

What had been professional turned personal. It was just the two of them in a snowy wonderland. It was bliss. Then came the accident.

"You made the right call, Kai. There was nothing you could do. We knew the risks."

Abby placed her hand on the back of his neck and drew his head toward hers until their foreheads touched. It was their greeting—the way they had begun and ended each day on the ice. Kai's throat tightened and his eyes welled in a mixture of remorse, anger, and relief. He drew back to once again look into the face of the woman who he had loved, then lost.

"You're here now," he whispered.

"Yes, I am."

"But how?"

"At first, I thought my mind was playing tricks—or, at the very least, my eyes were starting to adjust to the dark. It was the faintest of blue lights. Then it grew, and I could see the contours of the cave, tunnels branching off in all directions. I decided to do the only thing I could do. I followed the light. I had only an ice ax. I could see the light was fading, moving away. I was desperate and knew that I might lose my footing at any moment. It went on like that for hours. Then came the shivering. It crept in, the cold. When the warmth set in, I started to panic. I knew I was dying. I don't remember if I climbed the rest of the way or was pulled free, but when I woke, I was in a room, lying on a table and hooked up to an IV. That's all I remember."

"Who saved you?"

"Those who built the tunnels."

"*Built* them? You're telling me those tunnels are man-made?"

"I'd say more excavated than made, but yes. We weren't the first. They took me in, Kai. They shared everything with me. I've spent the last seven years trying to keep up with all they know. We've learned so much. And it's only the beginning. Come, I want you to meet the others."

Taking him by the hand, Abby led him to the opposite side of the chamber. The stone doorway drew back and they passed into a well-lit area, with doors to the right and laboratories behind glass to the left. There was not a soul in sight, but Kai could see that someone had been busy. The labs were filled with equipment, piles of paperwork, and whiteboards flush with formulas.

"This isn't the half of it," Abby said without breaking stride, heading for the door at the end of the corridor that opened into what might pass for an opulent hotel lobby. It was framed by twin staircases spiraling upward toward a high-arched ceiling. At the center of the hall lay a large slab carved from solid stone in the shape of a table. As Kai approached, he could see it shimmer and pulse with its own internal light. Three strangers stood around it.

"May I introduce you to your fellow travelers?" said Abby. "Carson Spinoza, Philomena Pettibone, and Spike Morrison."

Kai extended his hand and greeted each in turn.

"Fellow travelers, you say?"

"Yes. If you choose to join us."

"Join you for what?"

"A great adventure, Kai. And one that should please you... But first, let's talk!"

CHAPTER 22

Years of work and planning had brought them to this point. Abby looked around the room and considered how unique circumstances had brought together a NASA engineer, a shop owner, and an oil rigger. With the exception of Kai, she had played no part in selecting the team—which seemed odd, given her intimate involvement with every other aspect of the project. As such, the evening ahead held as much mystery for her as it did for the others.

It was hard not to jump the gun and dive right into the business at hand, but she knew she had to wait. Instinct dictated it. Chemistry was the important thing. She gave her dinner guests time to talk. Maybe they knew better than she did as to why they were there. They were taking turns, introducing themselves and searching for— without openly asking about—the possible thread that bound them all together.

"What about the box?" asked Philomena, directing her question to Abby, who, until that point, had remained quiet. "I still don't understand it... the message, that is."

"All great adventures begin with a call for a beginning. Would you agree? You might say the box marks our beginning. What say you, Mr. Morrison?"

"I prefer 'Spike,' and I have no fucking idea why I'm here. I guess it felt like a good idea at the time. Now, I'm not so sure."

"And you, Ms. Pettibone? Why are you here?"

"I can't say for sure. It showed up on the day of the sickness. The migraines and nausea. Is that a coincidence or is it related?"

"I've been wondering the same thing," said Carson. "I'd like to know—is this government-funded?"

Abby guffawed. "Far from it!"

"Then what's this all about? I think we're all entitled to some answers."

"And so, you'll have them."

"What exactly is this place?" asked Philomena.

"It's ground zero. A living lab. A test site for what's ahead."

"And what exactly is that?" Carson ventured.

Abby hesitated. "Before I answer that, perhaps you'll indulge me."

She stood and made her way across the room to where a large gold circle had been emblazoned on the back wall. She drew a laser pointer from her pocket. As she did so, the emblem faded to black. In its place appeared a larger revolving image of planet Earth. Abby took a deep breath and studied the expressions of her guests.

"Our planet is in crisis. You all know that. You each understand, in your own way, the truth of the matter. What you may not know is that it's worse than you think."

Abby paused, allowing her words to sink in.

"The fact is the planet's natural defenses are in full retreat. There is a point beyond which the Earth—like the human body—cannot and will not recover. Like our physiology, this world of ours has its own intricate set of interrelated systems. Central to its survival is its immune defense. Without it, the planet has nothing to protect it from disease."

"Disease?" asked Spike.

"Yes, disease... I'm talking about us... humans. We are a cancer on the body of Earth."

"So eliminate the humans and eliminate the problem? Is that what you're saying?" asked Philomena.

"Not exactly. It hasn't come to that yet. In hot spots around the world, gravitational and electromagnetic fields are commingling in ways that not only defy the principles of classical physics, but also point to a much deeper problem—something bound up with Earth's harmonics."

"I knew it!" cried Philomena, leaping from her chair, then sheepishly sitting back down. "My apologies. Please continue."

"We have our theory," continued Abby. "Perhaps you have one of your own, Ms. Pettibone. But first, ours. The Earth, it seems, is slowing down."

"Seriously?" asked Carson.

"I'm afraid so. If our calculations are correct, we are in what can only be called a death spiral."

"That doesn't sound good," said Spike.

"By syncing a network of high-density probes descending into the Earth's mantle, then pairing them with satellite input, we've observed a shift in atmospheric pressure. A slowdown, it seems, is inevitable. Hence the gravitational anomalies, or so we surmise."

"I'm not aware of any Earth probes," said Carson.

"I doubt you are. Their placement has remained a secret, at least until recently. I'll come to that shortly, but first, there's something more…"

"Can't wait," quipped Spike.

"Global warming has just handed us the first of a series of unprecedented effects. We knew the melting of the polar ice caps was a problem. What we hadn't counted on was the impact on Earth's alignment. We don't know if this is the cause or the consequence of spin reduction. What we do know is that the change has impacted Earth's axis—its 'tilt,' if you will. To grossly simplify, think of Earth as a gyroscope. As it begins to slow, it starts to wobble. When it stops… well… you get the picture…"

"Is this some joke," Spike muttered. "I don't like the sound of this."

"Nor do we," said Abby. "Beyond the damage caused by humans, melting ice, and reduced spin, there's a fourth dimension. I need to mention this as well."

"And I thought it couldn't get worse," said Kai.

"What exactly is the fourth dimension?" asked Spike.

"Einstein's theory of relativity. Gravity is at its center. Its presence distorts spacetime. If altered, it further warps the relationship of space to time. What we are experiencing is a series of cosmic *quarks*. These quarks are either triggering or responding to the shifts in Earth's natural state. We still don't know cause from effect. Dark matter—about which we know very little—has some hand in this. As I said… a perfect storm."

For what seemed like an eternity, the room remained silent. Abby gave them time. She knew it was a lot to take in.

Eventually, Carson spoke up.

"How sure are you about this?"

"Unfortunately, quite sure."

"And you're going to fix it?" asked Philomena.

"Well, I don't know about fixing it, but we have a plan."

"Let me guess," said Carson. "A plan to travel to Earth's core."

"Why, yes, Dr. Spinoza. How did you know?"

"Say what?" shouted Spike.

An audible gasp went up from the table. They looked from one to another. And suddenly it all became clear. They were there because they each held some secret knowledge of Earth's inner workings. Suddenly, the air in the grand hall felt very thin.

"I don't feel so well," said Philomena.

"So there *is* something down there?" asked Spike, momentarily casting aside all cynicism.

"Without a doubt. And we're going after it. The core holds the answers. If we have any chance of slowing or reversing the situation, we have to go. You can walk away. No questions asked. But if you choose to stay, you'll be sworn to secrecy."

"So let me get this straight," said Spike. "You're betting the future of the planet and the survival of all living things on a mission to the Earth's core? What in God's name are you hoping to find down there? And can someone please tell me how this crowd of misfits is gonna help?"

"He's not wrong, you know," said Kai, reflecting for a moment on his own limitations. "You're talking about forces well beyond our control."

"I thought so too. Until I was shown a new possibility."

"This is all too much. I know you, Abby," said Kai. "I know how talented and capable you are. But this goes well beyond our work in the Arctic all those years ago. You're talking about a whole new level."

"Indeed I am. I have so much to show you all. Let's not wait any longer."

"You have our full attention," said Carson.

Abby took a deep breath, sized up her audience one last time, then dove in, turning the group's attention back to the image of the revolving Earth.

"What we know is this. With absolute certainty, we are entering a new and precarious phase in Earth's history. It's been referred to as the sixth cycle of extinction. Under normal circumstances, there's no immediate cause for concern. The process can take thousands, even millions, of years. Unfortunately, our current situation isn't normal. It's worse than we imagined."

Abby could see their consternation, but rather than pause and allow for questions, she pushed on. "In fact, we may have less time than initially predicted."

"How much time?" asked Philomena.

"Years, maybe. A decade, if we're lucky."

"That's ridiculous," Carson snapped. "The scientific community has weighed in on this. Yeah, sure, there are signs of decline, but the cycle—as you just suggested—takes millennia. No one—not even the most extreme alarmist—has suggested imminent disaster."

Abby gave Carson a sympathetic gaze. "Unfortunately, they don't know what we know. Or, if some do know, they're not saying anything. The repercussions would be devastating. Global panic is the last thing we need. It's why—I assume—our benefactors have remained anonymous."

"You don't know who's behind this?" asked Kai, pointing around the room.

Abby could see how the years of pain and worry had worn away at the man she once loved. So often, these past many years, she had thought of reaching out, just to let him know she was alive. But it was forbidden. Nothing could jeopardize her work. She shot Kai a sympathetic glance. She could see he was judging her.

"At first, I insisted. But eventually I cared less about *who* they were, and more about *what* they knew. And oh, dear God, they know so much. More than all of us combined. But forgive me, I'm getting ahead of myself."

"How can you know what they're telling you is real?" asked Carson.

"One thing, and one thing alone," said Abby. "Evidence. It's all we have. We hope it leads us to the answers."

"Answers!" shouted Spike. "I don't even understand the question."

"What does any of this have to do with us?" asked Carson.

"With the exception of Kai here, I had no knowledge of any of you until just a few days ago. Those behind this venture know more than I thought possible. No one is here by chance. I can only assume that each of you has a critical part to play."

"If the answer is drilling for oil, then I'm your man. Beyond that, I don't know the first thing about geography, physics, glaciology, or astrology, for that matter. Hell, I barely got through school. I think there's been a mistake," said Spike.

"I doubt that. Our benefactors don't make mistakes. Whoever they are, they're well-connected. They've met my every request. We've achieved in less than ten years what would have taken a lifetime to create elsewhere."

"And have you stopped to consider their motive?" asked Philomena. "What's in it for them?"

Abby paused. Their questions were starting to make her question. She had been absorbed in the task at hand, but now, for the first time in a long time, reasonable people from the outside were asking reasonable questions.

"I don't know. I only know that they built this place and, from the beginning, offered everything required to carry out our research. If you bear with me, you may come to believe that our efforts have not been in vain."

"Very well, Dr. Clarke," said Carson. "Continue... please."

Abby returned their attention to the wall where the image of Earth continued its slow rotation.

"For 66 million years, this has been our home. Throughout this time, we've shared this planet with other forms of life. We've endured draughts, famine, disease, and war. And up until a few thousand years ago, we seemed to have found our natural place in the world—at the top of the food chain and, for the most part, in harmony with the natural world.

"It's hard to say precisely when all of this began to change. Perhaps it started when we hung up our foraging baskets and took up the plow. Or maybe it came later, with the invention of gunpowder or the printing press. Perhaps it was the discovery of oil and the combustion engine. I'll leave that question to the historians. But whatever the cause, it's led us to this moment. Human ingenuity is a double-edged sword. Are we better off? Maybe. This planet of ours has taken the brunt of it. Our findings suggest that we aren't entirely responsible for the current predicament, but we certainly haven't helped matters much. There's not one among you who doesn't understand the gravity of the situation. But here's the thing. For all the damage done, course correction may still be possible. To explain this, I'll need to go back— way back."

Theatrically, the lights in the chamber dimmed. The holographic image of Earth pulsated and grew rich in every detail. The mountainous regions assumed a three-dimensional majesty, the oceans turned a deep blue-green color, the coastal zones appeared animated, and there was a subtle feeling within the forested zones of a life force as old as the Earth itself. All eyes were riveted to the image as Abby took them back to a time long before humans.

"This planet of ours is a wonder. For millions of years, it ebbed and flowed, adjusting as best it could to altered conditions. Floods, earthquakes, and eruptions have annihilated species and reshaped the landscape. But time and again, life rebounds. To the best of our knowledge, there's no planet like it. We've learned in recent decades to understand its past by exploring its depths. And trust me when I tell you, we've learned more than we bargained for.

"Far from being a floating rock subject to the whims of the cosmos, this planet is self-regulating, imbued with essential properties—land, oceans, and atmosphere—that are intertwined and always evolving. It is a tightly coupled system whose constituent parts are greater than the whole. Earth, in other words, is an interdependent organism... a living mass.

More than once Earth has skirted death. Mass extinctions are part of her history. She made sacrifices. The remains of millions—perhaps billions—of species lay beneath our feet. They tell a story 4.5 billion years long. If Earth were an eighty-year-old woman, our knowledge of her would only begin around her sixty-fifth year. It was then, 444 million years ago, during the so-called Ordovician Period, that she experienced the first of five mass extinction events. Earth's magnetic field dipped to just one-tenth of its current strength. The sun's radiation poured through. It was carnage. All might have been lost, but then, quite miraculously, large deposits of iron at the Earth's core began to cool. That in turn created what we now refer to as polar drift. It set off a chain reaction, releasing magnesium and silicon, which, in turn, triggered an electrical current, in effect, jump-starting the magnetic field. Why did it happen? We have no idea. But evidence suggests that the planet responded by activating its own defense mechanisms, not unlike the way the white blood cells in our own bodies rush to fight an infection. Another event occurred during the late Devonian Period, some 360 million years back. And then a third, at the end of the Permian Period. The world lost eighty-six, seventy-five, and ninety-six percent of its species, respectively. Hence the term 'mass' extinction."·

The story of Earth's first three existential crises in combination with the slowly rotating image proved hypnotic. Abby thought for a moment how it had always been this way. How the crackling flames of a campfire and the sonorous tones of a storyteller could carry the listener to another time and place. It was this kind of deep and concentrated listening that offered her some hope for humanity. Abby gave her head a quick shake, then turned to face them.

"Am I moving too quickly?"

Only Carson turned to meet her eyes. The others sat mesmerized.

"Then allow me to continue," she said, clicking the remote and reanimating the image. They watched the Earth shift and morph in fast forward as another 400 million years passed. She paused the animation once more.

"Somewhere between 200 and 174 million years ago, it happened again. This time, the physical landscape beneath the Earth's crust shifted. And I don't mean gradually. It was all quite sudden. By our estimates, it occurred over a period of some 400 to 900 years. During that time, the landmass shifted an estimated twenty-six degrees south by southwest, prompted by a geomagnetic reversal. It was enough to usher in a mass extinction that would make the Jurassic episode— some 120 million years later—look mild by comparison. This is what it looked like."

Abby again pointed the remote at the image. The rotation began to slow, and as it did, the character of the landscape shifted with it. The oceans swirled and consumed large swaths of land. Animated eruptions pockmarked the surface. Colors changed and shifted in a patchwork of greens, blues, and browns. Forests sprang forth in place of deserts. Mountains rose and lakes were formed. Before their eyes, in a time-lapse sequence, the Earth was being transformed.

"Polar reversal. How is this even possible? As you can see, it added a whole new twist to the story. The last and most recent reversal took place just 42,000 years ago, and while less destructive than previous episodes, it was enough—some believe—to have eliminated the Neanderthals. Indeed, it's a miracle that sapiens survived. By studying ancient lava flows in parts of southern France or the remains of petrified kauri trees in New Zealand, we know the Earth endured a sudden and devastating shift in climate. Was it triggered by polar shift? Was the Earth's gravitational field affected? We don't know. What we do know is that Earth, once again, righted itself."

Abby froze the image. "This is Earth today."

"Ah, yes, it's lovely," said Philomena.

"And this," continued Abby, clicking the remote, "is our future."

All eyes were glued to the image. And as they watched, the world was transformed again. Continents split, re-formed, erupted, and were consumed by oceans. In one dramatic instant, the oceans parted, racing north and south, flooding the land. Gradually, one side of the planet turned dark, while the other turned orange and brazen. The hologram before them shifted from perfectly round to slightly oblong. The image slowed, then ground to a halt. All that was left was a sputtering aura of a blackened landscape, with spots of fire, surrounded by dark waters—a planetary death spiral.

"The model is not precise, but you get the picture."

She paused to let it all sink in. She felt a sick delight in watching their expressions, and then she smiled.

"Something funny about this?" asked Spike.

"No. Of course not, forgive me... But you see, this doesn't have to be our future. It will only come to pass if we do nothing."

"*We* again," said Philomena.

"Yes, *we*."

"Honey, it's *my* head that's spinning now," declared Philomna. "What can you—or any of us for that matter—do to keep this world of ours turning?"

Spike threw up his hands. "I'm sorry, but how is any of this even possible?"

"I'm glad you asked," replied Abby. "There is hope." And as if on cue, the image of the dead Earth, suspended before them, began to turn in reverse. The dark patches turned light brown, then to hues of green. Lakes and rivers reappeared. The ocean regained its aqua blue color.

"We believe the answer lies at the center of our Earth. It is the source of the gravitational and electromagnetic anomalies that I alluded to at the start. We are at the confluence of both natural and man-made events. We have one shot at this. If our theory proves correct, we may have the means to force a correction."

"What force do you have in mind?" asked Carson.

"I'll come to that later. First, professor, I offer you some additional evidence. Paleomagnetic signatures are reappearing in the rock samples we've been gathering for more than a decade. The twenty-six-degree geological lurch I mentioned was the result of what one might call a 'true polar wander,' in which the topmost layers of the planet, likely all the way down to the outer core, rotate significantly even as Earth maintains its spin on its axis. In effect, it is a major redistribution of mass toward the equator. The core, we believe, holds the secret to this unparalleled geomagnetic event."

"We appreciate the lesson, but what exactly are you suggesting?" asked Kai.

"Forgive me. In order to explain what I'm about to say, I thought it important to put things into context. As stated at the outset, our goal is to prevent—or at least delay—the next extinction cycle. By combining what we know from the last cycle and all that has come to pass over the course of the Industrial Revolution, we have formulated a theory."

Abby turned and looked directly at Carson. "Yes, Dr. Spinoza, a theory. You, of all people, can appreciate that."

She knew, thought Carson. This was a government-backed project. How else could she know?

"The events I've outlined from millions of years ago created a split in the Earth's core, a fissure that runs the length of the Earth's axis, essentially dividing the core into two halves. The eruptions that laced the Earth's surface are the result of the core releasing molten rock. It broke free from the mantle and exploded through the Earth's crust in thousands of locations. But this also triggered a counter-response—a rushing of the Earth's oceans to the north and south poles, creating what we refer to as the Great Reverse Cascade, with ocean water being driven through these channels back into the Earth's core through access points here, here, and here," she said, again pointing with the laser to the two poles, in addition to a third location separating South

America from Antarctica. "The cascade, we believe, carried with it some life force. Spirited, as it were, into middle Earth. Somewhere in or near the core, we believe *life*—in its many forms—found sanctuary and learned to thrive again there."

"You're saying there's life at Earth's center?"

"I'm saying there is a life force that emanates from the core, and we are going to find out what it is and whether it might help us rescue this planet."

Carson watched as Abby traced and retraced the three points of entry.

"So it's true?" asked Carson.

"Yes, professor. We believe it is."

Abby pivoted to face the man she once loved. "And Kai, you were right. We were there. The day we were torn apart was the day I encountered one of the great portals to the underworld. It is proof of a nineteenth-century theory that was once proposed, then quickly forgotten."

"Hollow Earth?"

"Yes," said Abby. "Hollow Earth."

Chapter 23

In 1818, an American eccentric by the name of John Cleves Symmes Jr. declared the Earth to be hollow. Its core, he claimed, was accessible via the north and south poles. This brazen appeal fell largely on deaf ears. To be frank, it was really more a declaration than a scientific theory. Although he had little scientific training to speak of, that didn't stop Symmes from distributing his *Circular No. 1* to the four corners of the Earth. He instructed that 500 copies be sent out, "one to each notable foreign government, reigning prince, legislature, city, college, and philosophical societies [*sic*], throughout the union, and to individual members of our National Legislature, as far as the... copies would go."[2]

LIGHT GIVES LIGHT, TO LIGHT DISCOVER—" AD INFINITUM."

ST. LOUIS, (Missouri Territory,)
North America, April 10, *A. D.* 1818.

TO ALL THE WORLD!

I declare the earth is hollow, and habitable within ; containing a number of solid concentrick spheres, one within the other, and that it is open at the poles 12 or 16 degrees ; I pledge my life in support of this truth, and am ready to explore the hollow, if the world will support and aid me in the undertaking.

Of Ohio, late Captain of Infantry.

N. B.—I have ready for the press, a Treatise on the principles of matter, wherein I show proofs of the above positions, account for various phenomena, and disclose *Doctor Darwin's Golden Secret.*

My terms, are the patronage of this and the new worlds.

I dedicate to my Wife and her ten Children.

I select *Doctor S. L. Mitchell,* Sir *H. Davy* and *Baron Alex. de Humboldt,* as my protectors.

I ask one hundred brave companions, well equipped, to start from Siberia in the fall season, with Reindeer and slays, on the ice of the frozen sea ; I engage we find warm and rich land, stocked with thrifty vegetables and animals if not men, on reaching one degree northward of latitude 82 ; we will return in the succeeding spring.   J. C. S.

---

2   As quoted in L. Sprague de Camp and Willy Ley, *Lands Beyond: A Fascinating Expedition into Unknown Lands* (1993), p. 296.

Symmes based his argument on Edmond Halley's 1691 lecture before the Royal Society of London. In order to explain certain electromagnetic anomalies, the legendary astronomer argued that there might exist "a much more ample Creation" in the ground beneath us. "Hollow Earth," he suggested, was a possibility. It was only by virtue of Halley's prior scientific accomplishments that his community of peers tolerated the suggestion. Once it had been presented, however, *An Account of the Cause of the Change of the Variation of the Magnetical Needle; With an Hypothesis of the Internal Parts of the Earth* was in quick order shelved and largely forgotten—considered by many to be a one-off and whimsical musing of a man pushing the limits of hypothetical speculation.

It was Symmes who unearthed the treatise and breathed new life into it. In his attempt to resurrect the theory, he pointed out that among the documents relating to Halley's lecture was a schema of inner Earth, comprising a series of concentric circles that had the ability to generate a magnetic resonance so powerful that they would allegedly be able to alter global wind patterns. In effect, Halley had argued that the Earth functioned as a kind of globe within a globe. Each of the spheres, he suggested, rotated in the same diurnal direction, but at slightly different velocities, enabled by an unknown liquid or hydraulic substance. "So then the External Parts of the Globe may well be reckoned as the Shell, and the Internal as a Nucleus or inner Globe included within ours, with a fluid medium between."[3] The rotations of these spheres, Halley speculated, were determined by the two fixed poles on the cortex of Earth and "a second moveable pair" at its nucleus. While there was no physical way to prove the existence of these interdependent magnetic poles, it was, in accordance with Halley's theory, a viable explanation.

Symmes might have wished that Halley had stopped there. But instead, the astronomer proceeded to dissect his own treatise, pointing out its many flaws and ultimately rendering the notion of Hollow Earth as more akin to fantasy than fact. Indeed, in his final analysis, Halley

---

3   *Philosophical Transactions of the Royal Society of London,* vol. 17, issue 196 (October 1692), p. 568.

landed on what many considered to be a most unscientific conclusion. "The Creator," he claimed, "would not mold a planetary habitation that wastes space. Our planet's very existence is the necessary expression of providential thrift, of creation's rational adherence to the precept of use-value."[4] In other words, why would God waste the time and energy to create such an odd set of geophysical exceptions to the general laws of physics? A puritanical God, Halley considered, would have had better things to do.

That might have been the end of it, the final blow to a far-reaching theory. But then, Halley did something that no one expected. He returned to the remote possibility of Hollow Earth once again, considering that if it did indeed exist, it would likely support other forms of life. The mere suggestion was enough to ignite the imagination of every dreamer and novelist on the planet. And, indeed, that is precisely what happened. Halley's scientific theory may have been put to bed, but it unleashed a new genre of literature, featuring fantasy voyages and science fiction, beginning with Johannes Kepler's *The Dream* (1608) and Francis Godwin's *The Man in the Moone* (1638), then extending to the works of Jules Verne, who throughout the late nineteenth century released classics such as *Twenty Thousand Leagues Under the Sea* (1870) and, of course, *Journey to the Centre of the Earth* (1864).

It was enough to keep the fantasy of Hollow Earth alive. But had it not been for Symmes' insistence that the Earth's interior was "hollow, habitable, and accessible," the scientific possibility might have faded into obscurity forever. Issuing his *Circular No. 1* was just the first step. In the years that followed, it became his mission to prove his theory. He began by lodging repeated requests to the U.S. Congress to sanction and fund an expedition to Antarctica in search of the elusive portal to Earth's core. And although all of his requests were rejected, he never became discouraged. He took his lecture on tour, presenting his thesis to anyone who would listen. Among the Chicago elite, he found a group of sympathizers (and prospective financiers), but this encounter came too late. Symmes passed away at the relatively young age of forty-nine,

---

4   Ibid. p. 574.

and buried with him—possibly forever—was his passion for proving the theory of Hollow Earth.

Symmes' legacy, alas, was very different to Halley's. Since Symmes was neither a sanctioned explorer nor an accredited scientist, he went down in history as a man who had been smitten by delusions of geophysical wonder, rather than as a credible empiricist with a viable theory. Proof of Hollow Earth had eluded him and, for the next 200 years, interest in it remained dormant—until, that is, someone had cause to resurrect it.

CHAPTER 24

Kai leaned back in his chair and pondered the woman he had known and loved before that fateful day. Over the past hour, with few interruptions, she had set out a planetary theory that defied conventional wisdom. His own academic training in the Earth sciences told him that her theories—while idiosyncratic—had merit. Abby had broken new ground. She was, in a word, *brilliant.* This was not the same eager and insistent young graduate student who had led him back to the Antarctic all those years ago. No. This was a woman transformed. Her passion for her work was evident. And to think she had achieved all of this operating in relative isolation! Who were these mentors of hers? What were they up to and why—of all the researchers in the field—had they chosen Abby? Was it circumstantial or had they anticipated her plunge into the ice tunnels in order to retrieve and enlist her?

With the exception of the light hanging above the round table that the group had gathered around—Earth's image slowly turning before them—the room was shrouded in darkness. Kai leaned back farther, tilting the chair and letting his head disappear into the shadows where he could see without being seen. From there, he gazed intently, watching Abby work the room, volley questions, and exhibit an astounding array of knowledge.

"Brilliant *and* beautiful," he thought to himself.

No sooner had the thought crossed his mind than Abby turned to look his way. A wry smile crept across her face and Kai wondered if he had not mistakenly said the words out loud.

"If you can hear me," he said to himself, "answer me this: do you still love me?"

As if on cue, Abby stepped back from the table and passed silently behind him. There, in the shadows, she drew her fingers through his hair, then, like an eclipse, emerged back into the light, where no one else was any the wiser.

The front legs of Kai's chair hit the floor with a clatter and the room went silent. There was only the sound of Abby's heels as she slowly circumnavigated the table, her eyes firmly fixed on him.

"Apologies," he said sheepishly. "It's late," he explained.

"I think we should call it a night," said Abby. Everyone around the table looked tired and spent. And understandably so. It was a lot to absorb. Philomena stood and the others followed suit. Abby went to each, holding out her hand and bidding them goodnight. As the sound of footsteps on stone tiles receded, Abby turned and found herself in Kai's arms. They stood holding each other as the image of Earth continued to gradually spin.

"I'm not the man I once was," he whispered. "I've changed."

"So have I," said Abby, pressing herself against him.

"I'd say so."

"You sound disappointed."

"Not at all. You're a miracle, Abby. This whole thing is a miracle. I don't even know where to begin."

"Let's begin where we left off," she said. And taking Kai by the hand, she led him into the darkness of the night and back to his room.

"Hollow Earth can wait," she said, closing the door behind them.

CHAPTER 25

The penthouse was dark when he entered. But by the light of the moon, he was able to make his way to the solitary desk that offered the best view of the city below. He sat down and reached beneath the desk to release the plasma screen. It rose gently before him and pinged into life. And in the blue glow of the room, he poured himself a cognac, warming the round-bottom glass in the palm of his large hand.

"It's late," came the voice on the screen.

"I guess that depends on where you are," he replied.

"Today, I am with the world."

"As am I." It was their customary greeting.

"What news?"

"At long last, they have gathered. Now the work begins.

"The work began long before. We have you to thank for that."

"It was never a choice."

"There is always a choice, and you chose well."

"This time, perhaps. But not at the beginning."

"You did what you felt you had to do. No one blames you for that... But enough of this. The only thing that matters is what lies before us. Will you keep us informed?"

"As best I can."

"Is there anything else you wish to tell us?"

"Not at this time."

"Then I wish you goodnight."

"And good day."

"It's all the same to us."

"Yes, I suppose it is. Goodbye then... for now."

The screen flickered and went dark, and for the next several hours, until the thin line of orange light appeared on the horizon, he sipped from the tumbler and thought about the world.

Chapter 26

The previous evening's lecture on the history—and future—of the Earth had had its intended effect. Over the course of her briefing, Abby had presented to the group evidence to confirm their long-held premonitions. Her discourse had closed the gap. Someone had brought them together for a reason. And between periods of dreaming and moments of awakening, each person passed the night wondering what was in store for them and how they might be called upon in the days ahead.

Peeling away from the big table in single file, the small party filed through a set of hallways hewn through solid granite. They sloped gradually downward, the sounds of their footsteps echoing. No one spoke. 100 meters in, they came to a dead end. Abby paused, then pressed her hand, fingers spread wide, against the cold black granite. There was a rush of air and the group found themselves staring into a large chamber teeming with engineers and other workers. Sounds of rivet guns, welding irons, and the hammering and pounding of metal filled the air. Sparks rained down on them as their eyes adjusted to the floodlit cavern.

"I give you *Orpheus!*" said Abby, gesturing skyward with a sweep of her arm.

The cavernous room was three times as high as it was wide. Steel cables secured a spherical object—the size of a small house—to the tall ceiling.

"It's a soccer ball," said Spike. "A giant fucking soccer ball."

Abby choked back a laugh. "Well, I suppose it bears a resemblance. But to be more precise, it is a *truncated icosahedron.*"

"A what?" asked Philomena.

"I'm speaking, of course, of its shape. An Archimedean solid, to be exact. One of thirteen convex isogonal non-prismatic solids whose faces are two or more types of regular polygons. It has twelve regular pentagonal faces, twenty regular hexagonal faces, sixty vertices, and ninety edges."

"That's great, but what does it do?" asked Carson.

"What does it do? Why, professor," said Abby, "what *doesn't* it do might be the more appropriate question. For now, let's call it an earth-ship. But no, that doesn't do it justice. It's so much more. It's many things wrapped in one."

Abby's excitement at being able to share this wondrous invention was palpable. She drew her hand to her chin and looked suddenly lost in thought. This was a different person from the calm and professo-rial character who had presided over the group, dispatching theories of global extinction and Hollow Earth. This Archimedean solid held a much deeper meaning for her. It was a life force, a product conceived over countless hours. It was—as she would later confide—her greatest invention. She stared up at the machine, draped in scaffolding and crawling with workers like bees tending to a hive. Sparks continued to spring from its metallic flanks and fall all around them. Abby stood directly beneath it while the others formed a circle around her. For a moment, she closed her eyes, her features fixed with an expression of pure adoration.

Then, in an instant, Abby found herself driven across the room, the sound of metal and chains crashing about them. She opened her eyes to see Spike on top of her, staring down.

"You okay?" he shouted.

"Yes... Yes, I'm fine," she replied.

He reached down and helped her up. Behind them, precisely where she had been standing, lay 200 pounds of block and tackle. It had fallen with enough force to crack the stone tiles. A team of engineers in white coats rushed forward, apologizing. But it was clear they were more concerned about the *Orpheus* than about the visitors.

"Did you see that?" said Philomena.

"Hardly," said Kai. "It was over before it happened."

Spike wore a guilty expression, as if he'd been caught doing some-thing wrong. "I'm sorry, professor. I hope I didn't hurt you."

"Hurt me? You saved me," she cried. "How did you know?"

"Know what?"

"How did you know that was going to happen?"

"I didn't. I just heard it give way."

"Spike. Even if you had, I can tell you with scientific certainty that no human could move that quickly... You knew *before* it happened!"

"That's bullshit! I just reacted."

"Instinct or intuition? Which, I wonder?"

"I'm not one of your fucking experiments. Anyone would have reacted the same way."

"But they didn't... You did! They were right."

"Who was right?"

"Our benefactors. I didn't quite understand it. The others here," she said with a gesture, "well, they made sense. But why you?"

"Well, I'm so goddamned pleased not to disappoint."

"I meant no offense. I only meant the others shared something in common."

"And what's that?"

"A discovery."

"And how do you know I haven't discovered something?"

"Well, someone thinks you know more than you're letting on. In time, Mr. Morrison. In time... Follow me, please."

Leading them to the edge of the great hall, Abby drew back the door to a caged lift. They stepped through and she pulled the gate to a close behind them. The lift shuddered, then began to rise. Above them, the *Orpheus* drew near. Cables hung from the ceiling like giant umbilical cords, attaching themselves to the metallic orb.

"These," said Abby," pointing at the larger of the cables, "are fuel lines. And those," she said, "are uploading data. Everything we need for our journey."

Philomena turned her attention from the *Orpheus* to look at Abby. "We're going on a trip?"

"Like no other."

Abby brought the cage to a halt. The door sprang back. Carson was the first to reach out and place his hand against it.

"An earthship," he said, more from wonderment than as a statement of fact.

The coating was cool to the touch, finely webbed. Not metal after all, but a fibrous composite, smooth and almost leathery.

"Unusual, isn't it professor? More than half our research effort went into the construction of the outer shell. It's vital, you see. It must withstand the harshest of conditions."

"What is it?" asked Carson.

"A kind of filio-carbon composite—a blend of rare earth and synthetic engineering. Ten times more durable than steel, yet supple and infused with millions of tiny air pockets to instantaneously adjust depth and buoyancy. But there's more. Much more," added Abby, reaching out to place her hand alongside Carson's.

A green-lit outline formed round her hand. And with a click and a hiss, a section of the ship receded. A doorway appeared, with another hiss. It slid open. Two tracks of light at their feet showed the way, and the group filed through, one after the other. The sides of the passageway were cylindrical. Twenty paces more, another door still. It, too, slid back, and they passed through to find themselves standing in a perfectly circular room—the core of the machine.

"We call this *the sanctum*," intoned Abby. "I dare say you will be spending much of your time here. It's the safest place on the ship."

"Good to know," said Spike.

Precisely 50 meters in circumference, the interior glowed in hues of blue. Hovering above them, seven glass orbs, each two meters in diameter, protruded from the curve of the ceiling. Each orb pulsed with internal light.

"And those?" asked Kai, pointing upward.

"Ah yes, the pods."

As if on command, the cylindrical objects glided out from their nesting place in the reserves of the ceiling. They floated gently along magnetic tracks, changing position, swirling, spinning, and eventually coming to rest. They stood three meters high, like oblong eggs.

There was a shift in the room, a lightness—not alarming, but subtle and only marginally detectable. Abby smiled. "Time for the big reveal," she thought.

"You're standing at the center of the ship that will deliver us to Earth's core. I won't bore you with tales of the many failed prototypes that came before it, but I assure you that it took all the brainpower and resources that we could muster. It is to the core what Apollo 11 was to the moon. It got there in stages. So will we."

"The core! Are you out of your flippin' mind?" Spike sputtered. "I don't need to be some goddamn scientist to know that we'd never survive at those temperatures."

"The *Orpheus* is built for those conditions. And there's more to the core than you might imagine. Let me explain. The Apollo was designed with three key functions in mind: propulsion, navigation, and a moon landing. The *Orpheus* has three core functions as well: submersion, navigation, and penetration. We have Stage 1 covered: we enter at a precise spot in the North Sea. Stage 2, that's over to you, professor."

"Me?"

"Yes, you, Carson. May I call you Carson? We were watching the day you made your big discovery."

"You've seen it?" cried Carson.

"We have. All 2,736 kilometers of subterranean trenches and tunnels, plying their way through oxides, silicates, and magma. You, my good doctor, broke the code. Now we just need to pinpoint the passageway to the core."

"You ransacked my lab! Shut it down!"

"Not us. There are others. Fortunately, we were tapped in. We were able to download the data before they got to it. Your secret is safe with us."

Carson's relief was apparent.

"Your work confirms what we long suspected. The core is accessible through Earth's mantle. Your findings have green-lit our little operation here. It came sooner than expected. We've had to step up our efforts. As explained, there's little time to waste. I know what you're thinking, professor."

"And what's that?"

"Are the tunnels by design?"

Carson betrayed a smile. "Who is this woman and how does she know these things," he wondered.

"You tell me, Professor Clarke. Are they?"

"Partly, is our best guess. You refer to them as the catacombs, do you not? Before agents absconded with your research, we did a remote capture of all your critical data. We extracted it there and rendered it here."

She slipped on a pair of gloves from the console, and with a wave of her hands, the dome above them sprang to life with high-definition images of subterranean tunnels. Carson had gazed upon them only once before. For the others, it was all new and breathtaking. Electromagnetic impulses delivered through the gloves allowed her to expand, zoom into, and fold sections of the catacombs, orchestrating her way into Earth's underbelly.

Carson felt a wave of emotion. His life's work. Here. Not lost. His eyes filled.

"I don't know what to say," he stammered. "This is everything to me. It's everything I worked for. How did you do it? Who are you?"

"We are allies, Carson. I do hope you'll forgive us. We aren't an organization prone to hacking data, but we saw this coming. We had to move fast. There was no time to warn you or enlist you as part of our mission. You wouldn't have believed us, anyway. I do hope this makes up for it," said Abby. "Now, let's have some fun."

Without saying another word, the pod closest to Abby parted just wide enough for her to enter. The orb closed around her, seamless. The group looked on as she assumed a crouched position, arms extended, palms facing upward.

"Initiate spin," she said—and the orb began to turn, slowly at first, then faster. She closed her eyes, and the others watched as she slowly began to rise until she was suspended within the spinning glass object. Now, folding her legs in mid-air and placing her hands on knees, she opened her eyes. Seeing the stunned expressions staring back, she smiled, then spoke.

"Here I am. And so will you also be," she said. Though separated and enclosed, her voice flowed through the membrane like water through a sieve. "Each pod has been programmed."

"Programmed for what?" asked Philomena, resisting the urge to reach out and touch the orb.

"Why... for you, of course. For all of you. They're state of the art, biorhythmically operated. We match your readings to the program and *voilà*—you become fetal savants. By lassoing the laws of physics, we've achieved animated suspension. Only when synchronized can the ship function... I'm sorry. I keep forgetting how much we have yet to share. Professor, let's start with you. If you will, please approach your pod."

Carson felt puzzled and awed all at the same time. Taking a deep breath, he stepped forward. The glass slid back and he stepped through, as she instructed.

"Calm, professor. It responds to your heart rate. Now, do as I did. Crouch, close your eyes, and stay very still."

Fighting the urge to pound on the glass and free himself, Carson tried to concentrate on remaining motionless.

"Be patient. You may feel a slight charge at first, but don't be alarmed."

Then, like a wave from head to toe, he felt the pulse pass through him, unleashing a flash of nausea which subsided as quickly as it began. He felt lighter and, looking down, he saw he was no longer standing, but was rather floating like a yolk within its eggshell.

"Easy, professor. Welcome to the state of quantum levitation."

Carson fought the temptation to resist. And when he did, he felt instantly at ease.

"There. Now how's that?"

"Strange," he replied. "Very strange. Yet somehow comforting. I'm actually floating."

"Let's just say that, at least for the moment, you are defying gravity. Now, how about the rest of you?"

One after another, the members of the group entered their respective pods. Some struggled more than others, but in only a few minutes they were comfortable—hovering, facing inward, staring out from their pods at each other.

"What happens next may be disconcerting for some of you, but please know this—no harm will come to you. It may feel like free-falling for a moment. Call it a willing suspension of disbelief."

And before anyone could say anything, five of the seven occupied pods rose skyward. They danced through the air, spinning and turning, yet maintaining perfect equilibrium at their center. There were a few screams and the occasional whoop, but—miraculously—no panic. Soon, the pods fell into a rhythm, a kind of orbit, swirling, looping, and circumambulating, yet always remaining equidistant from one another. Like motorcycle acrobats performing high-speed synchronized runs within a great metal sphere, the four newly inducted members of crew of the *Orpheus* were getting their first crash course in inner-Earth flight.

CHAPTER 27

On the banks of the river Idigna, Enoch thought back on all that had come to pass. By good fortune, he had arrived deep in the forest at the place the Nephilim had come to call home. The Twenty were there to greet him. And he—knowing that Lock and his army were only days away—fabricated a tale that he hoped the Nephilim would believe.

The prophecy foretold of a Twenty-first, who "walked with the One" and would guide the Nephilim to a place where they would fulfill their purpose on Earth. As a young plebe, living among The Twenty in the Upper Realm, Enoch had often wondered about the Book in which the Nephilim placed all their trust. For beings who spent their days prying into the natural wonders of the world, stopping at nothing to learn the truth, this blind faith struck him as odd and inconsistent. Under some pressure from Azazel, however, Enoch reluctantly accepted the honor and acquiesced. And on the full moon of his twentieth birthday, he was inducted into the order of the Nephilim. As emissary to The Twenty, he had opened the way for their eventual migration to the Lower Realm and contact with The Others. For a while, it had gone well. Until it no longer did.

Enoch's first encounter with death, at the hands of Lock, was proof that The Others had changed. They would stop at nothing until The Twenty were either destroyed or placed in chains. Knowing that the only way to save the Nephilim was to invoke the prophecy, he had arrived breathless at their forest home, prepared to tell them what he must.

"Exodus!" he declared. "You must leave the Lower Realm and travel to a distant land."

"But why? For what reason?" protested Kokabiel.

"Because the One commands it."

The Twenty—as one—grew quiet. They were taking stock of what Enoch was suggesting. Never impulsive, The Twenty sometimes took days to respond when presented with new information. This time, he hoped that would not be the case. They were in danger, and he could not risk telling them the true reasons why.

Acutely perceptive, Tamiel then spoke.

"You've had your first death, have you not?"

Enoch hesitated. They would want to know the circumstances and that might raise suspicions. He also knew that when it came to what they called the "little deaths," he could not lie.

"Yes," he hesitated. "I have made the journey. It was as you said it would be."

The Twenty closed in on him. One by one, they pressed their foreheads against his and welcomed him back into the world. They seemed pleased and perhaps even proud to learn that the gift of immortality had been passed on. Now they knew it would be the same for their own children.

"I thank you for your blessings," said Enoch, while searching for a way to draw them back to his real reason for being there. Then it came to him.

"It was in transition that he came to me."

"The One?" asked Danel.

"Yes. The One. No reason was given. But if you trust in the prophecy and you truly believe that I am the one chosen to speak on behalf of the One, then I urge you to make ready. We must leave!"

"And our families? What of them?"

"For the time being, they are to remain with you. The final judgment is at hand."

Enoch could see The Twenty mulling it over. He knew how their minds worked. If the One commanded it, then they must go. Gradually, but faster than Enoch might have anticipated, the enormity of what was being asked washed over them. The Twenty began nodding in unison. The One had been patient—waiting and witnessing their transgressions. They had sworn an oath, though none could remember when, to live apart from The Others, chaste and in service to the mysteries of the planet.

"This is good news... Good news indeed," Samyaza reassured them. "The One must see some merit in our union. Not all is lost."

Enoch saw hope in their eyes and felt ashamed. For just an instant, he thought about giving up the ruse and telling them what was about to befall them. How it was *not* the One that would determine their fate, but rather Lock and his minions. For all he knew, they might be set upon at any moment.

"There is no time to waste. Wake your families. Take only what you can carry. We leave tonight."

"As you bid, Enoch. We are grateful to you... for what you have done."

"I've done nothing. I've only carried with me the word of the One."

Enoch turned abruptly, hoping they had not seen through him. As he moved away from them, the fire flickered at his heels, and the shadows of the trees bobbed about in the waning light. He felt The Twenty and their eyes upon him. His heart was pounding. He was not accustomed to lying. Every day henceforth would be the same. He must embrace this charade with all his heart. There was no turning back. The future of the Nephilim depended on it.

All had come to pass as Enoch had foretold. The journey of exodus and the discovery of new lands had entered the annals of Nephilim lore—how The Twenty, with their families in tow, had crossed the great mountains, moved through parched terrain, come to a great expanse of water, and then crossed to floodplains that were far removed from The Others. Their story should be written by Enoch, they agreed, without whom none of their good fortune would have been possible.

Enoch's powers of observation had not gone unnoticed, and as time passed, they came to rely on him as their scribe and historian. He was now—like the others—bound in his commitment to plying his vocation and perfecting it as well he might.

He started by naming their new home Giza, meaning "border" or "threshold"—the spot that would forever separate the Nephilim from The Others and keep them safe. The Twenty were pleased, and while Enoch began documenting the tale of the Nephilim, they put their own skills to good use. Countless years spent in service to the order of all things—the natural world, from the elements of Earth to the heavens—had left them well equipped for a life of invention and new creation.

The lands they settled were wild, and remained that way, with the exception of their limited cultivation of rice, corn, and assorted fruits and vegetables. They planted only what they needed, not an acre more. The territory was divided by a wide and slow-moving river. On one side were forests. On the other side was an expanse of desert that spread as far as the eye could see to the south and the east. Half the year, it lay dry, cracked, and barren. During the other half, in the wake of receding flood waters, it gave birth to wildflowers. There was a logical explanation for why this happened. But, emblematic of how the Nephilim had come to see the world, they liked to say it was the season of *heaven on Earth*—that time each year when the sky relinquished its hold, in an instant, to send shards of rainbow earthbound to lie in heaps of color. The Nephilim had once believed that nothing would ever compare to the natural grace and beauty of the Lower Realm. But now, after many years, the floodplain of Giza proved itself a promised land beyond comparison.

Accordingly, The Twenty flourished. All, with the exception of Azazel, had married and borne children, demonstrating what was best in the blood-binding of the Nephilim with humans. Over time, Enoch found himself surrounded by cousins and an extended family. But whether by virtue of his circumstances, his difference in age, or his designation as the Twenty-first, he felt as though he never quite fit in. He was treated differently. The Nephilim, it seemed, had ascribed to him some undeserved status that left him partly revered and partly feared. Rather than concern himself with this, Enoch chose to spend his days circumnavigating Giza, observing the many changes and making note of them in his leather-bound book. In doing so, he unintentionally reinforced the idea that the Nephilim were under constant watch.

Because of—or perhaps in spite of—Enoch's continuing observation, the community went about its business by incorporating the twenty Great Blessings into the fabric of their lives. They did so by organizing themselves into Orders of Higher Learning. The result was predictable. Knowledge of the natural world accelerated and, with it, there was a renaissance of new discoveries. By virtue of their new circumstances and greater numbers, the Nephilim were gaining fresh insights. They applied all they learned, and Giza and the community thrived. Gradually, the fear of retribution from the One subsided. But, just to be sure, The Twenty conjured a plan.

"We will build a great structure to demonstrate our undying commitment to the One and the perpetuation of the Great Blessings."

Baraqiel was the first to suggest it. The idea was years in the making. Only by virtue of their Orders of Higher Learning and the collective insights that issued from them could they conceive of such an undertaking. Engineering such a feat demanded an interdisciplinary approach. It was not enough to know the dimensions and weights of the stones. The bindings of the minerals, the positions of the water tables, changing weather patterns, and the alignment of the stars all had central roles to play.

Baraqiel's Proposition, as it would later be known, ignited a level of enthusiasm uncharacteristic of the Nephilim. All the mundane tasks associated with building comfortable lives were cast aside in order to give full attention to their new enterprise.

By creating working groups, the Nephilim set a course to design and construct an edifice so awe-inspiring that it would, once complete, symbolize the quintessential joining of heaven and Earth. It was to be their crowning achievement, a testament to their abilities and their piety. On its completion, their pact with the One would be sanctified— and, once and for all, their debt would be fulfilled, or so they chose to believe. All that was left to do was to select the precise location. For this, they turned to Enoch.

It was Baraqiel who made the request. "You, 'the one who walks with the One,' have led us here. Now we ask that you choose the ground upon which we will build the Temple Mount. For the Book says: "He who walks with the One will venture to the place of *axis mundi*. And on that spot, he shall decree the raising of a great tribute. A gateway between Heaven and Earth. And all the world will rejoice!"

Axis mundi—the cosmic axis. There it was. Baraqiel had read from the prophecy of the Twenty-first and deduced that an accord with the One was still possible, but only if Enoch agreed to it.

Later that evening, he went to retrieve the Book. It had been carried by the Nephilim from the Upper Realm and ceremoniously placed at the center of Giza under the sign of the circle. By torchlight, Enoch read and reread the prophecy as recorded in the Book.

"He who walks with the One," he mumbled with disdain. "I walk with no one," he thought to himself. "How long must I continue this fantasy? The game is up. Perhaps it's time to come clean—to tell them that the exodus was a plan concocted to save them from Lock. The Others are the real threat. Not the One!"

What the Nephilim did not know was that Lock and his army were on the move. Enoch had hoped The Others would forget about The Twenty and would allow the Nephilim to live in peace, far away, no longer a threat to anyone. It was not to be.

From his frequent travels to the edge of the great waters, Enoch learned from those who traded up and down the coast that Lock was building enough ships to carry a thousand men. It would only be months before they made the crossing. They would pursue the Nephilim to the ends of the world. The Twenty could fight. But against a thousand armed and well-trained warriors, they and their families would have no chance. There was only one option left. Enoch hated the thought. The Nephilim would need to disappear for a while—to a place where they might never be found.

Chapter 28

In the northernmost reaches of the Norwegian peninsula, 223 nautical miles west of the Bilksvaer Fjord and a good three-day journey by land from the capital of Oslo, the mountains of Lofoten mark the coastline, its steep and craggy slopes punching through choppy seas and descending thousands of meters to the ocean floor. Waves rip and tear at the stony expanse, but its mass remains intact, impenetrable. All around, the ocean churns. Its surface lies dark, mottled, and uninviting. The winds ricochet off cliffs and reverberate back across the ocean landscape. In its midst lies one of the world's greatest oceanographic anomalies—a whirling mass of water a thousand meters across. Awe-inspiring from a distance, but terrifying up close it goes by the name of Moskstraumen. The word means *maelstrom*. Earth's whirling dervish.

Formed by a watery slipstream of torrents that surge between the islands of Moskenesøya and Mosken, this liquid morass produces a depression on the ocean's surface so apparent that it can be seen from space. Ships from all around keep a wide berth. Like a giant web woven across the ocean's surface, there is no escaping it once caught in its outer swirl. How the interplay between land and ocean creates the world's largest and most formidable downward-spiraling vortex remains one of the natural world's great unexplained mysteries.

Stretching from the tidal troughs of Vestfjorden that move toward the North Sea, this expanse of dyspeptic tide has long had a mythical reputation—so much so that humans have for centuries marked this spot as an entryway to the underworld. Ancient drawings on adjacent cliffs show images of humans and animals being trapped by the water and drawn downward. There is no single way of telling what may lie below—only an assortment of possibilities, as suggested by the cave drawings. While some show subterranean landscapes of perpetual suffering, others depict a distant world, rich and abundant.

For three days and three nights, a purpose-built ship carrying the *Orpheus* made its long approach toward the wanton embrace of Mosktraumen. Beneath layers of weatherproof tarp, the vessel that was to deliver the crew some 11,000 meters to the ocean floor sat indifferent and snug, strapped to the deck of the ship.

On the morning of the third day, all aboard were summoned to the bridge. There, the captain and a handful of crewmen jostled levers and throttles to continuously adjust the ship's position, occasionally throwing the engines into reverse to avoid the maelstrom's allure. From this vantage point, they had a bird's-eye view of what lay before them.

The captain offered a brief greeting, then slipped out from behind the chart table and threw back the door to the wing deck, stepping into the cold. The group looked on from behind the thick plate glass and watched him open the latch of a large metal container to reveal an industrial-sized drone, ringed by dozens of rotors, with an all-weather camera mounted to it. Returning to the warmth of the cabin, the captain picked up a set of controls topped by two antennas from behind the wheelhouse. Grasping the device between his swollen hands, he flipped a small lever, releasing a high-resolution screen from a slit in the ceiling.

"Keep your eyes on the screen. Let's give this whirlpool of ours a closer look."

The crew watched as the drone whirred to life, rose, then banked out and across the bow. On the screen above, images of the ocean came into view: nothing but swirling water and white-capped waves.

"A few seconds more," said the captain. "There. Our maelstrom."

Toggling the levers, the drone rose higher, sixty meters into the air, to reveal Mosktraumen's yawning maw, a circular wall of water, white-tipped and frothing, extending 100 meters in every direction. Dark and threatening, this liquid tornado plied itself ever deeper into the ocean, scarring the surface and driving billions of gallons of water downward.

Abby decided it was as good a time as any to let them know the rest.

"It would be wrong for me to suggest that we've assessed all the risks. We have not. What we do have is absolute confidence in the ability of the *Orpheus* to weather the entry and make the descent. Look deep, my friends," she said, pointing at the whirling maelstrom. "This is where it all begins, the swiftest and most assured route to the mantle and on to the catacombs.

"Why here?" asked Spike.

"Perhaps, professor," she said, looking at Carson, "you would like to answer that."

"You have a knack for knowing my mind. Don't you, Dr. Clarke?"

Abby smiled.

"Beneath the continents," began Carson, "Earth's crust is on average thirty kilometers thick. But along the ocean floor, it's less than five. It would take our most sophisticated machines, millions of dollars of investment, and more time than we have to drill through layers of igneous and sedimentary rock. And even if you were able to punch through to the mantle, there's no telling what would happen if tons of ocean water breached the catacombs. It could collapse the entire system."

"Yeah, I get that. But why *here* of all places?" asked Spike.

"Because our host here has seen my research. She knows this whirlpool feeds directly into the catacombs. It is the most expedient way to bypass layers of impenetrable stone and sediment."

"So the *Orpheus* is a turd and this is the toilet," scoffed Spike.

"A bit indelicate, but yes, I guess you could look at it that way."

"What the fuck are we doing?" shouted Spike. "You have us studying all this theoretical bullshit, planning for the mission, but what good is all that if we're likely dead the minute you push the button and flush us down? I'm done with this. I need a drink."

Exiting the wheelhouse and slamming the door in his wake, Spike descended the stairs and made his way to the galley. One by one, the others followed.

Abby let them file out. She might have seen this coming. She had done her best to convey to the crew all she knew, leaving the unknowns until last. "Need to deal with this head-on," she grumbled to herself.

Following the others, she sidled up to the dining table and reached for the nearest bottle. Emptying its contents, she then raised her glass.

"To the underworld!"

There was no response. Abby drank it down anyway. Were they lost to her? Any minute now, she wondered, would they say they'd had enough and walk away? Time for some much-needed inspiration.

"There's someone you haven't met," she offered.

The crew looked up from their drinks.

"Someone else, you say?"

"Yes," said Abby. "Our missing link."

CHAPTER 29

On the day of the full moon and the tenth anniversary of the exodus, Enoch entered the courtyard to see that all had been laid out in accordance with his instructions: a circle marked by torches, a square within it marked by candles, and, at the center, an altar covered with a precise topographical rendering of Giza. The detail and care that had been put into this miniature replica of their promised land, like the tiny trees descending across the undulating hills that lined the west bank, spoke volumes. Every structure, home, and courtyard had been rendered in perfect imitation. Enoch could see that The Twenty, who stood equidistant from one another and encircled the altar, were deeply proud of this small yet significant achievement.

Samyaza initiated the rites, and Baraqiel followed with an offering, explaining in uncharacteristically excited tones while pointing to the star-covered sky that his survey of the planets showed that the time for initiating their great project was near. Baraqiel turned to Enoch. All eyes were upon him. The only decision remaining was the precise placement of the cornerstone.

"You have bestowed upon me the task of selecting the location of the Temple Mount," said Enoch. "Your entrusting of this to me is a great honor. You've asked me to seek out the approval of the One and I have done so. But there is more to this decision. The One has spoken."

Enoch paused. There would be no going back from here. Clearing his throat, he shouted over the crowd: "All is not well."

Around him, he heard a collective gasp.

"The message in the stars, as Baraqiel has pointed out, speaks of a moment to come. But it is not what you think. There is a sickness in the world. It hails from the Lower Realm from whence we came. Much has transpired since our departure from the Lower Realm ten years ago. The people you once knew—some of whom we called friends—have changed. They have fallen from the path and now lay waste to the land around them. Conquest has long been their sole objective. As a people, they are waylaid by their own greed and avarice. They roam the Earth with an insatiable appetite."

Enoch paused to let his words settle. The mood suddenly shifted. Excitement gave way to foreboding.

Azazel stepped forward and stood before the gathering. He stole a glance at Enoch, then turned to face a throng of worried expressions.

"My son speaks the truth. We shared our knowledge with those who were not ready to hear it. I have myself to blame. For I was the one who gave them the means to forge weapons and wage war. I was blind to their true intentions. They are who they are because of us. Is it not so, Enoch?" he asked, turning to his son, then making way for what Enoch had to tell them next.

"In part, yes," rejoined Enoch. "Sharing all you knew with them was indiscreet. But it is your original transgression for which you must answer. Departing from the Upper Realm and joining with The Others was forbidden. And yet you defied what was written."

"But was it not the prophecy of the Twenty-first that led us there?" challenged Kokabiel.

"Is that not what you wished to believe? Do you blame me, Kokibiel?"

Enoch had no intention of shaming the brethren, but his words landed like hot embers.

"Leaving was our choice," said Samyaza, stepping forward. "The prophecy was merely the excuse we needed."

Blurted out in this way, it struck Enoch as more of a confession than a point of fact. It was to be a rare glimpse into how the Nephilim, perhaps, had begun to question the nature of their origins and the sanctity of the Book.

For a long time, The Twenty remained silent. They were thinking. Eventually, one of them spoke.

Are we to be punished?"

Enoch hesitated while staring into the kindly eyes of the wise Baraqiel. He swallowed hard, then pronounced the fateful words: "The day of judgment is at hand. Some, no doubt, will suffer more than others."

His words served to darken the mood further, and no sooner had he spoken than he was overcome with guilt. It was as if he had tripped the lock on the floodgates, only to find himself caught in the deluge. Remorse and regret flowed through and around him. What had he done? And yet what choice did he have? They would listen to no authority other than the presence they called the One. They had wanted it this way, he reminded himself, trying to dampen down the remorse that was welling up within him. It was more than he could bear. And yet he did not let them see it, but instead wore an expression of resolve. He had deceived them from the moment he first told them that he "walked with the One." Now he had no choice but to lie to them again. His deception, he assured himself, would be their salvation.

"All is not lost," Enoch tried to reassure them. "Alas, your Temple Mount shall be built—so wills the One—and it will serve a greater purpose."

There was a sudden glint of hope, and one among The Twenty spoke out.

"Tell us what you will, Enoch. We are prepared to do penance for our iniquities."

"First, there is something you should know. I said to you that some would suffer more than others. Now I will share with you the meaning of those words. The world—as we know it—will be destroyed. The waters across these floodplains and those to the north and across the great expanse and beyond will rise tenfold. Plants, creatures, and all other living things will be consumed."

Enoch's words were as unexpected as the reaction they caused. The Twenty—to a one—were visibly undone. Their lives were about to be upended. And yet it was the destruction of the world and all its abundance that concerned them most.

"Why *all* things?" Baraqiel asked beseechingly. "The land has harmed no one. Will the One not spare the Earth? If we must go, so be it. And if The Others perish, so be it. But spare the rest."

"All will be destroyed," declared Enoch, holding to his script and determined not to acquiesce.

The Twenty remained silent for some time, and Enoch allowed the vastness of what he was saying to sink in. How would he feel, he wondered, to hear such a thing? And how cruel of him to let them think it was possible.

Amaros, who was perhaps the most soft-spoken among them, then asked "What will become of us? Are we not immortal? Has this too been forsaken?"

"May your immortality not become your curse," cried Enoch. "You will live. But not here. Not in this place."

"Then where?" whispered Amaros, his question barely audible.

"Below!"

A look of confusion and astonishment washed across the gathering.

"Below?" asked Amaros, in disbelief.

"Below!" Enoch echoed.

He stepped down from where he was speaking and made his way toward the altar and the miniature model of Giza. The Twenty parted as he passed. He pointed toward the northern reach on the west bank, just beneath the terraced dikes and dams that served as the watery life force for the entire valley.

"Here—this is where you will build your Temple Mount. This is where you will erect your final resting place."

"So it is a tomb, not a temple, that you would have us build?" asked Samyaza.

"Yes... and no," replied Enoch. "It will stand as a lasting reminder of what might have been had the Nephilim and humans learned to live as one. Here," he said again, pointing to the place by the river, "lies your passage to the underworld. There you shall live until the One decides otherwise."

"Buried alive. This is your plan? What of our wives and children? How will they adapt to such a life?"

"As best they can. The women will suffer the most, for they are mortal. As for your children... your blood runs through their veins as my father's runs through mine. Our destinies are intertwined. They will journey with you and carry with them the curse of immortality. As I have said, some will suffer more than others."

"I think death would be preferable," uttered Amaros, and the others nodded in agreement.

"It is the will of the One that you survive. He may have plans for you yet."

In the days that followed, work on the Temple Mount began apace. Enoch had declared that, in accordance with a directive from the One, the Nephilim would have precisely 295 days to complete the task and make all their final preparations. From the Nephilim's point of view, it seemed like an impossibly short period of time. It would require all their combined knowledge and effort to succeed.

For days on end, the entire community worked in shifts, first excavating the earth, then cutting slabs of granite for the Temple Mount itself. The Twenty did most of the heavy lifting by cutting, shaping, and transporting the slabs back to the surface. It was brutal work. No mortal could have endured it. Each member of the brethren had the size and strength of ten men and the ability to withstand darkness, heat, and thin air without reprieve. They were tireless and determined. It would be this way for months on end. Gradually, an underground world took shape and The Twenty began to settle into the idea of starting life anew hundreds of meters below the surface.

When the first phase was completed, they held a brief ceremony. Again, as they had done at the beginning, the Nephilim looked to the stars for a sign that the One was pleased. Enoch, meanwhile, looked north. Through carrier pigeons, he gathered news from coastal villages and searched for signs that Lock and his armies were on their way.

As the Temple Mount grew, so did his respect and admiration for the Nephilim. Their time on this planet had taught them that discipline, above all other qualities, was the foundation upon which character, capabilities, and other skills were built. They had faced setbacks, both technical and logistical, but they were never dissuaded from the task at hand. If The Twenty could achieve this great feat, thought Enoch, what else might they have accomplished had a *détente* between the Nephilim and humans been possible?

Enoch watched them work and allowed his thoughts to unfurl.

"They must not be forgotten," he whispered to himself. "I'll see that they are not."

Sitting beneath the willows one evening, he shared with them a plan to erect two pillars. On them, he would record for all time the story and accomplishments of the Nephilim. They would be erected side by side at the base of the Temple Mount, there for anyone who survived to see and know the truth.

The light of the day was fading, and Enoch was chiseling a final row of hieroglyphics when Azazel appeared by his side. He stood watching for a while before speaking.

"What is the purpose of the pillars if—as you say—the world is soon to meet its end?"

Enoch was in no mood to explain himself.

"I said all living beings would be destroyed. But there will be life anew. The planet will endure, as it has through time. When the flood waters recede, life will return. This, the One has promised."

Enoch found it hard mouthing these words to his father, who somehow always had a way of seeing his true thoughts.

"Will the plants and trees bear witness? Will they speak of us? I think not. It seems more an act of vanity than posterity, my son. Your gesture is well intentioned, but we have no illusions. If what you tell us is true, the end of days for all two-legged beings is at hand."

Another period of silence passed, and Enoch was about to gesture that he would like to return to work when Azazel spoke again.

"I know what you are doing," he said.

"Do you speak of the pillars?"

"No, that is not my meaning."

"Then I'm not sure what you mean."

"Tell me about your walks with the One."

Enoch felt the blood run from his face. His arms went numb and his hands began to tingle. "No, not now," he thought to himself. "We are too close. The plan is almost complete." Enoch tried to compose himself.

"What would you like to know?"

"In all our time on this Earth, the entity we refer to as the One has never shown itself to us. Why would it choose to reveal itself to you?"

"It is the prophecy. You said so yourself."

Go gently, Enoch reminded himself. But the pressure of maintaining this ruse was too much to bear.

"Was it not the prophecy of the Twenty-first that led us to this? Do you think I have not asked myself why I must carry this burden and why I must deliver his message, thereby witnessing the pain and anguish it causes? I find no solace in this task. Urging the Nephilim and their families from the Lower Realm all those years ago gave me no pleasure. Such is the curse of the messenger. And know this! You think you can bribe destiny with this Temple Mount? I am not responsible for what may come. I am only accountable for communicating what has been ordained."

Azazel listened silently, but Enoch could not escape his father's penetrating gaze. He let his son finish, then gently reached out his hand and placed it over Enoch's. It was the most intimate gesture he had ever made, and it had the intended effect. Enoch's eyes welled, and he could feel in the moment that Azazel had seen through his plan from the beginning.

"Your secret is safe with me, Enoch," he whispered. "I come to you now only because I know you have suffered. I lived with The Others long before our brethren. I learned firsthand the way that jealousy and resentment can build in the human heart, how it can boil over and taint the rational mind. The human imagination is a blessing and a curse. Once they began to see us as the enemy, there was no turning back. I have waited in silence all these long years, like you, anticipating a time when Lock would come for us. I knew this would not end well, and I have feared for The Twenty, our community, and this place."

Enoch gasped, letting down his guard. "If you knew, why didn't you say something?"

"Because I believe in you, Enoch. You know what you are doing and why you are doing it. I know your mind better than you think. You are my son, after all."

"If there's a better way, please tell me."

"There is not. You know the Nephilim well. They are devout, committed to our laws, and firm in their belief in the Book and its prophecies. Even if you were to confess now, were you to tell them that you are not the chosen one and have never spoken with the One, they would not believe you. What is done is done. The Temple Mount is almost complete, and we will descend and live as instructed. If armies from the north were to arrive at this very moment, The Twenty would not stand and fight. Resistance would be in opposition to their very being and the covenant they established among themselves long ago."

"So you, too, question the existence of the One? How do you explain the ancient texts, the prophecies, the laws? What *do* you believe?"

"I believe that we are caretakers of this Earth. I believe that like the trees of the forest, we grow older and live longer than any other living thing. Nature has blessed us with the power to regenerate. This body is but a microcosm of the planet we inhabit. We will go on and endure and record for all time what has been and what will be. Perhaps it is enough that we are simply a part of the greater whole."

Enoch had never heard Azazel speak like this before. It was as if all his ideas about life had been knotted in his mind for centuries, but now, in a confessional moment, they started pouring out.

"What if we are wrong?" asked Enoch. "What if The Twenty could be convinced to stand against the armies? If they survived, they could carry on in the world, grow their ranks as the humans have, and create for this world something better and more lasting than power and conquest. Perhaps we have underestimated the brethren?"

"There have been days when I have thought as much. But it is not meant to be. As we descended from the Upper Realm to the Lower, then made our way here to Giza, so we will find our way in the under-world. We will embrace our time there, learn all we can, and make it a part of the long-running story of the Nephilim. Perhaps somewhere deep in Earth's crust there are answers to the great mysteries of this world. It is time for us to venture further."

For the first time, Enoch saw his father for the extraordinary being that he was. It was as if they had shared time and space for all these years but never truly witnessed one another.

"You will not come with us, Enoch. I will not allow it."

"What do you mean? It is part of the plan. I must go with you."

"You must not. You must remain here. You must move among The Others, learn their ways, and, whenever possible, safeguard the world from this path of destruction."

"How can I do such a thing alone?"

"You will never be alone. There are others who think and believe like us. Seek out those who share in our knowledge of the world. Guide them as you might. Our time will come, Enoch. The Nephilim will return. And when we do, there will be a reckoning. Until then, I bid you farewell, my son. I promise—we will meet again."

Enoch stood as his father turned to leave. There was no embrace. Not even a handshake. Yet, somehow, he felt that it was the most intimate exchange of their long lives. Enoch could not decide in the moment if his father's awareness of his mind and his angst was helpful or hurtful. He had been carrying the weight of this decision for so long. He felt briefly unburdened.

But then the guilt rushed in. "I've condemned them to a life of unspeakable misery. They will live in darkness, unable to live or die, and it will all be because of me." Enoch clenched his fists. "How will I live with this?"

As if in reply, a breeze cut its way across the surface of the river, making the long, drooping branches of the willow dance and sway about him. When it was safe, and once the story of the Nephilim had become widely known, he would return and free them. Then—just perhaps—there would be a reconciliation, a time when the Nephilim and humans would come to know each other once more.

CHAPTER 30

He was too large for the small cabin he occupied. He hated tight spaces. Always had. The bed groaned as he lifted his large frame and crossed the short distance to the porthole. The moon cut a silvery path across the dark surface of the water, and Enoch tried to recall the first time he felt her presence. He had circumnavigated the planet how many times now? Hard to say. And all the while, the moon remained his constant companion. Though she might cast a different pall in each place he journeyed to, the feeling of her was always the same.

His life was like an eternal wave, rolling from one side of the universe to the next, always forward. Everyone he had known and loved was left in his wake. They were mere shadows now, trailing behind in the remnants of his memories. Some—the lovers, the friends, the mentors—meant more to him than others. Their lives, in contrast to his own, were mere particles, appearing and disappearing, leaving an impression but never lasting. The transitions—or the "little deaths" as he came to call them—took their toll. At first, they were jarring. But, in time, he learned to make the leap from living to dying to living again, suppressing the pain and putting behind him what he could not take with him. Like a pendulum, his life was measured by the gravity of its own force. It would continue its long, languorous cycles until the end of time, or until time ended.

The very thought of all his past comings and goings left him feeling exhausted. And who wouldn't feel that way after a span of nearly 10,000 years. If it hadn't been for the "little deaths," he might have had no rest at all.

Retreating from the porthole, he slumped back onto the bed. Cupping his head in his two large hands, he tried to recall the high points—those brief, epiphanous moments when humankind appeared to regain its senses, putting aside its desires and cravings, to see, if only briefly, the possibility of a new way forward. How many times had he planted the seeds of new possibility, only to have them sabotaged by the vested interests of a powerful few? How long could he keep this up for? His father was right, the world was filled with those who sensed greater possibilities for the human race, who were prepared to speak out and die for it, if they must. And die they did. By the tens of millions. Poets, philosophers, revolutionaries, and warriors—all killed and buried. Each death was a loss. And yet, in death, many who fought for what was right would be remembered. Their ideas lived on. And from the golden threads of their noble efforts, Enoch was able to keep hope—and the prospect of a more virtuous humanity—alive.

How many disguises had he donned over time? How many personas had he assumed? No easy task for someone his size. Centuries of trial and error. He had learned, with practice, how to make his hands and feet look smaller. How to move through a crowd and blend in. How to go virtually unseen. There were times, of course, when he found the need to do just the opposite. To make himself larger than life, admired and feared. These moments marked the tight corners in his long existence. Presenting himself this way always came with consequences. It was always preferable to operate in the shadows, like an undercurrent, perpetually in motion and forever below the surface. Nothing good ever came from drawing too much attention to oneself. He practiced this the best he could.

His forays over the years had stacked up, one atop the other. One wrong move, and all his good efforts might come crashing down. His sole objective was, and would remain, to restore what had been lost. But there were other forces at play, many beyond his control. And for that reason alone, it had taken him longer—so much longer—than he ever could have imagined to arrive at this point. He had played the game well, but he was up against worthy opponents. They had proven themselves to be clever and agile. Beyond all else, they were adaptive. He had lived a thrust and parry existence. Try as his opponents might to eradicate the true memory of the Nephilim, he would never allow it. So many attempts had been made over the centuries to snuff them out, to cast The Twenty as enemies of men and to erase the record of how the Nephilim—in good faith—had bestowed upon humankind the gifts of knowing. By whatever means possible—confrontation, seduction, misdirection, or guile—he would keep their memory alive. Every situation required a different tactic and a different disguise to match it. He had played every conceivable role and sacrificed everything... for them... for the brethren. They deserved no less. He owed them that.

Closing his eyes, he traveled back to a time when things were less complicated. Would such a time ever return, he wondered? He considered sleep but waved it off. His mind was firmly fixed on the mission ahead. It had been years in the planning. No turning back now. They would slip below the ocean surface, unwitnessed. He had been operating behind the scenes for so long, he wondered why now, of all times, he suddenly wanted the world to know what he knew—and all of it. Was it because so much was at stake? He could not say.

This would be his last and final attempt. Time was up. The stage itself had risen up to join the ranks of players. The planet would wait no longer. This was the moment that would test humanity's ability to self-correct or suffer the consequences. What other species would knowingly and willingly drive itself to the point of extinction?

If this was to be his last venture, he would travel the path as himself. No fictitious identity required. No ruse. No deception. He would join the crew of the *Orpheus* and, when the moment presented itself, he would reveal to them the truth of 10,000 years.

None of the crew—not even Abby—understood how long the plans for the mission had been in the works for. Would he come clean? And reveal to them the full weight of their mission? Or would it be all too much? "They deserve the truth," he whispered. "No, stick to what you know. One step at a time." For now, he decided, it was enough for them to believe that they were on an errand to rescue the planet. The rest could wait.

He felt the muscles of his large frame begin to relax. Perhaps sleep would come at last. He thought of his fellow travelers. He wondered if they, too, lay awake, staring at the ceiling, contemplating their fate, resisting the fear. Like counting sheep, he went back over the details. And as he did so, the enormity of the task was laid bare.

No ship ever built for deep-sea exploration had endured what the *Orpheus* was about to endure. Even if they survived the maelstrom and somehow miraculously found themselves lodged below the ocean floor, would they find their way into the catacombs? He was counting on the Council to make this stage of the journey possible. Would they see there was no other way or would they refuse, as the crew of the *Orpheus* slowly suffocated hundreds of kilometers below the surface? He was betting that pragmatism—for they were always pragmatic— would sway them when it counted most.

Assuming he was right, and they did enter the catacombs, what next? Nearly 3,000 kilometers of mantle lay between them and the outer core. It was one thing to know the way—it was another to traverse it. It would be infinitely more dangerous than the quick descent from ocean surface to floor. Would the catacombs prove wide enough? Was the *Orpheus* strong enough? Would the crew be able to endure the journey? No human had ever been tested at such depths.

And then, of course, there was the matter of the core. Would they be incinerated? Or, as Abby hoped, would they have the means to make the crossing from the outer to the inner core? Was there, in fact, a Hollow Earth? He could think of no expedition in the history of man that was accompanied by so many uncertainties. Indeed, it made interplanetary space travel look safe and certain by comparison.

And yet here they were. The planet had grown tired of waiting... the Nephilim too. He tried not to let his ruminating thoughts get in the way. Belief was all that mattered now. Belief and faith in a ragtag crew.

"Have I chosen well?" he thought to himself. "Are they the ones?" Trained engineers would have been the more obvious choice, but he had hand-picked this crew for a reason. Had they known the effort that went into this, perhaps they would feel confident—even honored— that he believed they were, each one, a gift to the mission... and to the world. He had grown fond of them, too.

He pressed his hands against his temples, then threw back his head with a laugh. What madness. How had it all come to this? Why had he not stopped it when he might have? Had he known then what he knew now, no sacrifice would have been too great. His only choice was to trust in those who had been chosen.

Lying back on the narrow bed, he felt a sick foreboding. The ship rocked back and forth, its wooden frame groaning with every swell. He closed his eyes and allowed his mind to drift. He thought of those who had come before him: Gilgamesh, Odysseus, and, of course,

Orpheus—travelers to the underworld. It was a time-honored tradition. A hero's journey. Some voyaged for glory. Others for answers. "We go back for answers," he thought. "We go down for meaning. It has been that way since the beginning."

Would this downward journey be any different? They would know soon enough.

Chapter 31

Reverend Avon Caulfield sat twiddling his thumbs. His neck bulged at the collar and lines of sweat streamed from his temples. He was not accustomed to waiting. But, on this occasion, he thought it better not to complain. A private jet had arrived early that morning, whisking him from his palatial home on the outskirts of Chattanooga. Now, in the domed room, black-tiled and appointed with a single couch of deep burgundy leather, he waited.

Two plate glass doors slid back, and a woman in stilettos and a white, form-fitting Calvin Klein dress made her way across the room in five long strides, arm extended.

"Reverend Caulfield. A pleasure to meet you."

Avon pressed his thighs together and lifted his large frame from the couch. He received her hand and placed the other on top.

"Why, the pleasure is all mine, my dear."

She slid her hand out from beneath his sweaty palms. "Please follow me."

She continued across the wide hall to another set of thick glass doors. They, too, slid back, so as not to interrupt the clickety-clack of her Jimmy Choos. They entered a brightly lit corridor. Avon struggled to keep up. Another set of doors, but this time, they remained closed.

"They're all assembled, Reverend," she said.

"All of them?" he thought. But before he could inquire further, his escort punched in a code and the doors flew back. The Councilmen were seated, the chairman at the head. They swiveled in sync in their high-backed leather chairs, facing him as he entered. The woman gestured for him to take a seat at the far end of the table, opposite the chairman. Collecting himself, he tugged on the tight-fitting vest of his three-piece suit, adjusted his tie, and did as he was told. The perspiration sprang from his forehead and pooled beneath his collar.

"Our dear Lord certainly has y'all in a hot little corner of this fine world, does he not?" Avon flashed his made-for-media smile, but it had no effect. They remained expressionless, impossible to read.

"We are not here to discuss the weather, Reverend Caulfield," came a voice from the end of the table. "We have business to attend to and little time to waste."

Avon knew that voice from a half dozen brief calls placed over the last several months.

"We have need of your services. Would you care to hear more?"

Avon was not easily intimidated. There was a coldness in the man's tone, less urgent than determined. He knew in an instant to shelve any charm offensive. These characters meant business. It was why he had come all this way. Best he could do was to hear them out. At a glance, there was nothing overly impressive about them. All men—no surprise there. Difficult to gauge their ages, but from their time-worn expressions he assumed this group didn't take "no" for an answer.

The chairman allowed Avon to take it all in. "If you do have questions, this would be the time to ask."

Avon gathered himself, imagining himself at the pulpit, but it was no use. He felt small in the company of giants. He was aware of their reputation, or at least of what little was known of them. It was said that they held men's destinies in their hands. They had the power, influence, and, of course, the money to alter events of most any magnitude. What earthly role might he play in service to them, he wondered?

"I do apologize. I appear to be at a loss for words."

"How uncharacteristic," quipped the chairman. "Well then, if you have no burning questions, let us begin. We are the *Council*. Is this familiar to you?"

"By reputation only," replied Avon.

"The Knights of Pythias. The Ancient Order of the Foresters. The Illuminati. The Elders of Zion. All trifling, mitigating unions of men in search of meaning. Their missions, peripheral... inconsequential. We are the true Order. And so it is, Reverend, that our time is at hand."

Avon, not one to shy away from self-aggrandizement, was taken aback. A bold pronouncement, he thought, for a man who lived and operated in the shadows. Too bold, perhaps. "All very impressive," he heard himself mutter. "Did that sound patronizing?" he wondered to himself. "Stay cool Avon. Now think."

"But what does this have to do with me?" he ventured.

"*This* has nothing to do with you. Yet we may have some use for you."

"And what makes you think I'll play along?" It was the wrong tone. He could feel it. The chairman leveled his gaze, and Avon held his breath.

"*Good*, Reverend Caulfield. *Very* good. Direct and to the point. Let's just say that it plays to your advantage."

Whether imagined or not, the light and the mood in the room darkened.

"This you should know," said the chairman, edging himself out from behind the table, hands clasped behind his back. "Among all orders of men, we are the first. Our lineage reaches back before recorded history. I tell you this because it feeds the narrative that you, Reverend, will propagate. Does the term *Nephilim* mean anything to you?"

Avon tried to control his expression. "But yes, of course. The fallen ones."

"And what do you know of them?"

"Only what the Good Book tells us."

"What if I were to tell you there is more to the tale than what you might find in your *good* book?"

"I'd say that our Lord Almighty works in mysterious ways, and that if you tell me the Day of Reckoning is at hand, then we have much to do and little time to do it."

"I was hoping you'd say that, Reverend. This is the time for true believers."

"Forgive me, but what exactly *are* you saying?" asked Avon.

"That the Nephilim have returned. Indeed," he said, spreading his arms wide, "they are in our midst. *For they are demonic spirits, performing signs, who go abroad to the kings of the whole world, to assemble them for battle on the great day of God the Almighty.*"

Avon's lips moved, but he made no sound. Revelations 16:14. He wasn't sure if it was what this imposing figure of a man said or the way in which he said it, but it had the intended effect. Avon sat upright. He was transfixed. The chairman's eyes burned. Somehow, Avon knew that what he said or did next would change the course of his life, and perhaps the very course of history. Was he being trifled with? What cause prompted this man and this gathering to summon him to hear such news? Could it be true? Was the great day of reckoning at hand? What role might he possibly play? Was this destiny calling? Avon's thoughts must have betrayed him. For when he lifted his eyes, he could see the chairman staring back, a faint smile appearing at the corners of his dark mouth.

"Yes, Reverend. You see now, don't you, the possibilities all stretched out before you? What say you? Do you choose to play a role in this new narrative? He who hesitates..."

Confusion gave way to calm. In that instant, Avon saw the long arc of a new narrative unfold before him. It was a gift.

"Are you a God-fearing man?" he heard the chairman ask.

"I believe I am."

"Then hear what I have to say."

CHAPTER 32

Heaviness. That's what Carson felt as he regained consciousness. Then nausea. He resisted the urge to vomit by straightening his spine, dropping his shoulders, and taking long slow breaths. In... then out. His head hurt, and his brain felt liquid. He gently opened his eyes to see the others floating—still unconscious—in their gravity pods. Only Philomena was awake. She had a delicate constitution, and Carson worried about her. They locked eyes.

He cleared his throat, as if from a deep sleep. "Are you all right?" he asked her.

"I'm fine," she replied. "Just a bit shaken. What happened?"

"It looks like we all passed out. G-force. That was nothing like the simulator," he mumbled, shaking his head.

"Not even close," added Philomena.

From the moment when the *Orpheus* entered the maelstrom until the moment of its final submersion, the journey had lasted a mere fourteen minutes and twenty-two seconds. The pods had played their intended roles, maintaining equilibrium for each occupant and seeing them safely through thousands of pounds of atmospheric pressure. The *Orpheus* was still in one piece, as was its crew.

Abby woke and motioned for the pods to open. Gently, almost tenderly, so as to avoid losing orientation, each member stepped from their respective pod, testing their footing and reaching for one another, searching for balance. Abby, more sure-footed than the others, passed among them and, placing a hand on each shoulder, offered a few words of support. "Welcome to ground zero. Now, if you please, follow me. Go easy. You're still adapting."

The smooth lines of the inner sanctum shifted, and a door slid back, leading them all through a spiraling passageway up to the vessel's observation deck. As they entered, the room sprang to life with glowing green charts, tables, and data that only Abby seemed to fully grasp. She bounced from one side of the room to the other, pointing out this, then that. She was giddy—the effects, perhaps, of nitrogen narcosis or too much atmospheric pressure.

"Would you care to share your excitement?" asked Carson.

"Well, we're alive for starters," she replied.

"You sound surprised."

"Do I? Well, yes, perhaps a little."

Abby turned back to the panel of charts and began swiping through the tables and images on the screen in front of her. "18,000 atmospheres of pressure," she mumbled. "No apparent damage. All good." She felt restored, confident again. "If you feel the weight of the world, that's because you're under it. Want to see where we've landed?"

She tapped the screen before her and a panel of icons appeared. Holding her finger over the display, she said "Here we go." Another quick tap on the screen, and the crew could hear the gentle moan of an engine. The skin of the *Orpheus* slowly retracted, like the peeling of an apple. From the apex of the domed ceiling and down the convex sides of the ship, only six inches of reinforced plexiglass separated the crew from a watery death. Abby darkened the room and the panel lights went into sleep mode. "And now," she said, like a magician preparing to pull a rabbit out of a hat... She flipped a row of switches and floodlights clapped on. For only an instant, the shadows of a hundred deep-dwelling creatures swirled, before fleeing to the shadows.

The screen view pointed upward, and they could see the spindle of the maelstrom swirling above them. They were encapsulated in a silo of stone that, for the moment, sheltered them from the chaos above. The walls were dark and worn smooth, and the *Orpheus* was wedged in deep. Abby rotated the beams, tracing the walls and studying the floor beneath them.

"What now?" snapped Carson.

"We wait," she replied.

"Wait for what?" said Spike. "For this hellhole to crush us like a tin can?"

"Be patient, Mr. Morrison. I've been given assurances."

"Would you like to elaborate?" urged Carson.

"They know we are here. They said they would be ready."

"Who the hell is *they*?" demanded Spike.

CHAPTER 33

"Shut it down."

"I'm sorry, sir, what do you mean, 'Shut it down'?"

"You heard what I said. Shut it down."

"Which part?"

"All of it."

There were looks of shock and displeasure, but no one dared challenge. All eyes were on the chairman. He sat upright, fingers pressed lightly together, head bowed. Anyone who did not know him could be forgiven for thinking the man was at prayer. He was not.

"It's happening," he muttered, in such low tones that only those near to him could actually hear his words. But everyone understood what was at stake. Decades of drilling across thousands of locations across the globe had failed to yield what the chairman had dreamed of—a passageway to the core. The effort, instead, had set off a chain reaction of underground eruptions that now threatened to expose their plan.

"It's too soon," dared one brave member of the gathering. His protest was met with silence. He tested the waters again. "We're that close," he added.

The two were separated by the full expanse of the boardroom table.

"Not close enough," snapped the chairman. "And now this!" There would be no further protest. It was clear who was in charge.

It's these disruptions... these incidents," stammered the Council's chief engineer. "They're unexpected. We never modeled for this."

"And what did you model for?" probed the chairman.

"Well, sir, you know. We modeled for the breach. The breakthrough."

"Did it occur to you that there could be complications? Unforeseen events? Did your model allow for the possibility that our little project might exacerbate the problem?"

"We're dealing with a highly unstable environment. We've accounted for every possible scenario. Or at least I thought we had."

"I see."

The chairman released the man at the end of the table from his gaze, pivoted, and stood up. His thin waist and broad shoulders belied his age. Only the mane of white hair suggested he was much older than he appeared. He turned his back on the group of dark-suited men and stared up at the screen that showed an image, pockmarked with red, orange, and blue circles, thousands of pinpoints encircling the globe. They throbbed and pulsated to indicate if they were still live, compromised, or shut down.

"Which sites are we closest to?" asked the chairman.

"There. Off the coast of Finland. And there, just 100 kilometers due west of Nur-Sultan. Both sites are stable and we can go deeper still. These other sites—in the Mediterranean and the Gulf—well, we'll have to move fast. Capping them is the only way to contain it."

"Contain what?"

"The eruptions."

The chairman moved into the light of the projector. As pulsating red and orange dots appeared across his forehead, the hue of his skin turned pale blue.

"Need I remind you all what is at stake here? These... what did you call them? *incidents*... they're front-page news now. Scientists from here to Moscow are looking into them. It's time to change tactics. It's time to them in!"

A cackle of protest went up from the group, and the chairman waited patiently for the commotion to die down. Protest was meaningless at this point. Time for a new plan.

"Letting them in is the only way to know if they have the means to achieve their final objective. The approach by sea was a gamble. Yet the *Orpheus* has endured. Perhaps we've underestimated them. Our way seemed so much more..."—he fumbled for the right word—"*direct*. What are we missing here?"

To the others, he seemed momentarily and uncharacteristically disoriented.

"The tables have turned. Round one goes to the *Orpheus*. The stakes have changed and a new battlefront looms. Riddle me this," said the chairman. "If our bottom-feeders didn't have a plan for phase two and a means of approaching the core, why would they risk the descent in the first place?"

It was a reasonable question. No one present ventured a guess.

"But why let them in?" came the plea from one Council member.

"Because they know something we don't. And if we want to find out, we need to get close."

"And what about the drilling?" asked the same Council member, this time, in a whisper.

"Shut it down!" he thundered.

What the chairman was suggesting was beyond anything the Council members could fathom. Every effort had been made to plot and penetrate the Earth's crust. It was a project 200 years in the making. At first, they said the drilling was for well water to service large-scale farms and plantations. That played for a while, until they struck water. To keep drilling would raise suspicions. Then, a miracle. In small-town Texas, just 140 kilometers due east of modern-day Houston, Pattillo Higgins, the so-called "prophet of Spindletop," did what no other man had done before him—he struck oil. In doing so, he changed the course of history and created a cover for the Council that no one had dreamed possible. The oil boom would give them license to drill not hundreds but thousands of wells from every conceivable point on the planet, increasing the possibility of discovering a passage to the core in a fraction of the time that it might otherwise take. Better yet, it would become self-financing. Oil would pave the way, mollifying the masses and generating the kind of wealth necessary to fund the Council's grand ambitions. It was perfect. It would become a ruse of legendary proportions.

"Do you know what you're asking us to do?" asked a portly member of the group, who until that moment had remained quietly slumped in his chair. "Markets will collapse. We'll be ruined. Why shut it down? Can't we at least keep some of the wells running?"

The chairman shot a look at the speaker that buried the discussion once and for all.

"Oil was never the goal. Do you really need me to remind you of that?"

The man recoiled. "Forgive me, Mr. Chairman. I wasn't thinking. But if I may, how will we explain it... the shutdown, I mean?"

"Create something! There's no shortage of deceptive agency among you. Fabricate a tale. Concoct a story. Blame it on the Russians. I don't care what you do, just do it!"

"It's gonna hurt," the large man rejoined.

"It's time to get your head out of that feedbag. We knew this might be a possibility. It won't be the first shock to the system. We've stockpiled for this moment. Call on our friends in the Middle East. Now go do what you must."

The chairman was right. Deception was a Council trademark. Their collective power to devise a universal diversion knew no limits.

The news broke at midnight GMT. It began with a reported incident in Taiwan. By noon the next day, Hong Kong, Southern China, and parts of the Philippines were reporting cases. Responses varied, with some governments moving quickly to lock down, while others—worried that economic decline would invite political instability—held off.

As the virus spread, markets faltered. It took less than a week for the World Health Organization to declare a global pandemic. One after the other, with countries on lockdown and companies in disarray, markets wobbled, then toppled. Entire economies followed. It was carnage. Commodities were the hardest hit, including gold, platinum, copper, and oil... especially oil. Prices plummeted, cascading downward, with no end in sight. Markets reeled as one exchange after another reported catastrophic losses.

In a matter of days, the Council members disbanded, flying off in their private jets to begin planning the tales they would tell their shareholders. Only the chairman remained. He sat alone in the boardroom, with only flickering news feeds displayed across a phalanx of high-definition monitors, watching the world collapse. Muted images of bank runs, riots, burning buildings, and pleas for assistance were interspersed with news anchors making baseless conjectures and testing their pseudo-theories.

From Beijing to Buenos Aires, the air was thick with panic. It was a world in crisis. Behind the chairman, on the big screen, hundreds of tiny lights blinked across a three-dimensional world map. One after the other, the little lights twinkled, faded, then went out—the sight of a thousand oil wells being capped and decommissioned. Refineries everywhere ground to a halt. A global travel ban was in full effect. It was as if the world had come to a standstill.

The Council members videoconferenced from locations around the world. They were witnessing the death of a 200-year-old industry.

"I commend you," said the chairman. "Our little ruse has worked."

The soft glow from the screen added a pallor to the chairman's complexion. The Council had accomplished two important outcomes in one deft move: a smokescreen for the shuttering of global oil production *and* economic breakdown courtesy of a mysterious virus. It was a plot worthy of the Council, and even the chairman seemed uncharacteristically jubilant. It was proof that only they had the power to alter the course of world events, a notion as terrifying as it was gratifying.

The ploy had added benefits, too. For instance, those scientists who had been deployed to determine the cause of the gravitational anomalies that started with the disappearance of Wit Thompson were recalled. From one side of the world to the other, environmentalists, geologists, oceanographers, and physicists were told to pack up and go home. With the global economy in a tailspin, funding dried up.

"No more probing scientists," the chairman grumbled.

For now, their secret plan to find a passageway to the core was safely hidden away. The suffering caused was merely an unfortunate by-product—collateral damage. Humans had suffered before, and they would suffer again. It had been this way from the very beginning. Strange, thought the chairman, that no matter how extreme, hope always returned.

"When it is done, all will be forgiven," he whispered out loud. "And no one will be any the wiser."

There was no need to raise his voice. The others had heard, and they understood this to be true.

CHAPTER 34

Sometimes in the darkness, one can see more clearly. He knew—well before the crew—that the *Orpheus* had touched down. Even though it was hidden by the absence of light, it remained visible to Otto, with his refined ability to perceive what cannot be seen. He watched as they navigated the silo floor. He knew what they were looking for. He also knew that unless he assisted, the maelstrom would eventually shift, pounding their tiny ship into oblivion. He felt flush with the power to change the course of everything. He had his orders, but—for the time being at least—he was savoring the sense of control.

He knew momentarily what he would have to do, and he blanched at the thought of welcoming them into his world. He had grown accustomed to this place. He reveled in its deep isolation. He was well suited to this life, one ruled by discipline and scientific pursuit. An empirical mind does not preclude an imaginative one, though. He allowed himself to play with certain ideas. Indeed, he had come to fancy himself as a kind of lord of the underworld—an arbiter of the dead.

Decades had passed since his surface-dwelling days. His "formidable years," as he liked to think of them, spent living among those who knew nothing of his kind or his origins. Had he chosen to remain among them, his life might have turned out differently. Instead, he disappeared from the world of humans, never to be heard from again. Retreating back to the depths, he continued his research, alone and without distraction.

Deep down, it was easy to lose track of time. In fact, time had lost all meaning. He cared for only one thing—the meaning and purpose of dark matter. No theoretical physicist alive had broken the code. Roll back this single mystery, he believed, and the answers to all the world's wonders would be revealed.

Otto hated distractions. But this one could not be avoided. He could brood all he wanted, but that would not make the *Orpheus* go away. It sat at the threshold to his world and his work. The orders were clear: "Let them in." Still, he resisted. He trusted no one. Serving as host to a wayward team of surface dwellers was not part of the plan. Or, at least, not part of *his* plan. What did they want?

"They want what we want," the chairman had told him.

"Then why let them in?" he protested.

"Because time is running out and you have failed. We are no closer now than we were in the beginning. Theories. That's all you offer us."

"Theories are key. They could end the search and offer us the one thing we all desire."

"Perhaps we placed too much hope in you. Time for a new approach."

"So you think opening the door to a group of strangers will solve the problem? What's to prevent them from stealing what we know and completing the journey without us?"

"For someone with your intellect, you're having a hard time following. First, I'm not asking, I'm telling. Second, they won't need to steal anything. You're going to give it to them. And third, when it comes to the journey to Earth's core, you're going with them! Have I made myself clear?"

"Perfectly."

CHAPTER 35

While the *Orpheus* lay locked in the grips of the silo with the maelstrom raging above, only Carson remained awake. The other crew members had peeled away, retreating to their pods to rest and consider their fate. Alone, Carson continuously scrutinized the digital schematics that wormed their way through the overhanging image of Earth's mantle. He filed through the scans one microlayer at a time, searching like a digital detective for any clue that might lead them to the elusive point of entry to Earth's catacombs. He narrowed his gaze and pursed his lips, allowing his mind to wander back to his early discovery at NASA. His theories on muon tomography were controversial at best, but he had never backed down. He persisted with his superiors. By making regular trips to Capitol Hill, hat in hand, he had received the backing he required, but always at a cost.

Funding was everything. It had taken them six years and more than $400 million to crack the code and build the technology, but they had done it. Muons, tiny charged particles produced by cosmic rays, had the unique capability of being able to penetrate rock—to see through to the Earth's interior—unlike any competing technology. Trying to explain this to the Congressional Appropriations Committee year in and year out had almost been as exhausting as the research effort itself. At long last, though, his approach had worked. The images spiraling above him at this very moment were evidence of that.

As these thoughts—and more—were passing through his head, the ship shuddered. Reaching across the control panel, he gave two quick taps, activating spotlights and illuminating the ocean floor. Taking hold of the joystick, he maneuvered the lights, panning them over the ship's surroundings. There, to starboard, a massive hole appeared, deep in the western wall. It formed a large perfect arc from the sandy bottom, rising 100 meters or more. Not wanting to wake the others, and knowing that any wasted minute could result in a breach, he eased the throttle forward. The *Orpheus* groaned. The downward thrust of the currents had driven the ship deep into the sandy bottom. Even so, he was able to move it forward, rolling ever so slowly toward the opening. Using the floodlights to peer into the cave, Carson let his hand drop from the controls and leaned back in his chair.

"Incredible," he gasped. "Simply incredible."

CHAPTER 36

Otto stood looking through the porthole into the decompression chamber. The water level was falling, and within minutes, he saw the top of the ship emerge, then its midline, and then finally the whole *Orpheus*, in all her glory, reflected in the surrounding pools of water. For an instant, he considered turning away and leaving these unwanted guests trapped. "What a nuisance," he thought to himself.

Taking hold of the wheel that opened the hatch to the chamber, he gave it a hard turn. The door flew back with a hiss, and he stepped through.

Inside, the crew were assembled in the control room, standing in anticipation as the ship's outer lining slowly drew back to reveal its new surroundings. The walls of the cave-like structure—still flowing with sea water—curved upward to a domed ceiling, the *Orpheus* at its center. At the foot of the ship, but not too close, stood a cloaked figure.

"Darth Mal," uttered Spike.

"Or the Grim Reaper," ventured Carson.

"Dear God," said Abby, spinning about and heading for the exit.

"Abby, what's going on here?" Kai called after her. "You said nothing about other people down here."

Abby wasn't listening. "Stay calm," she thought to herself. Nothing had prepared her for this. She was a geophysicist, after all—not an anthropologist. Show her a thousand meters of raw earth and she could dissect and discern its inherent qualities, analyze its mineral composition, and derive a view on its origins and contribution to the makeup of the planet. Bring her face-to-face with an eight-foot-tall creature cloaked in black, however, and the only things she had to offer were a handshake and a hello. If nothing else, she had to maintain the appearance of control.

Turning, she said "Well, let's not keep him—or it—waiting."

In single file, the crew walked the gangway that stretched from the ship's midline to the ground below. Abby led the way. The figure remained perfectly still, his face concealed by the hood. The shroud, hung heavy over bent shoulders, shimmered black. They drew close. Abby was the first to speak.

"Where to begin...? We are..."

"I know who you are," a voice interrupted.

Two deathly pale hands emerged from beneath the folds and turned back the hood of the cloak. Abby recoiled, as did the others.

"Not what you expected?" he asked.

It had been quite some time since Otto had had a glimpse of himself. Vanity was a luxury he could little afford. Both the passage of time and the conditions at these depths had transformed him. His elongated head, small ears, and bulging eyes were as much a result of subatmospheric pressure and artificial lighting as they were aspects of genetic adaptation. Standing there now, he took some satisfaction in seeing their combined expressions of horror and pity.

"Not much to look at, eh?" he quipped with the hint of a grin.

"Forgive us, we just..."

"An apology is unnecessary. I am Otto Trubolt... *Dr.* Otto Trubolt. I am the sole administrator of this station, and I suppose that makes you my guests."

Something in his voice made them feel more wary than welcome.

"Is it just the five of you?"

"No, we are six," Abby replied.

"And where is the sixth?"

From the opening in the ship, Enoch appeared.

"Ah, the sixth."

Descending the gangplank, he crossed the short distance to join them.

"He's a big one, is he not?" quipped Otto—which seemed strange coming from someone of equal height.

Only days earlier, Enoch had appeared from nowhere. After landing on the ship's deck, he descended to one of the empty cabins below. Only then was Abby alerted to his presence. She went immediately to meet the stranger, who she had imagined was there on behalf of the mission's benefactors. She had had to duck down to step across the threshold, and as she did so, the figure rose from the bed. He was enormous, she thought—more genie than man. He wore foul weather gear, heavy wool pants tucked into the tops of his leather boots, and a black turtleneck. Across his shoulders hung a tent-sized trench coat, heavy and oiled. Rivulets of water cascaded along its flanks, forming small pools of water on the polished wood floor. He was larger than the average man in every way. Even his head looked slightly too big atop his broad shoulders. His hands were large and weathered, the color of tawny leather. His face was windburned and creased. And yet behind this ruggedly handsome *façade* was a lightness and alacrity that immediately put her at ease.

As she entered the room, he offered her a gentle smile and extended a large hand. The feeling of familiarity was overwhelming. It was as if they had known each other for ages, their meeting being a joyful reunion. He asked her to take a seat, and when she did so, Enoch apologized for showing up unannounced. The situation, he explained, required his presence.

For the next hour, she listened while he outlined the expectations and hopes of the benefactors. He described how, over recent days, the outbreak of a virus had precipitated a global lockdown. Economies would soon crumble. He insisted that nothing should stop Abby and the crew from staying the course and following through with the plan.

Abby had questions. But, for the moment, Enoch insisted that he was not in a position to share more than he already had. In the days ahead, he assured her, the full purpose of the mission would come to light. It was then that he told her he would be joining them on their journey. Watching the two tall figures now in a silent standoff, Abby wondered if she might have made a mistake in not pressing Enoch for more answers.

After what struck the crew as an uncomfortably long period of time, the two strangers disengaged. No words had passed between them, but Abby and the others had the distinct feeling that somehow volumes of information had been exchanged.

"Follow me," demanded Otto.

In single file, the crew members filed through the hatch, entering a long tunnel, before emerging into a dimly lit room.

"I wasn't expecting guests," he snapped, making no effort to hide his irritation.

Each interconnected room hummed with a soft, green glow. The walls were cut from solid rock, all crafted with sharp right angles and a polished finish. Whatever this place was, it was purpose-built—but for what? Eventually, they came to a large metal door affixed with a wheel and a pressure gauge. For an instant, it appeared that he was ushering them back to the *Orpheus*.

"I'm unaccustomed to pleasantries, and frankly I see no utility in them. I hope you don't think me rude, but there is little time, and we have much to discuss."

With that, Otto placed his enormous hands on the wheel and turned it until the door gasped. The air density shifted, and the crew clasped their hands to their ears.

Philomena swooned. Her legs buckled. Spike steadied himself against the wall and reached for her at the same time, saving her head from hitting the floor.

"Are you all right?" he asked.

"Yes, I'm fine. Just need a second."

"Jesus, my head," moaned Spike.

"Of course. I wasn't thinking. The pressure is difficult at first, but you get used to it," Otto assured them.

They stepped through, and after wheeling the door shut behind them, Otto stood drumming his fingers against the metal. Minutes passed and the pressure changed again. Their host then reached down and wheeled open the opposing door.

"Mind your step. It's a long way down."

In almost complete darkness, they moved in single file down a flight of winding steps. With only the slick curved walls to guide them, they spiraled their way downward. At the bottom was another door and yet another pressure lock, and once again the crew members were overcome with dizziness, pummeled by the change in pressure. Otto stooped low to step across the threshold, and the others followed, finding themselves in a domed room like the inside of a giant egg. At the room's center sat a square box made of dark metal, mounted on a large slab of pure granite. Computer terminals, servers, and data storage units lined the periphery, blinking and humming. Otto let the crew take it all in before breaking the silence.

"What you see before you is my life's work. I've sacrificed everything, and I can see by your expressions that you're probably wondering what madman would commit himself to this extent and for what purpose. Let me explain. I am a physicist by training. I won't bore you with my qualifications. And even if I did, you would only question me further. For countless years, I have focused on one thing only." Otto turned to look directly at Abby. "Quintessence—the elusive fifth force."

Otto's blunt declaration caught Abby off guard. Her shocked expression almost made him laugh. "Yes, Professor Clarke, an area of shared interest, I do believe."

"How do you know who I am?"

"I know many things about you. We've been working toward the same ends."

"Have we?"

"Yes, we have. You and I both know that time is running out. Our planet is dying. Answers lie deep within the Earth's core. While our methods may differ, we are in pursuit of the same thing."

This creature's matter-of-fact pronouncement felt abrupt. Until that moment, Abby had been under the impression that only she, the crew, and the benefactors of the mission fully understood what was at stake. She felt her mind racing. Who was this stranger? How did he know these things? And, more importantly, who else knew? They had chosen the maelstrom as the point of descent because she was told it was here that they might access the catacombs. There were other options, but until this moment, she could not imagine why her benefactors had insisted on this one. She knew nothing beyond this. Otto and this place had all come as a surprise. So much so that it left her wondering if she and this strange fellow were both agents of the same sponsor.

Abby looked up to see Otto staring at her, as if her mind and its workings were entirely available to him. There was a twinkle in his ghastly bulging eyes that made her feel squeamish.

"Who do you work for?" Abby demanded, taking the offensive.

"Professor, there's no need for distress. Your secrets are safe with me. Perhaps there is something we can do for each other?"

"And what might that be?"

"Well, clearly you have convened this team of travelers for a subterranean journey. You've come this far, and against all odds, I might add. The *Orpheus* has proved herself worthy, or at least up to this point. Since you had not expected to find me, you must have had plans for safe passage through the catacombs. I can only wonder how you hoped to achieve such an impossible task."

Otto did not know, realized Abby. Here he was, stuck in this lab deep in Earth, but he had no idea that they were in possession of the digital maps that would lead them to the core.

"How long have you been here?"

What happened next came unexpectedly. Otto let out a cackle that reverberated through the egg-shaped room, loud and uncouth. The deep-set lines in his pallid face reformed themselves, and for a moment he looked delighted and a tad surprised.

"How long, you ask? Time isn't the question, professor. It's matter that matters."

"You don't say?" said Kai, growing mildly irritated with Otto's elusiveness.

"Oh, but I do say."

Kai bit. "Okay, enough with the smoke and mirrors. I think it's time for you, Dr. Trubolt—or whoever you are—to come clean. Who do you work for? Why are you here? And what does this have to do with us?"

"Until yesterday, *this* had nothing to do with *you*. But when I received word that someone was lurking about my doorstep, things changed. It seems that serendipity has seen fit to conjoin our destinies."

Otto paused, then began circumventing the room with long strides. "For more years than I care to recall, I've been here, watching, waiting, and working."

"Watching for what?" asked Philomena.

"Professor Clarke, would you like to explain, or shall I?"

Abby took a hard look at Otto, who had resumed his pacing, before turning to face her colleagues. She hesitated, staring at the ground—and he pounced.

"Ah, so it seems I'm not alone when it comes to secrets. You haven't told them, have you?"

Abby looked like a schoolgirl caught cheating.

"I was waiting for the right moment," she confessed.

"I see. I see... Would you say this is the right moment?"

Abby wasn't accustomed to being toyed with. And she most definitely didn't like Otto forcing her hand.

Turning to the group, she said: "There's more to this mission than meets the eye."

"Why am I not surprised," quipped Spike.

Abby searched their faces. They had only come to know each other for a few days, but already the sense of commitment she felt to them bore a hole in her. "They deserve better," she thought to herself. "I need to trust them, and they need to trust me."

"A journey to Earth's core comes in stages. I didn't feel this part of the story was germane. But Dr. Trubolt here wants a confession."

"We're listening," said Philomena, with a mixture of curiosity and some recognition that Abby, in her own way, was trying to protect them.

"In physics, there are four observed fundamental forces or interactions that form the basis of all known interactions in nature: gravitational, electromagnetic, strong nuclear, and weak nuclear forces. Some theoretical work points to a 'fifth force.' The characteristics of this fifth force depend on which theory one follows. Some postulate it is a force roughly the strength of gravity but much weaker than electromagnetism or nuclear force.

"And what is the source of that 'force,' if you please, professor?" asked Otto, clearly delighted with the teacher–student dynamic that had now been established.

Abby winced. She didn't like being patronized.

"Dark matter."

"Dark matter, you say," chided Otto. "Thank you, professor. As you will no doubt have experienced, our Dr. Clarke here is somewhat of an expert in the field of electromagnetic engineering. The *Orpheus* is testimony to that. Electromagnetism has a role to play, no doubt. However, it is but one of the prime forces. There are others, are there not? Professor, what say you? Am I correct in assuming—at least as of late—that you've been a fan of general relativity? And yet there are anomalies in the behavior of our planet that have led you to believe that other physical influences may be afoot. Am I correct, Dr. Clarke?"

"Yes... Perhaps."

"So, this dark matter... Would you say it holds some importance as it relates to this *mission* of yours?"

The more Otto spoke, the more Abby disliked him. She felt betrayed. Exposed. It was not supposed to happen this way. It was enough that the crew had agreed to forego their own safety to travel to the center of the Earth. The role of dark matter could wait, could it not?

"Please share with our friends what you know about our shadowy substance. Or, to put it differently, how does one observe what one cannot see? We must infer its presence, must we not? It's all quite maddening... the waiting, I mean."

With raised eyebrows, Otto waited for Abby's reply, but all of a sudden she appeared lost in thought.

"'As if all there were, were fireflies—and from them you could infer the meadow.'"[5]

"What was that, professor?"

"Nothing," said Abby. "Just something I heard from someone I once knew."

"Fireflies, you say. Indeed, it is the perfect metaphor. And like the firefly, we watch for its illumination, but know not where or when it will choose to glow."

Watching Otto toy with Abby was like watching a lion play with a mouse. In an instant, he cast her aside. This was his domain, after all.

"You're looking at my life," Otto intoned, gesturing to the lab and all its instruments. "For countless years, I've been waiting, watching, and listening for what my fellow physicists so blandly refer to as 'weakly interacting massive particles'—WIMPs, for short. Only here, deep in the Earth's crust, can we drown out the cosmic noise to gain a glimpse of the blue-hued trail of a single, virtually weightless neutrino as it collides with an atom, scattering its electrons at the speed of light. I have come to see myself as more of a detective than a scientist. I search for evidence, clues, fingerprints—hints of the greater crime that has been committed. But in this instance, there is no crime. Only connection."

It had been a long time since Otto had an audience, and he was taking full advantage of the moment.

---

5   Rebecca Elson, *A Responsibility to Awe* (2001).

"If it is so elusive, how consequential could it be?" ventured Carson, who knew a thing or two about dark matter. Otto did not disappoint. Swiveling around, he took two quick steps toward Carson so that he might look down on him.

"Has everything I've said been lost on you? Do you not see that what we are talking about is the very fabric that binds our universe together? Dark matter is fundamental to *everything*. Without it, superclusters, galaxies, planets, humans, fleas, and bacilli would not exist. To prove and decipher the existence of dark matter... would be to approach 'the revelation of a new order, a new universe, in which even light will be known differently, and darkness as well.' At this very moment, our cosmos—and, more immediately, this planet—are being tested by the principal forces that allow each and every one of us to exist. We are, if you will, at both a theoretical as well as an existential crossroads, and this lab is testimony to that fact. My work, you see, is the glue that binds our work together. There is no such thing as coincidence. We are here for a reason. Recent events have conspired to bring us together. Why else would I be here wiling away the years in this underground bunker, while the rest of you are off doing whatever it is that the rest of you do?"

He was dismissive. Abby could see that the others were quickly learning to dislike Otto as much as she did.

"For God's sake, just get to the point!"

The sound of Enoch's voice came like the shattering of a plate. Everyone turned to look at the stranger who Abby had called "our missing link." Since his introduction to the group on the eve of their departure, Enoch had said little. He was there, he explained, to "observe" the mission. Nothing more.

"Ah, so the giant speaks," said Otto with a grin. "But make no mistake, *God* has nothing to do with this!"

Like a lunar eclipse, Otto's mood darkened. Enoch had struck a nerve and Otto made no effort to hide his disdain.

"You fools," he hissed. "You have no idea what you're up against. While you've been consumed with your little toy submarine, the world has gone to hell."

"What do you mean? What's happened?" asked Philomena, fighting to suppress a feeling of foreboding that had lingered for days.

"A little bit of everything, you might say. I'm sure you all recall that peculiar incident with SkyBound's CEO, Wit Thompson? Dr. Horner, I'm sure, can tell you all about it."

"What does that have to do with anything?" Kai snapped.

"Feeling a bit guilty, are we?" mocked Otto.

Kai lunged forward, but Abby stepped in between them.

"Not here. Not now," she whispered to him, before turning to Otto. "Go on."

A Cheshire grin spread across the oblong face, making this creature from the underworld look all the more hideous.

"It has started," said Otto, his eyes glimmering. "We predicted it would."

"What's started?" asked Abby.

Otto gave a soft chuckle. "The rapture!"

"What the hell are you talking about?" charged Kai.

"By the thousands. Maybe tens of thousands by now. Hard to say. They started off calling them *disappearances*. Mostly at high altitude, but not always. Some called it a hoax. But it's more than that. Oh yes, much more than that. For now, at least, it's turned into a kind of phenomenological pandemic. The *born-agains* are beside themselves. They've been activated, you might say. It's the metaphysical moment of truth they've all been waiting for. It may be the first thing in centuries that our religious orders can agree on. Fear is a powerful motivator. And, to plan, people are flocking back to God, begging for mercy." Otto chortled. "It's all so perfect!"

"*Perfect!*" cried Kai. "What could be perfect about millions living in fear and thousands disappearing?"

"It's a diversion, you fool," Otto snapped. "No one has figured it out. Not yet, at least. The scientific community can't explain it. But we know their type, don't we, professor?" said Otto, turning toward Abby. "Conjecture leads to theories and theories to proof, and that takes time."

"Time for what?" asked Philomena.

"Time for what?" repeated Otto, sarcastically. "Why, my dear, time to save the planet, of course."

CHAPTER 37

The good Reverend Avon Caulfield sat behind the big, thick plate glass table that served as his desk, a kaleidoscope of colors cascading down on him from the stained-glass skylights and spreading throughout the loft. The suite of white-satin-covered sofas to the left and the small altar with the golden cross to the right accented the signature of the room's triangular footprint—an architectural trinity.

Indeed, the Great Ascension Baptist Church was *the* leading example of spherical triangle transformation architecture. Many would lay claim to its unique design. But, truth be told, it was Avon who had envisioned it. Its design, he claimed, had come to him in a dream.

On the day it was completed, he had arranged a christening and spared no expense. His congregation had showed up *en masse*. Every moment was choreographed to a tee. With the press in full attendance, he declared "God is our chief architect, and I... little more than his lowly draftsman." There was no denying it—it was a megachurch of *GODacious* proportions.

The church's foundation was constructed around the shape of an icosahedron—a convex regular icosahedron, to be exact—that contained twenty triangular faces, with five meeting at the vertex. As odd as it appeared from the outside, the inside created a feeling of airy expansiveness. The congregation applauded the achievement, and there was nary a worshiper who said that they had not felt the presence of God within. The great arched ceilings screamed *ascendance*, in accordance with the name of the church itself.

The place where Avon sat was positioned at the apex of the building. It was, in a word, *spectacular!* Located with symbolic intentionality directly above the altar, the triangular structure left anyone who stepped into the room with the impression that Avon had a direct line to God. Two of the three walls of glass rose at forty-five-degree angles, clear glass blending into stained glass at their highest points. The third wall stood at ninety degrees and offered a full and unobstructed view of the nave, where congregations of thousands gathered each Sunday.

On this particular Sunday morning, Avon stood centered in his prism of light as his flock entered the hall, filling the church row by row. A phalanx of the faithful, heads lifted, admired the good Reverend behind glass. With his arms outstretched in flowing robes, he was a sight to behold. Church attendance was up—*way up!* Pandemics had a way of putting the fear of God into people. The chairman was right; he said they would come, and they did. Avon had only to do what he did best—tell people what they wanted to hear. In this case, it was about the choice they would need to make.

Only days earlier, he had sat in audience with the chairman and the Council. What he had learned during the course of that discussion changed everything—it was as if his destiny had been revealed to him. Whether the Nephilim truly existed or not was immaterial: it was the narrative that mattered most. He had been offered the chance to take the world stage, and he took it—anointed, as it were, by the Council itself. Minutes from now, he would unveil a tale worthy of his Great Ascension Baptist Church. It would put him on top. Nothing would be the same again, or so he imagined.

Avon had a thing about punctuality. He expected the same from his followers. Each Sunday service began the same way. At 8:56a.m., the organ would announce the start of the service. At 8:58a.m., he would descend from the office to the pulpit below, making three full turns along the spiral staircase. And at precisely 9:00a.m., he would raise his arms to reveal two crimson wings beneath folds of black silk. The organ—timed to perfection—would release its final triumphant note at that very—synchronized—moment.

With the minutes ticking down, Avon looked out from his glassy chamber to admire the packed house. Reaching beneath his vestment, he withdrew a silk handkerchief with the oversized monogram "AC," then wiped the sweat from his forehead and the back of his neck. No one stirred. They only watched as this mountain of a man closed his eyes. The calm before the storm. Then thunder!

"*Praise* be to God!" he shouted.

"Praise be to God! Hallelujah!" roared the response.

"Can I get an amen?" boomed Avon.

"Amen," cried the congregation.

"I said, can I get an amen?"

"Aaaaamen!" the words echoed through the chamber.

"Mmm, mmm, mmm, *God* is merciful... *Praise* the Lord!"

Already the temperature in the church had started to rise.

"We are the Lord's army. Praise God. We are one in the eyes of the Lord. His Holy Spirit stirs in our hearts. Is this *not* why you have come here today?"

"Save me, Jesus!" the parishioners cried out in unison.

"Praise be!" sang Avon.

He looked up from the sea of onlookers, who were swaying, crying, and singing the Lord's praises. TV cameras covered him from every angle, transmitting his message to the world. A Sunday audience of millions at this very moment hung on his every word.

The events of recent days had set the scene. No other evangelical preacher alive could have scripted it better. Outside, a pandemic was raging. Thousands were dying. Thousands more were being raptured. There, he said it, *raptured!* Emancipated from the Earth by being inexplicably lifted up and catapulted outward, into the heavens. The live footage did not lie. From Nepal to Chile, from Switzerland to New Zealand, first by the dozens, then by the thousands, anyone who lived above 3,000 meters or so risked being swept away. As a result, believers flocked to mountaintops all around the world, while others fled the high country to seek refuge in the lowlands.

A general dis-ease settled over the planet. People were beginning to panic. The death count from the virus grew, as did the number of gravitational disruptions. *Disruptions*—that's what they called them. While the scientific community flailed in its attempt to explain the phenomenon, people continued disappearing, and indiscriminately so, no less. The narrative was constantly shifting. One day, some poor innocent was a victim. The next day, it was one of God's chosen ones. The lines between the physical and metaphysical began to blur, and as they did so, support for the theory of divine intervention took hold.

The profligates of panic did not disappoint. They wove their webs and whipped communities into states of emotional frenzy. Televangelists everywhere battled to be heard. But only one of them knew the truth—or at least, part of the truth. The pandemic and the economic pandemonium that followed was the work of the Council, so he had been told. It was the necessary backdrop—they explained to him—for what must be done next. What remained unexplained was the gravitational anomaly. If this was the Council's doing, they made no show of enlightening Avon on this point.

"Use your imagination, Reverend," the chairman advised. "Or better yet, tell them the truth... Tell them the angels of God are among them and are here to do God's work. Tell them..." the chairman instructed, "that the *Nephilim* have returned."

The notion was irresistible. The Good Book had promised it. Now he would be the one to portend the moment. As members of the congregation poured through the doors of the church, Avon contemplated the words that he would use to describe the choice that they would all need to make. "Side with God," he would tell them, "or perish in the plague."

Sweat poured from his temples. The vestment felt tighter than usual around his thick torso. Twenty minutes from now, he would be the subject of headlines around the world. The prophet Avon. It had a nice ring to it, he thought.

Chapter 38

The human body was not built to endure thousands of pounds of atmospheric pressure for any extended period of time. Otto's lab and the adjoining rooms were designed to withstand the pressure, but that did little to ease the general discomfort felt by the crew of the *Orpheus*. Slumped against the wall at the far end of the lab, Spike and Philomena sat shoulder to shoulder. They watched as the tall, pallid figure of Otto Trubolt navigated his way around the black box at the center of the room, pointing out to the others the workings of his dark matter experiments. Occasionally, he would gesture with an extended arm and elongated fingers to the monitors that lined the wall.

Philomena felt uneasy.

"I don't trust him," she whispered.

"I'd call that good instinct," said Spike.

"There's something he's not telling us. Something important. But what?"

"How do you mean?"

"I can't pinpoint it. It's just a feeling."

Even though he was a good fifteen meters away, Otto turned and looked directly at Philomena. She stared back.

"He didn't..."

"I think he did," whispered Spike.

"How could he possibly hear us from there?"

"Must be the shape of his head."

Otto beckoned them to follow, then reached overhead and flipped a switch, activating a retractable screen.

Turning to Spike and Philomena, he said, "I don't mean to disturb your little exchange, but I am approaching the apex of my tale. Perhaps the two of you would like to join us."

"Might as well," yawned Spike, lifting himself up and brushing past Otto as he made his way to the opposite side of the room.

"Now that I've shared my theory on dark matter and explained to you why I believe it holds the key to unlocking the mysteries of our universe, there remain certain unknowns. There is the problem of gravity. Well, not so much a problem—rather, the question of gravity. It would appear that the over-celebrated Albert Einstein fell short in his estimations. His tidy little theory of relativity has a few holes in it, gravity being the biggest. Would you care to elaborate, Dr. Clarke?" he asked, turning once again with a grin to face Abby.

"It's just a theory," countered Abby.

"If you say so. But please, if you wouldn't mind, share with us your understanding."

"If you insist."

"Oh, but I do."

Abby made her way to the front of the room, took a deep breath, and began.

"When general relativity was first published, a problem arose: it appeared that energy might not be conserved in strongly curved spacetime. It was well known that certain quantities in nature are always conserved: the amount of energy (including energy in the form of mass), the amount of electric charge, the amount of momentum, and so on and so forth. In a remarkable feat of mathematical alchemy, the German mathematician Emmy Noether proved that each of these conserved quantities was associated with a particular symmetry, a change that doesn't *change* anything."

Abby could see that, with the exception of Otto and perhaps Carson, the others were lost.

"I'm sorry. Not very helpful, I know. Allow me to try again... For a while, Noether's formula put things to rest. But then there were anomalies. As the rotation of the Earth began to slow at an almost undetectable rate, it created a new set of phenomena. All of a sudden, it threw off the cosmic symmetry that underpins Einstein's theory. A small band of scientists detected the change and knew something was off, but what? There's a concept closely related to symmetry called 'duality.' Dualities are not new to physics. The wave–particle duality, for instance—the fact that the same quantum system can be best described as either a wave or a particle, depending on the context—has been around since the beginning of quantum mechanics. But newfound dualities have revealed surprising relationships. For example, a three-dimensional world without gravity can be mathematically equivalent, or dual, to a four-dimensional world with gravity."

Again, blank stares.

"It comes down to this," continued Abby. "Matter and energy themselves are less fundamental than the underlying relationship between them. Symmetry-based reasoning predicted a slew of things that haven't shown up in any experiments, including the 'supersymmetric' particles that could have served as the missing dark matter of the cosmos and explained why gravity is so weak compared to electromagnetism and all the other forces. This, I believe, is what Dr. Trubolt is attempting to prove." She turned to face him. "Is that correct, professor? Is dark matter the missing link in our cosmic tale—the slowing of Earth's rotation, the gravitational anomalies, the climactic and environmental unwinding of the ecosystem? Is dark matter the dark lord behind our existential march toward the sixth extinction?"

"Exquisite," said Otto, as if to praise a star student. "And quite dramatic, Dr. Clarke, if I do say so myself."

Abby looked more distraught and confused than pleased by his shallow praise.

"It's more than a theory," insisted Otto.

"How can you be sure?" Abby challenged.

"Do you have any idea how long I've been here? Do you think I would be so foolish as to suggest otherwise unless I had proof of what I say? I know your final objective, and it is to retrieve the secrets of the planet that most certainly lie at its core. This is but a pit stop on your journey to the center of the Earth. I applaud you. And I assure you that we are in search of the same thing."

"Are we?"

"Yes, I believe so. And I believe that if we combine our efforts, we might improve the chance of success."

"What are you asking?"

"I'm asking to join you and your crew on this journey."

"And why would we allow that?"

"Dark matter has been my life's mission. I believe it dwells in concentrated amounts within the reaches of this planet. Allow me to accompany you, and I will bring the full weight of my knowledge to bear. I believe the subatomic world holds answers for us all. A chain reaction has been unleashed. Earth is in a tailspin. Time—now, more than ever—does matter. If my theory proves correct, we may be able to slow down, and perhaps even reverse, the damage that has been done. That should be reason enough for you to take me with you."

Chapter 39

When Carson was younger, he kept a tall, thick, plate glass terrarium in his bedroom. That made him the first kid on his block to own an ant farm. The idea came to him while on a family camping trip in Utah's Moab Valley. Among the scrub and cactus, anthills padded the landscape. While his brothers and sisters played Capture the Flag among the rocky outcroppings, he prodded and probed the anthills to get a better look at their subterranean design. Unsatiated, he tossed away the stick and took a shovel to a mound, slicing away half the hill and unleashing panic. From the intricate latticework of the colony poured thousands of ferocious and vengeful red ants. It was a sudden onslaught. Within seconds, Carson's shoes and jeans were covered. The maddened insects charged up his legs and let loose a flurry of stinging bites that forced him to drop the shovel and run screaming back to the campsite. His father held onto him while his mother brushed and plucked the red devils from Carson's flesh. Red welts and a fever followed.

For the whole of the next day, Carson stayed in his tent and hallucinated. He dreamed of the underworld and a journey through endless loops of subterranean passageways. He imagined his way deep into the Earth's crust, where the tunnels grew wider. And there, colonies of creatures—half-human, half-insect—built great structures of surpassing beauty. In this place, their work was never done. Duties were assigned and everyone had a role to play. To live was to dig... and dig deep. No one in that place ever stopped to question why.

When the fever broke, Carson returned to his senses. Around the campfire he told his family what he had seen. There was a concerned look on his mother's face, while his siblings chided him.

"Stop now, you're upsetting him," his mother warned them. "You've had a nightmare, Carson. You're all right now." But he wasn't all right. He had seen them: the catacombs. Nothing could change that.

As members of the crew milled about the bridge making ready, Otto and Abby spoke in quiet consultation. She had agreed in principle to allow Otto to join them, but on the condition that he divulge all he knew. She had long suspected that dark matter had a part to play. The fact that Otto shared this belief was both comforting and distressing. To include Otto in the mission felt risky. Could she afford to include him? Then again, could she afford not to?

As Abby pondered her next move, Carson contemplated the digital cartography that had dominated his waking and dreaming states for so long. The three-dimensional rendering of the catacombs spreading out below them, cascading like spaghetti through 2,500 kilometers of highly pressurized rock oxides and silicates, was awe-inspiring, to say the least. Earth's mantle was navigable after all. At least in theory.

Enoch drew alongside Carson and gazed into the abyss with him.

"How will you manage?" he asked.

"It's the threshold that concerns me," replied Carson, trying not to show his surprise in Enoch's sudden interest. "Pick the wrong point of entry, and it's a dead end."

"I believe I might be of assistance," interrupted Otto. Though he had been standing across the room, whispering with Abby, somehow he had overheard them. Joining them, he reached out and placed the tip of his boney index finger against the screen.

"Do you see this?" Otto asked. Carson magnified the area and, sure enough, there appeared the faint outline of a perfectly oval opening into the rock. Beyond it, something quite unexpected—a great cavern. He refreshed the image and, indeed, there was structure to it. A honeycomb of outcroppings, bridges, passageways, and dwellings lined the walls.

"That doesn't make sense," said Carson.

"What doesn't?" asked Otto.

"It's perfect."

"Yes, it is, isn't it?"

"What are we looking at?"

The others gathered around the console to get a better look.

"Atlantis?"

"How quaint, Ms. Pettibone. But not so. Atlantis is but a fairytale. This is something quite different. She is called *Zalmoxis*. Another, lesser-known, underworld city.

"People lived here?"

"People, you say. No, not quite, Ms. Pettibone.

"Then who? Why?"

"Now *there* is a tale worth telling."

"You're full of surprises, Dr. Trubolt," said Abby. "I said you could join us on the condition that you come clean. What other secrets are you hiding?"

"I'm hiding nothing. It's all there before you."

Muon tomography was promising, but not perfect. Intermittent portions of the image were washed out. Carson called them "blind spots"—sections that remained impenetrable, even to muons. Artificial intelligence did the rest, filling in the map to complete the picture. There were no guarantees that this subterranean cartography was entirely accurate, but it was the best they had. Abby swiveled in her chair and turned to face the others. "Buckle up. We're going for a ride."

CHAPTER 40

As far as earthcraft go, the *Orpheus* was no ordinary ship. Its 11,000-meter journey from the surface to the ocean floor was a feat that no other man-made vessel could have survived. That small achievement, however, was nothing compared to what lay before them. The next leg of the journey would take advantage of new engineering fundamentals. Suspended by the creation of its own electromagnetic field, this craft, the first of its kind, was about to revolutionize subterranean travel. If successful, the launch site would be remembered forever—it would be to inner-Earth travel what Kitty Hawk was to aeronautics. Bottom line: the accuracy of Carson's charts would determine whether they all lived or died.

"Are you sure about this?" asked Abby, sidling up to Carson.

"Absolutely not," he replied with a hint of a smile.

"Then let's see what this ship can do."

Abby felt like her entire life had come down to this very moment— all her research and training, including the hours of experimentation, with its failures and adjustments. If the *Orpheus* performed as designed, and they survived, the question still remained: would they be on time? The planet was in a death spiral. Even if Abby's theories proved to be correct, would they be able to correct the planet's course? What hubris to think their mission would succeed!

Electromagnetic flux compression, or EMFC, lay at the heart of the design of the *Orpheus*. By generating its own electromagnetic field, the ship could achieve a state of animated suspension. Its effectiveness, however, was dependent on the integrity of the catacombs themselves. The notion of subterranean travel had come to Abby while she was lying at the bottom of the ice cave, waiting for hypothermia to set in. Separated from Kai and with no way out, she had contemplated the end. They say that your life flashes before you when you are faced with death. Abby had a different vision—of making deep-level Arctic cave exploration possible. Otherwise, traditional spelunking was slow business. EMFC was the way: it operated on the principle that if one could confine plasma in adequate amounts by driving charged particles through a large ring, it would be possible to generate fusion. The Tomahawk Principle, they called it. By sustaining the charge, a magnetic field equivalent to 1,200 teslas could effectively lift and propel an object forward through a state of animated suspension. She saw it as a kind of electromagnetic version of pneumatic tube transport, where compressed air creates a partial vacuum to deliver objects through a network of tubes. In order for it to work, a rock-solid contained field is essential. Snow caves were not that. A test of EMFC transport in tunnels of ice would cause a seismic catastrophe. Freezing to death all those years ago, these were her last thoughts, just before the lights appeared and she felt her body being lifted.

She had seen or spoken to no one since her rescue. The recovery ward appeared to be fully automated. She wanted for nothing as her strength gradually returned. During that time, the dream of EMFC transferal kept returning to her.

Days later, while sitting up in bed for the first time, she looked up just in time to see a note being slipped beneath the door. Easing herself out of the bed, she shuffled over to retrieve it. The envelope was elegant, made of parchment, and sealed with the shape of a perfect gold circle. "Who seals anything with wax anymore?" she wondered as she broke it open and withdrew two small pieces of paper. One was a telegraphic transfer slip; the other, a handwritten note. The wire transfer showed the date, the account, and the amount deposited, with the notation "for EMFC research." Abby's eyes bugged out when she saw the amount—$137 million—a grant from the gods! Flipping over the note, she examined an elegant cursive script. It read: "Project *Orpheus*. Say nothing."

Secrecy seemed a fair price to pay. But who were these saviors? And how did they even know what had been running through her mind?

In the weeks that followed, once she had fully recovered, she received further instructions. A second envelope appeared. This one with detailed instructions. A lab had been prepared for her in the Nordics. She was to relocate immediately. Twenty-four hours later, she touched down on an isolated island in the North Sea. There she was greeted by a team of top physicists and engineers. She had heard of some, but others were as mysterious to her as she was to them. This was her team now, she was told. But why her? Over the course of three remarkable hours, the answer became clear.

It had taken years to achieve her dream, with many failures along the way. Now was the moment of truth. Abby took hold of the controls, activating the electromagnetic shield. The only thing protecting the crew from certain death was the compressed lining of the ship's walls. As the lights dimmed, she engaged the generator, which set off a whirring sound. It grew louder, and the craft began to shake—gently at first, then more violently. Abby stayed focused, trying to ignore the anxious expressions on the faces of her fellow crew members.

"Headsets!" she shouted, and everyone did as she commanded. Seconds later, a wallop and a whine—and, just like that, the *Orpheus* lifted off the ground, gently bobbing and turning, orienting itself in an electromagnetic field of its own making.

"Engage," said Abby, her voice coming clear and strong through the comms system. There was an eruption, and the *Orpheus* bounded backward, but then regained its center. By directing a shock wave at the wall before them, she blew a hole the size of a bus through it. She had half expected the chamber to fill with sea water, but it did not. Instead, it opened onto a cavern.

Crossing the threshold, the *Orpheus* dipped, then started to swivel. The size of the cavern forced the ship to adjust. Traversing the expanse in search of the opening to the catacombs would require care and precision. As the world's first EMFC-enabled earthcraft drifted forward, only one question remained for her: would it hold?

The feeling of being locked inside an electromagnetic flux pulsating within a 1,200-tesla-strong field is a difficult thing to describe. Contained within concentric layers of reinforced alloy, the crew of the *Orpheus* were sheltered from the fusion. All they felt was a gentle tingling. Like a current, it penetrated the ship's core and entered the body, an affable and virtually undetectable dose of free-flowing electrical impulse. It was mildly arousing, and not at all unpleasant. As if sensing what the others were feeling, Abby spoke up.

"Strange, isn't it?" Her voice sounded crisp and clear through the headsets.

"I could get used to this," moaned Spike.

"Enjoy it while you can. We're in hover mode. Once we pass through this sector and enter the catacombs, nothing will be quite the same."

As she spoke, the crew kept their eyes locked on the monitor. They could see the *Orpheus* skirting the outer walls. Abby tested the controls, turning and pivoting the ship, nudging the throttle forward then backward, like a kid in a hot rod pumping the accelerator and staring down an open road. She tried lurching the craft into the side walls, but the electromagnetic field kept the ship precisely centered in the long, sloping chamber. The floodlights offered eighteen to twenty meters of visibility, but not much more.

"There," she said, "just ahead." She flipped off the floodlights and a soft green glow accented the darkness stretching out in front of the ship.

"Whatever it is, it feels unnatural," said Philomena. "Over there!" she pointed.

Like mountains emerging from the mist, a subterranean landscape gradually appeared before them.

"Zalmoxis," said Otto. "You're looking at what's left of an ancient civilization. Indulge me, Dr. Clarke. Throttle forward, if you would be so kind."

Abby complied, and the *Orpheus* nosed forward. As it did so, the light grew brighter.

"There it is," announced Otto. "The source."

Looming up before them, like an egg thrust from the floor of the inner chamber, stood the source of the soft green light. It illuminated the entire chamber, hundreds of meters up and down, from side to side. From the smooth carved surface of this subterranean chamber sprang architectural wonders cut with sandalwood precision. In honeycomb fashion, hundreds of portals and doorways of every shape, size, and degree of ornamentation reached out to greet them. Running around and through them were elaborate waterways, cascading waterfalls, fountains, and reflection pools.

Spike moved forward to stand alongside Otto.

"I've seen this before," he said, in a whisper. "I thought it was just a dream. I know where it is."

"Where what is?" asked Abby.

"The opening... the way down."

Otto, who stood silhouetted against the viewing deck, large hands pressed against the glass, spun to face Spike.

"No one knows. Not even those who lived here!"

"Who in the name of God would live down here?" said Philomena. "There's nothing!"

"Nothing, you say?" challenged Otto.

"*You* lived here, didn't you?" she asked.

"If living is what you would call it."

"But how?" rejoined Abby. "Why?"

"Because he had no choice," said Spike. "Where are the others?" he asked.

A look of surprise burst across Otto's face.

"Well, well, well... it would appear our oil rigger has something more to offer than false bravado. What else do you see in that tormented mind of yours?" he asked, drawing close and tapping Spike's forehead with the tip of his boney finger.

With lightning response, Spike grabbed Otto's wrist and chicken-winged him into submission. He had the creature on his knees, holding him fast from behind. Applying pressure and bringing his mouth close to Otto's ear, he hissed "Don't you ever fucking touch me again."

Otto grimaced and Spike let go, shoving him away. After finding his way back upright, Otto turned and the crew braced for what would come next. But he only grinned.

"Now, was that necessary, Mr. Morrison? Do I threaten you?"

"I don't trust you," charged Spike.

"I was simply pointing out that you seemed to know things."

"I don't *know* anything. I just see things," he said, suddenly sounding less defensive.

"In good time, Mr. Morrison. In good time." said Otto. "But let's not spoil the mood, shall we? This is a moment of celebration, is it not?"

Otto drew himself up to his full height and searched the room.

"Carson, my good professor. This moment belongs to you. You've done it, you see. You've uncovered a great secret. This city and the catacombs that lead from it are the stuff of legend. If I were to tell you what lengths others have gone to in the hope of finding a way to Earth's core, you wouldn't believe me."

"You mean others have tried?" asked Abby.

"Tried and failed. Or so it is said."

"We won't fail," said Spike, who stood once more with his face pressed against the window, searching the light. The orb glowed bright before them, swirling with incandescence.

"That's it," he said. "Our way through."

CHAPTER 41

When Carson was fourteen years old, his life was upended. His father, a professor of philosophy at Wellesley College, had received a teaching grant from Loyola. They were to spend the summer packing, then make the drive to Chicago. This would mean no trip to Lake Winnipesaukee—where Carson could be alone to do what he loved most: fishing.

The annual trips to the family cottage were ritualistic. Each time they arrived, he would run for the shed, work the cast-iron latch, and throw back the door. Through dust and cobwebs, he would make his way to the back corner and find his two best friends: his fishing rod and tackle box. Every day thereafter was a reverie. On the water, he would silently guide the red cedar hull of the old canoe in and out of the inlets along the lakefront. He rarely saw other fishermen, even at the height of the season. Sometimes he would stay out after dark and pull in his line, nestle down into the center of the boat, use his life jacket as a pillow, and stare up into a sky flush with stars and distant galaxies. Carson saw his life unfolding that way, drifting on a vast body of water with only the heavens for company.

"No cabin this year, sport," he heard his father say. "Don't look so glum. Chicago's a new adventure."

The long drive and hours spent looking out at Lake Erie did little to lighten Carson's mood. He remained despondent and brooding throughout. The house provided by the university only made things worse. It was cramped and locked between narrow streets. Lake Michigan was only three blocks away, but there were no inlets and no forests—no nature at all—as far as he could tell. Only buildings and people. The summer was shaping up to be a disaster! Most days, he took to his room. He wasn't much of a reader, but in the absence of the great outdoors, books proved a kind of companion. One morning after breakfast, there was a knock on his bedroom door. He put his book down and braced for what came next.

"Come on, sport, I'm taking you on a trip to the cosmos. Grab your things. We're leaving in ten minutes," his father said, turning and exiting as quickly as he had come in.

The short drive along the lakefront felt like a taunt, and when they arrived at the Adler Planetarium, Carson was loaded with excuses for giving the Adler a miss.

"Looks like a tomb," Carson muttered under his breath as they mounted the long set of marble steps. The twelve-sided building crowned with its massive dome shimmered pink and gray in the mid-morning light. After heading through the front door and into the atrium, he stopped and gazed up at the hanging display of planets, each disproportional, from one to the next. His father went to the window and bought two tickets. While they waited for the show to begin, he wandered among the exhibits—"Our Solar System," then "Mission Moon," then "Through the Looking Glass"—moving clock-wise through each one. His father was up ahead, accosting a tour guide and peppering him with questions. Carson rolled his eyes and kept walking until he came to the final exhibit. Above the door were the words "There is No Plan(et) B: An Astronomer's Ode to Earth."

"Cute," he thought, passing into the darkened room. Though the museum was crowded that morning, here he was alone. It was dark. Too dark, he thought. Then, from the middle of the room, a faint glow. It revealed a sphere, turning gently. The light grew stronger and he saw a giant rendering of planet Earth, with its swirling montage of blues and greens. He approached, and as he did so, his movements triggered an audio track. "Welcome to planet Earth, our only known living planet." As the deep-toned voice proceeded to tell the story of Earth, large screens around the room offered syncopated images from its beginnings and over its lifecycle of 4.5 billion years. The display peeled away, revealing the different layers: the crust, mantle, and core.

In a flash, the vantage point shifted, and images of Earth from space were paraded before him. They had the intended effect. His vision turned blurry and, looking around to see if anyone was watching, he wiped away the tears. The exhibition faded out with footage of Earth's great achievements—its oceans, mountains, rivers, and forests. "Our only living planet," Carson whispered.

"Carson! Carson, you in here?"

He turned as the audio track ended and the lights grew bright.

"You all right?" his father asked. "Something wrong?"

"I'm good," replied Carson, brushing his hand once more across his eyes.

Up circular stairs, they moved to the second level, then through to a large domed room where a few dozen people were, at that moment, settling into comfy-looking recliners. They nudged their way past a young couple and took their seats. "Nice, eh?" said his father. Carson shrugged. But as the lights dimmed and a voice rose against the backdrop of music, he felt a lump form in his throat. His eyes were tearing up again. "What gives?" he thought to himself. After the next thirty minutes, his life would never again be the same.

The ship shuddered, almost violently, and Carson's childhood memory faded to black. No time for daydreaming. Through the dim light, he could see the electromagnetic pods floating and twirling in rhythm before him. The others—like him—were encased and moving in sync. The *Orpheus* was as battened down as much as possible, its outer layers synced and clasped tight, protecting the crew from the powerful rays that now sparked and reverberated across the surface of the ship. The image of a digital portal bobbed and swirled above them like a mystical halo. Beyond it, a thousand twists and turns would either lead them to their doom or their destination at the edge of the outer core.

All he had worked for came down to this very moment. Would the digital cartography that had been his life's work actually take them 500 leagues through rocky oxides and silicates? Would they survive? Or would it all end in misery? It was insane, really. They were moments away from catapulting themselves through a vast network of unexplored catacombs, powered by an electromagnetic charge strong enough to blow them apart. If the atmospheric pressure did not crush them, the impact would. You did not need a PhD to know that the odds of survival were not in their favor. Had he calculated the estimated response time to unseen or unmapped objects? Could they stop in time if a passageway was blocked? Carson's mind raced with everything that could possibly go wrong. There was still time. He could abort. "Wait!" he wanted to say. But it was too late. He could feel the *Orpheus* pulse with energy. The whir of the machine filled his ears, the headphones doing little to drown it out. His heart pounded. No time to panic, he thought to himself.

In a flash, the ship lurched forward. He fixed his gaze on the constellation of passageways that now filled the dome. No turning back now. He felt his nails dig into his palms. Though the ship vibrated wildly, he and the others were as cocooned and protected as possible. Like Alice down the rabbit hole, they were in free fall at one moment and redirected the next. Gravity and trajectory determined their pace and speed. Nothing more. The digital display of the catacombs before them was too terrible to watch and too enthralling not to. It was more than the human brain could process.

Whether it was the jarring of the ship, the rising atmospheric pressure, the visual overload, or a combination of everything, it all ended in blackout. The last thing Carson remembered was a blaring at his temples and a tightness in his chest. Despite his blurred vision, he could see the temperature in the sanctum spiking. Indicator lights up and down the control panel flashed red and green. Until now, it had all been theory. The catacombs, the *Orpheus*, the principles of electromagnetic travel. Now, though, scientist and subject were one. Fate or folly? It was the last thought he had before a burst of light, then the sudden onset of darkness.

Floating on the waters of creation, Carson dreamed the world into being. It began with a breath and a sigh. Time entered first, stretching out across the waters to the horizon and beyond. Then came sound. It started as a whisper, then it grew, branching out in layers until the hum of all things—living and dead—formed in the deep inner ear and in the reserves of a place called consciousness. A wind stirred for the first time, and the feeling of the breeze on skin made touch possible. Carson felt his body, supple and fluid. He waited... floating... sensing... eyes shut... breathing. He wondered "Am I dead? Is this death?" But the wind assured him: "Not dead. Just resting."

Through the lids of his closed eyes, he sensed the first rays of light, subtle and brooding—then expanding, bright and electric.

"Why can't I open my eyes?" he asked himself.

"Because you cannot see," came the reply.

"Help me see. I want to see." he pleaded.

"Not until you are ready?"

"And when will I be ready?"

"When time allows."

While the warm waters of creation lapped over his thighs and across his arms, he became aware. He was not floating unassisted. He was buoyed up, suspended. He felt the smooth, cool liquid gentle beneath him. With a slow, undulating, and sumptuous motion, it embraced him in silky smooth coils, powerful but not threatening. In this watery cradle, he felt his arms, limp by his side, rise and fall with the rhythm of the tides. He felt wave after wave lapping his body into life. With soft hands and delicate fingers, he reached for the cord that rose skyward from his belly. Somewhere above him came muted tones, in a rhythm of chanting. With his eyes still closed, Carson imagined a world like no other. In his mind's eye, he saw them forming—the oceans, mountains, rivers, and forests. He dreamed into existence a world he had always imagined—the world as it was meant to be.

"Why can't I move?"

"Why must you move?" the voice whispered.

"Am I dreaming?"

"What is dreaming?"

"Dreaming is imagining while asleep."

"Are you asleep?"

"No... I don't think so..."

"Then you must be imagining."

Carson felt for the familiar. A foothold in a timeless ocean. What had floating felt like at first? Perhaps the answer lay upon the lakes in his grandfather's canoe. And so he went there, to that place. He stretched his lithe body across the bottom, where the ribbed gunwales curved beneath him and the smell of sun-warmed earthworms filled his nostrils. He strained his ears and heard the gentle wisp of the wind as it brushed through the pines that marked the shoreline. He was adrift, moving farther out now, he thought. Soon it would be dark. His parents would be on the porch, looking out across the lake, waiting for him to return.

He lifted his eyelids ever so slightly, letting in a sliver of golden light. He imagined light as liquid, gently bathing his eyes in soft tones. He opened them further, and deep in the heavens, he saw the first signs of a starlit sky pulsing beyond a misty veil. It took him a few minutes to realize it was not the sky, but rather the domed ceiling of the *Orpheus*. He shifted his body and felt it gently float and readjust itself. He was still secure in his pod. An unhatched chick. Slowly he came to his senses.

"Hello," he ventured. "Can you hear me?" No reply. Like coming out of a deep sleep, his mind was groggy and his body was slow to respond, with a feeling of heaviness and lightness all at once.

"Hello," he said, a bit louder this time.

"Yes, yes, I'm here," came a voice.

Carson leaned forward, bringing himself into an upright position. There, as they had been at the beginning, were his fellow crew members, secure in their floating orbs. The *Orpheus* gently pulsated. It had survived. They had survived.

"Is everyone all right?" came Abby's welcomed voice. One after the other, the members of the crew responded.

"Where are we?" whispered Philomena. Only the faintest light illuminated the control room. The vibrant lights that had revealed the outline of the catacombs were all but extinguished.

"Go easy," said Abby. "Let's take a minute."

They all sat up.

"Oh, my stomach," complained Kai, who had never once experienced altitude sickness on any of his expeditions. This was different. He groaned and turned his head to find Abby staring back at him. Her face was not what he expected. She was ecstatic.

"My God, I think we've done it!" she cried.

"Done what?"

"Done the impossible. Carson, your map... your amazing, subterranean, muon-generating, labyrinth-detecting holograph... Holy Christ, I think it worked!"

"And what makes you so sure?"

"We wouldn't be talking now if it hadn't," she said, letting go a nervous laugh.

CHAPTER 42

Abby surveyed the room. Her pod parted and she floated from it, weightless. Gravity had no sway here. Pushing off and propelling herself from one orb to the next, she released each member, setting them adrift. Through the gangway, she led the way and the others floated along behind her. She started by reading out the ship's vitals. "Temperature: 59.44 degrees Celsius. Atmospheric pressure: 228 giga-pascals. Depth: 3,010 kilometers." The hull of the *Orpheus* had with-stood it all. They were alive—the ship was still functional.

Abby flipped the switch to allow the outer shell to retract, and as she did so, the light filtered through.

"A window onto a brave, new world," she said, shielding her eyes.

With hands pressed against the thick glass and feet floating out behind her, she leaned in, wide-eyed. The others followed her. It was a wondrous light. It broke at first from the apex of the ceiling, then spread out like a wing, flooding the control room with hues of green, yellow, and amber. It was brilliant and subtle all at once, an aurora of liquid light.

"Plasma," exclaimed Abby. "We've landed in an ocean of pure plasma. I knew it. I just knew it. It's a miracle. We're adrift, my friends, and moving through the outer core. No molten iron or nickel magma. Not in the least. Our best minds were wrong. We were right!"

Eyes open, hands pressed to the glass, it was impossible to say which way was down and which way was up. They were adrift, no doubt, caught up in the current of a borderless river. Tiny orbed objects like hand-blown glass floated alongside them. They danced and swayed with prism-perfect light. Captive rainbows.

"Like your green glowing ovoid... The one lighting your under-ground city," Abby said to Otto. "Thousands of them."

Abby pushed away from the dome and headed down to the control panel, hand over hand. She keyed in a few numbers, then returned to the dome, searching the fluid expanse that stretched out before them.

"There," she said. "Just off to the left." Sliding into the field of vision appeared the thick, silvery coat of Earth's outer core. It grew before their eyes, and it was hard to tell if it was moving toward them or they toward it.

"We are in orbit," said Abby. "Inner orbit. And that…" she pointed, "is our final destination."

"I don't understand," said Kai.

"That's your atom," she said, pointing at the outer core. "Or, as we hypothesized, it's the core functioning like an atom. Within its confines you'll find a swarm of subatomic activity. When one or more electrons tear free, they leave behind protons and neutrons. Those electron-free atoms are called ions. They are positively charged, and when commingled with negatively charged electrons, we get plasma. The core is producing plasma!"

"You knew this?" asked Carson.

"We hypothesized, yes," she replied. "What we know is this. Atoms are capable of ejecting electrons when subjected to some combination of intense heat, high energy, and electromagnetic fields. What you have before you," she said, pointing back to the sea of plasma that now surrounded the ship, "is the perfect mixture of charged particles and high-voltage electricity. Plasma, once created, establishes an ionosphere."

She reiterated: "We are in orbit, moving at nearly 2,455 kilometers per hour. Next stop, magnetic north."

As if on cue, a massive sphere a hundred times the size of the *Orpheus* revealed itself directly ahead. It loomed large, suspended in a great swirl of plasma. Like a ship skirting a rocky shore, the crew braced for impact. Collision seemed certain. Only Abby remained calm. The *Orpheus* suddenly shifted leeward and entered a slipstream that sent the vessel skimming over the deep, pockmarked surface. It was over in a flash. Magnetic north was seen trailing off behind them. Disaster averted.

"It moves within a magnetic field of its own making. It repels anything it comes in close contact with, the *Orpheus* included. Not too long from now, we'll see her mate. Magnetic south. These are the twin spheres that generate spin—Earth's engine room."

"Lord, have mercy," exclaimed Philomena. "So what of Hollow Earth?"

"I'm glad you asked," said Abby. She was on the verge of giddy.

"If we are right about this," she said, pointing to the ocean of plasma that swirled around them, "I have high hopes that our predictions of Hollow Earth will hold true. To find out, we need to navigate our way closer to the core, circumnavigate, then choose our moment. Timing is everything. We must be ready."

Abby floated across the room and gazed once more at the surroundings.

"You recall what I said about Earth's slowing rotation? Well, you might say we've just assumed a bird's-eye view. If our calculations are correct, we are approaching the reversal of the magnetic poles, which only happens once every 1,500 years. We believe there have been approximately 170 such reversals over the course of the Earth's 4.5-billion-year history. The time between these reversals has averaged 300,000 years. In geological terms, we are living in an age we refer to as the Brunhes Magnetic Chron—when the south magnetic pole is in the northern hemisphere and the north magnetic pole is in the southern hemisphere. For thousands of years, the Earth's magnetism has been trending toward zero, weakening at a rate of approximately five percent every hundred years. The slower the world turns, the weaker the Earth's magnetic force. We are at this moment suspended in the Earth's inner magnetic field—a field of plasma and electricity, stimulated and maintained by convection currents. All physical activity has conspired to adjust Earth's overarching gravitational field. The many "disappearances"—what our religious fanatics are calling "the rapture"—are the unintended, or perhaps intended, consequences of the pending reversal."

"And, let me guess, you plan to stop it?" quipped Spike.

"Not stop it, necessarily. But understand it, yes! We haven't come all this way for nothing. The answers lie there," she said, pointing again at the silvery crescent of the core that emerged through a mist of plasma-charged ions. It shimmered smooth, reflecting the liquid aurora.

"Is anyone else seeing a pattern here?" asked Spike. "Are you saying we're going to save the world by entering that core, to find God knows what, in order to 'understand' a phenomenon that happens once every 300,000 years that has people flying off the fucking planet at random? Are you out of your fucking mind?"

Abby flinched. She had been braced for this moment from the outset of the mission. She had the advantage of knowing—or at least believing—where they were headed. For the others, this was all new. Spike was angry, understandably. He and the others had a right to be. Her failing in that moment was in not seeing the absurdity of the situation through their eyes. For years, she had lived in a state of absolute reliance on mathematical formulations that pointed to the very real possibility that Earth's core was something far different from what classical theory had postulated. For them—in an instant—their long-held views about planet Earth had been upended. Not since Isaac Newton formulated the laws of motion and universal gravity more than 350 years ago had a discovery of such magnitude surfaced. The scientific repercussions were enormous, the practical and philosophical consequences even greater. Had they happened upon a new energy source? Could plasma signal the death knell for fossil fuels, once and for all? Tapping plasma would come with certain ecological conditions. "No more rote exploitation," thought Abby. "This time it would be different." Her mind was racing. "People might start to hope again," she ventured to herself.

"Are you even listening to me?" shouted Spike.

Abby suddenly realized her mind had drifted. "Of course," she said." I'm sorry. I see your point. We took risks."

"*Risks!* Now isn't that the biggest fucking understatement of the century?!"

Philomena reached out and laid her hand on Spike's arm. She sensed a pressure building up in him. He was seeing, perhaps, what the rest of them had not, or could not.

"What is it?" she asked.

"What do you mean?" he grumbled.

"You see something that we don't?"

"I see this whole goddamn situation for what it is. A fucking night-mare. Am I the only one who gets this? Don't the rest of you know what's coming next? Mark my words, it won't end well."

Something about the way Spike was behaving drew the crew toward him. Philomena persisted, her hand remaining gently on his arm.

"And what makes you say that?"

To the others, Spike looked wild-eyed and deranged. The snarky cynicism that served as his trademark had all but disappeared, replaced by fear.

"You keep talking about *timing*," he shouted, turning on Abby. "You scientists are so taken with your formulas and calculations. Did you factor in the time shift from the surface to the core? Do you not see that your so-called *timing* is going to get us killed? Why the hell am I telling you something you should know? How do I fucking even know this?"

Spike's words struck like arrows. The joy and confidence Abby had felt only moments earlier drained away.

"I... I... didn't consider..."

"You didn't consider... *you didn't fucking consider?!*" he shouted.

Philomena, keeping her hand on his arm, pivoted in midair and took Spike in a full embrace. He did not resist. Holding him—as a mother would a child—she felt his pain. He was still a boy—just 22 years old—and yet he carried within him the weight of countless tormented lives. She whispered.

"What do you see, Spike?"

"I see it all... the possibility... and everything in between."

Spike floated limp in Philomena's arms. He was spent. The fight drained out of him.

"He knows," he said, pointing dismissively at Otto and without lifting his head. "Ask him."

Abby floated across to come face to face with Otto, who wore at that moment an odd and sheepish grin.

"Is there something more you haven't told us?" she asked.

"Perhaps you've failed to ask the right question." he countered.

"Would you care to enlighten us, Dr. Trubolt?"

"If I must."

CHAPTER 43

Otto made his way to the spherical window that looked out over Earth's inner galaxy. His tall, dark figure was floating and turning before them, framed in cosmic light. The long tails of his trench coat slowly undulated—dark wings made for hovering. He withdrew his hands from the pockets and gestured to the sea of plasma. With his back to them, he began to speak.

"Another force is at play here. A dark force. All the mysteries of our universe are in front of you, in what you, Dr. Clarke, have correctly identified as our planet's inner ionosphere. For generations, our greatest scientists, astronomers, and astrophysicists have looked to the heavens for the answers. Yet all the while, the truth of it all lay here, deep in the bowels of planet Earth. It is in this place that we will put our greatest theories to the test. No more hypothesizing about whether the universe bends. No more high-browed theories about interplanetary gravitational forces. All that *can* be known *will* be known. Today marks the beginning of a scientific renaissance, and we are all—willing or not—party to it. I told you when we met that I was in search of dark matter. You assumed, in your elementary fashion, that I meant among the heavens. How wrong you were. I meant here. Or rather there," he said, pointing at the core. "At the center. A hermetically sealed repository of the elemental forces that created our great universe. So you see, Dr. Clarke, I believe there is more. Much more."

Abby, having just convinced herself of the reliable accuracy of her calculations and the prospect that their next discovery would prove true as well, was taken aback. "Not Hollow Earth?" she ventured.

"No. Something far more powerful and deeply tantalizing."

Abby recoiled as Otto shot her a broad, crooked smile. He had regained control of the narrative, and he knew it. "Look about you, friends. Our journey continues. Vasco de Gama, Christopher Columbus,

Marco Polo—names that will fade and be forgotten, pioneers of lesser discoveries. But dark matter? It's a new world of a whole new dimension. Generations from now, *Otto Trubolt* is the name they will remember."

Spike had heard enough. "Hey, Adonis, snap out of it. We're trapped 3,000 kilometers below the surface and playing a high-stakes game of pinball with two moon-sized magnets. Plan your ticker-tape parade later. What are we going to do now?"

Philomena laughed.

"Mock me if you will, oil rigger, but you're way out of your depth."

"You arrogant bastard." Spike launched himself at Otto, but in a zero-gravity environment, the gesture was futile. The effort, instead, made his head spin.

"Yes, Mr. Morrison, the pressure grows here, does it not? I've learned to live with it. Can you?"

Philomena floated forward, pulling Spike close and cradling him in midair. The gesture was both awkward and reassuring at the same time.

"Shall I continue?" proffered Otto.

"Please do," said Abby.

The interruption from Spike had rattled him, but he composed himself once more.

"What none of you understand is that this search has been ongoing for longer than any of you could possibly imagine. Centuries have come and gone. You were not the first to discover that our planet held great secrets. If you knew your own history, you'd know that without us none of this would have been possible. Why my forefathers trusted you, I'll never know. They gave you everything. Shared it all. And for what? To be consigned to life underground. Separated from the world and the things they loved..."

"What in God's name are you talking about?" interrupted Kai.

"I'm talking about what your kind did to my kind."

"Your kind?"

"The *Nephilim*," snapped Otto.

Everyone in the control room fell silent.

"Ah yes, I can see that some of you have heard of us."

"Fallen angels," said Philomena.

"Captured more than fallen, I'd say. Consigned beneath the surface for more time than I care to recall. But we are not to be kept down. We are a resilient lot. Some thought us dead and gone. But how can you kill something that cannot die?"

"You're talking nonsense," said Carson. "That's nothing but Old Testament mumbo jumbo. There's no evidence."

"No evidence, you say?" Otto pivoted in midair. "What sayest Enoch? Anything you'd care to add? I'm rather curious, myself. Oh yes, I know who you are. It was only a matter of time before our paths crossed, and now here we are, at the center of all things."

Enoch pushed himself forward and the crew parted to let him pass. He slowly circled Otto to again come face to face with him.

"I do remember you, but you are not the boy you once were."

"Nor are you, dear cousin," growled Otto.

"Cousin?" questioned Abby.

Otto's expression darkened. He held Enoch with his eyes.

"Cousins," he scoffed. "How quaint. I and the others knew him only as the Twenty-first. Isn't that right, Enoch? Or has time eroded your memory? I—for one—have forgotten nothing!"

"You are Ohyah. Son of Samyaza. Are you not?" asked Enoch. "Or are you Hahya?"

"That was the name of my twin brother," snapped Otto.

"Where is he? Where are the others?"

"All of them, gone! Along with the name Ohyah. I vowed never to use my Nephilim name again. That life is lost to me."

The memory appeared to suddenly fatigue him, and he floated his tall frame back down into the chair. Cupping his hands and pressing his forefingers to his thin, white lips, he closed his eyes, as if he were trying not to remember, but to forget. Moments passed, then quietly, at first, the one once known as Ohyah began to speak.

"Did you think we had all perished? Do you find it hard to believe that some of us—or at least one of us—survived?"

"All I know, I know from the brethren," hissed Enoch.

"Ah, yes, the brethren... *Cowards!* That's what they are. They left us to rot, but of course, you know all about that, don't you, son of Azazel?"

"Brethren? Azazel? What's going on here? Someone needs to explain," Abby chimed in.

243

Otto barely stirred. He let his gaze fall full on Enoch, who floated before him, somber and tight-lipped.

"Shall I begin, or would you prefer to enlighten our friends? Although I dare say our two tellings will most certainly differ.

"Be my guest," said Enoch.

"Remember me or not. It matters little. But I was there that day. And so were you, you self-righteous traitor. I might add that when the tomb was sealed, I stood among them. Your father assured us it was the only way. Had we known what horrible suffering would follow, none of us would have agreed to dwell in darkness throughout the ages.

"What do you mean by 'the ages'?" asked Philomena.

"I'm talking about thousands of years, Ms. Pettibone. We are of Nephilim stock, he and I. Although, as you can see, time has treated one of us more kindly."

"So, you..."

"Yes, Mr. Morrison. My appearance is not quite human for a reason. Then again, under different circumstances, had I not spent the lion's share of my existence underground, he and I would not look so dissimilar. This is what a lifetime of subterranean dwelling will do to a carbon-based creature."

"I did it to save you... All of you!" When Enoch spoke, his voice emerged thinner and softer than intended.

"Ah, so you see yourself as a savior?"

"Nothing of the kind."

"How about the moment you shut us off from the only world we'd known, drawing the great stone over us and leaving us to rot?"

"Say what you will. I know the truth of it, as do you."

"Then pray tell, dear cousin, what prevented you from retrieving us as you promised?"

"Circumstances changed. I had no choice."

"What the hell is going on here?" shouted Spike. "Some kind of family feud? Personally, I don't give a shit. In case you haven't noticed, we're floating in a pool of plasma and circling the drain. How 'bout we focus on that."

"I tend to agree with you," said Abby. "But if this story has some bearing on our mission, then we need to know, and we need to know now!"

"Very well, Dr. Clarke. You want the whole story? Then let's start at the beginning with the Great Flood. Or perhaps we should call it the Great Ruse. More a diversion than a flood. Would you agree, cousin?"

Enoch cringed. This long-lost relative had him in his grips now. The memory and the guilt that came with it washed over him. Enoch bowed his head and quietly listened. To him, it was an old story. For the others, it was a tale entirely new and unexpected. As Otto continued, he let go the sides of the chair, allowing his body to float upward.

"A divine act, they called it. The lands were to be flooded, wiping away all evidence that we ever existed. The only thing left standing was the temple itself—the structure built by our hands. And for what purpose? To conceal the truth. But there I go, telling you things that might be better told by Enoch. Let me instead tell you what life was like on the other side... beneath the surface... hidden away for all eternity.

"The wrath of the One is a powerful motivator. So we went down, interning ourselves beneath the Temple Mount. It was only temporary. Or so we were told. We descended, leaving only one of us behind— the 'chosen one.' He would be protected, safeguarded by our creator, and kept from harm until such time that we might be retrieved." Otto glared at Enoch. "Life underground is cruel. Darkness brings despair, and despair brings sickness and disease. The women—our mothers— were the first to go. One after the other, they died wretched deaths. For the rest of us, immortality felt like a curse... Oh, did I fail to mention this? How foolish of me, and yet how central to the plot."

Otto let the idea settle with his listeners. The expressions on their silly human faces had a way of exciting him, so he continued.

"Where was I? Ah, yes, our subterranean existence. As months turned to years, we lost faith. Our liberator..." he paused, looking at Enoch, "never came for us. We were motherless and had only The Twenty to look up to. Pitiful excuses for fathers, they were. We were trapped, so it seemed, in a purgatory. No way to return to the surface, and nowhere to go farther down.

"Then we discovered the catacombs. Yes, Dr. Spinoza, we found them first. And through them, we felt our way into the Earth and she shared with us her secrets. In darkness, you might say, we found our way. We learned through touch and smell to blend with Earth's elements, drawing on our alchemist instincts. In such ways, we sparked some life into our hapless existence, and with time and patience we found ways to bind elements to generate heat, extract nutrients, and concoct treatments for the kinds of horrid illnesses that are borne in a lightless world. In other words, we *adapted*.

"Over those long years, we became unrecognizable from the tall and powerful surface dwellers that we once were. Yes, look at me now. A product of the underworld. Quite the contrast to my dear cousin here. Life among humans has been good to you, has it not?"

Enoch remained silent. There was nothing he could say. Layer by layer, the travesties that had been suffered by the Nephilim were laid bare. He, Enoch, was the villain in Otto's story. But this was neither the time nor the place to confront the grudge that this long-lost cousin held against him.

The crew stared at Enoch, waiting for him to respond. When he did not, Otto continued.

"I, on the other hand, have fallen into what one might call a state of disrepair. Appearances mean nothing in dark places. Over time, we came to accept our fate. I dare say, we turned our attentions elsewhere... to the unexplored depths. Then, a great discovery..."

Otto had the crew's full attention. Despite the horridness of the tale, he was beginning to enjoy the telling of it.

"Knowledge of a life-giving force from far below. It happened quite by accident, delivered up through one of the many magma pools that made our lives miserable, belching their flesh-burning toxins. The scalding of the lungs—even for an immortal—is a hideous affair. Then chipping away at a solidified mass one day, we discovered something quite extraordinary. It stood blocking one of the main passageways, eight meters high. A most wondrous thing."

"What was it?" Philomena asked.

Otto's eyes flew open. "Light. Beautiful, blinding light—painful to the eyes, at first, but worth the suffering. It was intoxicating and mysterious. An ovoid from the depths with its green swirling light. It was both a blessing and a curse. Until that day, we had been united in all things. No more, after that. A great debate ensued. Some saw it as a sign from the One. Perhaps we had not been forgotten. I thought the notion of divine intervention foolish and made my position known. I would have nothing to do with it. While my brothers and cousins went chasing after a dream, I joined with The Twenty, who saw the light as a gift—a way to make life better somehow. We set about learning to harness its power, allowing small slivers of incandescence through at first. Can you imagine, for a moment, what that can do to the mind—to live in darkness for so long, then once more see all that can be revealed? We learned to channel the light, directing it into the great underground canyons, where little by little we began to fashion a new way of life.

"How can I describe the joy of sight regained? Time had been cruel—deformities, adaptations, call them what you want. Our bodies had been degraded. We had become little more than bipedal moles, scurrying through passageways and hunting for food—living almost entirely by touch and smell. Sheer endurance. The orb and its inner light proved transformational for us. For the first time in countless decades, some semblance of joy was restored to us. We began to hope and dream again. It was a great awakening for our kind, or, at least, for some of us.

"For centuries thereafter, we lived by the light of that magnificent object. We counted cycles of time by the moments when we covered and uncovered that great object, creating our own days and nights. While The Twenty and I worked to make what living improvements we could, the others occupied their time by sending reconnaissance teams down to the depths. As time passed, my brothers, sisters, and cousins began to disappear. Soon," said Otto, narrowing his gaze and looking directly at Enoch, "The Twenty and I were all who were left. Indeed, they began to refer to *me* as the Twenty-first."

Otto was relentless. Thousands of years of his suffering were now being directed at Enoch. This was payback. The crew looked on, but Enoch refused to give his cousin the satisfaction of knowing how he too had suffered all those years, working feverishly to keep the hopes and dreams of the Nephilim alive.

"You have all seen what is left of our lost kingdom," Otto reminded them. "A mere shadow of its former self. But there was a time when it rivaled the planet's great cities. In its construction, the Nephilim proved once more their mastery in applied ingenuity. By pooling our collective knowledge in engineering, metallurgy, and alchemy, we were able to produce the architectural wonder that would come to be known as *Zalmoxis*, the Dark City. To control the flash floods and lava eruptions that tormented our ranks, we constructed elaborate aqueducts and catchments, gifting our community with hydropower, which turned the wheels of progress. Had it not been for the infatuation with our divine mission, more of my kind might have come to appreciate our achievements. Instead, our numbers dwindled. Over time, only myself and The Twenty remained, and then they too left.

"Left for where?" asked Kai.

"For the surface, of course."

"They returned?"

"That was always the plan."

"And what about you?" asked Philomena, drawing close to Otto, her eyes searching for the truth of the matter.

The creature's features darkened.

"I serve no one and no thing. My work is my mission and that's all you need know. It was my choice to remain down below. And except for a very brief period on the surface, I have dwelled in darkness, seen the light, remained a slave to my charge, and honored my quest for dark matter. For too long, perhaps, I held on to the possibility that some who journeyed below would return. They never did. I am the last of my generation. With the exception, that is, of one other."

Otto offered only a slight nod and the others turned to look at Enoch, who had retreated into the shadows at the edge of the control room, waiting patiently for the tale to end.

"Anything you'd like to add, cousin? Does my telling of our kind please you?"

"There's nothing pleasing about it."

"You have no idea."

Abby looked at Enoch and spoke. "Why the deception? Are you who he says you are?"

"I am," he confessed.

"And are you in concert with this creature?"

"I am not."

"Then why are you here?"

"To do what I can. Before it's too late."

"Maybe I missed something," said Spike, "but if what this freak here says is true, life as *we* know it is not life as *you* know it. When I'm dead, I'm dead. How about you?"

"There is truth in it. Call it a blessing or a curse, my life is a continuum. But I am not like him. We seek the same things, but not for the same reasons."

"I don't know who the hell to believe," snapped Kai. "I don't even know what I'm doing here."

"You're here because I need you to be here!" cried Abby. "You know about the Arctic passage. Your work points to it."

"That was a long time ago, Abby. A lot has changed... I've changed."

"The only thing that's changed is our circumstances. We do this together, or we don't do it at all. Together, I know, we can find our way back to the surface."

"Big assumption," chided Spike. "Isn't there still the small question of Hollow Earth? What if it's not as hollow as you hope?"

Otto read the room and said what he knew they were all thinking.

"Then all of you will die."

Chapter 44

When Abby finally found Kai, he was drifting about in the cargo bay, taking inventory and checking the crates of lab equipment that would be used to collect samples, assuming they arrived at Earth's core as planned.

"Old habit," he said. "Best to be prepared. Although, if we've forgotten something, I guess there's no going back for it."

She smiled and floated into his arms.

"I'm sorry," she said.

"Sorry for what?"

"For putting you through this."

"I've been through worse," he said with a pained smile.

Abby held him by the collar of his jacket and pulled him close, pressing her lips against his. Kai felt the angst well up inside him for every day they had been apart. He had been carrying it for so long. For years, it seemed like everything he cared about had simply disappeared. Knowing she was alive restored some hope. But his confidence in himself had long since perished.

"I'm a fraud, Abby. I'm not what you think I am. There was a time when, perhaps, I was onto something. But the world has moved on. I've failed more times than I'd like to recall. The Everest expeditions were just a way to cover up for all the loss—a way of surviving, of proving to myself that I wasn't an imposter. Then I lost the world's biggest CEO and got caught crying about it at 9,000 meters."

"Imposter?! What in God's name are you talking about? You're the most brilliant man I've ever known. Your research was ahead of its time. You had instinct, Kai. Beyond the reconnaissance, the measurements, and the math, you knew the tunnels existed—a passageway to Earth's core."

"Just a theory," whispered Kai. "Nothing more."

"Oh, but it is more... so much more."

"What aren't you telling me?"

"I'm not telling you anything you don't already know—it's our way out."

"Why wasn't it our way in? Why through the maelstrom?"

"The aquifers. The water tables. They're falling everywhere. You recall what I said the night we were reunited. Our research shows that water is rushing back to the Earth's core. But the reverse is true in the Antarctic. The tables there are rising. The pressure is building. It's as if the world's water supply is being rerouted, from the core outward."

"Are you kidding?"

"No. God no. Why would I kid about something like this? If our calculations are right, and we make it to the core, I think we'll find the place from where the pressure is building. Think of it as our quintessential search for the source of the Nile. It's hidden. But we'll find it. Together, we'll find it!"

CHAPTER 45

Avon caressed the contours of his corpulent belly, letting his hands roam in two large concentric circles. He moved his hands down and around, then up through the middle, repeating the motion and adjusting the pressure. He lay folded in the soft plush cushions of the red couch that sat at the center of his ample living room. He wore only black silk boxers and a grin on his face.

He had done it again—eaten too much. In the weeks since giving his heralded sermon, only his weight had risen faster than his fame. Corpulence, he reasoned, equated to *gravitas*. He had his followers where he wanted them, enmeshed in his echo chamber. The full weight of his social media presence was brought to bear, and wherever one turned, there was no escaping the promulgations of the good Reverend Avon Caulfield. He was the news. From Al Jazeera to Fox, everyone was talking about Avon and his prophecy. From the couch, Avon gazed up at the flat-screen TV mounted above the fireplace, relishing his most recent talk show performance.

"Armageddon! Is that what you're telling us?" challenged the interviewer.

"Are you blind to God's will? Do you need to be told what you yourself already know to be true?" came Avon's well-rehearsed reply.

Answering a question with another question was one of the tricks of his trade. Lying on the couch, he reveled in the interviewer's exasperation. "Got 'em tied round my little finger," he chuckled.

Events had conspired to reinforce the weight of Avon's message. 24/7 news feeds told of economic collapse, natural disasters, and plague. The world was sputtering into a state of chaos—all to plan. The chairman had told him what would come next and, true to his word, it happened as he said it would. The global shutdown of oil production was the first step. As expected, the markets responded with panic, precipitating a banking crisis in turn. Lending dried up and businesses lost confidence. Manufacturing ground to a halt, which meant shortages in everything from food to footwear. That caused public alarm, leading to riots and looting. Governments were overwhelmed, and as their services collapsed, people fled cities. Vigilante groups sprung up and formed their own small armies. The pandemic wasn't helping. Hospitals were filled to capacity and medical supplies were in short supply. People were dying and trust in the institutions that once served them had vanished. The world was turning paranoid, with fear of "the other" informing the ways in which communities made their decisions and struggled to survive. In a word, everything was chaos.

Throughout it all, people kept disappearing—carried off, as it were, by a gravitational anomaly that no one could explain. News agencies pounced on it and paraded, each morning, the numbers of those who had gone missing due to these inexplicable and recurring events. Scientists remained dumbfounded, opening the way for more supernatural explanations. That's where Avon came in—and the media ate it up.

Indeed, the Council had provided him with his own private jet, a new wardrobe, and enough talking points to keep him fresh and punchy for weeks on end. Avon's own media empire rode the wave, mastering the art of social media manipulation, but the impact of his own efforts paled in comparison to the Council's intelligence and communiqués. They knew what would happen *before* it happened. Their ability to predict events with such precision terrified Avon. But he was all in now. Without them, he would be unable to present himself to the press and the public as the prophet he professed to be. The chairman had remained true to his word. As long as Avon played along, all would be right. He came to believe that the Council was more powerful than anything he might have imagined. Their influence was unparalleled, and their pockets ran deep. They had a chokehold on the global economy, and it was the Council that would determine the future, not governments. The time of the nation state was ending. What might emerge from the ashes was anyone's guess. Global turmoil was Avon's cauldron. As long as he kept stirring, reason would not stick. He had faith in the Council and their sphere of influence. But even they could not—or would not—explain the thousands of disappearances that grew by the day. The rapture was the ideal ruse, a cover-up for the inexplicable. Yet the fact that even the Council seemed flummoxed by these events made him strangely uncomfortable. "Was this a case of divine intervention?" wondered Avon. The very idea made him question his faith.

While lying on the big couch, rubbing his belly and thinking about all that had conspired, he suddenly felt fatigued. A ruse, he decided, required a lot of effort and energy. Reaching for the remote, he flipped through the channels. Try as he might, it was difficult to avoid his own image. Occasionally, a rival popped up, some backwater preacher pushing his own brand of fire and brimstone. But they had nothing on him. Try as they might, they would never have what he had—the Council.

Just then, the doorbell rang. Avon grunted as he lifted himself off the couch and pulled on the black silk robe with his bright red monogrammed initials. He belched and rubbed his stomach again as he made his way across the living room and into the foyer, with its spiraling staircase leading to a suite of bed chambers. He felt himself harden as he reached for the door.

"My Lord, what a heavenly vision," he crooned.

"Thought you'd never answer," said the one.

"You gonna ask us in?" asked the other.

They were hardly distinguishable from one another. The Good Sisters, as they liked to be known, had perfected the art of the entrance. Avon stood aside and let the two women glide across the threshold. They said nothing as they mounted the staircase, sauntering their way up in perfect rhythm, letting their long jackets slip from their shoulders like snakes shedding their skin. They glistened. "Naked perfection," thought Avon, his robe wet with perspiration.

In the foyer, he heard his voice emanating from TV sets throughout the house.

From the living room: "Sinners take heed. God is merciful but only to those who bow before him."

From the study: "Know thy place. Make your confessions."

And from the kitchen: "They go by the name of The Twenty. They are the fallen. And they have returned to complete their work. We are the army of God, and we will not be put asunder!"

Man versus Nephilim, an age-old narrative, the ultimate battle, unearthed once more. It was genius. Why create a new narrative when the old one would do? It was embedded, was it not? Drilled deep into the human psyche from time immemorial. The Council, Avon came to understand, had a knack for weaving a good tale. No amount of wealth or political influence could rival the power of a great story. It made Avon's social media manipulations look like child's play.

"We write the script. You deliver it!" instructed the chairman. Avon knew his place. He was a tool, a single cog in the Council's machinery. He would play his part and retreat with the spoils—two of whom now waited for him in the bedroom above. Dropping his robe, he made for the stairway. Grabbing the railing, he gasped and roiled his way to the top. He would return to the pulpit tomorrow. Tonight, however, he had other plans.

Chapter 46

The chairman was careful to only feed Avon on a need-to-know basis. He was important, but by no means central to their plan. Events had not unfolded as expected. The Council was in reaction mode now. Maybe they had placed too much faith in Otto. Perhaps they should have paid more attention to competing forces. And then, of course, there was the matter of the planet's demise.

Otto and the Council—they were the leading experts, or so they believed, and in a league of their own. They had learned over the years to read the planet and interpret its signs. Their plan had been to go it alone from the start. Reaching the core and extracting its secrets would be justification for all their efforts and contrivances to date. At no point had they anticipated the need to join forces with anyone, most certainly not with a group of amateur explorers. And yet, quite unexpectedly, there they were—worthy rivals aided by an earthcraft that exceeded anything the Council might have conceived of.

The *Orpheus* was a miraculous accomplishment. At no point did the Council even consider the possibility of designing a ship to carry a manned crew. Drilling seemed a more practical approach. The ship's inventor, Abigail Clarke, had entirely escaped their attention. She came out of nowhere, reemerging after a decade, supposedly dead from a climbing accident in Antarctica. Clearly it had been the intention of this rival group to keep her work a secret. Her backers understood the importance of concealment. Who were they, the chairman wondered? And why had they selected a relatively unknown theoretical physicist to lead a mission of such existential importance? It was disquieting to think that another secret society existed with resources and insights to rival their own. The Council had served as Earth's helmsman throughout history. Who dared challenge what was God-given? For it was written: "*Let them have dominion over the fish of the sea, and over the birds of the air, and over the cattle, and over all the wild animals of the earth, and over every creeping thing that creeps upon the earth.*" Genesis 1:26–28. The Council had remained guardians of that divine promise.

Clearly, this rival had knowledge of their existence. It was unsettling. They were the ones who had always done the watching. It felt unnatural to be watched. These others, they had knowledge. They knew enough to land the *Orpheus* at the gateway to Zalmoxis. What else did they know? Was it Otto they wanted? Did he possess the knowledge they required to complete their mission? Were they after the same thing? If so, there was more at stake than the mere preservation of the planet.

Such were the thoughts that plagued the chairman's mind. The smokescreen of fabricated distractions was less of a concern now than the very real possibility that someone else had a means of penetrating the core. It had been the eternal mission of the Council to arrive at the center of all things. Only then might they discover, once and for all, the very source of their existence.

From one generation to the next, each Council chairman had played his part. Everyone who served was imbued with knowledge and possessed a unique skill to ensure that, with time and planning, they would prevail in retaining control. The only thing they had not anticipated was the rate at which the planet was collapsing. At first, they scoffed at the idea that their own activities had perpetuated the problem. The Industrial Revolution had been central in funding their endeavors. But no one had anticipated the degree of destruction that was necessary to achieve their ends. Now the race was on. Environmental degradation, melting ice caps, and global warming were all causes for concern. But in the Council's view, they were momentarily expendable, and not entirely irreversible. The gravitational anomalies, however—now *those* were unexpected. They were also inexplicable. They made the need to successfully arrive at the core all the more urgent. Otto, whose research to date had remained inconclusive, insisted that only at the planet's center would he be able to prove his thesis correct.

The chairman could only assume that the crew of the *Orpheus* were equally aware of the situation. In university and government research centers around the world, geophysicists were scrambling to come up with a meaningful explanation as to why people were disappearing from the surface of the planet. Sooner or later, he conjectured, someone would figure it out.

The chairman hated uncertainty. It made him uneasy. All he and the others could do now was wait. Their agent, Otto, had talked himself onto the *Orpheus*. They had to believe he would find a way.

There had been no communication since the ship disappeared into the catacombs. Had the *Orpheus* survived? Patience, he reminded himself. They could wait. There was always time.

CHAPTER 47

Caught in the current of the inner ionosphere, the crew found themselves in a state of animated suspension. They had beaten the odds to come this far. But now there was a new twist. Otto's revelation and his indictment of Enoch left the crew wondering if they were mere pawns in a bigger game. Abby had doubts as well. Until then, she had had every confidence in her benefactors. They had gotten them this far, after all. Sending an "observer" to join the crew at the eleventh hour felt strange, but she had full trust in them. Now, she was less sure.

As she and the others milled about the control room, moving between screens and reworking their calculations for the next stage of the mission, they kept their distance from Enoch, gravitating toward Otto, instead. Something in his tale of suffering had made him more human, more approachable. In different circumstances, discovering that a species of immortals had dwelled for centuries beneath the Earth's surface might have been cause for cognitive dissonance. Yet, over the last forty-eight hours, the crew had conquered a downward-spiraling maelstrom, discovered a lost subterranean city, penetrated the Earth's mantle, landed in a sea of plasma, and were now circumnavigating the Earth's core at nearly 2,500 kilometers per hour. By comparison, the notion of immortality seemed almost... normal.

Abby caught herself staring at Enoch from across the room. He looked distracted. He was fidgeting and appeared lost in thought. She could only imagine what was going through his head. He was here for a reason, she assured herself. There was some connection—but what? He was more than a mere observer.

Just then, the *Orpheus* shuddered. Abby snapped back to attention. The entire bridge had been struck by something that felt like an electromagnetic charge. The control panel lit up, flashing red and yellow.

"What's happening?" shouted Carson.

Abby lunged for her chair and, wheeling around, began punching in commands, hoping to put a stop to the incessant shaking.

"Dear God!" screamed Philomena, staring past the viewing deck into the rainbow world beyond.

Plastered against the glass were creatures unlike anything they had ever seen before. They were covered in a sleek red incandescent film that partly disguised their elongated heads, accented by two wide and bulbous eyes of black. They were humanoid, with extensions that might have served as arms and legs in a less fluid environment. Large separations along their necks and sides pulsated in a gill-like manner. Two dozen or more of them twirled frantically, like fish in a pond, making it difficult to say just how many there were. As the crew looked on, the creatures kept circling around, attaching themselves to the hull, then letting go when they found themselves overpowered by the force of the currents. The tormented expressions on their contorted faces only added to the confusion. Were they attacking the ship or trying to warn them?

"Help them!" cried Philomena, looking deep into their suffering eyes.

Otto moved close, pressing his face against the glass. One of the creatures returned the gesture. They were separated by only a few inches of clear composite.

"No one can help them," whispered Otto. "Now I know it's true."

"What's true?" begged Philomena. "What are you talking about?"

"They survived!"

"Who survived?"

"My kin."

During the days of the Great Divide, Otto refused to take sides. His attention was focused entirely on Zalmoxis. The underworld city had become, over the years, the object of his efforts and affections. It was a thing of beauty, as functional as it was sublime. And it was in this mix that he found a sense of purpose. The city had been fashioned from solid rock, carved away piece by piece, encasing the two-ton orb that swam with the green inner glow of liquid plasma.

The ovoid in their midst constituted the inflection point that took Otto and the others from a place of darkness and despair to one of light and promise. So fundamental was the ovoid as a symbol of their new beginning that it was decided that a city should be built around it, radiating out in concentric layers, ensuring that as the city grew, its borders would remain completely equidistant from the orb itself. That way, it could never be said that any member of the community had less access to its light than another. A new taxonomy emerged, giving way to a new way of thinking. For Otto, it was a license to invent.

Under the patronage of The Twenty, each member of the burgeoning community discovered a skill or passion and put it to work. In so doing, the ingenuity of the Nephilim was rekindled. From nothing, Zalmoxis emerged. Its edifices were to the city what a skeleton is to the body. The waterworks that underpinned the whole structure pumped life around the place, serving as its primary source of energy. All of this took time to build, of course: 228 years, 8 months, 2 weeks, 6 days, and 14 hours, to be exact. The boundaries of the metropolis were determined by the limitations of the orb's luminescence.

The completion of their underworld city should have been cause for celebration. Instead, it marked the beginning of what would come to be known as the Great Divide. No sooner had they set down their tools to admire their great accomplishment than the first of many disagreements broke out. Initially, it appeared to be nothing more than an intergenerational squabble. Life underground had had little effect on The Twenty. With so many years spent in the Upper Realm as well as in pursuit of knowledge, they understood that life was long and that circumstances, over time, would change. Their offspring— half-human, half-immortal—felt differently. Underworld internment proved hellish. If returning to the surface remained an impossibility for the foreseeable future, they reasoned, they would seek their salvation in the depths below, carving out a new frontier.

In defiance of The Twenty, these sons and daughters formed scouting parties. In groups of ten or more, they journeyed deep into the catacombs to search for a way through to a new world. If the light-giving orb was any indication, the planet's core most certainly had more to offer.

"This," whispered Otto, gesturing to the wild-eyed creatures beyond the viewing deck, "is what became of them."

Otto folded his arms and bowed his head.

"Nowhere to go, no way to escape. Death would have been kinder."

Otto panned the room to see the incredulous looks from the crew of the *Orpheus*, trying to make sense of it all. "Simple bastards," he thought to himself.

"You couldn't have known they would end up like this," said Kai.

"They were fanatics. Nothing good comes from that. They chose their path. I chose mine."

"What became of The Twenty?" asked Carson.

"For centuries, I went about my business and they went about theirs. Later, they came to me, saying it was time to go. "Go where?" I asked. "Back to the surface," they told me. At long last, they had found a way out, far from the reaches of Giza. They asked—only once—if I would come with them. I wanted no part of it. My life was Zalmoxis. More than a century would pass before I decided to follow. The way back was not easy. But eventually I broke through, up into a world bathed in light. It was almost more than I could bear. Can you imagine the sensory overload? Life was amplified, deafening at first. I could hear it all and all at once. On that first night, I sat for hours in a field, hands clasped over my ears, struggling to process everything. I nearly went mad. Eventually, I adjusted and set out in search of answers. If there had been a Great Flood, there was no evidence of it. Or perhaps the Earth had long since healed herself. So much color and abundance. Zalmoxis was a masterpiece. But when compared to life on the surface, my city lost its shimmer.

I traveled by night and disguised myself as best I could. People, I learned, were naturally distrustful. They were particularly wary of strangers, and I would have appeared most strange. I had questions that needed answering, so I made my way to what they called "a place of higher learning." A university. There, deep in the stacks of the library, I lived as a recluse. My appearance alone kept people away. Without distraction, I taught myself to read. Books were as mysterious to me as the cosmos itself. Eventually, I drifted into the field of theoretical physics. It unlocked the language I needed to give expression to my suspicions about the Earth and her hidden mysteries. At the university, they had a name for it. They called it 'dark matter.' The rest you know."

Otto took a deep breath and let out a sigh that sounded more like a moan. He looked haggard, as if all those years of suffering had suddenly caught up with him.

"Those creatures," he said, pointing back across the group and out into the plasma, "they are what remain of my kind—a lost generation. Captives of their own folly. If we could only communicate. Imagine what they might tell us."

"I don't know what to say," offered Abby. "Are they the reason you're here?"

"In part, yes."

"But there's something more, isn't there?" she asked. "What aren't you telling us?"

"I've told you quite enough already. I need to think now. I ask that you leave me alone."

Not waiting for a reply, Otto spun, then kicked his way to the portal that led to the pods.

Once he left the control room, the rest of the crew peeled away as well, most retreating to their pods to sleep and dream and wait for the moment when Abby called them back to complete the last stage of their mission. Only Enoch remained behind.

Chapter 48

Immortality is no guard against exhaustion. The floodgates of fatigue had been lifted, and Enoch—in defiance of low gravity—sat slumped in a corner of the control room, thinking back to a time when the Nephilim and humans lived in relative harmony.

There had been a brief point long ago when peaceful coexistence between the two species seemed possible. The Twenty had come down from the Upper Realm bearing gifts and carrying promises of a new way of life—one that combined the bounty of the Earth with a spirit of knowledge and innovation. Thinking back on it, Enoch tried to recapture that long-lost feeling of goodwill and kinship. For a moment in time, he felt that by virtue of his efforts and the nature of his hybrid being, he might help to bridge the gap that divided the Nephilim from humans.

It had all started out so well. The Nephilim had been well received. They found love, raised families, and unlocked new ways of communing with the natural world. He had seen The Twenty transforming before his very eyes, the layers of their proud intellects falling away to reveal a core of sentimental awakening. They learned to laugh and came to know the meaning of joy. It was a powerful distraction and one that drew Enoch's attention away from the other side of the equation.

As such, the harmony that grew between the Nephilim and their families became fodder for The Others, who came to resent The Twenty's newfound bliss. Humans, Enoch would soon come to discover, processed things differently. Knowledge—as bestowed upon them by The Twenty—only served to confuse their worldview. The elders and their stories paled in comparison to all that might potentially be achieved through the mixing of tonics, the binding of metals, the building of structures, and the conquest of others.

Before too long, The Twenty found themselves in the crosshairs of the likes of Lock. He was among the first to voice what The Others were feeling. And that is when the trouble began. These Nephilim, if not halted, would rise to become a super race, he claimed. What chance would humans have against a species of immortals? Fear is a powerful motivator, and it was only a matter of time before Lock made the case for hunting down and destroying them. Or, if they could not be destroyed, to imprison the Nephilim and their brood for all time.

"I did Lock's dirty work," thought Enoch. "*I* did this," he whispered out loud, staring out to where the squid-like creatures continued to circle around and thrash against the sides of the ship. "Look what's become of them."

Enoch looked down at his large hands, turning them over and back again. "At one time, we were not so different, both being products of Nephilim–human unions. But this," thought Enoch, seeing their bright red serpentine bodies flashing and coiling across the viewing deck, "is the dark side of immortality. No way to end the suffering. Trapped for eternity in this primordial soup."

As if on cue, one of the creatures attached its tentacles to the glass and pressed what passed for a face onto the surface, further contorting its features. It looked straight at Enoch, and for an instant he was reminded of that moment when he had pulled the capstone closed and sealed the Nephilim beneath the Temple Mount—all those terrified eyes of women and children looking up at him. He was protecting them from Lock and his marauders. That was his intention. His noble choice. Now he regretted all he had done.

It was hard to know who was to blame. Then again, perhaps blame had no part in this. Maybe this was fate. Had his father never left the Upper Realm and met his mother, perhaps the Nephilim and The Others would still be living parallel lives, woefully ignorant in their knowledge of one another—and unburdened. Instead, they merged. And the Nephilim, through no fault of their own, were demonized. There was not a human child alive or dead who had not been schooled to believe that the Nephilim were the source of all the world's misery— pure evil beings trapped in the depths of hell, with the ever-present possibility of one day returning.

As time passed, their fictionalized transgressions grew. How they had descended from on high and violated the women, putting in motion a campaign of lasciviousness and sin. How they had threatened humankind's God-given right to hold domain over the Earth. And how they had conspired to sow hatred in order to tear asunder the fabric of love that bound the people of the world together. The narrative ran deep, with humans prescribing all that was good to themselves and all that was evil to the Nephilim and their kind. "Vigilance!" shouted their priests and soothsayers. "Vigilance, lest they return!"

Enoch had hoped to keep the Nephilim hidden only until Lock and his army had lost interest and retreated from Giza. The Twenty and their families would never be found. Enoch made sure of that. Once the capstone had been hauled over the temple flooring, sealing them below, he withdrew to the banks of the river and let loose its water by destroying the dams, flooding the plains. By the time that Lock's armies had arrived, amassing themselves on the hills that ran alongside the river, only the apex of the Temple Mount could be seen protruding from the water and reflecting the sun's light. When the water receded, Enoch promised himself he would return. But when he did, the lands were occupied.

The Temple Mount was a sign, Lock told his people. So they migrated, in their thousands, to start living where the Nephilim had left off. Before the mass arrival, Lock removed the two pillars that had been raised to remind the world who the Nephilim were and what they stood for. Nowhere to be found. Lock took credit for the Temple Mount, calling it a gift to his people and a tribute to their sky god who had led them there. For Enoch, any hope of retrieving the Nephilim from beneath the temple was gone. He would need to find his way back to them by other means.

Cupping his head in his hands, Enoch let his mind drift back over the 10,000 years that had come and gone. During that time, he had traveled the world, searching for a way to reach the Nephilim and retrieve them as promised. Perhaps they would find their own way out, he hoped. But wherever he went, there was no trace. While he searched, he fought to keep their memory alive. This proved no easy task. Lock's fictions decrying the Nephilim traveled on the wings of storytellers. The more the human population grew, the more embedded the tales of the Nephilim atrocities became. For every truth Enoch planted, a thousand lies sprung up around it.

In Mesopotamia, Enoch crafted the tale of Gilgamesh and the story of an underworld filled with hope and possibility. Lock's descendants crushed the ancient city and buried the tablets and the tale with it. Enoch then wandered east and ended up in a place that would later be called the Orient. The people there had not heard of sky gods or conquests. They, like his mother and grandmother before her, seemed attuned to the natural world. Disguised as an ascetic, Enoch coined the name Laozi and in the wilderness wrote the *Tao Te Ching*. His teachings spread far and wide, giving life to the Taoist movement, which he hoped would create a permanent shift in worldview, to allow for the coexistence of the Nephilim and humans. But the armies raised by Lock's descendants put an end to that as well. As Mongol hordes, they used their skills in weaponry and horsemanship to sweep across the Orient and all the land to the west, extinguishing Taoist thought and calling for allegiance to one idea only—the supremacy of the Khan.

Returning to the land of Giza and the surrounding domains, Enoch would not be dissuaded. His eastern campaign had almost succeeded. He would try again. If the diaspora of humanity was able to harness stories to guide the practices and beliefs of people, perhaps he might do the same. Christianity, at that time, was on the rise. The generations of Roman rulers—direct descendants of Lock—had expanded their empire to the far reaches of Germania in the north, the African continent in the south, and the land of the Occident to the west. Given the state of constant warfare, the Roman ideologies garnered respect. But when there were no more wars to be waged, the primacy of their empire and way of life began to falter in the minds of those who yearned for a new way forward. What came to pass was a battle of narrative like no other. The Romans, sensing the shift in popular sentiment, seized upon Christianity and commissioned a telling of the life of Christ that was to be presided over by an official order of priests. To the people, it would appear that power was being transferred from state to church. In reality, it was a play for power and control. Enoch realized the deception and countered it by seeking out those who truly understood its meaning, coaxing from them the true nature of the Christian message: that love and kindness—not power—were the means of salvation and that the world was one in which the Nephilim and humans could and should peacefully coexist.

Once again, The League of Humans—as the order of Lock came to be known—held fast. In short order, they sniffed out Enoch's plot to undermine their power and declared heretical any books that had not been sanctioned by the Roman Catholic Church. The countermeasure of the Romans constituted a swift attack: free-thinking people from all walks of life were rounded up and slaughtered. Enoch had only one move left. He collected as best he could the books of the Gnostics and, sealing them away in large clay pots, he buried them—as he had the Nephilim—for safekeeping.

So went Enoch's life. He operated with secret knowledge in the same way that warriors conduct guerilla warfare. His stealth served as his primary weapon. Not knowing when or where he would plant seeds of the Nephilim and their thought kept the ancestors of Lock and The League of Humans on high alert for centuries on end. There were good days and bad. But in the end, the war of ideas was lost—for a time, at least.

Then The Twenty returned. It was a day Enoch would forever remember. A moment when all was forgiven and the rebuilding began—a moment that had led to the present.

Resting against the control room console and contemplating his long and fraught life, Enoch allowed a gentle smile to creep over his face. This moment had been over a hundred years in the making. He had once thought of himself as alone. But then suddenly, and unexpectedly, he was reunited with the brethren. It was not too late. Their life beneath the surface, as they had foretold, had brought forth new discoveries and new insights. Their time in the depths had not been squandered. They had returned with a boon, a gift for humanity and for all the world—and now was the time to make good on that promise.

Chapter 49

Enoch was hovering on the viewing deck, still reflecting on the past, when the others filtered back in. The poor creatures that had seemed so desperate had now gone. All that remained was the swirling plasma. By comparison, it was a joy to behold. Looming before them and drawing ever closer was the silvery outer lining of the inner core.

The next few hours were critical. They were in orbit, and if Abby's calculations were right, they would have one shot at entry at the precise moment when the magnetic force reached its lowest ebb. It was a race against time. Once the poles reversed—as they most surely would—the window of opportunity would close forever. And their fate would be no better than that of those other poor creatures.

Abby had been preparing for this moment for as long as Carson had been trying to unmask the mysteries of Earth's catacombs. His work had brought them this far. Now it was up to her to do the rest. She pushed across the room and floated down to rest by his side. He was meticulous, and she could see how focused he was in this moment.

"I've run through your computations a dozen times. I've tried to simulate it the best I can. By my estimates, we'll have less than seven minutes to make the jump. The second the reversal begins, the positive and negative charges in the ionosphere will be neutralized. If you're right, that's the moment when the core's outer layer will be its thinnest. To make it through, we'll need to rev up the EMFC."

"Tomahawk our way through," said Abby.

"I guess that's the technical term for it, yes."

"You don't sound hopeful."

"I'm not. Little room for error."

"We've made it this far. We'll make it the rest of the way. If my calculations are right, we'll need to sustain a level of 1,248 teslas for the full seven minutes. By directing the field toward the core, it should thin it out to allow us to punch through. There are, of course, a few unknowns, like the reaction from the plasma. Kicking on the EMFC is like dropping a hairdryer in a bathtub. It might be over before it begins."

"Kaboom!"

"Yeah, kaboom! Then there's the matter of the core itself. Assuming we make it through—and let's say we do—what's on the other side? Will the core's membrane rupture? And if so, will that cause the entire structure to collapse?"

"Let's say none of this happens and you're right about Hollow Earth. How will the ship transition from a surrounding liquid to a surrounding gas? Are we looking at a crash landing?"

Abby smiled despite herself. Here they were, two scientists, trying to weigh the probability of survival. They were empirical thinkers, both of them. Too many variables and uncertainties for their liking. If this were an experiment, they would scrap it on the spot and start all over. But this was no experiment. This was real time.

"The Australians have an expression I'm quite fond of," said Abby. "It's the kind of thing they say when they just don't know how things will turn out."

"Yeah, what's that?"

"Suck it and see!"

Carson laughed aloud, catching himself and everyone else by surprise. The other members of the crew stopped what they were doing and turned to see what was so funny.

"Listen," whispered Abby. "There's really no choice. If we don't try, we spend what time we have left in inner orbit. Forty-five... no... forty-four minutes from now, we'll either find what we came for or end it all in trying."

"Funny, isn't it?" said Carson. "The moment you realize there really is no choice, the stress of worrying about it kind of fades away."

Abby stood and turned to the others.

"Anyone have anything to say before we head to the pods?"

"Yeah," said Spike. "Where's the exit?"

"You're looking at it," she said, gesturing at the shiny gray mass of the core that rose up before them.

CHAPTER 50

Putting things in motion was like setting the timer on a homemade bomb. And, in effect, that's what the EMFC was. It would take a full three minutes for the electromagnetic force of the engines to reach the load threshold. If that did not set off a chain reaction, the *Orpheus* would make contact with the core, and they would know within minutes whether Abby's theory was right or tragically wrong.

It should have been enough to occupy Carson's mind. And yet the revelations of the preceding few hours were cause for distraction. If the stories Otto had shared with them were true, it would upend the way that he and all of humanity thought about themselves and the world around them. At this very moment, the crew were in the company of two immortals. How was that even possible? If they were to be believed, their lives had spanned more than ten millennia. He was no biologist, but he had enough scientific training to know that the human body—or any living organism, for that matter—had a limited lifespan. Of course, that was not necessarily true at a cellular level. For genomes, cells, and certain organisms, regeneration was the natural order. Morphogenetics characterized by phenotypic plasticity would determine a multicelled organism's ability to repair itself. Flatworms and salamanders, for instance, were equipped with a trigger response. If wounded, cells were activated, and regeneration began apace. Eventually, even salamanders died.

So what natural ability did the Nephilim and their offspring have that defied the laws of biology? "Maybe they are more vegetable than mammalian," thought Carson. He knew that plants were regenerative, some more than others. Fungi, for instance, could live forever under favorable conditions. They did this through a continual process of germination, sporing, and the formation of hyphae. By absorbing water through their walls, fungi activated cytoplasm, causing nuclear division. That, in turn, allowed cytoplasm to synthesize. Spherical walls formed around it to create polarity and, eventually, a hyphal apex formed—a kind of feeding tube to the outside world. The process could continue unabated if it was not interrupted. There's a theory, thought Carson—*Nephilim are plant-based!* "Was it too late to switch fields?" he wondered.

Just then, the ship's electromagnetic engines kicked in. He held his breath. There was no turning back now. The crew were arrayed in their pods in a state of total animated suspension. His last thoughts were those of mycelia, rooting their way through forest floors, extending their microscopically thin tendrils in search of their own kind. By interlocking one with another, they formed great circular colonies. Fairy rings, they were called, marking the way for those magical miniature creatures that nurtured the wood.

CHAPTER 51

There was no explosion. No sudden drop. In fact, there was nothing at all. The EMFC that had sent scintillating trickles of energy through the ship was still and the engines were silent. As the crew stared out from their pods, one at another, some wondered if they had simply failed, bounced off the core and catapulted back into a languid drift through the ionosphere.

Emerging from their pods, they felt the welcome return of gravity. And rather than float their way down the gangway, they walked in single file, grateful to have the use of their legs once more. "That's a good sign," thought Abby, as she and the others entered the control room that glowed red by the light of auxiliary power.

"We've lost power. We'll have to do it manually," said Abby, reaching for a metal winch that lay flush against the viewing platform. The crew gathered along the deck.

"I've got this," said Spike.

He pulled down on the lever and a thin stream of light shot through the opening, painting a line across the midsections of the assembled crew. He repeated the motion, and the sheathing drew back some more. Otto was the first to break rank and lunge forward, pressing his face against the glass.

"Keep going! Why are you stopping?" he shouted.

Spike pumped the handle up and down another dozen times, and the picture was complete.

"Dear God!" cried Philomena.

They all rushed forward, letting the light from the outside world break over them. What lay before them was a land of unsurpassed beauty. Verdant stretches of rolling hills tumbled toward them, accented by long lines of trees with branches coiling and reaching toward the plasma swirl of the outer core. They moved and swayed, not together, but independently, as if dancing to a thousand different tunes. Flowering vines coiled up along their thick trunks and stretched themselves across the lower boughs. Moving in and around the trees were streams and tiny tributaries of waterways. They streaked the landscape and glittered with the reflection of the aurora that penetrated the core's membrane.

"I'm having a Dorothy moment," Philomena mumbled, while the others could only gaze in wonderment.

Although they could not see it, they sensed the rhythmic pattern of the wind as it licked its way through manes of tall, velvety grass. The dome of the inner core stretched out to cap the landscape and, as they watched, it changed color from light purple to pink, then from yellow to aqua blue—like a painter's first brush strokes across a virgin canvas.

The ship had come to a stop in the middle of a low valley and rolled some distance from the outer reaches of the core's periphery, leaving in its wake a long line of crushed grass and flora. It was a single scar on the face of an otherwise pristine landscape.

For decades, the scientific community had speculated that Earth's core comprised a viscous mass of iron, silicon, and sulfur, churning at temperatures greater than 5,000 degrees Celsius. Hollow Earth theory was something quite different. Edmund Halley, of comet fame, was right! He had risked his reputation by suggesting that such a thing was possible. What would he say now, seeing Hollow Earth for himself?

"I don't know what I was expecting, but it wasn't this," intoned Abby. "I'm not sure how plant life is even possible, but here it is."

"Plants, maybe. But I've never seen vegetation like this before," noted Philomena.

"Is it breathable?" asked Carson. "The air?"

"Let's find out."

Abby retreated to the control deck. The reserve power was enough to give her a readout.

"Twenty-three degrees Celsius. A high concentration of oxygen. A PSI of 13.1. Gravity... well, how about that? 4.3 meters per second squared, half of what we're accustomed to."

"In other words," said Kai, "It's a spring day on inner Earth."

"Pretty much."

"Any reason why we shouldn't test it?" asked Carson.

"None that comes to mind. We're here, aren't we? Depressurizing now."

Abby flipped a switch and instantly the atmosphere shifted. A lightness took over. Descending through the gangway, they made their way from the control room to the exit way. Three days ago, they had entered the *Orpheus* through this opening, not sure if they would ever reemerge. The shock suits were lined up and waiting in cases against the inner wall, but there was no need for them. The outside world was stable and inviting. Abby engaged the door and, with a click and hiss of hydraulics, it slid back.

A warm breeze buffeted the crew. They breathed in the air and immediately felt lightheaded. Only Otto seemed unfazed. Bolting from the ship and down the gangway, he would be the first. No one moved as he lifted a foot and stepped down onto the surface. When he did so, Philomena drew in her breath. His black boot disappeared into the grass, settling at shin height.

"It's solid."

As if in response, the leaves among the trees began to rustle.

In single file, each of them descended the gangway, jumping off to land on terrain so spongy if felt like foam rubber. Philomena fell to her knees and brought her face close to the grass, inhaling its soft, flowery scent.

"Like heaven," she murmured.

Parting the grass, she looked closer. Then pushing it aside for a better look, she let out a gasp. The others circled around her and found themselves gazing into a translucent pool. Why they hadn't broken through and plunged into its depths, no one could say. There wasn't soil, only a thin transparent membrane that served as a window onto a vast network of undulating roots and tendrils. From beneath, this cavernous underworld shone with its own light, all in a purplish hue. How deep the pulsating network of roots and vines went was hard to say. But clearly this served as the land's underbelly, its nerve center, a mycorrhizal network pulsating as if triggered by tens of millions of choreographed synapses.

"Look!" they heard Otto shout. He was standing fifty meters away on the crest of a small hill, his long arm pointing toward something in the distance. The crew bounded after him, delighted by how easily and quickly they could move without gravity's restraint. Now they could see what Otto was pointing at. In the distance was a column of what appeared to be water, stretching from the land below to the inner core's apex far above. Even from this distance, they could hear its thunderous rumbling. They could see from the way the vegetation leaned out and away from it that the force of the cascade was generating the breeze that swirled about them.

"I feel incredible, how about you?" Philomena asked the others.

"I don't know if it's relief or joy, but I don't recall ever feeling so good," Abby replied.

Even Otto looked different. The stern expression that he wore like a mask had given way. He was smiling. As if caught in the act, he quickly turned, saying "Back to the ship. I need my equipment." The image of Otto bouncing back to the *Orpheus* was priceless—like a dog let off its leash, leaping its way through ocean surf. The crew broke into laughter, and all doing their best Otto imitations, they vaulted after him.

Enoch remained on the hill. His back to the crew, he stood transfixed and expressionless, staring at the great vortex in the distance. The search was almost over. "Soon we will know," he whispered to himself.

CHAPTER 52

Carson wondered how Columbus might have felt at the moment when he caught sight of the New World. Would he have felt relief, elation, or something in between? All new discoveries, he thought, were short-lived. Before you knew it, that eureka moment was over. It was the same with the crew of the *Orpheus*. They had work to do, and so they agreed to make their way toward the great pillar of water in the distance. It stood at the center of the landscape, as if holding aloft the dome of this magnificent underworld. There, perhaps, they would find answers. Better yet, in such a low-gravity environment, they could take the ship with them. It was that easy. By affixing ropes to her sides, then fanning out, the crew rolled the *Orpheus* forward with surprising ease.

Everyone had a job to do. Abby was in charge of the ship. Carson plotted the best approach. Kai was responsible for collecting water samples from the array of tributaries that branched their way across the landscape. Meanwhile, Philomena—pruning shears in hand— moved through an ocean of flora. She was like a celebrity trapped in a throng of adoring fans. As she passed, the plants leaned in and reached out, asking to be noticed and hoping for connection. Spike stayed close, as a bodyguard might, taking the clippings she handed him and placing each one in a hermetically sealed tube. It was trickier than it looked. These were no ordinary plants. Some resisted. Like touch-me-nots, some would recoil and retract, hugging the surface, to avoid Philomena's clippers. Others were playful, almost curious, reaching out to stroke her finger or coil about her wrist before offering them-selves up to her.

Philomena stopped. "Wait. It doesn't feel right," she whispered.

"How do you mean?" asked Spike.

"I wonder if I'm hurting them."

"They don't seem to mind."

Spike was right. Even for those that momentarily resisted, it appeared they were more shy than fearful. In their own time, the plants would guide Philomena's hand, self-selecting, allowing her to trim a sample here or a cutting there. Together, they came up with names. Like Eggplant Molly for a purplish tuber that poked its head out from the ground in one place, then disappeared and popped up elsewhere. And Goldilocks for a willowlike tree with a habit of twitching her leaves, like a girl flicking hair from her face. They made a game of it, trying to outdo one another. Of course, not all vegetation was animated. Some of the larger trees stood stoic and indifferent, not minding one way or the other if Philomena clipped them away or left them alone.

"Are they edible?" asked Spike, plucking a softball-sized red fruit with yellow dimples from a nearby tree, then holding it up to his nose.

"I wouldn't want to be the one to find out," said Philomena, clearly a bit miffed at Spike for taking from the tree something that was not offered. "I'd suggest you wait. We can test them later."

Hours had passed since they set out, and yet not one of the crew members felt tired or winded. In fact, with every step, they felt energized. It was as if the vegetation brushing up against their legs was urging them forward.

"Should we rest?" asked Abby.

"Not now," said Otto. "We're less than an hour away."

"What is it, exactly, you're looking for?" asked Carson.

"The same thing you're looking for, professor... answers."

"Maybe the answers are right here," said Carson, gesturing to the surrounding land. "Maybe you're missing the whole point."

"And what is the point, professor?"

"All I meant is that sometimes it's the things right in front of you that matter most."

"I think not," snapped Otto. "It's the things that go unseen."

"What's the difference?"

Philomena overheard the exchange, stepped between them, and smiled up at Otto.

"I believe what Carson is saying is that one should never forget to stop and smell the flowers."

"I think we could all use a break," said Abby, throwing down her rope. The others followed suit, and the *Orpheus* rolled to a standstill.

"Take ten," said Abby.

They had come to rest on a hill's crest. All around them, the land spread out in perfect stretches of grassland, accented by groves of trees and a network of rivers that flowed out from the aqueous spout rising from the land and disappearing into the upper reaches of the core's great domed ceiling. It shimmered and reflected the light from the aurora beyond. The sight was intoxicating. It drew them forward like a beacon amid a verdant ocean. If ever there was a Garden of Eden, this was it.

While the others luxuriated in the tall grass, looking up into the dome's shimmering canopy, Philomena rolled onto her stomach and pressed her face into the soft ground. She breathed deeply and the scent of life filled her nostrils. She turned her head and held her ear to the ground. Closing her eyes, she listened. The mysteries of the mycorrhiza that swirled just beneath her outstretched body excited her. There, she thought, they would find the force that animated these plants and gave them character.

"Otto," she said, rolling back over and sitting up so that her head poked just above the grass.

"Yes?"

"Take out your instruments."

"And why should I do that?"

"Because I have a theory."

"You do, huh?"

"Humor me."

Otto did not reply, but instead rolled his bulbous eyes, rose to his feet, and walked to the ship. He returned moments later carrying a silver suitcase. Laying it beside Philomena, he flipped the lock and threw back the cover. Placed in form-fitting foam rubber cutouts were dozens of metal probes, insertion tools, and detectors.

"May I?" Philomena asked, gesturing toward one of the probes.

"Be my guest."

Lifting the probe from the case, she held it out, balanced between her two hands like Excalibur, then, without saying a word, she plunged the end of the probe into the ground. It was like driving a pin into plastic. There was a sharp snap, and Philomena was thrown back onto the grass."

Carson and the others leapt to their feet.

"Are you all right?"

I'm fine. Just fine," she said, sitting upright. Her hair was charged and stood up on end. It had a halo effect. The others laughed, and Carson reached out a hand to help her up. As soon as he did so, he too received a jolt.

"You're static!" he cried.

"I feel fine," she replied.

"You should see yourself," chuckled Spike.

"Electrons," grunted Otto, turning away and gingerly attaching the meter to the probe. "They repel one another. And they don't like you much, either."

For the next thirty minutes, the crew watched on as Otto intermittently inserted into the ground one filament after another, taking measurements, then repeating the steps.

Spike leaned down and whispered to Philomena, whose hair had recovered. "What's he looking for?"

"Who knows. Maybe his bacterial brothers—agrobacterium, azospirillum, azotobacter, flavobacterium, gluconobacter, and herbaspirillum," she said, rattling off the names of her favorite microbials.

"You are a strange one. You know that right?" quipped Spike.

"Takes one to know one," she replied, playfully tousling his hair before springing away to run headlong across the open field.

There was no escaping the lightness that had enveloped the crew. It was like a megadose of nitrous oxide carried on the wind. What initially appeared to be relief at having landed safely in this fantastic panorama was actually a mild form of intoxication, as if every node of sensory perception was all at once filled up by sights, scents, and textures never before experienced.

While the crew members took it all in, Otto worked in silence, rebuffing all questions. Enoch was way out ahead. They could see his large frame among the fields of flowers, with Philomena making her way toward him. Abby wondered if she should not go after him and keep him close. She was about to say something when Otto suddenly sprang to his feet and looked to the vortex in the distance, then back down at the probe.

"It's here."

"What's here?" asked Carson.

"Neutrinos. In concentrations I never thought possible. We're being fed by them."

"What do you mean, fed?" asked Abby.

"Ghost particles. Completely invisible to the naked eye and to most every instrument known to man. But here they are, nonetheless, moving all about and through us. We feel the way we do because they carry with them the energy of the cosmos. These plants. Those trees. All of it. Right here, beneath our feet. It's what we've been looking for."

"And what, exactly, is that?" asked Kai.

"Regenerative energy. The fifth force. The founding principle of immortality!"

CHAPTER 53

With every footstep across the strange and beautiful land, Enoch felt a turning. Barely detectable at first, it was more a feeling than a distinct impression. Euphoria, perhaps, at arriving at their destination alive and in one piece? No, it was not that. Gratitude for the *Orpheus* and its crew? No, not that either. The feeling was more visceral—more primal. It was like the slow and sensual shedding of old skin. Exposing what had once been hidden and inviting his entire being to experience life anew.

Instinctively, Enoch had removed his boots the minute he set foot on Hollow Earth. As he walked barefoot across the landscape, the combination of low gravity and soft vegetation underfoot sent sensuous waves of energy up his legs and across his thighs. With every step, he resisted the temptation to lie down and let wisps of grass and tiny vines creep their way up and across his body. The land was beckoning to him. Calling him home. Stopping, for a moment, he panned around his surroundings. How miraculous to discover at Earth's core a land of such surpassing richness and splendor! How extraordinary to think that, in so many ways, the vast cosmos around had proven more accessible to humans than this hidden miracle inside—*this* Hollow Earth. Until now, he had believed that the most perfect place on Earth was alongside the river of his youth, beneath the willow tree. It was— and would remain—his place of resurrection. There, he felt regenerated. Here, however, he felt reborn.

Enoch turned at the sound of light footsteps from behind. Philomena came bounding toward him, her frizzy hair keeping time with her stride, an enormous smile stretched across her doll-like face. She had a gift—perhaps the greatest gift of them all. She was tuned in to something larger. She understood, perhaps without being able to precisely explain it, how all life-forms were born of energy. The planet was energy's petri dish, fed and nourished by frequencies, some detectable and some not. She had learned this while studying the principles of Earth acupuncture back in Manitou Springs, although Enoch had sensed her special gift long before that.

How many explorers from times past, having set foot in a new land, had chosen to appropriate rather than understand what they had discovered? Philomena—and the others—represented a new breed of explorer. Their work here over the coming days would lay the groundwork for a new beginning. A chance to turn back the clock for humanity—and the Nephilim. The world had gone wrong, and he knew he was partly to blame. This was his chance to make it right. Due to the Nephilim having been locked away beneath the earth for all those years, humanity had been left unchecked. The world turned for them, so they believed.

"How cruel," thought Enoch, "to discover Hollow Earth only to be too late." Had the planet reached its tipping point or was there still time to undo what had been done?

"Enoch. Slow down. What's the rush?"

Philomena slowed to a jog, cradling something in her right hand.

"Look at this one," she said, holding up what appeared to be a simple twine of braided grass. "Blow on it."

He bent down and gently blew. It quivered, then unfurled, revealing dozens of translucent feelers, like dragonfly wings.

"It's the carbon dioxide from your breath. Isn't it amazing?"

"Extraordinary," he replied.

Through the trees, the other members of the crew could be seen moving through the valley, the *Orpheus* lassoed and pulled along behind them. The great spout in the distance drew them in like a magnet. Otto was out in front, carrying the metal case with its instruments. Every twenty meters or so he would drop down to one knee, remove a probe from the case, and plunge it into the ground. He seemed oblivious to, or perhaps unaffected by, the static shock that had knocked Philomena to the ground. He was moving faster now. Enoch and Philomena moved down and alongside the hill to join them, just as Spike was loading a final tray of saplings onto the ship.

"Quite a haul," he said, looking almost pleased. "What do you plan to do with all of this?" he asked Philomena.

"Find out what they know," she said, in a matter-of-fact way.

The slope of the hill had grown steeper, and now everyone had to lean in to haul the *Orpheus* to the top. As they approached the crest, the sight before them almost caused them to let go of the ropes. Thrusting up and out from the surface below stood a geyser of swirling liquid. It spiraled 500 meters or more into the air before disappearing through the crown of the inner core and into the aurora beyond. Standing just before it was a tree, magnificent in its own right, yet dwarfing all the others. It stood alone just fifty meters or so from the upward-spiraling maelstrom. It swayed back and forth, enshrouded in a rainbow-colored mist.

Slowly, the crew moved down the far side of the hill to where the land flattened out. From there, they crossed another 100 meters to stand beneath the thick boughs and foliage of the magnificent tree.

Enoch stood stone-still. What were the odds? A willow, its massive limbs heavily bent with long reaches of bright green leaves. They fluttered and twirled in the wind, and in his mind's eye, he saw his own willow by the river. That was *his axis mundi*. This was *the axis mundi*. The tree that marked the center of all creation. Was it a coincidence? Or was this his dream of the world?

The roar of the great column of water reverberated, and the ground beneath their feet shook from its power. All around the tree, the terrain was void of vegetation. Where the trunk penetrated the surface, roots blossomed and fanned out in all directions. As if standing on a lake of clear ice, the crew could see beneath their feet the flashing and pulsing of a million tiny lights.

"Christmas on steroids," muttered Spike.

"It's the scent," said Philomena, closing her eyes and breathing in the air around her. "Like the holidays, when the whole house smells of pine."

"Pine? This is no pine. What evergreen flowers are like this?" challenged Abby. "I've seen my share of dogwoods, but this one is something special."

Carson looked at the others, then back at the tree. He was no dendrologist, but he knew a maple tree when he saw one. Slowly, he let his eyes move up to follow the line of the trunk, where branches sprouted leaves of red, orange, and yellow. It reminded him of the lakeside in autumn and the trees that gathered around his grandparents' cottage.

"What the...?" Kai shouted above the din. "Have none of you seen a banyan before? What pine or dogwood has a trunk like that?"

"Banyans don't produce these," said Abby, holding up a flower the size of her hand. "Dogwood for sure."

The others looked at one another to see if this might, in fact, be some kind of joke.

"We call those pinecones where I come from," said Philomena, confirming to the others that Philomena had lost her mind.

"Aspen. Everyone knows an aspen, don't they?" asked Spike, suddenly coming to his senses. "What the hell's going on? Is this one of your tricks, Trubolt?"

Otto did not reply. He stood in rapt attention, staring into the field of energy that rushed upward from the roots, making the tree morph and shift in rapid succession. He saw what they saw—and more.

"This is no tree and every tree, all at once," he said. "Or perhaps I've misspoken. This is the One tree."

For the last few kilometers, as they had approached this spot, Otto's readings had shown accelerated levels of subatomic activity. The ground was pulsating with the kind of dark energy that he had spent a lifetime searching for. The closer they drew to the vortex, the greater the activity. But there was more. The patterns were changing, becoming more erratic, almost distressed. But that was ridiculous. How can one attribute a feeling of distress to a subatomic energy field? That would be to subjugate the laws of quantum theory to some irrational state. And that was more than his mind would allow.

"*Defies logic, doesn't it?*" asked Enoch.

Otto looked up to see Enoch eyeballing him from across the way. The two had not spoken since the ship landed. Perhaps Otto had misheard.

Then again: "*I said, it defies logic, doesn't it? You realize this changes everything?!*"

Enoch was speaking to him from ten meters away, but his lips weren't moving.

"Did you think you were the only one who could read the thoughts of others? I've been listening, Ohyah. I know what you've come for, and I know who you serve."

"I serve no one," he grimaced, locking eyes with Enoch.

"You and I both know that's not true. Would you hand it all over to those who would misuse it?"

Otto gave a quick shake, trying to cast Enoch out of his head. It was no use. Could he sense his doubts as well?

"Who are you to speak about misuse of power? You condemned us all. You made that decision. We had no say in it."

"My father knew. The Twenty understood. They've put it behind them. What about you, Ohyah? Can you do the same?"

"Never!" cried Otto, realizing too late that he had shouted out loud.

"Is there a problem?" asked Abby, turning to see the two of them in a standoff.

"Nothing. None of your concern," snapped Otto.

"Quite the contrary," she countered. "I'd say this is *all* our concern. Can you explain this? Why do each of us see something different?"

Otto composed himself, yet he could not help but wonder what else Enoch had learned by eavesdropping on his thoughts. It was safe to assume he knew everything. Otto realized he would now need to improvise. "A diversion," he thought. "Keep him guessing."

Backing away from the tree and the beating sound of billions of liters of water heading skyward, Otto drew the crew after him. They circled around and he looked deep into their sorry eyes. They understood so little. Glancing once more at Enoch, he felt a rare moment of agreement pass between them.

"Are you familiar with Schrödinger's Cat?" he asked, looking down at Abby.

"But of course."

"Then you know one of the first rules of quantum theory is that one thing can exist in many different states at the same moment."

"Superposition."

"Precisely."

"But that was nothing but a thought experiment," countered Abby.

"For Schrödinger, it was. For us, it appears to be something quite observable."

"You're playing with words, doctor. What are you saying?

"Schrödinger had his cat. We have our tree."

"It means," said Enoch, "that how we choose to perceive the world is how it will come to be. You see a dogwood tree because that's what you choose to see. The same holds true for all of you. Philomena sees pine. Kai, a banyan. You, a dogwood. I see a willow."

"But in actuality, what tree is it, really?" asked Carson.

"It is all things, all at once," mumbled Otto.

"What does egghead here see that none of us see?" asked Spike. "Am I right? Are you seeing something else?"

"Very perceptive, Mr. Morrison. I too have a gift. I see past the one and into the many."

"And what does that look like, Obi Wan?"

"Like the answer to all our questions."

CHAPTER 54

In the hours that followed, the group busied themselves by offloading various items from the ship—food, other supplies, and the equipment they would need to determine if, indeed, what was happening here was having some bearing on the state of the planet. What concerned them most was that in order to know if a change had occurred, they had to have a baseline from which to measure that change. Arriving within the bounds of Hollow Earth was like being born again—moving from a warm, dark, watery place to a world where the old senses were utterly inadequate. Here, in Hollow Earth, they had to unlearn what they had learned. Only by doing so could they hope to breathe—and live—again.

In the presence of the tree—or what they perceived as a tree—sight, it seemed, had betrayed them. When the senses falter, the mind plays tricks. Enoch, through time and experience, well understood the tendency of humans to substitute with memory what might otherwise seem obvious. Individually, humans were unreliable in this way. And yet the fact that they all interpreted the phenomenon in front of them as *a tree*—albeit one of different varieties—revealed, on some level, that they all perceived the world in a similar way. This was the best explanation that Enoch could come up with, so he shared it with the rest of them.

"I don't buy it," said Spike. "Now that we know that we all see something different, what if we agreed to try to see it as just one kind of tree? Abby's dogwood, for instance. What if we sat around and she described what she saw so that we too started to see a dogwood? Or what if we borrow a page from the book of Dr. Know-It-All over there and try *not* to see it as a tree at all, but as something entirely different instead? Would it be possible? Would we see it as dark energy or does it only work if you're a half-breed? No offense."

"None taken," replied Enoch. "I see," he said, turning his head, "I still see a willow. Even if I try to tell myself it's a mirage, or some kind of subatomic phenomenon, for me, it remains a willow."

"Then why does *he* see that it's *more* than a tree?" shouted Spike, pointing an accusing finger at Otto, who stood brooding and pondering the shape-shifting dendron.

"If you would all stop your blathering and let me think..." he growled.

While they argued, Philomena circumnavigated the tree, walking slowly, trying to see it from every possible angle. But the more she focused, the more fixated she became on it being a pine and nothing else. While she did not dare approach the trunk and test the strength of the thin membrane of ground surrounding it, she was able to just reach the lowest branches on tiptoe and feel the smooth pine needles in their neat little rows. She ran her thumb and forefinger over them time and again, before returning to the group and sitting down cross-legged.

"I have an idea. Instead of trying to see it as the same, what if we pick another plant—like these, for instance," she said, springing to her feet and walking to a pair of red flowering shrubs no more than ten meters apart.

"Humor me. Kai, Abby—come over here, please. Both of you sit down, side by side, and face that bush. Carson, Spike—sit here. Same thing, but face the other way and look at the other plant." Once they were situated, Philomena leaned down and whispered something, first to Kai and Abby and then to Carson and Spike.

"Let's start with ten minutes. Now do what I've asked and please concentrate. Enoch, Otto, please don't interfere... Go."

Philomena sank down into the grass close enough to see, but far enough away to avoid being a distraction. Otto and Enoch stood behind her. Five minutes passed, and Philomena started to think that maybe she had got it wrong. She was no scientist. "Anyway," she thought to herself, "it was just an idea."

Eight minutes passed, then nine, and she was about to call it off when it happened. The bush to the left under the watch of Kai and Abby began to vibrate, its tiny branches seeming almost to sit up and look taller. A minute later, the number of crimson flowers had doubled. To the right, the bush was waning. The few blooms it had were falling off. It looked tired and wilted. Enoch sighed with approval, and Philomena leapt to her feet.

"It worked! Oh, dear Lord, it worked!" she shouted, rushing toward the bushes.

"Look, look!" she cried. The four who were seated stood to look at one plant, then the other. They were mystified. Philomena, meanwhile, turned childlike, jumping up and down and clapping her hands, so pleased she was with herself.

"What did you whisper to them?" asked Enoch.

"Over here, I asked them to think of the plant as parched and dying. Over there, I said to imagine watering her with your minds. Do you see? Do you know what this means?"

"I'm not certain I do," said Carson.

"It means we have the power to control the outcome. At least here, in this place, we do."

Philomena walked to the bush that had wilted. She held her hands over it and whispered a little prayer. The plant quivered, and before their eyes, new green shoots appeared from its tiny branches and formed into buds.

"The only question now is how?" said Kai.

"Did you not hear what I said about all this dark energy?" chimed Otto.

"Perhaps there is some connection, but that doesn't explain how it works through us, does it?" Abby noted. "And if this does have something to do with your subatomic world, what are the implications?"

"Is it conscious?" asked Enoch. "Dark energy... is it conscious?" he asked again.

"What kind of ridiculous question is that?" Otto shot back, still miffed and confused by Enoch's earlier ability to read his thoughts.

"I'll be more specific. Does this help to explain the behavior of subatomic particles? Is this why photons and neutrinos behave differently when observed?"

The question was like a slap across the face. Otto had never considered *why* particles in his quantum world behaved the way they did. He only noted the fact that they *did*.

"Do you realize what you are suggesting?" asked Otto.

"I think I do," Enoch replied.

"Harness the power of dark energy..." Otto hesitated, "and one would have the power to control the universe."

"Perhaps a bit ambitious, but in theory, yes!"

Otto looked suddenly shaken.

"We have to get started," he cried. "Not a minute to spare. We need data. Proof!"

"Knock yourself out," said Spike. "I have better things to do."

"I'll come with you," said Philomena, reaching for Spike's hand.

Cutting a wide path around the tree, the others looked on as the odd couple made for the vortex beyond the tree that rose from the translucent floor and extended upward as high as the eye could see, where it disappeared into a dome of swirling water.

CHAPTER 55

Enoch sat apart from the others, his back resting against the curved flanks of the *Orpheus*. The mist that emanated from the spouting water glistened as it fell, casting rainbows in every direction. He could feel the ground rise up to meet him, grateful for the moisture expressed in gentle hues of green. Here, the land was not only lush, but alive. From his vantage point, he could see for miles in every direction—a tapestry of grasslands, flowering fields, forests, and undulating hills. They ebbed and flowed in color and arrangement, creating an odd sense of perpetual movement, as if the ground itself were shifting and changing in sync with the gentle breeze that pulsed outward from the spiraling column of pure liquid and frolicked its way to the far reaches of the surrounding landscape.

He looked down at his outstretched legs to see wisps of tall grass bending and curling themselves around them. They appeared to act in concert, moving up and down, gently brushing and probing, as if trying to understand the object that had come to rest among them. They seemed as curious about Enoch as he was about them. What land was this? A community of sentient plant life—untouched, so it seemed, by anyone or anything. With no marauding herbivores or insects to contend with, it had flourished. It was the original garden. A botanist's dream.

At the center of it all was the tree. The tree from his childhood, a thing of surpassing beauty, perfect in every way, and so clearly a weeping willow with its sweeping crown and long drooping branches that cascaded in folds to lightly stroke the ground. It shimmered with the silvery undersides of the fluttering green leaves, and the trunk itself—gray, rough, and ridged—clung to the ground with roots that spread out and around, just visible beneath the translucent surface. Was all this real or an illusion?

They had done the impossible, traveling nearly 3,000 kilometers through the Earth to arrive at its core. Their discovery would turn on its head the closely held views of humans and the Nephilim alike. For thousands of years, both species had looked to the heavens, believing that some transcendent power would provide. And yet all along, it was the Earth beneath their feet that would offer the answers to life's most profound questions. The gifts of this planet were given freely. The Nephilim had understood this from the very beginning. They took from it only what they could use. Humans, on the whole, were different. They knew no limits. Why, wondered Enoch, was it so?

Long ago, The Twenty had done their best to show The Others how the planet and the cosmos all hung in the balance. They had urged them to explore the deep mysteries, to probe beneath the surface in search of what was most essential. But to no avail. Had The Twenty understood this about The Others, they might have seen, in time, the folly of their good intentions. By sharing their knowledge of the Earth and its bounties, they unleashed in humans an insatiable appetite. There would be no gratitude—only hate and jealousy. Even worse, by vesting in humans, the Nephilim had seeded their own demise.

The Twenty—so imbued with wisdom—were, at the end of the day, gullible by nature. If only Enoch had understood then what he knew now. He might have taken another course of action. In some ways, he was no better than those who would have harmed them. He too had exploited them, using their guilelessness against them, invoking "the One" to ensure their supplication.

The Great Flood was nothing more than a ruse—a means to bend the Nephilim to his will and send them scurrying to the underworld, where they would rot and wait for him to one day liberate them. For he was the Twenty-first, the one promised to them. And Enoch—on the premise of safeguarding them—exploited that belief. Otto was right. He had given The Twenty and their families no say in the matter, but instead consigned them to a life of misery. Over time, he convinced himself that he had done what he had to do. By burying them, he protected them. How could he have known that they would be lost in a subterranean world for thousands of years? Otto was a remnant of that long period of suffering—he hated Enoch, and understandably so.

With the Nephilim out of the way, humans had flourished at the expense of all other forms of life. Worst of all, they had done so at the expense of their own long-term survival. The planet was dying, having been denuded and depleted. How ironic, thought Enoch, that at the eleventh hour the descendants of Lock were in a sprint to save what they had spent centuries destroying. Or perhaps their intentions had nothing to do with the planet. Were they in search of something else? Otto knew. But the truth could not be pried from him. He kept his ultimate plan hidden away, well beyond Enoch's ability to read his thoughts.

Without the *Orpheus*, its crew, and the vast resources commandeered by the mission's patrons, none of this would have been possible. Hollow Earth would have remained a renegade theory. The world would slowly stop revolving. And the planet and all its inhabitants would most surely be faced with the daunting prospect of a sixth extinction.

A thought then occurred to Enoch. Human ambition knew no limitations. Human ascent was in full stride. It was an aspect of the species' condition that from the beginning had confounded the Nephilim. And here, at the center of the Earth, dark matter in sufficient quantities in combination with human determination would have the ability to influence any conceivable outcome. "Power," thought Enoch. "That's what this is all about."

CHAPTER 56

As the idea firmly lodged itself in Enoch's head, a cry rose up from across the valley.

"Come! Come now!" shouted Philomena.

Kai and the others turned and ran toward her. "Where's Spike?" he shouted.

"There," she said, pointing at the geyser that sprang and spun its way up from the surface. Squinting, they could see a figure standing before it.

Rushing across the fields, the grass parted before them. They came to a halt. Spike was standing less than a meter from the torrent, as if preparing to step through. Kai crept forward and was about to grab his shoulder when Philomena stopped him.

"Don't! Look!" she said.

Kai turned to see as, one by one, each member stepped forward to flank Spike on the right and the left. They stood silent and incredulous. Then Kai caught, in the silvery waves of water, an image of himself. As he stood staring in amazement, he could see his reflection morph and shift. Single-frame moments flashed and whirled before him as if he were trapped in some spectacular house of mirrors. He felt dizzy and nauseous, but try as he might, he could not tear his attention away from the kaleidoscope of images. They flitted and turned before him, folding one on the other. It was a complete archive of his life... of many lives!

Nearby, Philomena was on her knees, staring into the watery abyss, with Carson and Abby beside her. Spike's shoulders shook as tears streamed down his face, lips quivering.

"What are they looking at?" asked Otto, drawing alongside Enoch.

"I have no idea," said Enoch, narrowing his gaze and peering deep into the wall of dark matter–infused water.

"Professor!" shouted Enoch above the din of the cascade. "Carson! What is it? What are you looking at?" Enoch moved closer, leaned in, and called again. "Carson. Talk to me. What's happening?"

"It's... it's..."

"It's what?"

Carson went catatonic once more, and Enoch withdrew and returned to where Otto stood, looking desperately from side to side, trying to see what the others saw. Nothing would shake them. They were transfixed. Enoch and Otto resigned themselves to waiting it out.

Thirty minutes or more passed, when, as suddenly as it had begun, the spell was broken. The five crew members collapsed, as if simultaneously dropped by a force that moments earlier would not let them go.

Enoch rushed forward, rolling Philomena over, placing her head in his lap. Her eyes were wide open, and she stared past him into the great beyond.

"She's in shock!" shouted Enoch. "Fetch some water."

Otto drew close and gently poured water between Philomena's slightly parted lips. She sputtered and gagged, then sat up, coming to.

"What happened?" cried Enoch. "Where did you go?"

"Everywhere," whispered Philomena. "*I am everywhere.*"

"What's this nonsense?" flashed Otto, clearly perturbed by being left in the dark. "Enough of this!"

Rising, he proceeded to douse the others with the remaining water. Each sat up in turn, shook it off, and tried as best they might to describe what had just happened. Eventually, it all came pouring out.

"The tree," said Abby, pointing back across the way. "It was a warning."

"A warning of what?" urged Otto.

"Of this," she said, turning to stare back into the wall of water.

"She's going back in," said Enoch.

Otto sprang forward, grabbing Abby by the shoulders and forcing her to look straight at him. "No, you don't!" he cried. "I want answers!"

The others stirred.

"Déjà vu?" asked Kai.

"More like magic mushrooms," offered Philomena, still swooning.

"There are no words," said Abby. "I'm not sure I even know what it means, or if it means anything at all."

Otto reached for his instruments. He had taken dozens of readings since they penetrated the core. He plunged the probe deep through the fibrous layer of the surface to the threshold of the geyser. The meter squealed. The readout was irrefutable.

"I'll tell you what it means," said Otto, rising to his feet and turning to face the geyser. His tall and angular figure cut a dark silhouette.

"Whatever it is, you don't look happy about it," said Carson.

Pointing to Enoch and himself, Otto said, "You have glimpsed what some of us never will."

"And what, precisely, is that?"

"The multiverse. Proof that the quantum field exists. It is here that dark matter plays its part. It is here, in concentrations found perhaps nowhere else in the universe, that we can see in ways that otherwise we could not. I say 'we', but what I mean is *you*," he said, pointing from one member of the crew to the next. Then nodding to Enoch: "*Not* us."

The looks of confusion on their faces reminded Otto of how little they understood. One short life was not enough for them to grasp the meaning of it all. But, of course, that was precisely the problem, he thought.

"Enoch, I know you understand. Tell our friends here what's at stake."

"Life itself," said Enoch.

"What are you saying?" asked Abby.

Otto cut in. "We're saying that we—unlike you—have but one life to live."

"But that makes no sense," said Carson. "You are the ones with a claim on immortality, not us."

"Perhaps in this world," allowed Otto. "But through there," he said, "you live on forever. I look, and I see nothing. You look, and you see all the possibilities of lives lived and yet unlived. Infinite lives, in other realms, in perpetuity, in parallel worlds. You've been given a great gift, a chance to glimpse the many and endless aspects of what you know as your *selves*. This," he said, pointing to the vortex, "is a window onto other worlds. It's also proof of what I've long suspected."

"Which is?" ventured Abby.

"That dark matter is the source of all things. Harness its power and shape the world however you see fit. The possibilities are endless. The power that comes with it is absolute! Only here, in these concentrations, does it reveal itself. It was lost... Now, it has been found!"

"Lost? What do you mean?" challenged Abby.

"Have you forgotten your childhood stories? Do you not know what this is that stands before you?"

"For God's sake, what are you babbling on about?" demanded Kai.

"*Yggdrasil*," cried Otto. "Of Celtic lore. Or perhaps *The Tree of Good and Evil* is a myth more familiar to you? The Persians called it *Gaokerena*. In China, it is *Fusang*. The symbol of the tree is as old as civilization itself. The tree itself may have eluded us, but not its meaning!"

"What meaning?" asked Spike.

"Knowledge, of course. The kind of knowledge that begets everlasting life. Partake of the tree, and you shall die and be reborn as a higher version of yourself. *Behold!*" cried Otto with a sweep of his arm. "See how it rises from this place to the dome above, how it branches out in all directions as it penetrates the core itself. Could this be the Tree of Life you've heard tell of? Are we Adam and Eve returned once more? The message was clear: 'eat of the fruit' and you shall have everlasting life! Just a metaphor, you say? I think not! Draw near. Reach out. Sample for yourselves the fruit of this tree. Are you not drawn to it? Is it not calling out?"

"Yes... yes, it is," confessed Philomena.

"There is something at play, it's true," agreed Carson.

"Then what's stopping you? Immortality is yours for the taking. The search for meaning ends here! This is *your* moment. This is *your* truth."

"And what of yours?" challenged Philomena, resisting for the moment the temptation to place her hand against the shimmering torrent.

Her words hit hard, dousing in an instant the delight that Otto had felt in presenting his little theory.

"The One's way of cheating us, I'd wager. The Twenty were forbidden from mixing with The Others, but they did so anyway. He and I are what remain of their trysts. Their blood flows in ours. Their curse is now our curse. We were told immortality was a blessing bestowed upon us. Now, we know the truth. It was a sentencing. One life to live. Nothing more. I look into this liquid expanse and I see *nothing*—no other lives, no other possibilities. Immortality, in our case," he said, gesturing to Enoch, "is limited to this one world. However long it lasts, so—I believe—shall we."

Otto's long arms hung by his side. His head bowed. He was spent. What joy he had felt in his discovery was suddenly snuffed out. It was hard not to feel sorry for the poor creature.

"If there is truth in what you say," ventured Abby, "and what we have before us gives every human the opportunity to step off into any number of parallel worlds, no one will care if this planet lives or dies. People will take the easy way out. They'll leave in droves. We set out to save the planet. Are you saying we just give up now?"

Otto stared back at Abby, flabbergasted.

"Give up? What in the world are you giving up? You might lose a planet, but you've gained your immortality. Does this not answer humanity's greatest single question: *what's life about?* Well, here it is... parallel worlds! For you humans, life *is* eternal. Perhaps this explains why your kind has so abused this planet. Somewhere, lurking in that scrawny gray matter you call brains, ran the subliminal notion of life after death. Now you know the truth of it. Be off with you! Take whatever path you choose. It's all the same to me! I have better things to do. The Council waits and I must deliver!"

The vitriol was shocking. It was as if every ounce of resentment Otto held for the human species came gushing out in one raging torrent. He resented everything about humanity. And yet he was conspiring to deliver the secrets of Hollow Earth to some group called the Council, come what may.

CHAPTER 57

Otto realized the minute he said it that he had let slip reference to the Council. He had done well to keep this a secret, perhaps even from Enoch, but now it was out in the open.

"The Council again. Who are they and what do you owe them?" demanded Kai.

"They are no concern of yours," snapped Otto. "Evidence of the multiverse—that's what we've been searching for," he said, pointing at the vortex. "Control this, and you control the destiny of humans! The planet is dying. This is their exit strategy. Once the Council is alerted, the selection will begin."

"What selection?" asked Kai.

"Let's call it Noah's Ark 2.0. A chance for those who can afford it to pick their new world."

"And for those who can't?" pressed Kai.

"They'll be all right. No one really dies. Everyone moves on. It's just that some will be able to choose their new lives, and others won't."

"Are you mad?" shouted Spike.

"I don't know, are you? Do you question your sanity when you stare into this watery abyss? What's real and what's not? I'll tell you what's real. This is real! Your humanity is a gift and, I dare say, it's entirely wasted on you."

"Look into the vortex, Sasquatch, I'd say you're the one getting wasted. This Council has played you," chided Spike. "You were nothing but a bottom-feeder stuck in a cave when we found you. Abby here, she's the real hero. Without the *Orpheus*, you'd still be sitting in your dark little lab playing checkers with sub-particles."

"Step lightly, boy. Don't trifle with me."

"I'm not trifling. It's your Council taskmasters pulling the wool over your big bulbous eyes. Looks like they got the Dark Lord just where they want him."

Otto's expression shifted from annoyed to incensed. Spike had hit a nerve—now to twist the knife.

"Come on, you satanic sack of shit, do your worst."

Otto lunged and caught Spike by the collar, clutching at him with both hands. Spike countered. For a moment, the two figures were locked, legs spread wide, leaning one against the other. The crew shouted for them to break it up, but an old familiar feeling had taken hold. Spike was back on the football field, exploding off the front line, locking up his opponent and driving him backward. He felt pure rage, with images of every failed moment in his life welling up inside him. The anger and disappointment surged through his body and amplified the appearance of his powerful frame.

He had imagined this moment. Indeed, he had seen it... all of it. He had thought it was madness: images of a descent to the underworld, secret passages, strange encounters, a kaleidoscopic realm, and a vortex casting images of his infinite lives—those that were and those that would never be. It came to him in a single flash of blue light, from deep within a bore hole as he was atop an ocean oil rig. He had known nothing but fear and confusion ever since.

The shouts coming from the others were distant now and fading fast. He felt the drive in his legs and, looking across Otto's shoulder, found himself once again entranced by the cascading reflections of his alternative lives dancing across a liquid screen. Why this life? Why not any of these others? Perhaps it wasn't too late. This might be his only chance. He would end it now.

Spike let out a roar and, with all his strength, drove Otto backward toward the geyser. Otto was half a meter taller than Spike, but he had neither the strength nor the will to resist. Almost unexpectedly, Spike felt the creature surrender, as if he understood and was prepared to sacrifice himself to a higher force. In a flash, they were gone, jetted upward the minute they made contact. Philomena screamed and rushed forward, but Carson caught her and held her back.

"It's done," he whispered. "They're gone."

CHAPTER 58

Otto's words reverberated long after he disappeared. Abby had suspected from the beginning that he knew more than he was letting on. It was a risk letting him join the mission. But what choice did she have? Too many uncertainties. Discovering a theoretical physicist at the threshold to the underworld felt like a resource not to be squandered. Her plan entailed finding answers to slow the planet's demise. His plan had been to affirm the probability of human immortality. Before her, at that very moment, was a vortex so charged with dark matter that—if they thought it through—might perhaps be harnessed in the service of both endgames.

Where was Spike now, she wondered? Had he survived? And, if so, would there ever be a way of knowing for sure. As for Otto, if his theory held true, he was spiraling in a world neither here nor there. Purgatory, at best. Hell, at worst.

Over the course of their journey, dozens of theories long held as scientific fact had been refuted—entirely overturned, in fact. Their discovery would rewrite the annals of all ten branches of Earth science. The big bang and the very origins of the planet might be called into question. And then, of course, there was the quantum world. If Otto was right and the concentration of dark matter at the core was demonstrative proof of parallel worlds, the entire field of physics would be upended. As much as she hated to admit it, had he returned to the surface, Otto Trubolt might have displaced Albert Einstein as the greatest physicist of all time. The fact that she and Otto were conjoined in some way in their thinking about dark matter gave her small comfort. She could see how limited her own theories were compared to his. While her hopes and aspirations had been centered on understanding dark matter as a force capable of safeguarding the planet and restoring it to health, Otto had ventured with them for one reason and one reason only—to prove *himself* right!

None of this, she thought, would ever matter if they did not find a way back to the surface.

"We need to talk," said Kai.

Abby, so lost in thought, barely heard him come up behind her.

"I suppose we do," she replied, turning and unexpectedly pulling him close, her arms wound tightly around his neck.

Kai said nothing. He would let her hold on as long as she liked.

"What's our next move?" he whispered.

"To get out of here," she said. "And I don't mean by hurling ourselves into the vortex and going our separate ways."

"Maybe the vortex isn't such a bad idea."

"No Kai, I..."

"I don't mean separately," he interrupted. "I mean together."

Abby leaned back and looked up at him. Her quizzical gaze was all the encouragement he needed.

"I mean," Kai continued, "what if our geyser is more than a portal to other worlds? What if it's a jet stream back to the surface? I've been sitting with Carson, running through some of the data. If our calculations are correct, based on the estimated propulsion of the geyser, Antarctica is directly above us."

"3,000 kilometers above us," Abby reminded him. "The force of the geyser would need to be moving at somewhere in the range of 1,200 kilometers per hour to spring us from here to there."

"It's about half that, in fact, and we only need to clear the outer core and the inner ionosphere. Carson's maps show a direct line through the mantle. Come with me. I'll show you."

Kai and Abby headed away from the vortex and back to the ship. As they approached, Carson stepped out to meet them. He was visibly shaken, as if he had just seen a ghost.

"You won't believe this," he said, turning to lead them back into the ship's core.

They entered the control room and Carson, without breaking stride, activated the overhead map to once again reveal the intricate system of interwoven passageways. He rotated the optics and pointed the viewer to a gaping hole at its center.

"From a surface-to-center perspective, this portal," he said, gesturing toward the image's apex, "was largely undetectable. You can see here how it penetrates the dome of the core, and then gradually narrows as it climbs through the mantle. The vortex, with its high concentrations of dark matter, narrows and accelerates here," he said, pointing at the 1,700 kilometer mark. From that point to the surface, it becomes virtually invisible, a kind of black hole shielded by heavy concentrations of subatomic particles."

"My God," gasped Abby. "Kai, that's directly beneath the ice caves, close to where you and I were separated. If this is true, then you were right from the beginning. There is another passage to Earth's core, only hidden."

CHAPTER 59

In the days that followed, the crew moved about with renewed vigor. Hope has that effect. It restores human spirit. While Carson and Kai continued to work and rework the data, Abby prepared the *Orpheus*. Philomena, meanwhile, gathered plant and mineral samples, carefully storing and labeling them as best she could. Wandering the perimeter of the geyser with shearing clippers and a floppy hat, she looked like a country maid tending her backyard garden. From time to time, she could be seen lugging Otto's equipment to one section of the surrounding hills and then another, plunging—as he had—the probe through the thin surface, doing her best to jot down the readings before moving on.

Enoch moved among them like a ghost. Otto's revelations about parallel worlds and the essential differences between the Nephilim and humans had left him feeling distant from the others. As had been the case so many times before, his human nature felt melancholy, while his Nephilim side urged him to stay focused in order to deal with the problem before him. The problem, of course, was existential. To think oneself immortal for nearly 10,000 years and then one day discover that life is not linear, but instead multidimensional... well, the very idea left him feeling debilitated. Even the Nephilim are prone to depression. And that is precisely what he felt in those intervening days. He spent long hours sitting cross-legged, gazing intently into the great wall of water, hoping, if only for an instant, to catch a glimpse of just one other life. But no matter how long and how intently he stared, he saw only shadows and heard only the roar of billions of gallons of dark matter–infused water jetting up into the ionosphere.

By closing his eyes, he imagined the early morning mist that rose from the forest floors of his childhood. He dreamed of returning one last time to the willow that overhung the river, and he wondered if by stepping into the vortex he would die and be reborn again in that familiar place. Or perhaps, as Otto had suggested, he would disappear forever. The multiverse was not inviting. It was a feeling—and Enoch had long ago learned to honor what he felt deepest.

While the other members of the crew remained busy preparing for the return, Enoch contemplated what would follow if they were indeed to be successful. How would they be received? The Council would be waiting. They wanted control and Enoch knew their ways well enough to know that nothing would stop them from containing the situation. They had proven themselves in this regard from one century to the next. Of course, there were other forces at play. And the Council, now aware that they had a rival, would spare no effort seeking out and destroying anyone who opposed them. Enoch had been a thorn in the side of the Council for as long as he could remember. He knew its members. They would stop at nothing. Enoch must get to The Twenty first. If he failed to do so, the whole situation might unravel and there would be nothing he could do to save the *Orpheus* and its crew from what would most surely follow.

In his thousands of years of existence, Enoch had never known a moment when so much was at stake. Worst of all, he had to figure things out on his own. Revealing to Abby now the role he had played from the beginning would only raise more questions. What would she say if he were to confess to the part he played in convincing The Twenty to believe in her and her planetary theories? How could he explain all that he had done to secretly fund the *Orpheus* project, while also diverting attention from it? And, even worse, what would the others think of him if they knew he had been spying on them for years, keeping track of their lives and discoveries, and ultimately selecting them from among thousands in the hope that they would play their part as circumstance required? Yes, Enoch reassured himself, it was too much to share. Not at this moment, at least. Better to keep them focused on the return journey. If they did not make it, it would not matter anyway.

CHAPTER 60

The *Orpheus* seemed oddly out of place, situated halfway between the shape-shifting tree and the great upward-spiraling column. The crew had eased it into place before making final preparations. Two of the thick ropes were affixed to the windward and leeward sides of the ship, fanning out to the left and the right of the geyser. Carson, never satisfied, remained in the control room, working on his calculations for the hundredth time. Abby and Kai had long since surrendered to the probability that they had less than a fifty-fifty chance.

"He's only doing this because he's not going," Kai said.

"Can you blame him?" asked Philomena. "He and I aren't the ones being launched into oblivion."

"And I suppose that's less precarious than remaining here, waiting out your days, and wondering—without knowing—if the world is about to come to an end."

"Slower or faster, we all end up in the same place," she said, flashing an awkward smile.

"We'll be back for you," assured Abby. "It's bureaucracy that worries me, not the return trip. Who knows what we'll run into when we tell the world what we've found."

"Just my luck that Carson's computations limited the crew to three instead of five," said Philomena. "But, if I'm being honest, I kind of like it here. It feels... well... it feels like home."

"Coming from you, I almost believe it," said Kai, stepping forward to give her one final hug goodbye.

Just then, Carson came trotting down the gangway. "It's as complete as it's going to get. Time for you to fly," he said.

"We're ready," said Abby. "Shall we?" she said, gesturing to Kai and Enoch.

The three of them walked slowly up the gangway, each of them looking back over their shoulders one more time to see Carson and Philomena standing in the tall grass, hills rolling in every direction. Even the flora seemed aware that their guests were about to depart. In all directions, it appeared that the trees and flowers were leaning inward, beckoning after the ship and the crew.

The portal to the *Orpheus* closed behind them, and Carson and Philomena stood, rope in hand, on either side of the ship.

"Ready?" Carson shouted above the din of the cascading water.

"Ready!" Philomena shouted back.

Together they pulled on the long ropes. The *Orpheus* rocked in its place, then rolled closer to the great wall of water. They only needed to move it five meters—in such a low-gravity environment, the ship eased into the geyser almost effortlessly. Letting go of the ropes, they jumped back just in time to see the ship rocket upward, disappearing into the void almost instantaneously. There was a flash, and Carson felt the gravity shift. He fell to his knees and clenched his teeth.

The pain between his ears soon receded, and he lay back in the grass feeling Philomena next to him, her hand in his.

"What now?" he asked.

"We learn to live," he heard her reply.

Carson turned his head to look at her as flowering ferns gently coiled round her, framing her body and crowning her head. Her eyes were closed and she wore a soft smile, surrendering to the million tiny green tendrils whispering to her about things she somehow already knew.

Carson did not reply, but merely gave her hand a squeeze. Then, gazing up and into the apex of the core—where water penetrated the dome and disappeared into the great beyond—he found himself once more floating in his grandfather's canoe, bobbing in still waters. Staring up into a swirling sky of rainbow plasma, he watched as long, languorous ripples pulsated down and across the translucent dome from where the *Orpheus*, like a stone, had momentarily disturbed the still waters of the wondrous womb—Earth's core. She was gone now, jettisoned to a place far away, with only ripples to remind them that she ever existed.

"Will we ever see them again?" Philomena's voice sounded, as if from far away.

"God willing," he said. "God willing."

Epilogue

For an instant, Enoch floated at the center of all things—suspended in his pod at the heart of the *Orpheus*, at the locus of the vortex, within the planet's core. And at that moment—only milliseconds before the ship exploded upward, into the ionosphere and through Earth's mantle—he had a vision.

It came to him in a flash, like a thousand intersecting beams of light. In that vision, he was dark matter itself, racing upward, evacuating the core, and departing the planet. He was the effluvial stream expelled from the blowhole of a world grown weary. He was Jonah, in the belly of the whale, on the brink of emancipation, knowing—in that instant—that the answers to life lay inward, not outward.

The Nephilim had always understood this. And for this reason, they viewed their 10,000 years of internment in the underworld as a gift, not a curse. It allowed for a period of deep introspection. When they emerged, they did so in awe. And it was only by virtue of living within her that they were able to attune themselves to the pulse of the planet. The Twenty went down as acolytes and returned as *satori*—enlightened ones, anointed in the knowledge that "the One" was not some distant and transcendent overlord, but rather the jagged little edges of Earth herself.

On the day that Enoch reunited with The Twenty, it was on the occasion of one of his many "little deaths." Waking by the river and allowing his eyes to adjust to the swaying boughs of the willow, he felt them form around him—twenty white-bearded heads all in a circle, smiling down upon him. They raised him up and, in turn, embraced their chosen one—the Twenty-first among them. Helping him to the river's edge, they watched from the banks as he made his way through the currents once again, to mount the boulder and await the wind. Once reanimated, he would never again be alone. The Twenty were with him. And, together, they charted a course to counter those who had robbed rather than rewarded the planet they were born to.

Two centuries of planning had led them to the core. Along the way, they had discovered that there were those among the race of humans who sensed the shape of the world and those who did not. Like gravity, those who did emitted a weak, subatomic pulse. Kept apart, they were inconsequential. But when brought together, they exhibited a cumulative strength, a core energy, a gravitational pull.

Indeed, gravity—from the start—had been trying to show what could otherwise not be explained. And so it was that Enoch glimpsed in his vision the image of Wit Thompson, the SkyBound CEO, who only months earlier had mysteriously disappeared into the stratosphere from the top of Mount Everest. A "gravitational anomaly," they called it. But now, as he rested momentarily at the Earth's core, Enoch knew it was more than that. There were those like Philomena who were contemplative, connected, and inextricably bound to the planet. And then there were those like Wit Thompson—egotistical and exploitative. One was grounded. One was not.

Enoch considered for a moment the profiles of the thousands who had suddenly found themselves "emancipated" from the planet. Who were they and what were they made of, he wondered? Was it possible that dark matter had some hand in this? And could it be that like the planet itself—expelling dark matter from its core as it slowly dies—humans without the capacity to ground themselves were also depleting their systems of the dark energy that was required to keep them bound to the Earth itself? It seemed improbable, at best. And yet, as Enoch floated in a state of animated suspension, he entertained the possibility. As the G-forces rendered him unconscious and he felt his world fade to black, he knew that somewhere in this mixture of science and imagination he would one day discover the truth of it.